if tomorrow doesn't come

if tomorrow doesn't come

Jen St. Jude

BLOOMSBURY

NEW YORK LONDON OXFORD NEW DELHI SYDNEY

BLOOMSBURY YA
Bloomsbury Publishing Inc., part of Bloomsbury Publishing Plc
1385 Broadway, New York, NY 10018

BLOOMSBURY and the Diana logo are trademarks of Bloomsbury Publishing Plc

First published in the United States of America in May 2023 by Bloomsbury YA

Bloomsbury books may be purchased for business or promotional use. For information on
bulk purchases please contact Macmillan Corporate and Premium Sales Department at
specialmarkets@macmillan.com

Library of Congress Cataloging-in-Publication Data
Names: St. Jude, Jen, author.
Title: If tomorrow doesn't come / by Jen St. Jude.
Other titles: If tomorrow does not come
Description: New York : Bloomsbury Children's Books, 2023.
Summary: Nineteen-year-old Avery plans to end her life but changes her mind when
she learns an asteroid is heading toward Earth, and with nine days left to live, long-held
secrets begin to come out and Avery finally begins to heal.
Identifiers: LCCN 2022047371 (print) | LCCN 2022047372 (e-book)
ISBN 978-1-5476-1136-2 (hardcover) • ISBN 978-1-5476-1137-9 (e-book)
Subjects: CYAC: Natural disasters—Fiction. | Depression, Mental—Fiction. |
Secrets—Fiction. | LGBTQ+ people—Fiction. | Family life—Fiction.
Classification: LCC PZ7.1.S7188 If 2023 (print) | LCC PZ7.1.S7188 (e-book) |
DDC [Fic]—dc23
LC record available at https://lccn.loc.gov/2022047371
LC e-book record available at https://lccn.loc.gov/2022047372

Book design by John Candell
Typeset by Westchester Publishing Services
Printed and bound in the U.S.A.
2 4 6 8 10 9 7 5 3 1

To find out more about our authors and books visit www.bloomsbury.com
and sign up for our newsletters.

To Krupa: With you, the answers are so damn easy.

& for Connor: I will always be running through orchards, flashlight in hand, looking for you.

author's note

Dear Reader,

Avery Byrne, the narrator of my YA debut, *If Tomorrow Doesn't Come*, doesn't know how to keep living. Her depression is a state, a feeling, a place: where things will never get better, not ever. Where she doesn't deserve anything better, anyway. Where the world keeps spinning in technicolor around her, but she's trapped in her own little gray apocalypse, alone. Then she learns an asteroid is hurtling toward Earth, and she has nine days left to live. Suddenly, her own private apocalypse is not so private. It's everywhere. It's everyone's. And they must all learn how to survive it, together.

Isolation is depression's greatest weapon. It makes us believe that our pain is our fault, that our struggles are personal failures. Young people are especially susceptible to this type of shame, since you have not had the chance to build communities outside your immediate environment. It may be especially hard for young people to imagine a better tomorrow because you have not lived it—and if you are queer or otherwise marginalized in society, you may have never even seen it.

If Tomorrow Doesn't Come is my small way of saying that you don't have to hurt alone, and that even in your darkest, most painful moments, you are still worthy of love and all of life's infinite possibilities. I want you to know that queer love is hopeful and holy. I want you to feel like life's most spectacular, electric, perfect moments can come right after its worst ones. No one is broken beyond repair, even if healing is slow and nonlinear.

The world may end someday, but not yet. Not today. For now, we're all here together, and that can be enough. Tomorrow can be different. Tomorrow can be better. If we let it come.

—Jen St. Jude

if tomorrow
doesn't
come

the end

I wanted to hide my body somewhere no one would have to find it.

Midway through my freshman year, I settled on the Saco River—a hungry stretch of icebergs and fog that slipped by the edge of campus. I liked the river because when I stood on its edge, it always felt like morning, even at sunset, even at midnight. I also liked it because it was practical and clean. It would take me away, wash every part of me. Bury me in its silt.

On a frigid February night, I cleaned my side of the room by moonlight as my roommate slept soundlessly. I deleted every photo of myself from social media and then sat on my bed writing goodbye notes on loose-leaf paper. I put the letters on my desk, tucked myself into my bed, and listened to an audiobook until our window glowed with the first sign of dawn.

On my final morning, the morning of my nineteenth birthday, I put on my blue coat and gold sneakers, smoothed my hair in the mirror without looking myself in the eyes, and left my dorm room one last time. I crossed Eaton College's campus in the shadows of mountains, and stumbled through a wall of evergreen trees to a dock winged by canoes. Everything looked so beautiful, but I didn't know how to feel it.

The boats crashed around me as I knelt on the icy wood, sadness like sand in my blood. In the broken glass of rushing water, I almost expected to see not my own reflection but the face of my aunt Devin, my mother's sister who, on the day I was born, waded out into the Irish Sea and stayed there. Everyone said I looked like her because of my penny-red hair and blue eyes. But I didn't see her face in front of me, only mine. I was alone.

My jeans soaked through to the skin. My heart raced until my ribs shivered. I brushed tears away so I could see one more sunrise, but the sun blinked open too quickly for color.

I'd always been a little broken, but at least before Eaton I'd fooled people into thinking I was talented, sparkling, and smart. Now, I felt like I wasn't even a person at all. I didn't want anything. I hoped for nothing. No one needed me. The sadness had spread from my brain to my bones. It lived in my body. I didn't think it would ever go away. How could it? It could only get worse when my parents found out I had failed a class. When they discovered I'd been essentially kicked off the soccer team. It could only get worse when Cass fell in love with somebody new, and I had to watch it happen. Then what?

Then nothing.

I got to my feet and leaned over the water, ready to fall into the rushing, into the stillness. I tried to catch my reflection one more time, but I didn't know the girl who flickered below me, and I didn't know how to save her. I dared her to want something, to wish for something. *Anything.* I begged her. I missed, not for the first time, having someone to pray to.

I inched to the very edge. Held my breath. Prepared to jump. And then my cell phone vibrated and Eaton's emergency alert system started screaming.

Even through the forest, I could hear the sirens blaring. That meant we needed to get into the closest building and lock the doors. The bells of the chapel chimed too, signaling six o'clock naively, innocently. I scrambled backward up the dock to hide in a cluster of trees and wrestled my phone out of my pocket.

The screen showed my best friend, Cass Joshi-Aguilar, in a black suit with her head thrown back in laughter underneath New York City streetlights. One of her new friends had taken the photo, and I'd ripped it from her

Instagram profile. Every time I looked at it, I forgot to breathe. Every time Cass called, I waited until the last ring so I could take in the shock of her smile, the hint of her collarbone where her shirt was unbuttoned, and the blur of her hand running through her hair. God, she was perfect.

I didn't want to answer it, but it was the first I'd heard from her since I saw her in January and told her that I hated her. I hadn't been surprised, after that, when she didn't text me at midnight on my birthday like she usually did. Now she was calling me, and I didn't want to lose my nerve to jump, but I did want to hear her voice one more time, to change my last words to her. I didn't hate her. I was in love with her. Goddammit. I hit the button to accept the call and moved deeper into the trees, as if she'd see less of me.

"Hey." I tried to sound like I was waking up, but the alarms were obvious, even at their distance.

"Avery. What the hell, right?" On her end, sirens wailed too, which was not unusual for New York City, but added to the cacophony in my brain. I pictured her standing at her alley-facing window, running her hand through her hair or crossing her arm against her chest.

"What the hell *what*?"

"You don't know?"

"Know?"

She inhaled like she was pissed off, and for a second I

thought she somehow knew what I'd been doing. But she was just trying to catch her breath.

"Someone hacked NASA's emails and found out there's an asteroid headed toward Arizona."

"Huh?"

"Or, like, they don't know totally where, but it's eight miles wide."

"So . . ." So, there was an asteroid coming. And people were unhappy about it. Cass was unhappy about it. I tried to piece together her words but couldn't even breathe through the fog of becoming again.

"So, we're cooked!" She laughed horribly. "They're saying it's bigger than the dinosaur one. Isn't everyone freaking out there?"

I glanced toward campus, felt its pulsing. "Are you messing with me?"

"No," her voice cracked. "I'm not; it's everywhere. Fucking Google it."

I couldn't process what she was saying, not really, so when I didn't say anything, she added, "They're saying we have nine days." Her breath quickened. I heard her slamming things around. I pictured her packing up her sticker-covered laptop and her treasured fashion collages.

"Where are you?"

"I'm still at my apartment, but I'm heading to the bus station to try to get to Boston. I'll catch another bus home from there. I'm assuming my parents are trying to get back from Fiji, but I haven't talked to them. You should be looking for a way home too." Cass's parents had been planning their trip to Fiji for years. They called it their empty-nest honeymoon. Cass called it their cincuentañera even though they were well into their fifties already.

I turned to look back at the river and let myself be hypnotized by its current. Did I believe what Cass was saying? No. It had to be a hoax, right? An internet rumor gone viral? Was I even talking to Cass on the phone for real, or was this my body's way of tricking me into staying alive?

"I have to go, Cass," I said, and started walking back to the edge of the dock. I had to hang up. Had to jump. Had to say goodbye. I pulled the phone from my ear, but I found I couldn't hit the End Call button.

"Wait, Avery," she said, her voice suddenly so small and far away.

"Yeah?"

"I need you to promise me you'll be there when I get home, okay?"

"I can't do that."

I bent down to touch the water but quickly pulled my hand back, stung by its chill.

"Why? You have to promise me. Avery? You have to. Promise me even if it's a lie. I need you." She started to cry, too, and though my body was almost too tired to feel anything, the sound of her tears made my heart cave in.

She needed me again. It had been a while. And when had I ever been able to say no to Cass, really? Not ever. Certainly not now. Even if I didn't believe what she was saying about the asteroid, she was offering me one more chance to see her, to say the words I'd been tracing over and over in my mind every time I looked at her: *I'm sorry* and *I love you* and *goodbye.*

But could I do it, make it through more days? Did I want to?

I felt something close inside me, a door to the rest I'd promised myself. The salvation, the escape. I bit my lip in frustration, so hard it bled.

"I'll be there," I whispered, though I didn't know if I was lying or not.

"Thank you," she said, and then she was gone.

I bent down one last time to splash the freezing water on my face, to break my promise to myself so I could keep one to her. Maybe I wouldn't make it until the asteroid hit, but I could do just one more day, couldn't I? For her. For my family. One more. One.

I stood up and turned back toward campus. I laughed, wild, angry laughter. Because on that morning, I'd thought it would finally be over.

Instead, I ran. I wept. I began again.

I shoved my phone back in my pocket and jogged across the cemetery, and the knee I injured in my final soccer game screamed with every step. As I approached the center quad, the emergency alarm system grew louder. Students streamed across the yard, grabbed their friends by the shoulders, and hovered in clusters around cell phone screens, calling the names of the people they loved. I knew no one there would call for me. I hadn't made a single close friend in all my months at school, not on the soccer team or off it. I didn't want anyone to *really* know me. And they hadn't tried to, anyway.

Granite Hall, a white building with dark purple shutters, had its doors propped open. I followed the waves of bodies flowing inside. In the first classroom, students squeezed in to stare at a video projected on the whiteboard. Banners framed CNN anchors and scrolled across the top and bottom of the screen. Their voices thundered at full volume, but I couldn't hear whole sentences, only words, as my eyes adjusted to the speeding pixels.

But then, the CNN anchor, an older man with a frown and wide eyes said, ". . . more energy than every nuclear bomb on Earth, and it's moving at fifty times the speed of sound . . ." My throat tightened as I tried to keep up with the rolling text.

HACKER REVEALS ASTEROID HEADING TOWARD EARTH . . .
ORIGINALLY DETECTED BY MISSION DEEP IMPACT . . .

"Eight miles wide," the anchor said. "Wow."

He held up one finger to tell us to be patient while he talked to a producer off-screen and came back with a voice louder and stranger than before: "This might be the answer to our hubris. This is, perhaps, the end of our planet, at least as we know it. You heard it here. First. On CNN."

The room spun around me, and my classmates' faces looked like they were warped by funhouse mirrors. The room vibrated with their horror. So it was real, then. Cass was right. An asteroid was really headed straight for us. On the day I wanted to die. What the *fuck*. I laughed out loud, so hard I had to put my hands on my knees, until someone smacked my arm.

I turned to see my roommate and teammate, Aisha Shagari, glaring at me. It was 6 a.m. and the world was ending, but she already looked ready for the day in her new winter boots, still-pristine white peacoat, and headscarf to match. She clutched her gold locket against her chest.

"It's not funny, Avery," she said with tears in her eyes. "How dare you?"

"I'm sorry," I said. "I don't think it's funny either. I'm just . . ."

"Messed up?" someone said nearby.

"Yeah. I'm messed up," I said, and then I felt like crying again. Sobbing. Because the world was ending, and everyone I loved might die, not just me.

I had to go home. I had to be there for my family, and for Cass. The river would wait for me.

If we survived.

Aisha started to walk away from me, and I chased after her out of the building and back into the fresh sunlight. "I'm sorry," I said again.

"Don't be sorry," she said. "Just wake up. Where have you been all morning? We have to get out of here. I have to go home." A new wind whipped us in the face. "I have to get my passport and get back to Nigeria," she said, her voice cracking. "I booked a flight on my mother's debit card that leaves from Logan in seven hours. Would you go find a car headed to Boston? Please?"

"Of course," I said, this small mission anchoring me to my body again. This was how I was going to get through this and get to Cass: little task by little task, one foot clumsily in front of the other. I sprinted into the parking lot to see who I could find and saw the lot was already half-empty. Most of the remaining cars were snowed in. My classmates clawed at the tires with shovels, SOLO cups, dining hall trays, and bare hands. Many had carved their destinations into the snow on their windshields: *Boston, Philadelphia, Portland, Montreal*.

"Do you have room for one more?" I asked Billy Carter, one of the guys standing in front of a Boston car. He was the sports editor at the *Eaton Moose Tracks* and had interviewed me during soccer season. He cracked ice with the corner of a shovel and grunted. He had two guys helping him free the back tires, and they were blasting rap from inside the Subaru.

I'd asked for Aisha, not me, I realized. But Cass *needed* me, and I wanted desperately to see her one more time. If we took I-93, our hometown, Kilkenny, was on the way to Boston. I could have Billy drop me off at our exit, and my family could get me from there. And then, Cass would meet me there. We'd be home together. I could say goodbye. My eyes prickled with tears of exhaustion.

"Sorry, Avery," Billy said. "We're full."

Standing next to another Boston-bound car was Meredith Wyn, the pitcher for the softball team, whom I'd secretly hooked up with all fall.

"We can fit you, Red, but we're just about ready to rock and roll. Leaving as soon as the car's free." She bent down to kiss me goodbye, something she'd never done in public before, and for some reason I let her, even though I couldn't feel my face or limbs.

Everyone was getting the hell out of Conway. I ran to our room to find Aisha. She was sitting on her plastic mattress, head in her hands, wilting in a way that was so unlike her.

"Meredith has room," I said breathlessly, and waited for her relief. Instead, she looked up at me and stared.

"You should just go," she said. "I can't find my passport."

"Oh, no. Well, we'll find it! You'll get there, okay? You will." As soon as I said it, I realized she might not get home at all, and my stomach twisted for her. *Were planes still flying, people still working? Were airports open? Could she even get to Boston?* "Forget it, there are a few cars outside about to leave, and I don't think your passport is going to be the issue."

"I need my passport," she whispered. "I don't understand. I never lose *anything*."

Humoring her, I bent down and dug around for it in her tangled chaos of belongings. I didn't know what a Nigerian passport looked like, but I thought I'd recognize it if I saw it. When I finally looked at my phone, I saw fifteen minutes had gone by. Meredith had obviously left, but I was determined to help Aisha. I needed something I could keep my mind on, something that would keep my hands busy.

"Run into the parking lot," I told her. "See if someone will wait for us, okay?" She nodded, the plastic mattress rising as she stood. While she was gone, I continued to frantically sort through her things, pausing only momentarily when I came across a photo of her family or a letter from her grandma.

We'd lived together for months, but I never *knew* her. Every time I thought we might have shared a moment—a knowing glance across the weight room, an inside joke I felt like I was in on—it was quickly followed by a stiff silence, and I could never tell if it was my fault or hers.

I had a photo of my family on my desk. I'd told her about everyone: my parents, my brother Peter, his wife Georgia, their son Teddy. I also had a photo of my mother and her younger sister, Devin, my lookalike, whom I'd never met. Her suicide was the reason my parents had moved from Kilkenny, Ireland, to Kilkenny, New Hampshire, when I was only six months old. They wanted to get as far away from the Irish Sea as they could, but lacked imagination when it came to finding a home with a new name.

Mom had no idea I'd stolen the fading photo of her and Devin laughing in a field as teenagers, seemingly happy. Mom would have thought it was morbid, would have hated the way I talked about Aunt Devin, as if I'd known her. As if she was ever mine to lose. But I loved that photo— Devin smiling so big, even though she was desperately sad. Or maybe in that moment she *was* genuinely happy. I loved that version of the story too.

Because anyone who came into our room commented on how much Aunt Devin and I looked alike, Aisha must have heard me talk about that photo ten times. Still, it wasn't until December when we were drifting off to sleep one night that she told me she'd had an older sister.

"We lost her," she said.

"I'm so sorry." I sat up in bed in case she wanted to talk about it more. "Not that you owe me anything, but why didn't you tell me before?" She looked at me as if I were a child.

"I've known you less than one year, and you think I'd give you my heart?"

I felt cheap, then, for exposing my family—especially Aunt Devin—so frequently, so soon.

"You're right," I said. "Like I said, you don't owe me anything. I just thought . . ."

"You think too much." And then Aisha had turned over on her side and went to sleep.

Now I knelt on the grimy carpet of our floor, careful not to touch her colorful, intricate prayer mat. I continued to dig through her belongings like they were hay and her passport the needle. At one point I found a photo of Aisha with her sister, whose name I still didn't know. The sister had been much older, it seemed. Aisha was a kid, sitting in her lap, smiling freely. She was wearing the same locket she still wore every day, the one she only removed for games and practice. In the photo, her sister had powdered their eyes with blue shadow and painted their lips with magenta lipstick. I felt a pang of longing on her behalf. She was so, so far from home.

As if on cue, my phone buzzed violently and lit up with texts from my family.

Dad Byrne: **Avery, do you need us to come get you?**

Peter Lasky: **Ave, you ok??**

Mom Byrne: **Call us ASAP**

They were awake. They knew, about the asteroid and the nine days and . . . what might happen after. I hovered my fingers over our group text and tried to think of something, anything, to say that might comfort them. Before I came up with a single word, my mom's number and photo sparked on my screen instead. I didn't want to answer, to hear the grief in her voice, but I knew if I didn't, she'd be sick with worry. I hit Accept.

"Hey, Mom?"

"Avery, where are you?" She was electric with fear. This was why I hadn't answered her calls for days: her voice always convinced me to try to live one more time. Especially when I didn't want to.

"I'm in my dorm."

"Have you seen the news? People are rioting, panicking. And, Avery, the asteroid! I'm in bits. Are you safe? Tell me you're safe." I wanted to laugh and cry at the same time.

"Yeah," I said. "I'm safe."

"Do you need someone to come get you?"

"No, I found a ride," I lied. I didn't want her to worry about me more than she had to. She was always so worried about me.

"Good. Please, Avery. Come home as soon as you can and keep me posted."

"Okay," I said. "I love you."

When Aisha came back into the room, she had beads of sweat gathered at her temples. "Mina Patel," she said. "Leaving in ten minutes." We spent that time digging through the madness. No passport.

"Aisha, I'm sorry, but I think we should——"

"I know," she said, exasperated. "I know. Okay. Let's go." She grabbed the small bag she'd packed, and we booked it—but Mina was gone.

"You were right," she said, the two of us standing like statues in the middle of the empty lot. "I should have left with one of the earlier cars."

"It's going to be okay. You're going to get to Boston, you'll get on that plane, and you'll get out of here. You're going to get home." I had started to doubt that, but it was the only thing I could think to say.

"Why are you helping me?"

It was a question I couldn't answer honestly. *Aisha, you're an anchor. Aisha, I don't know how to be alive right now, but I have to get to Kilkenny to see Cass one last time, to be with my family. Drag me with you.*

"I'm trying to distract myself," I said. A van drove by, one of those big, creepy white vans with tinted windows that transports prisoners. Or paint supplies. Or acts as the stakeout post for a heist. Taped to its rearview window was a piece of paper with the word *Boston* scrawled across it. Aisha and I took off running. "WAIT!" we screamed. The van slowed to a roll.

"Do you have room?" Aisha exhaled, leaning on the van for support. The driver was an Eaton custodian, Melanie, whom I recognized from our dorm.

"Yeah," she said, "but let's go." Aisha didn't even think about it; she slid the heavy door open and put her leg up to get in.

My phone buzzed again. Cass.

"I'm so sorry," I said to everyone in the van. "Can you hold on just a second?" I didn't wait for them to respond. I touched the screen to answer the call.

"Avery," Cass said in a voice I'd never heard from her before: metallic and fearful. "I'm on the bus to Boston, but I don't think I'll be able to get one from there to New Hampshire. They said there won't be any buses leaving from Boston at all anymore. I don't know what to do."

"What?"

"I'm going to try to find a car; it just might be a while. I don't know, I'll do anything. I'll get to you, I promise."

I considered my options, which were few: I could stick to my original plan and have Melanie drop me off in Kilkenny. Or, I could risk not making it back to Kilkenny and continue on with Aisha to Boston, meet up with Cass, and, together, figure out what we should do next. Didn't feel like a hard decision. Didn't feel like a decision at all.

"When you get to South Station, stay there," I said. "I'm coming." Aisha offered me her hand and moved her knees to the side.

"Don't you dare," Cass said. "They're saying it's a nightmare in Boston."

I would get home, but first I'd blow right by Kilkenny. I'd go to Cass. It would all be okay. It had to be. I let Aisha hoist me up.

"I'm coming," I said, and hung up on her. I put my phone in my pocket, and the door of the van slid closed.

To Aisha I said, "Cass is going to Boston."

"So, you are too," she said. It wasn't a question.

fourteen and six years to impact

My brother, Peter, and I were well-behaved when we were growing up, mostly because our parents put the fear of God in us. We never fought, rarely had to sit in time-out, and when we went to Mass, we knelt in pews and *listened* (unlike the rowdy young heathens relegated to the children's room). And yet, when Peter and I discovered a tattered shoebox under my parents' bed when he was eight and I was five, we pulled it out even though we both knew we shouldn't. We found photographs, envelopes, ticket stubs, and clippings inside. In every photo, the same woman: red hair, blue eyes. Just like me.

"That's Aunt Devin," Peter whispered, and my blood chilled. I knew she was Mom's sister, and that she had passed away, but my parents only talked about "what

Devin did" in hushed tones with each other, never us. Peter picked up a newspaper article and started reading it.

"February second—Avery, that's your birthday!—Police believe Devin Walsh entered the sea between Seapoint and the West Pier in south Dublin."

"What's entered?" I asked, as quietly as possible.

"I guess, like, walked into?"

"Is that why Mom cried on my birthday?" She'd spent my whole party at the local ice rink weeping in the bathroom. It had frightened me.

"Probably."

"Why did Aunt Devin do that?"

"I don't know." He shook his head and carefully put the box away. "We probably shouldn't be reading this."

Peter didn't know that I went back later and stole one of the photos, the one I displayed in my room at Eaton of Devin and Mom. And though I didn't understand it, not really, I couldn't stop thinking about What Devin Did.

That autumn, I climbed a chain-link fence and jumped into the deep end of our neighbors' undrained pool fully clothed. I don't know what I thought would happen, exactly—perhaps that I could find Aunt Devin, bring her back, and stop Mom from crying? Maybe I just wanted to know what it felt like.

In the ice water, every muscle lit up with a searing pain, and I clawed in the direction I thought was *up.*

I don't know if I'd have found my way to the surface if Mrs. Davidson hadn't been on her porch and heard the splash. She rescued me with the pool skimmer, and I was shaking but hot with shame as she wrapped me in towels at her kitchen table. She called my mom, who arrived within minutes, hysterical.

"Why did you do that, Avery?" she asked me on the way home. "You can't even swim. What's wrong with you?"

"I don't know," I said, finally starting to cry. "Aunt Devin did it too."

"How do you know about that?" She stopped walking and studied me, her long brown hair whipping in an October wind. I said nothing, afraid of getting Peter into trouble. She said her next words breathlessly: "Were you trying to kill yourself?"

I thought, *Aunt Devin killed herself? People* kill *themselves?* The shock of it rendered me speechless.

"You go to Hell if you kill yourself, Avery." She looked frightened. Was that where Aunt Devin was? Hell? Was that why my parents didn't talk about her? "Do you want to go to Hell?"

I shook my head no. Of course I didn't. I wanted to be with everyone else after this life. I didn't want to be without my parents or Peter. I cried in bed, later, wondering if I had accidentally damned myself. Was it already too late for me? I prayed the hardest I'd ever prayed:

I didn't mean it, God, I didn't know, please forgive me. What had I done?

After the pool incident, my parents tried to keep me away from water. When Cass invited me to her beach house in Hampton the summer after sixth grade, my parents said no. They said it was unsafe, that they'd worry too much. I didn't want them to worry, but I privately wondered if it was also because Cass was a lesbian. She'd been out for as long as I'd known her, and any time it came up around my parents, they just smiled tight-lipped smiles and changed the subject. But the next summer, they finally caved when I suggested Peter come too.

In the summer, at the beach house, Cass was golden. Her black hair was flecked with light, her brown skin warmed deeper from the ocean sun, and she smiled so easily. The two of us had gone to different elementary schools, so I hadn't known her when she and her parents had built the one-bedroom log cabin with their own hands. The house was small, but it had an ocean view, which Cass said calmed her Pisces moon sign. The Joshi-Aguilars spent the sunnier months sailing and swimming in the Atlantic's frigid waters by day, and playing old records and making virgin (and not-so-virgin) sangria by night.

On our first trip out on the sailboat, Peter gripped his life vest with both hands at all times. I was grateful mine covered most of my torso. It was the first time I remember feeling woefully self-conscious in my body, but I wasn't alone. Peter was older but still short, timid, and so embarrassed by his new curly body hair that he perpetually kept his T-shirt on. Though my hair was copper, my first sheen of leg hair grew in blond, and I only felt shame when the light hit it right. Cass had a thin, dark layer growing, but she acted like it was beautiful, so we believed her. When she emerged from the waves, droplets of water clung to her shins and board shorts. "Kinda looks like a night rain," she said, touching one bead with her finger. It did.

Cass seemed so comfortable in her body, so in command of the fabric, fiberglass, and bronze of the little ship. I loved to watch her smooth hands play the ropes like a harp. I loved how it felt, to be wind-smacked and sun-kissed, to be guided by my friend across the waters. She taught us how to steer through the wind and the traffic of other boats, but Peter and I were still terrified whenever she made us do anything alone.

"You think you got it?" she asked us after an hour of making us repeat her directions.

"No," we said in unison. Cass smiled mischievously. She unbuckled her life vest and let it drop.

"I think you do," she yelled and dove into the water. Peter and I looked at each other in horror. There were other boats only yards away.

"Get back here!" we called to Cass. "We're going to

hit someone!" She treaded water a few feet away from us and threw her head back to laugh.

"I'm not going to let you hit anything!" she said, coaching us through the motions. Only after we'd stabilized the boat did she swim up to its edges and hoist herself up and over the side.

"You're ridiculous!" Peter said, his salty brown curls whipping in and out of his eyes.

"Maybe," Cass said, "but you sailed."

"You could have drowned!" I said. My heart was racing; I'd been genuinely terrified for her. She shrugged, shoulders up to her ears.

"And I could have made friends with a dolphin, but neither of those things happened." I threw her life vest at her. She deflected it and instead reached out to hug me. Her soaked sports bra and shorts drenched me. I yelped, and Peter rolled his eyes.

"Get a room, you two," he said.

My whole body blushed, and I wondered why he'd said that. Had we hugged for a beat too long? Was it weird to touch each other that way, now that we were getting older? Did everyone think I was gay too, just because I was her friend? Did my brother think that? Had he seen something on my face when she touched me? Had *she*? Cass released me from her grip and turned to hug Peter, instead, and I exhaled.

"You're the worst!" he screeched.

"You're seventy percent water!" Cass retorted. "You're *of* the ocean."

"I'm *of* myself," he said, "and myself doesn't want to be wet."

"Too late," I said, and he flipped me off for the first time in our young lives.

"Peter!" we shrieked in delight. He added a second bird, and Cass hugged him again.

We anchored the boat, hosed the sand and seawater off our feet, and marched back to her parents' house. They lay on a mat on the floor surrounded by construction paper, those gummy glue sticks, and photos ripped out of *National Geographic.* Classical music tinkled out from an old-school boom box.

"Hi, mija," Mr. Aguilar said.

"Hi, Avery; hi, Peter," Mrs. Joshi added. "You want to join?"

"I'm making an oceanscape," Mr. Aguilar said, holding up his cerulean creation. Mrs. Joshi rolled her eyes.

"He thinks he's Hannah Höch," she said. Though I hadn't the slightest clue who that was, I met her glance with a knowing one. Cass's parents were both first-generation immigrants like I technically was (though I was born in Ireland, I didn't remember it, and I had never been back). They were much older than my parents; they met in medical school and were pediatric surgeons for a few decades before making enough money to retire at fifty and live carefully but comfortably. They took up log cabin building and sailing among other things—birding, competitive chess, cider brewing. As soon as Cass was old enough, they let her stay at my house while they backpacked across continents with blank notebooks they'd fill with their own private observations to be exchanged, read by each other, and then ceremoniously burned.

"I suck at arts and crafts," Peter said, carefully bending down to flip through an issue of *Smithsonian.* "But I like 'em."

"I'll make a collage," I said. "I just need to get the saltwater knots out of my hair."

"Come with me," Cass said. She took my hand and led me to the small bathroom in the corner. We took turns changing into dry soccer shorts and T-shirts, then we stood together at the pink porcelain sink decorated with unimpressive seashells. She stepped on a footstool to tower over me. She sprayed my hair with a mist that smelled like the ocean, then ran a brush through it gently. I could feel her breath on my ears when she put the brush back on the sink. She ran her fingers through my hair as a final touch, and my skin prickled.

"Better?" she asked.

"Better," I said, grinning at her in the mirror. "You're my detangler."

Ever since we'd met in sixth grade, she'd been exasperated with me every time I pulled headphones out of my pocket, knotted and balled.

"Avery, Avery, Avery," she'd say with an exaggerated sigh and a roll of her eyes. She'd take the white strings and pluck them apart, straighten them out, put them back in my hands, and shake her head. In the years to come, she'd do it automatically without a word or a joke. She did things for me without thinking. She tightened my lacrosse sticks. Separated a nest of necklaces. Zipped my dress zippers, moved my keys on and off keychains, helped me and Peter with Christmas lights, alphabetized my bookshelf.

"Your detangler? I don't know what that means," she said, but kept her fingers on my scalp.

"Me neither," I said. I imagined her sliding her arms around me from behind, holding me there. I could almost, *almost* feel it, but I knew it wouldn't happen, couldn't happen. Shouldn't happen. We stared at one another stacked in the mirror and dared each other to leave, but neither of us did. She kept running her hands through my hair. My hands gripped the edge of the sink tighter and tighter. And then there was a knock on the door, and my entire body jumped.

"I gotta go," Peter said.

"All good," Cass said. She moved my hair behind my ears and then stepped down from the step stool. Her voice was a little breathless, like I'd caught her doing something she wasn't supposed to.

All good.

For the rest of the afternoon, we sat cross-legged on the floor and made collages with her parents.

"For you," she said when she was done, and slid me her paper with swirls of red, letters at the center that spelled out *AVERY.* I kept both of ours, and Peter's too. I took them home and glued them into a forest-green scrapbook I got at the Mall of New Hampshire. I kept it by my bed every night.

Even when we were ripping magazines to jagged pieces, Cass's art was so cutting, so interesting—she stitched together faces, flowers, hands, and swatches of tiny newspaper print. She mashed up bookshelves, stoic women, skies on fire. Her collages looked like poetry. Mine looked like they were made by a child and were objectively boring, but I loved them still. I put giraffes in space, tree lines behind skyscrapers. I felt like I was creating a new world by gluing paper to paper. I felt like I was saving something. Like *we* were saving everything beautiful, glittering, and strange.

After Peter and I survived that first day in Hampton, my parents let me go back alone, sometimes for whole weekends. Cass taught me to swim by wading with me from the shore into blue-gray waters. She showed me how to float and tread, guided me to the places I could stand up. By the end of the summer, I could swim well enough to dive into the ocean after her when she left the sailboat anchored. We plunged in next to one another, light dancing on Cass's hair, salt stinging my eyes, the sky and sea swirling around us, pushing and pulling us farther away, closer together.

Each trip, I became less and less afraid, until I wasn't scared at all. Not when I swam without a life jacket, not when Cass hugged me for a beat too long, not when we collided with a boat of drunken college guys. Not even the muggy, August day when the sky blinked dark above us and lightning flashed on the horizon.

"Uh-oh," she said as she jumped up to lower the sails, to steer us to safety. "Avoid metal, if you can."

"But you're touching metal!"

"Well, I have to!"

I grabbed her by the hand as a bold wind howled around us, and she looked at me quizzically.

"If you get struck by lightning, I'm going down with you," I shouted.

"I can't sail with one hand."

"Just try!" She did, and I helped. We figured it out together. I attached the safety lines with my left hand while she pulled the tiller to steer with her right, and I couldn't forget, even for a second, that her fingers were locked into mine. I should have been terrified—the sky raging above us, the stretch of angry water before us— but I wasn't. I was with Cass. And after we'd anchored the boat and sprinted home in a downpour, her terrified, horrified, sick-with-worry parents opened the door to find us on their front steps soaked to the bone, laughing.

"You could have died!" Mr. Aguilar yelled, and I was

instantly grateful my parents didn't know we'd been out on the water.

"We didn't die, Dad," Cass said. "We were *electric.*"

We watched the rest of the storm from inside, clutching mugs of hot chai, just the two of us across from each other in the bay window of her bedroom. Rain beat against the roof, yellow lightning ripped the sky, and thunder interrupted the jazz record her parents were spinning in the next room.

I studied Cass as she studied the storm, her face lit by wonder, her smooth fingers gripping her mug so tightly. I missed her fingers clasping mine, but I knew I couldn't reach into the space between us and ask for them again. The threat had passed.

I thought, *I would hold your hand through anything. Even the dangerous things. Even the hard things. I always want to be your best friend.*

For the rest of the summer. For the rest of my life.

nine days
to impact

As Aisha and I drove away from Eaton, the tree line stretched out like a white, fuzzy tunnel. Melanie, ex-custodian, always-hero, could have been driving to Mars, and I would have gone with her. My eyes and brain couldn't focus enough to pay attention to where we were and which way the roads were splitting. In the passenger seat of the van, Melanie's daughter, Vanessa, colored in a coloring book. She looked to be around eight or nine. Every time we hit a bump in the road, she yelled, "*Mom!*" as her hand flew out of the lines. "You made me *scribble*."

Melanie said nothing, and we said nothing, because we didn't know how much the little girl knew. We didn't even know how much we knew, only that we were going to Boston, and it was the best we could do.

Wrecked cars lined the interstate on both sides. The road was edged with ice, so we stayed in the middle lane, unsalted I-93 rolling under the van's tires. Signs for New Hampshire towns scrolled outside the windows waving us *goodbye, goodbye, goodbye.*

Aisha and I were tucked in the middle row of the van. A very large, white, bowlegged pit bull sat in the third row, and she kept leaning forward to lick my ears. Her tongue made me want to crawl out of my skin. The dog belonged to Dr. Basil Talley, professor of American Literature at Eaton College, who was also sitting behind us. He was tall, trim, gray-bearded, and distinguished. He wore tweed suits all through New Hampshire winters. He'd grown up in Louisiana and attended university at our rival school, Dartmouth. He was well loved and well respected, the type of professor I'd dreamed of studying under before I went off to college. Instead, he actively *hated* me, and failed me in the American Short Story because I missed too many classes, turned in almost every single paper late, and "didn't speak enough." I hadn't told my parents yet. I didn't plan to.

Your papers are well constructed, he'd written, *but I have no idea who you are or what you stand for. In light of your apparent intelligence, I chalk that up to sheer laziness and a disregard for your academic potential. The entitlement of student athletes never fails to astound me.*

I resented him, but mostly I was mortified. I'd never

had a teacher hate me before. I'd never even gotten a B. He was the last person I wanted in the van with me, and I felt hot with humiliation.

Next to me, Aisha checked her flight information on her phone and rubbed her locket between her fingers.

"It still says it's on time," she said in a tight voice. I wanted to be encouraging, but I was scared for her. If buses weren't leaving anymore, like Cass said, why would flights be on schedule?

"Where are you headed, Dr. Talley?" I asked to break the silence. He looked at me with such neutrality I wondered if he even remembered I was his least favorite student.

"I suppose I'm going to Louisiana," he said. "I suppose I'm going anywhere I can." I could see Melanie looking at us in her rearview mirror, pleading with us to be quiet for her daughter's sake. I reached into my pocket to check my own phone's messages, but it wasn't there. And it wasn't on the floor, or in the door handle, or in the seat cushions. I checked again and again, frantically, but my hands hit only leather and crayon bits and carpet.

My phone was gone. Sweat ripped down my cheek. I couldn't breathe, suddenly, and I wanted to yell for Melanie to stop the car so I could get out and scream. But I had to get to Cass, so I stayed in that seat and gripped the handle on the door so hard my knuckles turned white.

I tried not to think about it: that I couldn't call her, couldn't call my family. I couldn't *stop* thinking about it.

We drove over part of a moose carcass with a sickening thump. It started to snow again. We passed a woman who was standing between exits using one arm to hitchhike and one arm to hold her baby. The sleeves of her sweatshirt were stiff with snow and ice. She had an eyebrow ring, and a small red backpack that looked so full the zipper might burst. We slowed and asked her where she was trying to go. "Canada," she said. "Montreal."

"You're on the wrong side of the highway, sweetheart," Melanie said. The woman started to cry. "Get in, I'll drive you over."

I opened the door and let her and the wide-eyed baby with frosty eyelashes squish in next to Aisha and me.

"What's in Canada?" Aisha asked her.

"Home."

"Do you want to come with us instead and fly out of Boston?"

"No," she said. "Haven't you heard about all the looting in big cities? Plus, you think planes are still in the air? I doubt it." Aisha and I made eye contact, and I could tell in real time she was starting to doubt it too. Panic lit her eyes.

"I'm sure they are," I said to try to comfort her, but she looked out the window, away from me. We drove the mother and the baby to the northbound side, where we had to leave them in the snow again. Aisha tried to give the woman her white peacoat, but she wouldn't take it. Dr. Talley tried to give her his Bible, but she refused that too.

"Come to Boston with us," Melanie pleaded. "For the baby." But the woman didn't look back at us as she walked into the ivory dust. After we'd driven away, Vanessa kept asking, "What's going to happen to that baby?"

Dr. Talley said to the dog more than anyone, "What's gone and what's past help should be past grief." Melanie ran her fingers through Vanessa's hair while she wailed. A Billy Joel–heavy playlist began again.

Three hours into our journey, I was high, manic. The closer we got to Boston, the more wired with hope I became. The drive hadn't been pleasant, but it also hadn't been impossible. I thought I would find Cass, Aisha would get on a plane, and Melanie, Vanessa, Dr. Talley, and the pit bull would all get put into their own puzzle-piece spaces. If the world had to end, everything would be right. We would all be with the people we loved most. In warm places. Wrapped in delicate quiet.

The mania rolled through my muscles in waves until it turned to exhaustion. I'd been up for close to forty-eight hours, and though I clung to consciousness by biting my tongue and pressing the back of my hand to the cold window, eventually my eyes shut, and I forgot to fight against sleep.

I don't know how long I was out. I don't know how many miles went by before I jerked awake, but I felt a moment of calm before the dread rooted itself in my stomach again. I checked the signs and saw we were close to Massachusetts. I turned to Aisha and saw she was reading something. Her hands trembled.

She was reading a letter.

She was reading a letter written in my handwriting.

She was reading the letter I'd left on the desk for her, meant only to be read when I was hidden in the river. In it, I told her I planned to die. I apologized for the trouble this would cause her. I said it was in no way her fault, wasn't anyone's fault, and there was no one and nothing in the world that could stop me.

Well, almost nothing. I reached for the paper, and she yanked it away from me.

"Aisha, please," I said. "It's mine." She looked at me with a combination of worry, pain, and disbelief.

"It's *mine*," she whispered. "It has my name on it."

I shook my head. I wanted it back. I wanted to rip it up and throw it out the car window. I kicked myself for falling asleep. For not throwing out the letters. For making her carry this thing when, after everything, she didn't have to. Now that I hadn't gone through with it, why did she—or anyone—have to know?

I wanted to explain myself. To lie my face off. In the silence of the van, I tried to think of ways to spin it: It was a homework assignment for my philosophy class. It was a joke. I didn't mean it. It was art? Anything I wanted to say, I couldn't say in front of Dr. Talley, Melanie, or Vanessa. I had to sit in silence while I watched Aisha read the letter again. Sweat slipped down the center of my chest. I could hardly breathe.

Fuck.

I could imagine in a flash our semester at Eaton on too-small twin beds, our long hours logged on the soccer field, in the gym, on the bus. I thought of the walls we had stacked between us to keep from knowing the person on the other side of our dorm room. Now, she knew too much. Way too much. And she couldn't look me in the eye.

"I'm sorry," I whispered. "You weren't supposed to find that. I mean, not anymore."

"Well, I did," she said, reaching for my hand. I didn't want to give it to her; I didn't deserve her kindness, her comfort. But I put my palm in hers, squeezed, and hoped it felt like an apology for burdening her. Though Aisha would know this thing about me forever, I would only be with her for the next hour, and then I would never see her again. I didn't know if that made me feel relieved or devastated.

We hit gridlock traffic when we got close to Boston, and I wondered if we would be able to get into the city at all. Horns blared incessantly. I longed for the Boston I used to know: brick-and-glass buildings cradled by the sea, frozen Bruins games, and the Public Garden's willow trees and neon pink tulips. I knew that was not what waited for us beyond the interstate.

Idling cars clogged the ramps off the highway. We probably jerked forward about an inch every ten minutes. Anxiety drummed through me. I didn't have a phone, and I had to get to South Station before Cass came and went and disappeared. There was no other option. The other side of the highway was also at a standstill. It made me sick, but I knew we'd deal with it. We had to get home. We'd do it. We'd find a way.

"It might be faster to walk," I said. People streamed by our windows on foot toward the city, dragging bags behind them in the snow.

"I agree," Aisha said. I was relieved to hear her voice sounding steady. "I can't miss my flight. They're all going to beat us. And my service seems clogged. My page won't refresh."

We were still about three miles out, and the snow was coming down in flakes as big as silver dollars. Aisha had only her small bag, and I had nothing at all, so that would help us travel more quickly. It also meant we didn't have any water, food, or extra layers. I hoped the traffic would suddenly dissipate so that we could all stay together, but it didn't.

"I'm going to walk too, Melanie," Dr. Talley announced. I clenched my teeth. Of course he was joining us.

"I can't leave the van," she said.

"Will you be all right alone? With Vanessa?"

"I'll be fine," she said, but her voice wavered. "You all do what you need to do, and I'm gonna do what I need to do."

I wanted to say something, anything, that would be enough to thank her for what she'd done for us, but my brain felt fuzzy and I could barely catch my breath. I opened the door and pressed myself between the crowds and the van so Aisha, Dr. Talley, and the dog could get out too.

"'Bye!" Vanessa said, using the word none of us wanted to say.

"Goodbye!" we all said, waving to her through the tinted van window as we walked away. My heart splintered a little bit more. Aisha grabbed one of Dr. Talley's bags and carried it on her shoulder, and Dr. Talley shoved the leash toward my hands. I bristled and tried to think of a way to reject it, but both Aisha and Dr. Talley had their hands full. I resented dogs: their ignorant happiness. Their naïve love. Their permanent state of tail-wagging purity. This was, according to Cass, my greatest flaw.

"What's her name?" Aisha asked, nodding toward the dog.

"Scout," Dr. Talley said. "Harper was a mentor of mine."

Naturally.

We walked for an hour, and I felt panic sinking deeper and deeper into my skin. I was dehydrated and dizzy, so I followed the dog's lead and prayed I wouldn't faint. A thick and ominous smoke hovered over the city like a wig. Sirens and alarm systems continued to screech and echo, unrelenting, but the traffic started to move again, and I felt a new surge of hope and fear.

I wondered if my parents were okay. If Peter and his family were okay. If we were even going to get out of *this* day alive. I wanted to see them again, hold them again. I needed to get Cass and get home. Suddenly I had never needed anything quite so badly in all my life. I'd forgotten how much it hurt to want things.

When we got closer to the city, about a mile out from downtown, the cars slowed to a roll up ahead. Pedestrians climbed onto their roofs and trunks and rode them like birds on an elephant.

I spotted a Logan Airport van in the middle of the three lanes. There were two tall men already riding on top of it.

"Look," I said, "that would be perfect. We can ride that van for a while."

"Good idea," Aisha said.

I made eye contact with the driver, a small man in a parka. I pointed to his roof. He gave me a thumbs-up without hesitation.

"Let's go," I said. The four of us sprinted between lanes and jogged to keep up with the flow of traffic. Once the airport van came to a stop, Aisha boosted me onto the roof and I helped her, Dr. Talley, and Scout scramble up after me. One family followed us, a mom and a dad and their two teenage girls.

"This is going to Logan, right?" Aisha asked. "I need to get to Logan Airport."

"Logan's been closed all day," one of the tall guys said, his backward ballcap ridged with ice. "No flights in or out." I bit down on my tongue to stop myself from crying out.

"But I have a flight. I have a boarding pass. It's booked." Aisha felt around for her phone, but when she pulled it out of her pocket, her fingers were too cold to open her lock screen. She blew on them to try to warm them up.

"If that's why you're going to Boston, you should turn around right now. It's not only shut down; it's blocked off with tanks. No use going into this hell if you don't have to. You might not make it out alive."

Aisha looked to me and her body went rigid. "What do I do?"

I wanted to panic too, but I knew her situation was unbearable, shattering. She needed someone to lean on. I could be that person. I could keep it together for a while, for her. I rubbed her back, but I wasn't sure if she could feel it. "We'll figure it out," I said. "We'll fix this. I'm not going to leave you behind." I plastered a false smile on my face, like I always did.

"Maybe you can hitchhike?" the mother suggested. "Where are you trying to go?"

"Kano, Nigeria," I said quietly, since Aisha couldn't.

"That's not going to happen," one of the daughters said, smacking her chewing gum. We all looked at her with collective fury.

"We'll figure it out. We'll figure it out," I said again. I didn't believe myself, and from the look on Aisha's face, I don't think she believed me either.

The Logan Airport van (not going to Logan Airport) crawled forward into smoke, sirens, and snow. *It looks apocalyptic*, I thought, and my stomach seized. It was.

We melted snow in our mouths to ease our thirst. We hid our hands anywhere we could to keep them warm. Pain iced our butts, ears, and toes. It seemed plausible we might freeze to death, but eventually the van made it onto Storrow Drive, where yesterday, cars would have been zooming by, weaving in and out of traffic to cut each other off, horns blaring. We climbed down off the roof and began to walk again. We put one foot in front of the other, moving in a sick little silence, onto the streets of Back Bay.

Broken glass shimmered in the snow in front of the shops on Newbury Street. In my summer memories, those shops were colorful and curated. In front of us, they were gutted and gaping. An entire building was on fire, its insides charred. Families huddled under blankets crying, watching it burn. The smoke made it hard to breathe. Cars jammed every street, and people darted around them, their arms full of food and boxes. How had the world—my world—shattered so swiftly?

We watched in horror as a guy in a Patriots hat punched an old man in the face, reached down to pick through his pockets, and ran off. The man with white hair lay facedown in the middle of the street, blood streaming from the open wound on his forehead. Without words, Aisha and I went to him and knelt beside him as if he were an injured teammate. We helped him roll onto his side, and I used my sleeve to wipe the blood out of his eyes.

"Can we help you?" I asked him.

"Let us help you," Aisha echoed when he didn't answer me.

"There's nowhere for me to go," he said. "Leave me here." Drool froze on his chin.

"We can't leave you," I said. "You need to get to a hospital." My stomach sunk as I wondered if hospitals were even open.

A street away, an ambulance inched down the sidewalks. Dr. Talley ran after it, his lanky body tumbling forward with Scout charging ahead of him. "Help!" he yelled, desperately. It was the first time I'd ever heard his voice rise above a dry, academic whisper. "Help!"

The ambulance slowed to a stop, but it couldn't get down the street, so Aisha and I picked the old man up. I felt surprised, at first, that we could move together without speaking. But hadn't we spent hours working in tandem on the field? We could anticipate each other's motions. The strength in her arms balanced the strength in mine. We stepped carefully, slowly, over debris and ice. My biceps strained under his weight, but I could tell we would make it.

"Okay, okay," the old man said, over and over, as if to convince himself something, anything was okay. He rolled his head back and forth. His blood stained the sleeves of my jacket.

When we reached the ambulance, Dr. Talley helped us lift the old man inside the vehicle. The EMT driver, a woman with an orange vest and tired eyes, put her hand on the man's face and said, matter-of-factly, "Sir, we're going to take care of you." Her voice was full of such certainty it calmed me down too. The man didn't say anything in response, but he stopped moaning as she took a wet cloth to his forehead.

"The hospitals are still open?" Aisha asked the woman.

"Sort of," she said, wincing as if in apology. As she slammed the ambulance's back door shut, she added, "We have more people than we can handle—and about half of our staff. We're doing our best."

"And the airport?"

"Closed. Even if they wanted to send planes out, no other airports are accepting them." Aisha knelt to the ground beside me and stifled a sob.

"And South Station?" I asked, but the EMT worker shut the driver's door before she could answer me.

She was still helping people. People were still helping people. Couldn't I? Wasn't that the only way I knew how to get through anything at all?

"Come with me," I shouted at Aisha and Dr. Talley over the wailing sirens. "Come to Kilkenny until things settle down. Then we'll get you back here when you can fly, I promise." They both stared at me blankly, but followed me as I started toward South Station. Though I was the one who had invited Aisha to my home, I felt anxious with her at my heels. She knew my ugly, harmful secret. She would always know it. Dr. Talley, too, knew some of my shame, my failure. But I still wanted them with me, despite it all. I still held on to them as we tripped over the cobblestones and ice and pulled each other to our feet.

We kept moving our aching bodies, and my brain vibrated with terrible questions: Would Cass get to South Station at all? Would I find her? If not, then what? *Then what?!* But the only thing I could do was keep walking toward her, or at least the place she was supposed to be. I would be there if she made it. I'd be waiting for her if she stepped off the bus. I'd keep my promise. That was the only thing I knew with certainty.

four years
to impact

I spent a lot of my young life trying to repent for diving into the neighbors' pool. I didn't want to go to Hell. I tried to be someone worthy of saving: by getting good grades, training hard for soccer, and praying even harder. As soon as I received Holy Communion, I became an altar server and sat on display on the stage at every Sunday Mass. I wore a white robe and a gold cross and helped the priest carry candles and books. If I was lucky, I got to ring the bell for consecration.

When I turned fourteen in eighth grade, I ran for head of our Catholic Charities program. Most girls who led it were at least sixteen, usually older, but I wowed the committee with an essay on purposeful philanthropy and ethical altruism. Although I'm sure it didn't hurt that my parents were prominent members of the community who read scripture at Mass weekly and always remembered cash for the collection basket. In the email the board sent offering me the position, they called my essay inspiring, forward-thinking, and wise beyond my years. I screenshotted it and sent it to Cass with the caption *Ah yes, the three tenets of the Catholic Church.* But they chose me out of twelve applicants. I was proud. It felt like it *meant* something. Something good.

Cass was both Jain and Catholic, or, as she called it, Catholish. Her parents made her attend both the temple and Mass every weekend so she could learn both religions and decide what she believed in for herself, but the Joshi-Aguilars went to a different parish in Manchester. The summer after freshman year, I convinced her to come to Catholic Girls' Camp with me and my mom who'd eagerly volunteered as a chaperone. It was basically a classic summer camp experience: friendship bracelets, pottery, canoeing, and hiking, with Bible readings and CCD classes by firelight. It was also one of my major tasks as the group leader to organize the nightly readings and act as a counselor. I was fifteen and proud. And *stressed.*

We drove up to Lake Winnipesaukee in a blue church van, its seats packed with girls and my mom at the wheel. We threw our bags into wooden lean-tos, put on matching fuchsia Our Lady of Mercy T-shirts, and marched through the woods singing songs about Jesus while slapping the mosquitos at our ankles. We ate food like oatmeal and mashed potatoes that had been dehydrated and then hydrated again, and you could taste it.

I handed out the schedules, woke everyone up on time, and led troops of girls to the camp's mess hall. It was exhausting. There was so much to keep track of, so many people to answer to.

"Avery!" I felt like my name was everywhere, and I had to be *on* all the time. I put Band-Aids on scraped knees, found extra bug spray for the sweet-blooded, coordinated meals for the kids with allergies. I liked being there for all of them, but I hated being the center of attention. At least it made my mom happy.

"I'm so proud of you," she kept saying, anytime we crossed paths. "And you know who else is? God." High praise.

Cass, on the other hand, kept me grounded. "Saint Avery!" she mimicked the other campers quietly as we walked through the shadows of trees to get to breakfast one morning. "Mother Avery! Nun? Avery! I didn't know there were New Hampshire celebrities until this trip."

"Oh, stop," I said. "It's my job! I'm the leader." I was still proud of that, but I was losing steam by the minute.

"Oh, *are* you the leader?" She shook a spider off her arm. "I never would have guessed."

"Geez."

"No, it's cool. It's just a little exhausting being your friend. You're in such high demand."

"It's a little exhausting being me." I flipped my hair. "But I guess that's my cross to bear."

"Too soon."

"Cass!"

"Avery!"

"Forgot to mention: If you don't make me a friendship bracelet today, I might have to ex-communicate you from the church."

"That's not very Christian of you."

"It's not, but I'm drunk with power."

"Excellent. I love when you're bossy."

We shared a lean-to with one other girl, Ella West, a big-eyed blond who loved horses, shopping, and monogrammed, pastel clothing. She was dating the son of a state senator and lived in one of the richest neighborhoods in town. She was pleasant enough, and when I couldn't think of anything to talk to her about, I would ask about her relationship with Noah, and she was more than happy to ramble on eternally.

Cass had an easier time connecting with her, though. They became fast friends. As I drifted off in my sleeping bag each night—run down and empty—I'd hear them chatting away about sailing and dogs and Playa del Carmen. They carried each other's backpacks, counted stars, split granola bars they had saved for each other. They were an unlikely pair, and I felt a twinge of jealousy every time Cass sat next to Ella at meals instead of next to me, even though it was because I was busy. I still got all of Cass's friendship bracelets, though. Or at least, so I hoped.

On the final night of camp, we all trudged down to the amphitheater, where everyone sat in theater-style rows. I was the emcee, and as I stood at the podium in the middle of the sea of faces, I tried to decide: Had I done enough? To be saved? To be loved? To be good?

A woman in a pink ballcap gave me a microphone, and my skin buzzed with the heat of the summer, the colors of the setting sun, and the murmurs of an excited crowd. I'd been going to camp since I was eleven. I'd always looked up to the girl who was the center of this moment, this beautiful testimonial, and now it was me.

And still I felt empty. And still I felt alone.

"Thank you, everyone, for coming tonight," I said, and had to pause a second to catch my breath. "I hope everyone had an amazing week." There were hoots and whistles, applause and amens. "We're here tonight so we can share final reflections. Form a line at the side of this stage and know we will absolutely get to everyone. When you're speaking, please know you're in a safe space. When you're listening, remember we're not here to judge each other. This is meant to bring us closer to God, Jesus, and the Holy Spirit. To begin, please recite the Lord's Prayer with me."

One by one, girls lined up to speak about their

connection to God, how He'd saved them, how He'd guided them. I listened to their stories of cancer, eating disorders, and recovery. They were moved to tears. Their belief looked *real*. You could tell it lived in their bodies. My skin prickled with envy, because when I thought of God, all I felt was shame. Fear. What did I have to do to feel *that* way—solid and holy? What did I have to do to earn that? I was a good daughter. I worked so hard, at everything. I was the *leader*. But it still didn't feel like enough.

Ella West, who had of course been sitting next to Cass, was one of the last girls in line, and by the time she was illuminated by the white floor lights, her hair looked completely glow-in-the-dark. She flashed a wide smile as she took the mic in her hand and looked positively joyful as she began to speak. Cass called, "Yeah, Ella!"

"Hi, ladies," she said. "I've had the best time this week getting to know you all, and I wanted to ask for some special prayers. There are wonderful people I've met this week who I feel deserve to be saved by the Lord's grace. But we have to help them get there. There are some people among us who are homosexuals, who I think are still virgins and capable of being saved but are going to eventually live in sin. I don't want that for them! God doesn't want that for them! They don't have to choose that."

"What the hell is wrong with you?" I said. I didn't realize I was still mic'd up, and my words echoed throughout the hall and ended in the crowd's collective gasp. My face shocked with blood, and I saw my mom turn and walk toward an exit. Cass, too, stood up from her seat and ran up the stairs. "Sorry," I mumbled, and then with more conviction, "I'm an ally, and that's really wrong, Ella."

I ripped my microphone off my T-shirt and threw it on the ground with a thud. I chased my mom and Cass into the night.

In front of the amphitheater, I found them sitting on a splintery bench. They both looked sick, and my throat closed up. I wasn't sure who I should apologize to or what I should apologize for, but I knew I should start.

"I'm sorry I swore, Mom," I said. "I just . . . what was that?"

"You should have stayed down there and defended me," Cass said.

"I did," I said. "Didn't you hear me?"

"Kind of, but your 'I'm an ally' was very no-homo." She crossed her arms against her chest like a shield, and I did too, ashamed of myself. Was she . . . mad at me? We'd never even argued before.

"She couldn't have been talking about you," Mom said to Cass. "Don't worry."

"She was absolutely talking about me," Cass said. "I'm a lesbian, Mrs. Byrne. You know that. Super gay and very proud of it. And Ella knows too. I told her.

This whole week she's been, like, flirting with me. And now this."

"I repeat: What the h—heck—is wrong with her?" I said.

"You can still be saved, Cass," Mom said, and folded her hands like she was praying. Like she was begging. "Ella's right. It's not too late. You can still go to Heaven, if you ask God to be forgiven for—"

"*Mom*, stop!" I cried out to cut her off, to spare Cass from whatever she was about to say next. I hugged my arms tighter against my chest and realized I was shaking—from rage or fear or both. "Jesus loves everyone just as they are." It felt like I was begging too.

"Save it, Avery," Cass said. "I don't even want to go to Heaven if it's all straight people. This religion is bullshit."

"Don't say things like that," Mom said, and made the sign of the cross. "You're a good girl, and a good friend to Avery. You deserve to be saved."

Cass stood up and put her hands on her head. "I need to go for a walk. Come with me?" Her eyes met mine. It felt like a dare.

"Yeah. Of course." I looked to my mom, and though I felt bad for leaving her with tears in her eyes, I had to make things right with Cass. I had to make sure she was okay. She took off in a jog down the forest path, and I followed her.

"Don't go to the water!" Mom called after me, but of course that was exactly where we were headed.

When we hit Lake Winnipesaukee, we slowed down and she put her hands on her knees to catch her breath. "I can't come back here," she said. "Not next year, not ever."

"Don't let someone like that take this away from you," I said. "This is yours just as much as it's hers. More, even."

"What's 'this'? Camp? Catholicism? Because nope. This is yours, Ave. You can have it."

"Not Catholicism, not camp. Christianity. Whatever that means to you." I tried to touch her arm, but she jerked away from me.

"What if it doesn't mean anything, huh?"

"Don't say that, Cass. You don't mean it."

"I do. How can you trust in any of it when people are like *that*? I thought she was my friend."

"It was cruel, what Ella did. But she's one girl. One person out of that whole group."

"The whole church thinks that way! Come on, Avery. You heard your own mother."

I wanted to protest again, to prove her wrong, but my mom's words ricocheted around in my brain: *You can still go to Heaven. You deserve to be saved.* But only if Cass changed who she was entirely. My mom had always thought that way, I knew that. But it was the first time I heard her say it out loud.

Cass was right, wasn't she? Even if Jesus loved everyone—that was like, his *whole* thing—our church didn't, not really. No wonder it didn't feel special or good to stand at the center with a microphone. No wonder I felt cold standing there, even in the summer wind. Did I have to choose, then, between the church—the thing that I always thought might save me—and my very best friend? I did. It kind of broke my heart.

But then, hadn't I already decided?

"I hope you know *I* don't think that way," I said, and when she smiled softly, I breathed again.

"I know," she said.

"And I'm sorry I said I'm an ally back there." She laughed a little, and slung her arm around my shoulders.

"No, it's okay. I was just upset. You meant well."

We sat on the grass at the edge of the lake, alone together. Her knee touched mine, and it was all I could think about, but neither of us moved to put inches between us. And there it was, finally, the spark I'd been waiting for all week, fear, awe, beauty, all at once. There was more holiness in the cricket cry, in the starlight, in the silver, moon-painted waters than I had felt all week. Loons sang to us, beautiful, bittersweet songs, and wandering fireflies lit the dark with golden sparks. No one from camp could see us. No one from church could touch us. And I thought, *No other heaven could ever compare to this one. It doesn't want us to grovel. It doesn't need us to change.*

"You know Ella was talking about you too, right?" Cass said.

"Me?"

"She thinks you and I are secretly dating."

I could feel my cheeks burn red and was grateful for the darkness. "Why does she think that?"

"How should I know?"

"Did you tell her we're not?"

"Obviously."

Ella couldn't know anything about me I didn't know about myself. Right? It wasn't that I thought being gay was a bad thing. Cass was my very favorite person, after all. But how did I know if I was gay too? How did anyone know? Was it normal to want to hold her hand by the water? And wouldn't anyone notice the moonlight in her hair, the way it cut across her face, how many times she'd rolled the sleeves of her T-shirt, the way her arms looked as she pulled her knees to her chest and stared out across the lake?

"Have you kissed anyone yet?" I couldn't believe the words that left my mouth. Cass turned to study me.

"No," she said slowly. "You know that."

"Do you want to?"

"I mean. Yeah." Her breath quickened. I hadn't kissed anyone either, but she didn't know that. I had certainly implied something had happened between me and a boy at soccer camp one summer, and I had been too embarrassed to take it back.

"What if we kissed here?" I said quickly. "Just to spite them." She smirked and looked away from me.

"Is that what allies do, Avery?"

"No," I said. "Sorry, I was—" *Kidding*, I was going to say, but before I could, she leaned over and pressed her lips to mine. She pulled them away lightning fast, and I reeled a little, put my fingers to my mouth.

"Oh God," I said, only because I was surprised—by the kiss, by how hard my heart hammered, but she looked stricken.

"Wow, you're freaking out, huh?" She crossed her arms. "Relax. You're not my type."

It felt like she'd slapped me.

"Oh, right. No, of course. But that'll show 'em." My words came out breathlessly. We were quiet for a few moments, and the heat between us was unbearable. Had I ruined everything? Our friendship and her first kiss? Mine? I exhaled with relief when she opened her mouth to speak.

"It's funny," she said quietly. "I came into tonight thinking so strongly I don't believe in God or Gods or whatever. I've been stewing over it all week, biting my tongue. But I'm looking at this." She spread her hands toward the water. "Feeling like *this*." She touched her chest. "There must be something, right? Do you feel it too?"

"Yes," I said, still breathless, still wounded. But I didn't mean God.

For the first time in my life, I didn't feel Him at all.

But my mind started to race. Without God, who was

I? Why were we here? What did this life mean, if we weren't trying to earn the afterlife?

Without Hell or Heaven, where did that leave me?

It left me there with Cass until my mom and a search team of girls came through the trees screaming for us.

"What were you doing out here?" Mom asked us. Cass and I locked eyes in the lake light, for maybe a second too long. But in that moment I knew we were choosing each other. That we always would choose each other—over Ella, over the church, over family, over God, even. It was scary. It was right. She was my *best friend*.

My friendship bracelets fell off in the shower a few weeks later, but the small white stripe of skin they protected lasted through the summer. So did the spray of freckles on my face, the sting on my lips, the empty sky, the prayerless nights. My questions.

nine days
to impact

When I visited Boston as a kid, it felt like anything could happen there: I got to throw peanut shells on the floor of Fenway Park. Pick out a coffee-based ice cream at J.P. Licks (not realizing it contained zero caffeine). Feed the chubby, too-friendly squirrels in Boston Common, who would waddle right up to take pieces of my cone from my hand.

But this was a different Boston. It was frigid, howling, and spinning as people ran around me, Aisha, Dr. Talley, and Scout. The walk from Storrow Drive to South Station should have taken forty-five minutes, and maybe it did, but it felt like hours. I sobbed without realizing it. Aisha sang to herself, manically. Dr. Talley stayed stoic. I'm sure someone would have tried to rob us if we had anything left to take, but all we had were our jackets, one satchel bag, and whatever was within them. It still felt like anything could happen in Boston, but this time, it wouldn't be anything good.

When the red banners of South Station broke into view, I took off running on legs I could no longer feel. I squeezed my way up the stairs of the bus terminal and thought I might be trampled by the stampede going in the opposite direction. I fought through bodies to get to a young woman in a blue megabus uniform.

"Where's the bus from New York?"

She pointed down the buzzing hallway. "There's a lot of buses coming from New York, honey. Only reason I'm still here is 'cause I'm waiting too." I tried to do the math in my head for the thousandth time that day, to calculate the rates at which Cass's bus could have traveled, if it traveled at all. *Had her ride been like ours? Could she get out of New York? Could she get into Boston?*

I caught my reflection in the glass wall behind the woman and ran toward it to wipe the matted hair out of my eyes. My lips and hands were bleeding, eyes swollen. My clothes were wet through to my muscles. I shouldn't have cared what I looked like. It was absurd to care, but I was about to see Cass, and I was unsalvageable. It was one more sliver of despair.

After I wiped the blood on my sleeves and brushed my hair with my fingers, I made my way to the New York terminal and stood by a bench I could cling to. On the TV monitors, news channels ran silent banners:

Asteroid Confirmed: 9 days remain. More at 11 p.m....
Nine days was nothing. Nine days was an eternity.

Scout barked somewhere behind me, and I felt Aisha and Dr. Talley approach. Though I didn't know it was possible, my panic ramped up when I realized I still hadn't had time to talk to Aisha. *Would she tell Cass about the letter?* I wanted to pull her away from Dr. Talley to plead with her, but I didn't want to miss Cass if she came through the crowd.

"Aisha," I said, hardly looking at her. "You won't tell anyone, right?"

"We have bigger concerns than that right now, Avery."

"I mean, of course, but . . ."

"What's the problem?" Dr. Talley asked.

"There's no problem," I said.

"No problem," Aisha echoed. She placed a hand on my back, and whispered, "But you should tell people, Avery. Or at least someone who's not me."

"I know," I said, though I didn't see the point in telling anyone now. "But—"

"I won't tell anyone," she said, "for now."

For now? "Thanks. Where is she?"

"She'll be here."

But for about an hour she wasn't, and my skin crawled with an unbearable poison. She wasn't there. She wasn't there. Cass wasn't there.

And then, she was.

She took tentative steps out of a bus door, her canvas duffel bag hugged against her chest. She'd pulled her hair back into a bun and was wearing her New York uniform: tight black pants, black tailored coat, black scarf, black boots, and a calculated cool expression, even amid all the chaos.

Her stony stare cracked open when she saw me, and beneath it was the girl I'd known most of my life. Relief erupted through me, and I couldn't keep it down. We ran to each other and collided violently. We tangled our limbs and then untangled them. We put hands on cheeks, laughed, and fell to the floor. It was almost like before. It was almost like the incident in New York hadn't happened at all.

"You look like you've been through hell," she said, running her fingers through the knots in my hair. She didn't know the half of it. I grabbed the front of her coat. I would have been happy to die right there, but Aisha hovered over us anxiously and Dr. Talley wasn't far behind.

"Aisha, hey." Cass stood up and pulled me with her.

"We have to go," Aisha said, and I remembered for the first time we were shipwrecked—on an island in a sea of chaos.

"You're both coming to Kilkenny," I said again. Scout barked. "All three of you." Dr. Talley opened his mouth, perhaps to protest, but jogged behind the rest of us as we left the station.

. . .

Outside, the cold sharpened, piercing through my jacket and jeans so thoroughly I felt naked. The four of us gripped on to handfuls of each other and stumbled through the crowd, looking for an opening.

"Maybe we can ride on a van like we did on the way here?" I shouted over the wailing sirens.

"Or sit in the back of a truck," Cass shouted back. "Have our *But I'm a Cheerleader* moment."

"Whatever, let's move toward the highway," Aisha said.

We made our way past the Boston Tea Party Ships & Museum, through the Rose Kennedy Greenway, where the brick pathways had been ripped up by tires, and past the New England Aquarium, where the seals did hypnotic laps in their outdoor tank. We passed the still-lit Waterfront Park, its ivy trellis haloed by blue-and-yellow Christmas lights. I looked for I-93 and found it by tracing the snake of cars leading down toward Faneuil Hall. Every car honked in standstill. And worse, as far as we could see, people had crammed onto every car's roof, into every truck bed. Perhaps if we split up, we could have squeezed in, but the five of us together were not going to make it.

"Maybe we should stay the night," Aisha said.

"No," I said quickly. "We have to get home."

"What if Logan opens again?"

"It's not gonna open again! Look around!" Cass yelled.

"Do not gang up on me because there're two of you

now," Aisha said. She looked to Dr. Talley for backup, but he quietly patted the dog, whose cries grew more frantic.

"Do you want to split up and stay here?" I asked.

"Of course not," she said. "But how are we getting out of here?"

"What if we look for an abandoned car and take the back roads?" I suggested.

"Who's going to leave their car?"

"People are leaving their cars."

"Only because they can't move them."

"If you see a vehicle older than 1990, alert me," Dr. Talley said. "I have dabbled in hot-wiring."

"I'm sorry, *what?*" Cass sounded more than a little impressed. I scanned the side streets around us, searching everywhere for an empty driver's seat. All I found were desperate faces.

"Oh, for goodness' sake. There!" Aisha said suddenly. I whipped my gaze to where she was pointing: a beat-up burgundy Toyota a few yards away, exhaust billowing out of the tail pipe, all four doors swung wide open. It looked like it was about to take flight. We all took off running.

"I'll drive!" Dr. Talley called.

"Head north," I said. We threw ourselves into the car, and Cass buried her face into my shoulder as Dr. Talley locked the doors, drove up on sidewalks, honked the horn at pedestrians, and headed away from the highway.

I looked out the back window, where fire, smog, and shrieking buried the city. Dr. Talley whipped the car at sharp angles around discarded, broken vehicles. Within minutes he'd clipped off both of the mirrors. Cass's fingers rattled on my arms.

"You're shaking," I whispered.

"I want to go home."

"We're going home," I said, but with her head on my shoulder, I was already halfway there.

About half an hour out of Boston, the roads opened and we cruised slowly but surely ahead with Dr. Talley at the wheel. Cass gently stroked the dog's ears while Aisha tuned the radio every few minutes, desperate for updates. Strangers' voices peppered us with information:

"Seven of the world's largest space programs have confirmed impact in just nine days, around eleven p.m., Eastern Standard Time."

"It's not looking good, Barbara, I'll tell you that. The bees are reacting. The bees! They know what they're talking about."

"Over twenty fatalities have been reported at the site of the Logan Airport brawl—"

"You gotta think we have the resources to get our most valuable people to Mars, you know? Like Noah's ark but for people who are the best at everything. For hottest woman, I'd pick—"

Aisha smashed the volume button to turn it off, and we sat in silence, simmering.

We started to run out of gas near the New Hampshire border, but Cass still had cell phone battery, so she texted everyone in my family to let them know our location. Within seconds, her phone vibrated and lit up with LAURA BYRNE. Cass tapped Speakerphone, and we braced ourselves.

"Cass?" Mom said in a thin, high-pitched voice.

"I'm here too," I said. "I lost my phone."

"Avery! Where are you?!"

"I'm in a car coming from Boston with Cass, Aisha, and one of my professors."

"Why were you in Boston? It's a war zone!"

"I'm safe, and I'll explain when I'm home, okay? We're approaching the border, and we're running out of gas."

"Dad and I are at Market Basket with Peter. We're in line for food baskets. They're throwing everything into bags and giving them away."

"I'm here for the cookies!" Dad yelled somewhere next to her.

"Could you come get us after?" I asked. There was scuffling and static.

"Avery?! It's Dad," a new voice said.

"Dad, could you come get us after?"

"Peter's on his way. We have to go, our battery is running down."

Sure enough, somewhere near Salem, our headlights splashed across Peter's red pickup truck, which was pulled over on the shoulder of the road.

"Stop the car," I said, and without a word, Dr. Talley pulled over behind him. As soon as I was out the door, Peter's arms wrapped around me so tightly I couldn't breathe.

"We all thought you were dead," he said. "Don't do that ever again. It's dangerous out here."

I pulled away to look at his face. His eyes were cloudy with exhaustion and fear, scanning me as if I were covered in words he couldn't decipher. Maybe that was true. Peter could read me better than anyone, so I broke away from him before he knew too much.

He stuck his hand out to Dr. Talley and Aisha.

"Peter Lasky," he said. "Avery's brother." Peter had taken Georgia's last name when they got married, and though it was cool, I still couldn't quite get used to it.

"Dr. Basil Talley. Former professor of literature."

"Aisha," she said. "I've seen you in Avery's photographs."

"Cool. I've seen you play."

Cass leapt on Peter, and he stumbled backward into the truck bed. "Pete!"

"Cass! My other sister."

"Ew," we both said. Dr. Talley towered over all of us and cast shadows in the headlights. He wrapped his fist tightly around the dog's collar, but she yanked his arm to roll onto her back and offer her belly up to Peter.

"Hey, girl," he said, kneeling to pet her until a passing car zipped within a foot of them.

"Let's get moving," Dr. Talley said. He pulled the dog onto her feet, and Peter pushed the seats forward so Dr. Talley and Scout could climb into the back seat of the pickup truck. Aisha climbed into the passenger seat.

"We can sit in the back," I said. "We've done it before."

Peter shrugged, so we hoisted ourselves over the side. We pulled slowly back onto the road and headed for Kilkenny, which wasn't any place special, but it was home. It was known for its apple orchards, sports teams, and marching band. It had two stretches of chain restaurants and strip malls. It had schools and soccer fields and churches. Also, in 1719, it was the first place in North America where the Irish planted potatoes, a fact my dad loved to tell every stranger who would listen.

In the bed of the truck, Cass and I sat shoulder to shoulder. She tried to say something to me, but I couldn't hear her over the howl of wind and tires on gravel. We slid onto our sides to try to hide from the sound, from the world.

"I'm scared," she shouted. I wanted to close the distance between us, to hold her. I put my shaking hand on her cheek. She put her fingers in my hair to try to untangle knots that wouldn't budge.

"I'm here," I shouted back. I rubbed my thumb across her cheekbone and tried to calm her, but I was scared too. Not because of the asteroid, but because I could smell the lilac in her hair. The warm cologne on her neck. If I reached forward, I would taste it too.

Like I had in New York. When I'd tried to kiss her, and then—

I turned away from her to face the sky and felt the wind on my skin. It hurt, but I let it. And I could only think two things:

I love her, I love her, I love her.

And:

She's better off without me.

I don't know which thought filled me with more sorrow, or if they were separate thoughts at all, but I didn't have time to decide. The truck slowed as we turned onto McIntosh Court. When we sat up, when we put more distance between us, I had to be just me again. It was as cold and as dark as it had been before. It was so quiet, even as my parents opened the garage door and yelled for us to hurry inside.

four years
to impact

When we were kids, Peter was weird. He wore a black cape around school, pretended to be a cat in public, and hissed at anyone who tried to give him shit for it. I was weird too, but I cared what *everyone* thought, and it felt like if God could read every single idea that was inside me, other people might be able to too. In the months after I jumped into the Davidsons' pool, I stopped speaking to everyone except for my family. I didn't want anyone to know me. I was ashamed of myself, and scared of doing something else that might send me to Hell. At home, I said things here and there to avoid any sort of serious intervention, but at school I refused to speak to anyone unless I was called on in class.

During recess, I'd hide in a hot yellow plastic tunnel

on the playground, sweating into my floral outfits, wishing I could disappear. Kids teased me and tried to drag me out until Peter found out. He was a fifth grader, and it was wildly uncool for him to associate with me, but he didn't care about cool. He'd sit outside the tunnel to keep me company and keep the other kids away. He'd move his hand around to catch the light and cast shadows into my yellow tube. He'd talk to me about Greek mythology and animals and cartoons. Every recess I stared at his silhouette, and I felt safe.

I spent all of middle school without him while he went off to high school, and I had no choice but to make it on my own. Lucky for me, it was the first time I could try out for the school soccer team, and when people realized I was damn good, actually—strong, tricky-footed, and far faster than even the eighth graders on the team—my classmates let me rewrite my reputation. And thank God, because I met Cass at tryouts for the very first time, and she got to know me as the quiet, rock star rookie. She didn't have to know about the pool or the playground, about the gravity of my fear or the depth of my sadness.

The first time she came over to our house, Peter and I led her up to the lookout tower in the apple orchard beyond our backyard, where we all talked for hours about aliens, basketball, and reincarnation. After she left, he said, "Your new friend is freaking awesome, Ave."

"You know she's, um, gay, right?" I said, and looked at my hands while I waited for him to respond.

"Oh, yeah?" he said. "That's cool." When I looked back at him, his smile seemed genuine, and I felt relieved my favorite person could see in her what I did: chemistry and comfort and light. I trusted Peter so much. His approval made me like Cass even more than I already did, which was a whole hell of a lot.

By the time I was in eighth grade, he was a senior with a red pickup truck who had stopped wearing a cape and become moderately popular because he was handsome and goofy and kind, but he still hung out with me. He never made me feel immature or silly; he asked for my opinions, and laughed at my jokes. He invited Cass and me to pile into his back seat with his friends and took us out to ice cream, to the mall, to lakes, forests, mountains, and oceans. I felt like he knew me better than anyone. I felt like I knew him better than anyone. When he went to college at UNH—even though it was only an hour away, even though he came home to visit all the time—it left me unmoored. Before, my parents split their focus between the two of us, but with me alone, they watched my every facial expression, my every move.

"Are you all right, there, Avery?" Dad would say if my face fell even a little bit at dinner.

"Oh, yeah, fine." I'd smile big and take an even bigger bite of my pot pie. "I got an A on the bio test I got back today."

"Wow, superstar," they'd say. "We're so proud of you."

It was hard but worth it, to perform on paper—in the classroom, on the soccer field. It made me look good. They thought I was thriving. I liked that they thought that about me. I *needed* them to think that about me.

But it wasn't real. I had a lot to fake.

For some reason, starting in ninth grade, I felt like crying pretty much all the time, and I didn't know why. If I didn't want my parents to ask me questions (and I very much didn't), I had to wait until they were asleep to cry in my room. And why? *Why?* Was it because I missed Peter? Because it was so damn exhausting to succeed like I did? Was it because the junior and senior boys had started making rude comments to me in the hallway, asking me what kind of underwear I was wearing, mocking me when it made me blush? They told me it was a compliment when I asked them to stop. That wasn't such a big deal, was it?

And I did miss Peter. I did. Every day.

In Durham, Peter grew a beard. He put on a few pounds and it suited him. When I went to visit him during his first semester, I realized he'd found his *people*, people who weren't me. He'd befriended practically everyone in his dorm, mostly down-to-earth, friendly kids from New Hampshire, but also students from all over the world. He started to roll with the art crowd, which was the absolute last crowd I thought he'd ever roll with. He'd been a science freak all through school. I thought he wanted to be a vet.

But I think he mostly wanted to be around Georgia Lasky, a girl he met the first week of college with big brown eyes, short blue hair, and a super fancy tattoo of a bee on the inside of one wrist and a flower on the inside of the other. She was from Brooklyn, came to UNH because she wanted fresh air, and loved to sketch the rows of peonies and poinsettias in the campus greenhouses. The first time I met her, she dragged me and Peter there. We sat across from her on wooden benches, surrounded by foliage and glass.

"Your brother is the *only* person I've ever met who likes art and science equally. Sees them as two sides of the same coin. As I do," she said. Peter grinned sheepishly, and I sent him a wide-eyed look that said, *Oh, is he really?* "Maple?" Georgia reached into her tote bag and then offered us sugar candy like they sold in the Purple Finch Orchard Country Store back home.

"Oh, wow, thanks," I said. "These are my favorite." She put the little hazel leaf in my hand. I popped it into my mouth and let it melt as I watched Georgia pull out her sketchpad. She started scribbling.

"She's so talented," Peter said, nervously folding and unfolding the cardboard box the candy came in. "I just like to watch her work."

"We sit here for hours," she said. "Talking." Blood rushed to his cheeks.

Good lord, he was smitten. I had never, ever seen Peter like that. I tried not to blow up his spot, to play it cool, to act like, *Oh, yeah, you know Kilkenny's own Peter Byrne. He totally loves to sit around looking at your face—I mean art—for hours.* As I watched her bring a sprout to life, I recognized the sharp curves and charcoal of her pencil.

"Wait, did you design your own tattoos?" I asked.

"You noticed?" She held her wrists out so I could look at them more closely.

"They're beautiful," I said. "What did your parents say?"

She smirked, licked her thumb, and dragged it across her left wrist. The ink smudged.

"They're not permanent. I draw them on every morning. Always the same. Always ever so different."

"Whoa, they look real."

"I know," she said, and went back to sketching. "This way I can change them if I want to. But I don't think I will."

Later, when we were alone again, passing a soccer ball back and forth outside his dorm, Peter said, "So? What did you think of her?"

What did I think of her? I thought she was lovely, if a little manic-pixie-dream-girl with the big eyes and the blue hair. But I couldn't say that, of course. I gave him the same assurance he had given me years earlier.

"I think she's freaking awesome, dude."

"Right? She is." He caught the ball on his foot and narrowed his eyebrows. I thought he was going to tell me something scandalous. Instead, he said, "I really do like art, though, actually. That part's real too." He passed the ball back to me, and I hit it with one strike.

"Yeah," I said. "Of course."

Months later, I got a phone call from him late at night. My phone vibrated so violently it fell off my desk and thumped on the wooden floor.

"Are you with Mom and Dad?" he asked when I finally picked up, and I could tell he'd been crying by the way he had to catch his breath in between words.

"No, I'm in my room," I said, pushing my biology homework to the side. "Why, what's up?" There was a long pause, and I waited for him to tell me Georgia broke up with him.

"I messed up," he whispered.

"What happened? Are you okay?"

"Georgia's pregnant."

"Oh." It was . . . not what I had been expecting. "Oh. Wow."

"Yeah."

"Have you told Mom and Dad?"

"No, God no. Don't you dare."

"Is she going to get, you know?" I wanted to say *abortion*, but it still felt like a forbidden word.

"We're kind of thinking we want to keep it," he said. "Not it, sorry. Him, her, them. Is that completely irrational?"

I chewed my lip and considered that he was nineteen years old, a freshman in college, and he didn't *really* know Georgia, even if she was friendly and whimsical. He didn't know her at all. I considered that him having a child would mean he was a father first, a partner second, a brother a very, very distant third. I lay down on my bedroom floor and stared up at the ceiling, nauseous, trying to say the right thing. Trying not to be selfish.

"I mean, it's not the *best* timing," I said. "Are you going to drop out of school? Live at home? Mom and Dad are going to lose their minds if you don't marry her first." I added quickly, "But you know I'll support you no matter what, right?"

"Right. I know. Of course you will."

After we hung up, I stayed there flat on my floor watching the popcorn ceiling twirl into static. I tried to breathe, and I started crying without even knowing why. I guess I should have considered Peter might have a child eventually, but I hadn't been expecting it then, and I wasn't prepared. A new fear twisted inside me: What if the baby got my genes? Aunt Devin's genes? What if they had red hair and blue eyes and a paper soul? What if someday they lost me in the same way I lost Aunt Devin? I couldn't be an aunt. I was fifteen. Peter shouldn't have this kid. Peter couldn't have this kid.

Theodore Simon Lasky was born eight months later with thick brown hair and gray eyes. **Cutest baby,** Cass texted, **but does Pete know he gave that poor kid 2 of the 3 chipmunk names?**

OH NOOOOOOOOO, I texted back, but all I could feel was relief. Logically, I knew my hair and eyes weren't my curse, but I held on to that fact anyway: He didn't look like me. He didn't look like Aunt Devin. He'd be okay.

My parents' first reaction to the pregnancy news was nothing short of terrifying. They blasted Peter in the living room with their loud, rough Irish accents, shouting all the predictable laments about premarital sex and familial responsibility. And yet they still called Teddy a blessing at every turn and melted the instant they held him in their arms for the first time. They invited Peter and Georgia to live in our house, and while I was happy to have Peter back in my everyday life, the baby's crying kept me up late at night even when I had big tests or important games, and there wasn't anything I could say about it.

Plus, Peter was too busy to hang out with me anymore.

He and Georgia eloped, and he took her last name. They both transferred to UNH Manchester, where they gave up their art degrees to focus on science, because that was where the money was: Georgia became a nurse in training at Parkland Medical Center, and Peter substitute-taught at Kilkenny High while he took night classes. They eventually saved up enough money to rent the house next door to my parents' when it came on the market. They built a life. They gave us all a new center of the family; everything revolved around Teddy—all conversation, schedules, and thoughts of the future.

Which was good, because I couldn't imagine my own future.

Which was good, because even then, I wondered if I would have one.

It was good, because maybe, maybe, maybe, with Teddy in their lives, they wouldn't miss me so much if one day I decided I couldn't do it anymore. They'd all be okay, if one day I was gone. They would have each other.

nine days
to impact

As soon as I entered the house, my parents threw their arms around me. For the briefest instant, I forgot about the asteroid, about Boston, about every ugly thing that was to come. When they let me go, I saw how tired and disturbed they looked. Mom's face was puffy and splotched with patches of pink. Dad's was gaunt, his gray eyes haunted. I couldn't tell if he saw me at all. They ushered everyone into the living room, and the dog ran past them to jump onto the couch.

"Hey!" Mom yelped, but then remembered the circumstances and let the dog stay curled up on the cushions. Who cared if they got ruined, now? When Dr. Talley reached out to shake their hands, my blood burned a little. I held my breath. I was so focused on Aisha telling everyone about my suicide note that I hadn't stopped to wonder if Dr. Talley would tell my parents about my failing grade in his class. I exhaled when he moved away from them to take his place next to Scout on the couch.

"Cass, you made it," Dad said, pulling her into a hug.

"Thank God," Mom said. "I've been praying non-stop." She reached over to rub Aisha's back. Both of my parents *loved* Aisha. They'd made it a point to talk to her after games, and to cheer for her as loudly as they cheered for me, if not louder. It was, of course, because she was a stellar player, so easy to root for. But I think they also did it because they knew her parents were far away, and they both knew what it was like to be so far from family. I think they also did it because they thought if they could get close to her, they might be able to find out what was going on with me. I'd been so tight-lipped about school. For good reason.

"Get anything good at Market Basket?" Peter asked. Dad gestured to the kitchen, where he'd stacked crates of food. Some were comprised of cookies alone: Oreos, Chips Ahoy!, Nutter Butters, even a dusty box of Thin Mints, leftover from the last time an ambitious Girl Scout knocked on our door. Even in an apocalypse, Dad had a sweet tooth.

"It's enough . . . for now."

"We have about a year's worth of apples frozen in our garage fridge too," Mom added. "We'll be okay."

A year?

"Can we put the news on?" Aisha asked. "I need to know everything."

I didn't know if I wanted to know everything—the way I would die, unplanned and uncontrolled. The ways I might watch my family and friends die too. I tried to find a news channel, but for a few moments, the TV glowed silently on the mantel, static filling the gaps between news stations cutting in and out.

"What do you know so far?" Aisha asked. My parents shared a stricken look and dared each other to speak.

"We've heard a lot of things," Dad said, opaquely.

"But there's hope," Mom interjected. "They're going to try to redirect it or weaken it. And even if it hits, we're prepared."

"Who's 'they'? Redirect it how?" Aisha said.

My mom shot my dad a weary look. "The militaries are trying . . . things."

"It would take approximately seven to ten years to develop the technology to deflect an asteroid of this size," Dr. Talley said. I had the urge to say, *Thanks for your expertise, Dr. of Literature*, but I held my tongue. "We have nine *days*."

"Dan Allah," Aisha said at the same time Peter said, "Fuck."

"I'm gonna go home," he said to my parents, and then to me, "Come by after, okay?" I nodded but was unnerved by my parents' immobility, their fixed gazes that didn't even flicker in his direction as he crept back out through the garage.

Cass knelt on the floor, buckling under the weight of it all. My body was numb and carbonated. *Nine more days than expected*, I thought, and wondered suddenly if I had actually died that morning and this was my personal hell, forced to watch the people I loved collapse into despair and then die over and over again. But I sat exhausted, shivering, and wet in my living room. This was happening. I was still alive. Still here.

Finally, sound rocketed out of the TV as I landed on a channel that worked. A nuclear bomb blossomed across the screen. A deep disembodied voice that might as well have been ripped from a 1950s radio program floated over the fiery images.

"These images are merely examples of what the impact could look like. It will likely be beyond anything our minds can fathom, more devastating than any weapon of mass destruction, and impossible to capture by any recording device."

"Enough of *that*," I said, clicking ahead to the next channel with sound.

The president of the United States stood at a podium surrounded by solemn-faced politicians and members of the military. She looked as strong and elegant as ever. She oozed confidence and compassion. I had a glint of hope she might comfort us as she always did in times of tragedy. But the instant she started to speak, I heard her sadness and fear.

"Some American citizens believe we withheld information to deceive, to subdue the masses. While it's true the United States government had intelligence that had not yet been shared with the public, there was a plan to reveal the information and simultaneously develop infrastructures across the nation that would ensure the crisis was dealt with responsibly. Intel was leaked before these measures could be taken. As a result . . ." She paused to look up at the sky. "As a result, our nation has seen unprecedented waves of violence and destruction." The news cut to footage of burning buildings, people brawling, lying in the streets bleeding. Men beating cars with baseball bats. Wild, rapid gunfire. Dad took the remote and zapped the TV off.

"Tomorrow we begin," he said. Mom clung to his arm.

"Begin what?" I asked, looking between the two of them, still shaking from the horrors on the screen.

"Turning our basement into a bunker."

Dr. Talley chuckled, but no one else seemed to notice.

"How do you do that?" Cass asked.

"Stockpile food. Create living spaces. Secure the foundation." Dad clapped his hands. "We're far enough from the impact to potentially survive the fallout. If there's any chance at making it through this, we're going to do it. There's room for all of us." He motioned to Dr. Talley and Aisha.

"Oh, no," Aisha said. "As soon as I can get out of here, I'm going home." We all opened our mouths to speak and shut them quickly, deciding better of it. I felt a pang of relief to hear she was leaving, that she couldn't tell anyone I was suicidal, and then the kickback of guilt.

"Of course," Mom said. "But until then, you're welcome here and welcome to all we have."

"Thank you," Aisha said softly. "Do you have a computer I can use? I need to get online."

"Here," Dad said. "I'll show you around the house. You too." He gestured toward Dr. Talley, and the dog jumped up instinctively. As they left the room, I heard Dad telling them, "Did you know the first potato in the country was planted here? In the whole nation! Isn't that something?"

Mom stared at Cass and me with a brutal intensity.

"Girls, what happened in Boston? Where were you when you found out? How'd you get back from New York? Where are your parents, Cass?"

We answered her questions with overlapping monologues: Cass's true, mine completely fabricated: *I was in the library where I fell asleep. I woke up. I heard the news.* I was grateful Aisha wasn't there to call me out.

"Let's go to Peter's," I whispered to Cass when my father returned to the room alone, and my parents started having their own hushed conversation. She looked at me blankly before registering what I'd said, then stood up and leaned on me to steady herself.

"We're going next door," I said to my parents, who nodded a little too enthusiastically.

Peter and Georgia's house was just through the trees. Outside, the night was eerily quiet. Cass gripped the edge of the truck to catch her breath after only a few steps. I tried to rub her arm, but she pushed my hand away.

"I'm processing," she said. Maybe it wasn't like my New York visit had never happened, then. I crossed my arms and tried to think of something to say that would be comforting.

"Do you want to try to get to Fiji, if things do open up?" I didn't want her to say yes. I didn't want her to leave. But I didn't want her to waste her final days on me, a total shell of a person. If she wanted to meet up with her parents, then she should. Cass squinted at me.

"No one is getting out of here," she hissed. "No one is going to Fiji or Nigeria or Louisiana. My parents aren't coming home. You know that. Everyone knows that." She crouched down, shut her eyes, and screamed into the sleeve of her jacket.

Somewhere in the distance—though not distant enough—gunshots popped.

"Hunters," we said together. It wasn't an uncommon sound during hunting season, but that had ended months before, and the sound chilled me. We were already undone, but the gunshots were enough to push Cass to her feet, past me and through the woods.

When we reached the front of Peter's blue Cape house, we could see lights pulsing inside. Cass knocked on the front door, and we waited a beat before we heard footsteps that could only belong to Peter. He peered out the frosted window, and I watched the flame in his eyes flicker from fear to recognition. He opened the door quickly and we stepped into the foyer.

"Hey," he said, and threw his arms around us both. He smelled like he always did these days, like his house, a scent that was new and different. Was it laundry detergent? Cheerios? Georgia's small frame cast a shadow as she entered the doorway. She was wearing a big T-shirt as a nightgown with socks pulled up to her knees. Her hair was tinted purple.

"Come here," Cass said. As Georgia folded herself into the blob of us, I was reminded that we had bodies. Bodies we'd often criticized, sized up, and hated. Bodies we'd hurt and loved with. Bodies that were resilient, fragile, soft, hard, warm, cold. My body loved their bodies. My body knew their bodies. Maybe if we gripped each other tightly enough, we could become anchors. Maybe if we pressed hard enough, we could melt into each another.

We didn't. We split apart, slowly, and sat on the floor in their front foyer.

"Where's Teddy?" I asked. Georgia motioned upstairs.

"Sleeping," Peter said. "Cass, we didn't get a chance to talk about how you got home. I hate to say it, but I sort of thought you wouldn't." Cass ran her hand through her hair, and stared at the floor, as if she hated whatever she was remembering.

"I know," she said. She rubbed her eyes like she was trying to forget. "I was up all night working on my designs for this big fashion show that I got into, Mx. and Match. I'm like—or I *was* like—manic about it. Obsessed with it. I've been working on my designs twenty-four seven. So I was still awake this morning when it went down. I was on one of the first buses out of the city, but it still took forever. I saw . . . some shit."

"Damn," he said. "I'm so happy you're here."

"Let's go in the living room," Georgia suggested, and motioned for us to hand her our jackets. "We opened a bottle of wine."

The living room was a minefield of plastic cars, foam puzzle pieces, bowling pins, and rag dolls. Cass and I sat on the droopy cushions of their yellow love seat while Georgia got us glasses and filled them with ruby-red liquid. I tipped half of the glass into my mouth in one gulp, and it moved like mercury down my throat. Cass copied me, and I had the overwhelming urge to kiss her before I remembered myself.

"So," Peter said, "Mom and Dad told you about the bunker?"

"Yeah." I laughed a little. "Do they seriously think they can save us?"

He bristled. "Yeah, of course." Peter looked away from me, and I realized what I'd actually asked him was, *Do you seriously think you can save Teddy?*

Peter ran into the kitchen and came back with a stack of computer paper covered in pen scribbles. "So, here's the US, right? If the asteroid hits where they're saying it will, in Arizona, scientists say this is the zone of impact." He traced a circle whose perimeter ended somewhere near West Virginia.

"So, the East Coast is probably safe from the energy of the blast," Georgia said. "*If* it lands where it's supposed to."

"Which doesn't mean we're in the clear," Peter said, shuffling the papers around, pulling out different sketches and circled words. "Immediate impact could include dust that blacks out the sun for years. Shifts in the earth's plates. Earthquakes and hurricanes. And long-term? We're looking at years of winter. Deep winter."

"Then there's the acid rain. Species extinction. Environmental shifts."

"Not to mention structural collapse. And that's *if* it hits where they say it will, on land," Peter added.

"If it doesn't?" Cass asked.

"If it hits the ocean, it'll basically spray so much moisture into the air there'll be torrential rain everywhere. Flooding. Maybe more tidal waves."

The dramatic irony of Peter's statement was almost unbearable. "So . . ." I swallowed, "we'd drown?"

Peter stared at me for a beat too long. "I mean. Probably. Yeah."

"But it's not supposed to hit water," Georgia reassured us, "so it's really a matter of having a sturdy shelter and enough supplies to last until it's safe to emerge."

"Which could be years. Hence, basement bunker." Peter gestured toward our parents' house.

Cass looked skeptical. "How does one 'build a bunker,' though? If this is all I get, I don't want to spend the rest of my days playing *Queer Eye: Apocalypse Edition.*"

"Mom and Dad's house was built during the Cold War. The foundation's solid. We need to get supplies. If we do this right, it won't be the rest of your days. We can survive this."

I didn't know if I wanted to survive this, but I couldn't say that. What if this worked and I had to live in a bunker with everyone for years? What would everyone learn about me? What would I put them through?

"Has Teddy noticed anything weird?" I asked to shift the subject. Peter and Georgia shook their heads quickly, too quickly.

"We deserve Oscars," Georgia said.

"Yeah, I don't think he knows." Peter broke eye contact. He was lying. Three and a half years was too young to understand, but it was old enough to *know.*

"Can I charge my phone?" Cass asked. "I talked to my parents this morning, but I need to call them again soon." Peter motioned toward the white charger dangling from an outlet.

"Get on our Wi-Fi," Peter said. "Our cell service stopped working maybe twenty minutes ago. I think it's signal congestion."

"Either that or they're trying to control how information is spreading. Where are your parents?" Georgia asked.

"Fuckin' Fiji," Cass said brightly. "So that's cool."

"Are they freaking out?"

"No. You've met my parents, right? They've always wanted me to be independent, self-sufficient. When I talked to them this morning, they told me to make the most of this because *they* were going to."

"In Fiji?" Georgia asked.

"In Fiji," Cass echoed, taking another swig of wine. "I mean, good for them, I guess. Until tsunamis come." A darkness flickered across her face. "And your parents, Georgia?" Cass asked.

"They're still in Brooklyn." She wrung her hands in her lap. "I want them to come here, but it's too dangerous, at least right now. My dad's in his seventies."

"Guys?" a little voice called from upstairs. "Are the ladies here?"

Peter had trained Teddy to call us ladies because (a) it

sounded hilarious in his little voice and (b) I absolutely hated that term. In what context, other than a stranger berating you in public or a girlboss workout video, were you ever called "lady"? At the sound of his son's voice, Peter stood up, but Georgia put her arm out to stop him.

"Your sister's here," she said as she left the room. Peter watched Georgia go, then looked at us, let his guard down.

"He's just a kid," he said, helplessly. We moved apart so Peter could sit between us. We rubbed his back. My fingers grazed Cass's frequently, and on purpose.

"We don't know what you're going through," I said, "but we're here." But what could we even say or do? Peter was losing every version of his kid he thought he'd know.

"I know it's painful to feel hopeful, but maybe we should," Cass said. "Who does it hurt?"

But I knew hope wasn't a choice.

"It could be a mistake," Peter said, "but what if it's not?"

"If we're not going to make it, what do you hope for?" Cass asked. I didn't like imagining that, the two of them and everyone else dead in only days. I could hardly breathe. I could hardly think. I pressed on my injured knee just to keep from screaming.

"Peace," Peter said. "Mercy. You?"

"I hope to live the shit out of the next few days: see everything and feel everything and scream and claw and burn. Like, basically live out *The L Word* theme song."

They both looked to me.

"What about you, Avery?" Peter asked.

I almost laughed. It didn't matter to me. I didn't want anything. "I, um." I tipped the rest of the wine down my throat and started pouring more while I tried to think of something true to say.

"Oh God, your hands," Peter said, unwittingly saving me from myself. Cass and I looked down. Our hands were cut and scraped and cracked from our journey home. Blood burned in between my knuckles.

"I'll go get some Band-Aids." Peter patted us on the knees and left the room. Cass and I looked at each other, and I put my glass on the table.

When she teared up again, and put her head in her hands, I wanted to inch toward her, to put an arm around her, but she felt miles away. I wished for the desperation from the truck bed or the urgency of the asteroid to push us together, but we both breathed separately and it felt like we were back in her dorm room in New York yet again. My back aching on a cold tile floor. Her arms around someone else, inches away from me. Her cologne still clinging to the cotton of my clothes. The weeks of silence after.

When Peter returned, he put the box of glow-in-the-dark children's Band-Aids on the table in front of us, but he didn't sit down.

"Stay as long as you want, but I have to get to bed."

He suddenly looked like he could barely keep his eyes open. "We have a bunker to build first thing tomorrow."

"Right," I said. "'Night, Peter."

"Thanks for the wine," Cass said. She'd unwrapped a bright pink bandage and tried to wrap it around her middle finger. She had the angle all wrong. I moved over and motioned for her to give me her hand instead, and when she did, I carefully unpeeled the edges to reset it. I reached for an electric green one, too, and when I turned my head, I saw Peter lingering in the doorway, watching us.

"You okay?" I said.

"You two *do* know, right?"

"Know what?" we said. He twisted his face a little, as if deciding what to say.

"Never mind. Get some rest, okay?" He disappeared up the stairs, and Cass and I were left alone in the living room. I put one last Band-Aid on her thumb, and when she pulled her hand away, she gasped and covered her mouth. She looked horrified.

"What's wrong?" I said, as if the world wasn't ending. It took her a minute to speak, and when she did, it came out as a whisper.

"Avery. It's your birthday. It's your fucking birthday."

"Oh, right," I said, relieved it wasn't something terrible and new. "I forgot."

"We all forgot! Oh my God, I'm the worst."

"It's fine! Who cares when—" I gestured at the world.

"Plus, we already celebrated, remember?" She'd come over during winter break for cake with my family and orchard flashlight tag. And then I'd said I hated her, which I'm pretty sure made *me* the worst, but neither of us brought it up.

"It's not fine." She pushed hair out of my face, and her hand lingered on my cheek. It was enough to undo me. "Lookout tower?"

"Lookout tower."

We put our coats back on, and she followed me through the pitch-black hallways. We tumbled out of the Laskys' back door and into the cold, open night. Snow laced the sky again. Big, soft flakes landed in our hair. The Purple Finch Apple Orchard stretched before us, the glass of frozen branches glittering in moonlight. I took off running, even though my bruised knee ached with every step, and she trailed behind me.

"No fair, I'm a goalie!" she called like she always did, and I couldn't help but laugh out loud.

"I'm injured!" I called.

"You're still Avery freaking Byrne!"

"You're still Cass Joshi-Aguilar!"

We breathed white puffs of air toward the sky until we reached the lookout tower, a tall, splintery wooden structure the orchard owner, Mr. Connor, used to survey the rows of trees in autumn. He was kind enough to let us claim it as our tree house every other season. We clambered up the icy wooden stairs, the railings stinging my battered hands.

"Avery, why do I feel like I've been chasing you my whole life?" Cass said as she climbed to the top, wiped her hands on her pants. She threw her head back and put her arms out. She looked so gorgeous under the spray of stars, in the snowfall. I could have stared at her all night, but I followed her gaze. A star cut across the darkness like the strike of a match.

"I can't stop thinking about how a star is going to kill us," she said, her voice cracking. "I don't want to die. I was just becoming myself."

I barely knew what to say. I did want to die. But not like this. Not with my family. Not with her. They had to make it. They had to.

"We don't know what's going to happen yet," I said. "Maybe they'll deflect it; maybe the bunker will work. Maybe we can live." I wanted to reach in between her ribs and hold her heart in my fist until it calmed.

"Do you actually believe that?" She searched my eyes. I could tell she wanted the truth.

"I don't know," I whispered. "Do you?"

"I want to," she said, then shook her head. "You know what? No. I'll have a nervous breakdown tomorrow. For now?" She checked her watch. "For now, we celebrate the last hour of your birthday." She pulled a lighter from her pocket, sparked the flame, and used her coat sleeve to protect it from the wind. I watched shadows cut her face into a collage of features, the flame burning in her chestnut eyes, and I thought, *I'm not supposed to be here. I'm supposed to be gone. How am I going to ruin all of this, all of us, yet again?* But I was very much alive, and very much in love with her, and, impossibly, I thought I could smell apple blossoms.

"Pretend there's a cake. Pretend all our old friends are here. Pretend there's a piñata and a disco ball and a jumpy castle and a water slide. There's a fondue fountain and a mountain of chocolate-covered strawberries and a hot, tattooed DJ who knows all your favorite songs by heart and she's just pumping them out one after the next, bam, bam, bam, and—"

"Cass, Cass, Cass." I stopped her, but I smiled despite myself. "You know I don't need all that." *Just you, here*, I didn't say.

"Fine. The cake at least, then. With rainbow sprinkles. Close your eyes. Make a wish."

I blew out the lighter's flame without thinking of anything at all, and she cheered. Without the small heat, we realized suddenly how cold we were, how tired.

"Annual *Beckham* rewatch until we fall asleep?" she said.

"Best birthday *ever*," I said, and we laughed so we didn't cry. It broke the terrible silence of the night, and I followed her out of the sky toward warmth, toward home.

three years
to impact

Sophomore fall, Cass begged me to dress up with her as the main characters from the 2002 movie *Bend It Like Beckham*.

"It's like this old lesbian movie about soccer," she said. "How have you never seen it?"

"I mean, I don't know. I wasn't even born when it came out."

"Yeah, but there's such a *dearth* of lesbian movies, I have to dig." We'd been studying for the SATs, and Cass was using every opportunity to throw in one of our buzzwords.

"Wait, so like, we'd be dressing up as a couple?" I asked. Heat crept up my cheeks.

"They're actually just friends. But one's white and one's Brown."

"I thought you said it was a lesbian movie."

"I mean it is. Or it's not, but it should be. It's Sapphic soccer subtext. You have to watch it."

I did watch it late one night, alone, after all my homework was done. I streamed it on my phone so I could talk to Cass about it the next day. *I don't get what's so gay about it*, I thought as I watched the two main characters sneak glances at each other and trade little touches that lasted a breath too long. *I mean, our friendship is basically exactly like this.* Was there something I'd missed? As soon as the credits rolled, I slid the cursor back to the beginning and fast-forwarded to all my favorite parts. When I finally went to sleep, it was two in the morning.

"It was definitely queer," I said the next day, leaned up against the locker next to hers. "Or at least, their hair, their clothes, their vibes. That coach was so useless. He could have been replaced by a traffic cone." She patted me on the head.

"You're the gayest straight girl I know, Avery." Before I had the chance to even react, she continued: "So, you're in? For the costumes?"

"Yeah, sure. No one is going to get it, but sure." Or at least I hoped that if someone got the costume, they wouldn't get the subtext.

A week before actual Halloween, Peter drove us in his truck to drop us off at Spooky World's Nightmare New

England, a haunted house built into our local mini golf course. It was Cass's fifteenth birthday, and the two of us wore matching red-and-white soccer jerseys with soccer socks up to our knees and plastic candy baskets shaped like soccer balls Cass found at Party City. They bumped together as we walked, clapping and sending vibrations up my arm.

Our friend Omar Pérez worked at one of their six haunted houses, but he would never tell us which character he played just to make us anxious. Even worse, he worked in a claustrophobic tube of a house, a one-hallway situation where the walls were made of billowing plastic that puffed out as you went and hit you in unexpected moments. Omar was Cass's friend more than he was mine. I got the feeling he didn't like me, but he seemed to accept Cass and I were a package deal.

Inside the house where he worked, we held on to the back of each other's jerseys so we wouldn't get separated. Fake smoke wet the air, and a soundtrack of screaming popped around strategically placed speakers. As we inched forward, I felt the walls closing in on me from every direction. High schoolers in gory makeup and masks jumped out from behind random trapdoors. We passed a woman in a cage who cried to us for help, men on a table being sawed in two, "old ladies" trying to convince us to drink "poison." Cass stared one of the women in the eyes, took the vial from her hands, and downed it. She made a face.

"It's lemonade," she announced loudly. "But I was not prepared."

Toward the end of the maze, a deranged clown with fangs and a bloody neck leapt out, grabbing us both by the shoulders. I almost clocked him in the face.

"It's me!" Omar whispered. He removed his fake teeth. "I got you good!"

"Of course they made you the clown," Cass said. "Very on-brand, cabrón."

"Maybe next year a spot will open up for you, Cass, but all the brujas lesbianas were accounted for."

"Damn, missed my calling."

"I'm off in fifteen; can you wait so I can catch a ride home?"

We stood outside under a full moon in the middle of the crowd while Omar finished his shift. I bought candy apples for both of us, but they were hard to eat. We cracked the ruby shells with our front teeth and picked the shards off in little pieces that coated our fingertips with syrup. By the time I got through to the apple, I wanted to drop it in the mud, so I did.

"Why doesn't Omar like me?" I asked Cass, not for the first time. She rolled her eyes and took a bite of her apple. She'd carefully and patiently chipped away at her own shell.

"Not this again. Omar likes you just fine," she said. "Everyone likes you, Avery. What's not to like?" When

I was quiet, she touched my arm and said, "Remember when Omar dove under the table in Mr. Heath's class?"

Despite myself, I collapsed into a fit of giggles that lit my whole body right up, and then she did too, and we hung on to each other to keep from falling over.

Cass and I had a whole library of inside jokes, and the right eye contact at the wrong time got us into a whole lot of trouble. Once we got each other going, we couldn't stop laughing until we were on the floor with stomach aches and shirt collars wet with our own tears. This happened at soccer camp, in biology class, and—extremely unfortunately—Catholic Mass.

And it was exactly what was happening in the haunted house parking lot until we heard someone yell, "Avery! Cass! My babies!" A gaggle of older girls from our soccer team approached us, leaning on each other and shrieking. They seemed drunk and wore unintentionally matching jackets and knee-high boots. We weren't supposed to be drinking at all, obviously, but especially not during the season, so it made my skin crawl to see the captain, Kayla Powell, struggling to stay on her feet. It was enough to help me get my laughter under control, although Cass kept going beside me.

"Aw, so cute, you two still wear costumes?" she said like she didn't think it was cute at all. I tried to hide my soccer ball full of bite-size candies behind my back.

"Oh my God, like, matching costumes," Penny Bryant chimed in.

"Like a couple's costume," Sara Lowenstein screamed. Though everyone fawned over us, I could feel my face get hot. So, it wasn't subtext. Just text, then.

"Do you two want to drink with us?" Kayla whisper-shouted.

"Oh, no," I said, "we can't, we're—"

"Can I talk to you for a sec?" Cass said quickly and dragged me away from the girls before I could finish. "Let's do it."

"No way. If we get caught, we'll get suspended."

"We're not going to get caught. Come on! One drink, and then you can invite them to my quinceañera next month. My dad said I can invite a few more people."

"What? Why can't *you* invite them? We see them, like, every day." She shook my shoulders.

"Avery, they don't give a shit about me, and you know it. They're obsessed with you, their little superstar. Please? Do it for me. It would be so cool if they came. I would feel so cool." She rubbed her thumbs on my collarbones. *Do it for me* rolled around in my head. I sighed loudly, mostly because I knew I was going to cave. It was her birthday, after all.

"Fine," I said, and followed her and them back to Sara's car. They popped the trunk, and while Penny acted as lookout, Sara poured vodka into red SOLO cups and handed one to each of us along with orange slices she pulled out of a big Ziploc bag. The citrus bloomed under my nose.

"What is this, halftime?" I asked.

"You're dressed for it," Kayla said with some bite. When my face fell, she threw an arm around me and kissed my temple. Her vodka sloshed over the side of her cup and splashed near my sneakers. "I'm kidding. You're *so* my favorite underclassman," she slurred. "Can I play with your hair? It's the best color. You're so pretty." Cass raised her eyebrows at me and bit her lip to hold back laughter. "Who are you dating?"

"I'm too busy to date," I said. I spent most of my free time with Cass. I didn't want that to change. "I have to keep my grades up, and I work at the movie theater, and, you know, training. I want to play at Eaton College." I'd seen the campus on a brochure in the guidance counselor's office, and it was *beautiful.* I could picture myself there, playing in a purple jersey under blazing foliage and a mountainous horizon. It was an Ivy too. If I got into Eaton, that would mean I'd made it. That I was *actually* good. *Actually* thriving.

"Cheers to that," Penny said. On the count of three, we tipped the liquor down our throats, and while everyone else made faces, I let it burn. I remembered to put the fruit in my mouth when everyone else did, and my edges softened a bit.

Suddenly, I felt someone tap my shoulder. I imagined a cop or parent or our coach behind me. I felt my whole future evaporating before I spun around and saw it was Omar. Only Omar.

"Boo," he said.

"Jesus Christ, you look scarier now than you did in there," Cass said. She wasn't wrong. Omar had ditched his wig, but his makeup was badly scrubbed off and streaks of black pooled underneath his eyes. He'd put his glasses back on. "Everyone, this is Omar."

"He's cute," Penny said. "Avery, why don't you date him?"

"*He's* cute?" Cass asked incredulously. "He looks like the Creature from the Black Lagoon. Plus, he's gay."

"I'll have you know I am wildly handsome outside of murderous clown makeup," Omar said. "And, like, wicked rich because I have this job and all, so tell all the cute men in your life."

"What about you, Cass?" Sara said. She threw her orange rind on the ground. "Do you have cute men in your life?" We exchanged a look that said, *They clearly haven't been paying attention.*

"Alas, I'm single. And gay as hell."

"We love that," Kayla said, and started braiding my hair. "It's like, live your truth."

"So brave," Sara echoed.

"Have you kissed a girl before?" Penny asked, leaning in for Cass's answer.

"Once," she said. My heart raced, and though I tried to catch Cass's gaze to beg her to not tell the story of the two of us on the lakeshore at church camp, she didn't look at me. "But it was a long time ago."

"You should all come to Cass's quinceañera next month," I said loudly, to change the subject. They all let out excited squeals, and though I was dizzy from the vodka, when Cass smiled, I decided it had been worth it.

"Oh my God, yes, we'd love to!" Kayla spoke for all of them. "Are you going to wear a big, glittery ball gown?"

"And a tiara?" Penny said.

"Will you have a waltz?"

A flicker of something like fear crossed Cass's face. Did she think she'd made a mistake, inviting these girls who didn't care about her, or, despite what she thought, care about me? I wanted to yell at them for no reason, then, but her smile returned and she waved her hands in the air.

"No dress, no tiara, no waltz," she said. "It's not going to be very traditional, just a big birthday party. My dad wanted me to have one, just an excuse to get the family together, but he'll let me do what I want. He's cool."

Two weeks later, I was lying on my bed draped over my chemistry homework when Cass called me on the phone. It took her a minute to speak.

"What's wrong?" I asked.

"My dad is *not* being cool," she said through tears. The sound of her crying broke me in two, and within seconds I was brushing my hair, pulling on jeans, begging Peter to drive me to her house. I quickly said hi to Mr. Aguilar and Mrs. Joshi before charging up the stairs, and though they were sipping chai and playing cards, they were more solemn than normal. I could tell they knew why I was there.

I found Cass in her room sobbing into her buffalo plaid pillow. I had only seen her cry twice before: when she broke her arm on Omar's trampoline, and during a lacrosse game where the opposing team's fans shouted, "The Kilkenny goalie is a boy! It's cheating!"

Cass shopped in the "boys'" section at most stores and loved it when Omar or I called her handsome, but getting cruelly misgendered by strangers in front of the whole school was another thing entirely. I wanted to scream, *It's called swagger, you assholes!* but I thought they'd kick me out of the game. I swung by her cage to comfort her, but before I could get words out, she pointed her stick at the center of the field and said, "Just play. Embarrass them." I did.

But I'd never seen her cry like *this*, the uncontrollable full-body sobbing that guaranteed a two-day headache and eyes swollen half shut. I sat next to her on the bed and rubbed her back.

"Talk to me," I said.

"He made it seems like this party would be for *me*. It was supposed to be fun."

"It won't be fun?"

"No. We've been arguing about every detail. He said, 'What do you want to wear?' I said, a suit, and I want to cut my hair. Not even that short! Like, to my shoulders. He said, 'Cassandra, why can't you give me one day? You're my only child. My whole family will be there; I've never forced you to learn Spanish or be more feminine. Why can't you give me one day where we stick to tradition?'"

"Did you say it's supposed to be *your* day? That it's for you most of all?"

She started crying again. "You should just go."

"What? Why?"

"You're not going to get it. You're so white." It was a lament, not an accusation. I started to protest, but I swallowed my words.

"I'm sorry."

"Stop apologizing. It's not something you did; it's who you are. No matter how much you care about me, you will never know how it feels to *be* me. And it makes me sad."

"You're right," I said. "But I want to know as much as I can. I can read more about it, I can——"

"Avery. You can't study your way into understanding. You can't read a book and get it. You think because you're smart you can know everything, and that's not how the world works."

I wish I'd said, *You're right. I don't understand. I can't know. I'll never know. But I can also try harder to see you. All of you.*

But I didn't. I sat beside her quietly, shamefully, until she was ready to speak again.

"I don't know who I want to be on the day. Everyone I know will be *watching* me. My family has never been all together like this. What if my Joshi cousins think I'm too Mexican and my Aguilar cousins think I'm too Indian and *all* of them think I'm too American, and too butch? Or too femme! If my dad gets his way. And then the *soccer seniors*—oh my GOD, Avery, why did you invite them?" She hugged her pillow to her chest.

"Cass. First of all, you made me invite them. Second of all, every single person you just listed loves you. So much. They're flying in from all over the world to show up for *you*."

"But who even am I? I feel like I'm ten people and no one all at once. I show different sides of myself to different groups of people. I can't even find one single formal outfit I want to wear on an infinite internet. I'm a mess."

"What sides do you show to me? Because I love them all. Other people will too."

She rolled her eyes, but inched closer to me. She started braiding the fringe on her quilt, and I watched her fingers move. There was not enough space or gravity between our hands and our knees. There was way too much.

"And," I said, "if anyone ruins your quince, I will physically fight them. I'll bring hockey gloves so I can drop them all dramatically. Even your dad. Don't play with me, Mr. Aguilar. I work out." I flexed my biceps and motioned for her to feel it.

"Pure steel," she said, finally smirking. "I feel so much safer now."

She wiped at her eyes. When her breath steadied, she spoke again. "You know why you've always been my best friend?" she said.

"Because we play the same sports and because I'm impossibly funny and cool?"

"Absolutely not," she deadpanned, but when I scoffed, she smiled for real. "Outside of my parents, you care more about my happiness than, like, anyone. You actively try to make every day better for me. It's annoying when you try to fix things and you shouldn't or you can't. But don't think I don't notice the trying."

I reached over, then, to squeeze her hand. Maybe I held on too long. Maybe I shouldn't have let it go.

Weeks later, I was back in her bedroom, but we were very much not alone. The women of her family leaned in to share mirror space, trade jewelry, and pin each other's hair before heading to the church. They swirled around Cass, doting on her, fixing her hot-pink suit—a Cass and Mr. Aguilar compromise—and though I was supposed to be there to help her get ready, I don't think I got a single word in. Still, I was honored to be there, near her. It felt like I'd been let in on a secret, like I got to see new sides of her. I loved them all. When she mouthed to me across the room, "Do I look okay?" I gave her a double thumbs-up, and her shoulders relaxed.

In the church basement after the ceremony, she awkwardly accepted la ultima muñeca, which she joked was her primera muñeca. She made sarcastic eye contact with me across the room when she showed off its dead-eyed porcelain face. She danced with her father to "Tiempo de Vals," and when her cousins on both sides surprised her with a group dance choreographed to a mash-up of Spanish and Indian songs, I saw her cry for the fourth time. But this time, they were happy tears. I couldn't take it. I cried too.

During dinner, I sat at a table with the other soccer girls. They screamed out loud when they saw me and hugged me until my curls were flat. Kayla Powell, whose blond hair was pinned up on her head, and whose own teal sequined dress would have been glam enough if *she* were a quinceañera, leaned over to squeeze my arm.

"You look stunning, Avery," she said. "Why won't you let me set you up with someone? My neighbor is so hot for you. He says you're like a pure, little Irish rose."

"It's English rose." Penny Bryant rolled her eyes. "What a genius."

"Well," I said, "there's actually a Yeats poem, and a folk song, and this creepy nursery rhyme that isn't actually Irish, but—" Then I started to feel like my dad with his Kilkenny potatoes and shut up. "Anyway, you all look great too."

"I've never been to anything like this," Kayla said. "It's so much fun. So colorful."

"I love the music," Penny said, "and Cass's suit. Although hot pink was a *choice*."

Kayla leaned forward and dropped her voice. "Okay, I wasn't going to say anything because I know she's your bestie, but why didn't she wear a dress?"

"She told you she wasn't going to wear a dress," I said defensively.

"It's just like, time and place. Even if she didn't want a ball gown, she would have looked so good in something simple and cute like this." She tugged on the skirt of my green lace dress, the one Mom had picked out for me because she hoped a boy would invite me to a school dance.

"No, she wouldn't have," I said. They burst out into laughter.

"Ouch!" Penny said.

"Tell us how you really feel, Avery," Kayla said.

"Stop," I pleaded. "You know that's not what I meant. She looks good in everything. She just wouldn't look like herself. She wouldn't look like *our* Cass."

"*Your* Cass," Kayla teased. I couldn't tell if her tone was accusing me, us, of something, but for once, I didn't correct her.

"My Cass," I said, and put my hand over my heart. I made a very serious face to make it look like a joke, if they needed it to be one.

And in a way, it was. Cass wasn't mine, or at least not only mine. She was so bright she could belong to everyone and no one, just like the sun, just like the stars.

Cass was one person and ten people all at once.

From across the room, we locked eyes as she was being group-hugged by her family, and I made a heart with my hands. She did it back, before disappearing into the crowd again.

She was my Cass.

She was so much more.

eight days
to impact

Cass and I woke up in my bed in the same positions we accidentally fell asleep in, my laptop still glowing between us with the final credits screen. She propped her head up on her hand, and I watched her expression morph from grogginess, to confusion, to sinking grief.

"So it wasn't a nightmare," she said.

The asteroid was real. I was alive. We had, maybe, days to live. I was devastated. I was so relieved.

My dad pounded on my door and then opened it without any prompting.

"Hey!" I yelled, and Cass scrambled as far away from me as she could, even though we hadn't even been touching.

"Everyone in the basement in ten minutes," he said.

"God, really?"

"Avery. Ten minutes."

We spent the next nine minutes lying there like sponges, trying to absorb everything from the day before. Cass moved between laughing and weeping in a way that would have been disturbing in any other circumstance. She was unhinged, manic, and it made so much sense. I was the abnormal one: made of stone, somehow solid for the first time in so long. I was comfortable in this ending, like I'd always known it was coming, like I'd wanted it for so long and here it was.

I spent the tenth minute looking for one of my socks under the covers and brushing my teeth, and an eleventh minute stumbling down the two flights of stairs to the basement. Aisha stood with her arms crossed in a corner, game face on. Though I knew my parents were not above dragging me out of bed, I was surprised they had done the same to her. I waved to her, and she nodded in my direction.

Peter, Georgia, and Teddy were there too. Teddy sat in the corner on a pillow someone had thrown down for him on the concrete, crayons scattered around him like a moat. He looked up to smirk at Cass and me before waving half-heartedly.

"Hi, ladies," he said in his high little voice before going back to his drawing.

"Hi, Ted," Cass said, and ran over to ruffle his hair.

He laughed but smoothed it back into place. He was three and a half, wonderfully polite, smart, and curious. He liked picking clovers. His eyes lit up when he talked to you. I loved him, but I was never overly affectionate with him. I was actively trying to remove myself from his heart. I needed him *not* to love me. I needed him not to need me. I didn't want him to ever have to lose me.

"Okay," Mom said. "Everyone, get comfortable." Our basement wasn't finished, but I loved the smell of the cement and old boxes. And that was all that was down there: elementary school homework assignments, free T-shirts that hadn't been worn in years, tattered paperback books.

"But not too comfortable," Dad said. "We're going to put you to work."

My parents had taped white pieces of paper to the wall and scribbled on them with pungent black Sharpie. The first sheet—made up of eight pieces of copy paper— contained a list: *Necessities: Food, water, sanitation, communication, defense, exercise, insulation, visibility, mobility, and FUN!*

It was clear my dad had slapped that last one up there.

"We're going to get through this," Mom said. "Maybe the"—she looked at Teddy—"*blizzard* will be as bad as they say it is. Maybe it will be worse. Maybe it will be nothing at all, but we will be prepared. I'll spend every single waking moment trying to save you all."

"Going into downtown or Manchester is too dangerous right now," Dad said. "We read places like Home
Depot and Walmart are battlefields. They've probably
already been picked clean, anyway, so we have to scour
abandoned houses in the neighborhood to find everything
we need. And look for cookies. I repeat, look for cookies."

"We need supplies for"—Mom quickly counted
around the room—"nine people. One dog." I waited for
Aisha to protest, to say she was leaving as soon as she
could, but she looked at the ground. Dad pointed at the
items on the necessities list.

"Food, water," he said. "We'll empty the well so it's
accessible. We have a serious stock of apples. We'll freeze
them until we can't freeze anymore."

"Sanitation," Mom said. "We'll make a makeshift
bathroom. Look for hand sanitizer, soap, medications,
cleaning solutions. Every single roll of toilet paper or
paper products you can find."

"Communication," Dad said. "Radios. Computers.
Routers. Cell phones. Batteries. Walkie-talkies."

"Defense," Mom said. "I think you get that one. Exercise:
think of routines we could do. Avery, Cass, Aisha: soccer,
lacrosse stuff. Georgia: yoga. Peter . . . never mind."

"I do yoga sometimes!" Peter said.

"And you think you know your children," Mom said.
"Insulation: we'll patch the foundation. Visibility: look
for flares, flashlights, candles, matches."

"Mobility," Dad said, "means we'll all have escape bags packed and ready to go at all times. And *fun*," he said, wiggling his fingers. "Fun means things we can all do to keep from killing each other."

"Why?" Teddy said from the corner. I didn't know what he was questioning or how much he understood, though I knew it was probably far more than we wanted him to.

"There's a bad storm coming," Georgia said. She bent down to sit cross-legged next to him. "There's going to be a blizzard, and we're all going to go camping here at Nana and Papa's house. Won't that be fun?"

He scanned the room of faces, as if trying to decide the answer to her question based on the vibes we projected his way. He looked back at his mother, then shook his head.

"It will be fun!" Peter said. "Right, everyone?"

"Yeah!" we all yelled.

"Why are you all so prepared for this?" Aisha said from the corner of the room.

"We met in the Irish Army," Dad said.

"Irish people are *always* thinking about death," Peter said at the same time.

Mom rolled her eyes. "Dad, the Laskys, and I are going to work on insulation and everything here," she said.

"The three of us will go out to look for food and water," Aisha said in the same urgent tone Coach Cather used when we weren't properly covering our marks. Cass squinted at her, then at me, then back at my parents again.

"We're really doing this? I mean, okay. I guess," she said under her breath.

We made for the stairs, but Mom stopped us with a single finger.

"Wait, wait, wait," she said. "Do not talk to people you don't know. And do not enter someone's house if they're in it." She held my face in her hands. "I love you. Be careful."

"I will," I promised, and I meant it.

Outside, Cass walked toward Peter's red pickup truck.

"Should we drive?"

"Nah, let's stay on foot," I said. I wanted to feel the muscles in my legs and the burn of cold air in my throat. I wanted to be stuck between sky and gravel, to smell wisps of the orchard, to stay near houses I knew from porch to porch.

"Game plan," Aisha said as she pulled the zipper up higher on her white coat. "I grabbed four duffel bags and some trash bags. Let's go to the farthest houses first so we can create a known perimeter." She and I started walking, but Cass stayed rooted to the driveway.

"This feels like a waste of time," Cass said, looking at the two of us in disbelief. "If we only have eight days left—"

"It will be more," Aisha said. "This can work."

"And if it doesn't? I'm not going to spend what time I have left doing all this. I want to actually *live*."

"Must be nice," Aisha said, "to only think about yourself."

I quickly interrupted before Cass could snap back. "Aisha, I thought you were leaving as soon as you could?"

She looked hurt. I hadn't meant for it to come out the way it did. "And I thought you said I was welcome here."

"You are, of course you are. It's just last night you were saying you wanted no part in this. And now?"

"Last night I spent hours reading every single thing I could, and it became crystal clear I will not be able to go home to Nigeria."

"Are you sure?" I said. "I mean, I know things are chaotic now, but in a few days?"

"No," she said. "I have no choice but to try to survive in your basement and pray I make it out alive and so does my family."

"Can we circle back to the thing where you said it must be nice for me to only care about myself?" Cass snapped. "It's not selfish to want things. It's not selfish to have an opinion. It's not selfish to freak out when I might be dying." She put her hands over her face as if she wanted to disappear completely. "Why aren't either of you out here screaming about what you want to do in the next few days? Don't you get it? We really might die."

My stomach dropped because Aisha kept opening her mouth and shutting it like she wanted to say something but wasn't sure she should. I drilled a stare into her and shook my head. *Please, no,* I thought. *Please don't tell her.*

Aisha pursed her lips one final time, then turned to Cass instead. "You're being unfair," she said, "and presumptuous."

"Can we all be careful with what we say?" I said. "We can't take it back, not now."

"Jesus, Avery," Cass said. "Just because you do whatever people want you to do doesn't make you a better person than me."

Ouch.

A window on the front of my house slid open, and I looked up to see Dr. Talley's face pressed to the screen.

"I can hear every tempestuous conversation you have," he said, "and I have concluded you three need a dog."

"I hate dogs," I said.

"We can't walk around with—" Aisha started, but Dr. Talley pulled away from the window and a moment later the dog was springing out the open front door, her muscles twitching happily as she dove headfirst into snow. She rolled onto her back and wiggled around, making soft grunting sounds and unhinging her mouth to let her tongue loll about.

"You see?" Dr. Talley's voice came from somewhere inside the house. "Pure distraction from your squabble." The leash landed with a thud on the porch steps, and Dr. Talley slammed the door shut.

"C'mere, dog," I said with the best dog voice I could muster. I ran toward the leash, but Scout beat me to it and grabbed it in her mouth. She crouched down with her butt in the air.

This was only one of the reasons why I couldn't stand dogs. They had a buoyancy that defied logic. I did not relate to their levity. Her tail danced across her back, and she dared me to chase her. From the corner of my eye, I saw Aisha walking down the driveway by herself and Cass crouching on the pavement with her head in her hands. So I was on my own, then.

After precious minutes of running in circles, I gave up. I threw myself into the snow and rolled onto my back. Dr. Talley could lose Scout if he wanted to. I didn't care. What did it matter?

The ground chilled through my jacket, and snow nipped at my ears. A formation of birds sliced across the gray sky. I liked the lactic acid in my throat and muscles. I liked knowing how many tomorrows I had to live through. Maybe I'd just lie there until it all went dark.

But the dog, no longer amused by her own game, dropped her leash by my head so she could stoop down to lick my face. I squealed to cover myself.

"Yuck!" I yelled. "Gah!" And then I saw Cass in a blur of silver and black gently tackling Scout to the ground. The dog turned her attention to Cass and started licking the bottom of her chin.

"Avery, I saved you," Cass said, "now you have to save me!" I reached over, grabbed Scout's collar, and clipped the leash to it in one quick swoop.

"Gotcha," I said, though being leashed did little to ease the dog's excitement. Cass grabbed a ball of snow and threw it at me and Scout. Scout tried to bite the snowball, so it exploded in her face like a firework.

"So that's how it is," I said, trying to form a ball of my own. Instead, I threw a spray of loose flakes at Cass. She tried to bite it too.

"I didn't mean what I said, Ave. About you doing what everyone tells you to do. I'm sorry."

"You weren't wrong."

"I'm full of shit, anyway. I don't know what I want either. I want to burn and feel and do all that living stuff, but I don't even know how to do that. Where would I even go? What would I even do?"

"I don't think you can force living," I said. I knew that as well as anyone. "But we'll try. I don't really want to do this shit either, Cass, but I feel like we should for the rest of them. Don't you want to try to survive?" She nodded, but her eyes brimmed with tears. I wiped them away. I wanted to kiss her, too, but the moment was too sad, and she didn't want that, and she was already walking away from me.

"Let's go," she said. "We have to find Aisha."

We caught up to Aisha two streets away where she was walking steadily forward, white clouds of moisture blinking out in front of her.

"I'm sorry for my outburst," Cass said too loudly through broken breath.

Aisha looked her up and down. "It's fine," she said. "I'm sorry I said you are selfish."

We walked in silence past houses I'd grown up with, but they all looked new, as if they'd been reconstructed overnight. Half of them were already abandoned, their garage doors gaping open, trails of belongings strewn across yards.

We passed a headless doll, a mangled bicycle, an entire bed dismantled, the sheets caught on nearby trees, flapping in the wind. A pizza was positioned perfectly in the middle of the street, and while I let the dog take a few desperate bites, I had to talk myself out of doing the same. My stomach wrenched with hunger, and it finally occurred to me I hadn't eaten for days.

"Oh God!" Cass exclaimed. She pointed at someone's yard, beyond a pine tree that had been shielding our view as we approached. My eyes settled first on a single ruby drop of blood, then a short trail of them, and then a big, sickening indent where more blood had settled. Aisha gasped, and my vision spun. I forced myself to scan the rest of the yard for a human body or a wounded moose, but the snow was still clean.

"Where did that come from?" Aisha said.

"I don't know," I said. My relief was quickly replaced by a litany of gruesome possibilities: Someone had been murdered. An animal had been slain. This was the grisly aftermath of the gunshots Cass and I heard the night before.

"Maybe we shouldn't be out here like this," Cass said. "A woman of color and a lesbian and a lesbian of color? Without cell phone service or swords? Woof."

"Cass, it's my neighborhood," I said, though I was rattled too.

"Exactly."

"We have to do this," Aisha said, plowing forward. "I don't have a choice." Cass, Scout, and I jogged after her.

I didn't look back.

Once we'd walked for about fifteen minutes, we identified the houses that looked abandoned and walked up the driveway of the biggest one first. It was a McMansion that had probably been thrown together before the housing crises. Bright, spacious, and beautiful, but not built to last. *A terrible investment*, my dad had said. *They don't even use real wood in houses these days.* A fine investment, it seemed now.

We entered through the garage. There was a freezer by the door, and when I opened it up, I saw slabs of meat wrapped in cellophane and stacked in neat columns. Masking tape across the plastic declared, VENISON. I shuddered.

"Nope. Not looking at that," Cass said, as she stuffed batteries and flashlights into one of our bags. "Pretending that does not exist." She was a lifelong vegetarian who had no problem showing her disdain for meat-eaters publicly or privately. It only took her six months to convince me to take up her dietary habits, but I didn't feel like I was in any position to preach after an entire childhood of animal eating.

"Oh God," Aisha said, "do you think that blood was from a deer?"

"Possibly," I said, trying to push the image from my mind.

Aisha put the venison in her bag, anyway.

"How much you wanna bet there's a moose head mounted somewhere up in here?" Cass said. "This seems like a disembodied-moose-head type of family."

From the garage, we entered the living room where ivory-white carpets remained white, and black leather couches popped with blood-red accent pillows. In the kitchen, the granite counters were spotless. All I could salvage from their fridge was barely expired yogurt and a half-eaten jar of sour pickles whose juice I poured down the drain to lighten my load. Their cabinets were stocked with every type of cereal. I grabbed Frosted Mini-Wheats and Froot Loops.

"Are we sure they're not using this stuff?" I said, pulling out a half-eaten box of Lucky Charms.

Cass waved her arms around the empty kitchen. "They're not here, so, no, they're not using this stuff."

"I'm saying, if we're stealing from other people, then what can we say when they come for us?"

What if it hadn't been hunters after all? What if people were angry and scared and lashing out? What if we pissed someone off out here and they came for my family?

"We just have to make sure someone's home at all times," Cass said. "From what I heard on my trip home from New York, people are leaving well enough alone if you're still on your property. That seems to be the current code of conduct."

"Let's hope so," I said, and continued stuffing boxes in a bag. But the sight of the fresh blood seeped through my mind again. Something violent and brutal had taken place close to my home, close to my family. Close to Teddy. I had to steady myself by leaning up against the counter. There were so many more days to survive.

Back in our basement, I unloaded all the food, board games, and supplies we'd gathered. My parents stood on ladders in different corners of the room, paintbrushes in hand, wet construction glue in buckets by their feet. I was relieved to find music was blasting way too loud for them to ask us any real questions. Kidz Bop echoed off the bare walls, and Georgia held Teddy to her chest while they spun around dancing. Peter danced near them awkwardly and terribly, and my heart melted.

"Ladies!" Teddy yelled. "You have to dance!" A chipmunk version of "Single Ladies" came on, and he screamed with delight.

"Right on time," Cass said as she came down the basement stairs. I held my hand out to her. She rolled her eyes but dropped her bag and glided toward me. My parents continued to plaster the cracks in the walls with their mixture, but they also belted out the lyrics until they drowned out the song entirely with their misinterpretations of the words and Irish accents.

Peter danced around us like a grandfather might. When I accidentally bumped into him, he pulled me into a hug and whispered in my ear, "Everything's going to be okay. We're going to make it." A vague, beautiful thing that felt like something like hope or happiness flickered through me, painfully, and then it was gone.

Teddy's eyes were wide with glee as Georgia dipped him backward. "Again!" he yelled when the song ended. Though we played it one more time, it had lost whatever had made it sparkle. I looked around the basement and tried to picture all of us living there for months, years, on end. I was terrified of what would be happening above us after the asteroid hit but felt even more suffocated by the things Cass and my family might learn about me in a tight space over a long time. The things I almost did. The thing I might still do. Would Aisha tell them about the letter? Would Dr. Talley tell them about my failing grade? Or would they see all the ways I was broken on their own? Would I fall apart again in front of them, completely?

Still, I'd been hopeful or happy or something for a moment, and I clung to that, remembered it as I watched everyone try to cheer Teddy up by swinging their exhausted arms. I tried to conjure it again by thinking to myself, *These are the best people, and they're mine.*

But my brain couldn't help but add, *They're mine, and they deserve better than me.* I kept smiling even though I didn't feel like it, something I'd practiced to perfection over the past few years. I didn't want them to know I was thinking, *I don't belong here. I'm going to burden you. I'm going to hurt you.*

The music played on.

two years
to impact

Junior year, the boys' lacrosse captain, Clayton Fielder, cornered me in the hallway by plowing his shoulder into my locker. I'd had to talk to him a lot that spring since I'd been named captain along with one of the seniors, but it didn't mean I enjoyed it. Whenever he talked to me, he looked down my shirt and he constantly tried to cheat off me in our shared calc class.

"Avery Byrne," he said. "You're captain. I'm captain. You're sexy, I'm sexy. What do you say we lead together and unify our kingdoms?"

"Sorry, what?" I asked, genuinely confused. We'd already scrimmaged twice. Did we really need to do it again?

"I'm asking you to prom," he said, "duh." The

invitation was so bumbling it was almost endearing, but it was Clayton Fielder, so not quite.

I quickly racked my brain for excuses. I already had a date? But then he'd ask me who it was. Club soccer tournament out of state? But what if I ended up going to prom, after all? I wanted to go with my friend Cass? But what if he thought I meant *with* Cass and told everyone that, and then it got back to my parents? What if it got around the whole school and I had to spend the next six months denying it and listening to Cass tell people I wasn't her type?

"I mean . . . why not?" I said as Clayton stuck his fist out to bump mine. I tapped his half-heartedly.

"I'm going to prom with Avery Byrne!" he howled into the hallway. People whooped as he spun away from me, and I felt a door inside me close, though I wasn't sure what was on the other side of it.

I found Cass lounging in the forum, a hallway with uncomfortable couches and bulletin boards covered in club advertisements.

"Why the long face, Ave?" she said. I sat down beside her and put my head on her shoulder.

"It's been . . . a day."

"I want to hear about that. But can I ask you something first before I explode?"

"Yeah, of course," I said. "What's up?"

She got off the couch, reached into her unzipped backpack, and pulled out a piece of computer paper with jagged magazine pieces glued to it. It looked like the collages we made together while lying on the floor of her parents' house, a hybrid of dream board and ransom note. She put it in my hands as she sat back down beside me, and it took me a few seconds to process what it said. Slowly, my brain made out soccer fields, sailboats, rooftops, apple orchards. In the middle, five symbols: *PROM?*

"Who's this for?" I asked, running my fingertips over Cass's colorful paper world, feeling them get hot with jealousy.

"It's for you," she said.

"From who?" I managed breathlessly.

"Me, obviously." She started bouncing her knee.

It was for me. For prom. From Cass. People milled around us, and it felt like they were staring. Was she actually asking me to go with her as her real date? She wouldn't do something like that so publicly, so unceremoniously with no explanation. She couldn't. How could she? My heart pounded so loud I could hardly hear my next words.

"Wait, are you making fun of me?"

"What? No. I'm asking if you want to go to prom with me. Why?"

"Clayton asked me, like, two seconds ago. Very publicly. And it was embarrassing."

"Clayton Fielder? Ew. You let him down easy?"

"I . . . said I'd go with him." It had not fully occurred to me I could have said no.

Cass covered her face, tossed her head back, and groaned.

"Ah, that sounds like the groan of someone who found out Clayton asked Avery to the prom," Omar said as he came out of nowhere to sit on the wooden arm of her couch. "And she said yes." Cass punched his knee.

"How did you hear that already? I mean, really. Clayton Fielder." She said his name like a diagnosis and took the paper out of my hands. She crumpled it up and put it back in her backpack. Omar pretended to shudder.

"The horror," he said. "Avery, how dare you want to participate in a decades-old high school tradition?"

"With Clayton, though," Cass said. "You want to go with me, Omes?"

I felt something drop in my stomach. I was right to think she was asking me as a friend if her next invitation was to Omar.

He crossed his arms in smug satisfaction.

"Avery's not the only one with news," he said. "I asked Violet Connor and she said yes."

"Congrats!" I said, though all I knew of Violet was she dressed in mostly purple, played clarinet in the marching band, and her father ran the Purple Finch Apple Orchard, which practically made him Kilkenny royalty. Cass groaned again and slumped deeper into her chair.

"You're going with a *girl*? The betrayal." She pointed at both of us. "The betrayal runs so deep."

"Violet's my friend!" Omar said. "Plus, I already told you to ask Serenity."

"Serenity White?" I asked, my voice high enough to reveal my own sting of betrayal. Serenity was a strikingly gorgeous point guard on Cass's travel basketball team. Cass hadn't told me there was something going on between them, but apparently, she'd told Omar. Though Cass hadn't even asked her yet, I knew Serenity White would go to prom on Cass's arm, and it was all my fault. Or Omar's for asking Violet, or Clayton's for asking me. Mostly mine for saying yes.

"Huh, yeah," she said. "I think I will."

Suddenly, all I wanted to do was rewind time by one hour. I'd take a different route away from my locker. I'd agree to go to prom with my best friend. We'd shop for outfits and take pictures together and maybe fall asleep together in sweatpants under the stars.

In our study hall later that day, I passed Cass a note that read, *Were you really asking me to go with you?* I looked away as she scribbled a response, my heart nearly punching out of my chest. I didn't know what I wanted her to write, but my breath caught when she slid the note back.

Yeah?? So?? You're my best friend. Don't make it weird.

"I'm not," I mouthed back, but when she shook her head and looked away from me, I knew it was too late. She threw her crumpled collage in the trash can as we left the room, and before I went home that day, I plucked it out. I took it home, flattened it under dictionaries, and pasted it in my scrapbook. I put it on one of the last pages so she probably would never find it, but so I could flip to it anytime I wanted to torture myself with what might have been, if only I'd been braver.

Three weeks later. Prom. My mom did my hair and makeup in our downstairs bathroom, and I wore yet another dress she'd picked out. My ridiculous father stood outside the house with a baseball bat while we waited for Clayton to come pick me up.

"Oh my God, Dad."

"I'm just joking around!"

"Just put it away before he gets here," I said. "This is embarrassing. I don't need a man to protect me like this."

"It's a gag, darling. But a man *should* protect you like that."

"I was in the army too," Mom said, as she emerged from the front door to wait with us. "Give *me* the bat."

"Nobody needs a bat!" I said, as I saw Clayton's hulking black Escalade barreling down our street.

"Well, you look absolutely *beautiful*, Avery. And he's handsome too, that Clayton. I Googled him. If you're not careful tonight, you might fall in love."

"Ah sure, look it," I said, copying their accents, and my dad almost ruffled my hair before he remembered how long it had taken Mom to pin it.

They snapped pictures of the two of us posing stiffly in our backyard, the orchard behind us, and then Clayton and I drove off to meet his friends who were loud and boisterous and didn't really give me the time of day. I crossed my arms a lot and sipped illegal champagne in a garish white Hummer stretch limo. I sat at their dinner table, tried to make small talk, and sent longing glances across the room to Omar and Cass, who'd refused to be looped into large group activities.

"You're throwing me to the wolves!" I'd lamented.

"Avery," Cass said, "you're Little Red Riding Hood."

She'd spent the entire week leading up to prom teasing me about Clayton, leaning in at random moments to whisper in my ear, "Avery Byrne, does my robust masculinity make you feel like a tiny porcelain doll?"; "Avery Byrne, do my sick lax skills keep you up at night?"; "Avery Byrne, does my Axe body spray and King Mode hair gel combo send you into erotic bliss?"

Each time, I smacked her arm and rolled my eyes, but I couldn't help but smile. As we sat around tables with black tablecloths and sweating water glasses and made small talk, Clayton pulled his hair gel out of his pocket and started reapplying it without even looking in a mirror or phone camera. I made the mistake of looking over at my friends' table, making eye contact with Cass, and bursting out into terrible, horrible, painful laughter. All eyes turned to me.

I wanted to sink into the floor or drown in my overdressed salad, but all I could do was choke down freezing tap water and gigantic ice cubes and try to explain to Clayton and his friends I thought of something funny, that was all, nothing happened, everything was fine. I did everything in my power not to look back at Cass as I finally, finally composed myself, though I knew she was probably doing the same, telling Serenity and Omar the whole story, all of them laughing more at me than with me.

Without looking at photos, I don't remember what Clayton wore, but Serenity wore a black satin dress that poured down her body, the moon to Cass's kurta pajama, a sun: a stunning red two-piece ensemble embellished with gold beading. She wore silver most of the time, but on special occasions like her quinceañera and family weddings, all gold. It radiated. Once the music hit, they slowly, finally merged their little group with mine, and I spent the next few hours trying to hold my emerald strapless dress up, while repeatedly moving Clayton's hands off my ass and screaming the lyrics to every song that came on.

All night, everyone stared at Cass and Serenity, in part because they were the only queer couple there, but also because they were the best dancers by far. Cass grew up dancing with both the Indian and Mexican sides of her family, whereas my family stayed at our tables during weddings to sip wine and only stood up for the Village People's "YMCA." At prom, during the final slow song, my heart quickened with both anxiety and longing as I watched them move in their private galaxy around the gym. I had one hand on Clayton's shoulder. The other held my dress up. I turned my head at an angle where he'd think I was resting it against his chest, but really, I was watching Cass guide Serenity across the floor, whispering something mysterious in her ear. Even though we were so far away in so many ways, I still felt tethered to her. There was an invisible rope between us in any room, and it tugged on me then. Yanked.

I felt, all night, on the verge of tears I didn't understand. Sure, Clayton wasn't my dream date and prom was just okay, but I'd never had any high hopes for it. Why was I so upset, so fragile? Why did my heart feel like it was being squeezed in a fist?

I told myself over and over again, *I want to be dancing with my friend.*

But then, in my periphery, I saw Cass with her hands on Serenity's hips. I watched her move her and be moved by her. For the first time, I understood in my skin and not just my brain that girls could be together like *that*, and

Cass was with a girl like *that*, and that girl was not me. And I had always wanted it to be me.

My ribs iced over and cracked one by one right down my chest. My hands, knees, neck, back, hair all burned in the places Cass had touched me recently and froze again without her hands there still. I pulled my own hands away from the boy in front of me and crossed them over my chest.

"Oh my God. I'm in love with her."

"What?" Clayton yelled over the music. Only then did I realize I'd said it out loud. I shook my head and backed away from him, nauseous with certainty, stunned by string lights, looking anywhere in the room but at Cass and Serenity. Cass was in love with Serenity, or something like it.

And I was in love with Cass. I always had been. I probably always would be. I loved her. I loved her. I loved her. My God, how had I never realized? It almost brought me to my knees. I wanted to tell everyone and no one. I wanted to find Omar, but the lights came up to expose me.

I gripped on to Clayton's suit jacket to stay standing.

"Do you want to go to my house or Sharkman's party?" Clayton asked me through the disappointed buzz. He put one hand on my hip and one in my hair. I backed away.

"I actually have to go home," I lied. "My parents are really strict. Thank you for a nice night, though."

"Can I come to your house?"

"No," I said. I beelined it to Omar's side, and together we left for a different party at Milan Leoni's house, where we'd already stashed clothes and sleeping bags earlier that afternoon. Violet's dad was waiting to pick her right up at the high school—simultaneously knocking my parents out of the running for most vigilant parents of the year and forcing her and Omar into a side-hug goodbye.

I sat in the passenger seat of Omar's Honda as we drove down familiar streets in a world that felt new to me. I was so rarely alone with Omar, and when I was, I felt like every word out of my mouth was met with his side-eye.

"So, Avery," he said with a little rearview mirror smile. "How was prom with Captain Clayton?" I rolled my eyes and felt completely pinned down by the weight in my mouth. I tried to get the heavy words off the tip of my tongue: *I'm in love with Cass. I've always known, and I never knew. What do I do? What should I fucking do?*

"It was fine," I said.

"Only fine? You and Clayton would make a wicked good-looking couple." I stifled a laugh and bit my lip, still dying to get the words out. But God, they were so heavy, so heavy I knew they'd flip me inside out.

"God, Omar. No."

"I'm *saying*," he said. "It's prom night. It's like a witching hour situation. Connections are made."

I pulled my phone out and drafted a text to Peter: Umm . . . I think I'm in love with Cass? I hit Send and put my phone back in my purse, afraid of what he'd say and what he wouldn't. At least if I died in some freak car accident, she'd know. Peter could tell her. It was out there now, in the universe, even if I couldn't speak it.

"Did you have fun with Violet?" I said.

"Totally," he said. "She's wicked fun. Can I tell you something, though? I was jealous of Cass and Serenity. Like, I wish I was brave enough to ask a guy."

"Why didn't you?"

"I don't know. I don't have a crush right now. And I thought I'd have more fun not worrying about what people would say about me. But like, who cares?"

"They did look amazing together," I said weakly.

"They did, right? No offense, Avery, but I told her not to ask you. She did it anyway. But now look."

"You told her not to ask me?" My voice came out smaller than I wanted it to.

"Yeah. I know she's your best friend, but she's mine too."

"You wanted her to ask you instead?"

"No." He sucked his teeth, exasperated. "Not exactly. It's just—I used to be like her."

"Used to be like her how?"

"I don't want to say too much."

"I feel like you're not saying anything at all." He slowed to stop for a red light and turned to look at me.

"Avery, look. I'll just say this: It's good she went with Serenity. They're good together."

"We wouldn't be?" As soon as I said the words, I wanted to take them back. He looked at me sideways before focusing again on the road.

"You're straight, so no. You wouldn't be."

"What if I wasn't?" My brain begged me to shut up. I couldn't even say it, present tense: *What if I'm not?*

"Well, you are," he said, getting annoyed. "Aren't you?"

What could I say? I didn't want to tell him how I felt before I told her, before I talked to Peter. I had only just come out to *myself*; I wasn't about to come out to Omar. When I said nothing, he continued, "If I'm being real, I think you use Cass for attention. You treat her like she's your boyfriend, and the second you get a real one, you're gonna drop her. That's facts."

I felt like he'd knocked the wind right out of me. I bit my tongue to keep from crying and stared out the window. What if he was right? What if I was just jealous and possessive? How was I supposed to tell the difference?

But, no. I was in love with Cass. Everything in me was screaming that I was, that I always had been, and how had I not known that?

"I don't use her," I said, and felt embarrassed because he could probably tell I was on the verge of tears.

"I'm not trying to be mean," he said. "I've been there, you know?" *Been where?* I wanted to ask, but he added,

"If you care about her, and I know you do, you'll let her go. You'll let her be happy."

He was right, even if he was wrong about me using her for attention. Even if I was in love with her, she'd be better off without me. She'd be better off with a girl who would go with her to prom without asking a million ridiculous questions, who would dance with her openly, who was probably somewhere, right now, kissing her. Loving her in the way she deserved to be loved. I plastered a concrete smile to my lips for Omar, and I nodded.

At Milan's, Omar and I sat with a couple of other kids in sweatpants and sweatshirts by the fire pit and ate potato chips. We set marshmallows on fire and beat them with sticks when, still lit, they slid off our skewers and onto the grass.

"Aren't we all supposed to be losing our virginity right now?" Milan said.

"Cass still isn't here," Felix Hall said smugly as he churned a perfectly golden marshmallow.

"Her date looked like a movie star," Milan said, then scrunched her nose. "Do you think they're really hooking up right now?" When it was quiet, I realized she was asking me.

"How would I know?" I flushed.

"I thought you two tell each other everything."

"I'm sure she'll tell me after."

I felt someone sit next to me and sling their arm around my shoulder. For a horrifying instant, I thought it might be Clayton. But it was Cass, with her hair in a braid and a big grin on her face. She'd changed into Adidas track pants and her lacrosse coat and had wiped off all her makeup. She was so clean, so warm, so beautiful, so handsome I could hardly stop myself from putting my hands on her cheeks and pulling her lips to mine.

"Hey!" I said, a little too enthusiastically.

"Cass!" the others cheered.

"Yo," she said and held out a hand. "Marshmallow me."

"Where's Serenity?" Omar asked.

"I dropped her off. She has church in the morning."

"I respect that," Atticus Romney said.

"But did you take her to church tonight?" Felix said coyly. I wanted to throw up.

"Inappropriate!" Milan threw a marshmallow at Felix, who dodged it.

Cass bit her lip. "Felix, you're literally the worst. But also, I don't kiss and tell."

My stomach tightened.

"A noble disposition," Milan said, "but zero fun. We wanted someone to get laid tonight."

"Then why are you all out here hiding from your dates?" Cass asked. We shrugged collectively.

"I'm Mormon," Atticus droned.

"Swipin' on Grindr," Omar said.

"Clayton's gross," I said, and the others threw their voices into the chorus of excuses.

"All right, all right," Cass said. "Are we capable of talking about people's outfits tonight without being catty bitches?"

"Yes," Milan said, "but first can I say *one* bitchy thing?"

"I thought you'd never ask." Cass popped a marshmallow turned cinder into her mouth.

About an hour later, Cass, Omar, and I had fixed our sleeping bags in a corner of Milan's finished basement. We lay on our stomachs in the dark, whispering so Milan's mom didn't hear us when she made her rounds, which she made more frequently to our corner like a weird, homophobic helicopter.

"So," Omar said, "you kissed. Now tell." I clenched my teeth and fought the urge to put my hand over her mouth.

"It didn't happen," Cass said. "I was adding to the cloud of mystery surrounding my majestic reputation."

"You don't like her like that?" Omar asked.

"I *do*," Cass said. "I really, really do. I'm so into her. She's such a happy person. So full of life. It's contagious."

I nodded quickly, even though neither of them could see me. I was so . . . *not* that. I dug my fingernails into my fingertips.

"That's great," I said.

"It was nice to go with someone who actually wanted to go with me. It was really nice."

"Yeah," I said, stomach souring. "I'm happy for you, Cass." I was. Of course I was. But.

"And what about Clayton?" Cass said. "Did his testosterone hair slime seduce you? If you tell me you kissed him, Avery, I swear to God . . ."

"Cass, ew. First of all, you *can't* make me laugh like that; I almost spit my water out all over the table. Second of all, on top of everything else—and to be clear there's a lot—I found out tonight he's a Republican."

"ABORT MISSION, ABORT MISSION," Omar said.

"Just don't say 'abort' around him," Cass said.

"Cass!" I said, and Omar laughed into his pillow. "You're awful."

"I know," she sighed. "Universe, forgive me."

"We're all awful," Omar said. "Except for Catholic Charities Avery. That's it, isn't it? You went with Clayton as charity."

"Too mean," I said. "He has some redeeming qualities, like . . ."

"Ugh, we get it, Avery, you're not awful," Cass said with a sigh, and then to me, "You are the exact opposite of awful. You are incapable of being awful. You are a do-gooder Christian who, like, cares about people for some reason."

"Why do I feel like you're insulting me?" I said.

"Because nice people are dull and/or self-righteous and/or hypocrites."

"Ouch." Is this what Cass and Omar talked about when I wasn't around? How I used her, how I was impossibly straight, how I was dull and self-righteous, and a hypocrite? God, I'd known Omar didn't like me, and she'd denied it.

"Avery, geez, you're none of those things," Cass said.

"We're giving you a hard time," Omar said, as if I should know.

"You're gonna be the senior girl all the little underclassmen look up to. You know that, right?" Cass said. "I saw it tonight. People revolve around you. You're kind. You're going to be captain of the soccer team; you're already captain of the lacrosse team. Straight A's. Hot as shit."

I'd watched her all night, but clearly, she'd looked out for me too. I wanted to ask her why, and what about Serenity, and what if I told her there could be an us? What then? But I couldn't ruin this night for her, not when she was so happy about Serenity.

"That's ridiculous," I said, and looked at my pillow.

Cass's eyes must have adjusted to the darkness, because she said, "See? You take compliments like the Catholic you are."

Milan's mom called down for us to go to sleep, and after the whole room filled with giggling and shushing and breathing, we started to drift off. Cass was using her arms as a pillow, and I positioned my hand to be so close to hers that it could seem like an accident if we touched in the night. But Omar's words rang in my head: *Let her go. Let her be happy.*

Once I was sure the two of them were asleep, I finally let myself cry into my pillow until sleep closed in on me.

In the morning, I woke up to a text from Peter responding to my confession: **Umm . . . Avery. LOL. You really didn't know?**

eight days to impact

That night, we sat in the orchard under a silver moon: Cass, Peter, Aisha, Georgia, and me, a fire between us, cases of cider stacked beside us. My cells were still. My breath came steady. Cass sat on the ground between my knees, and Peter sat to my right in a lawn chair still iced to the ground. I tossed apple after apple into the flames because I liked the smoke and cracking.

We were talking about where we were and what we were doing when we heard about the asteroid. The stories were only skeletons, but everyone was so eager to tell their own, to visit the people they were before. Everyone except me.

"We were soaking oatmeal together before Teddy woke up," Georgia said. She talked about the bliss of their routine, the glory of the mundanity. I couldn't see her bee and flower tattoos under her jacket sleeves, but I knew they were there. Always different, always the same.

"I checked Twitter and could barely process it . . ." Peter shook his head. "I dropped my phone."

"That's where we go blank," Georgia said. "Because it's hard to remember taking in that information. Understanding it."

"I still don't understand," Cass said. "I was at a class-mate's apartment working on my designs for Mx. and Match, this huge fashion show Pratt does during spring semester. I was the only freshman who got in! And my clothes were *good*; I had this really sweet plaid theme."

"Plaid? For queers? Groundbreaking," I said, and she got up to fake-tackle me.

"No!" she laughed. "It was like plaid piping on black suits and surprising pattern combinations and . . . damn, I'm so crushed. That was my biggest dream for so long, to have a whole collection in a show like that, and it was just weeks away. I worked so hard, and I was *so close* too. And now—" Her voice caught, and she sat back down between my knees to lean back into me. I felt bad for cracking a joke, even though she'd laughed. I wanted to rub her shoulders, but I didn't know if she would want that, and I felt everyone watching us.

"You should have brought your designs here!" Georgia said. "We would have modeled them for you."

"I would have slayed, as they say," Peter said.

"I know! I'm mad at myself. I was also, uh, a little high." She mimed smoking weed with the wistfulness of an Old Hollywood cigarette. "So I didn't exactly have my act together. What about you, Aisha?"

"I was sleeping," she said, and pulled the five blankets she was wrapped in closer to her chest. "And then praying. And then looking for Avery." She didn't elaborate; she let her words hang there in the smoke of the flames. We locked eyes, but I looked away quickly. "And you, Avery?" she said with a hint of urging.

"I was in the library finishing up an essay for Dr. Talley. And then Cass called me."

Cass leaned back into me, harder. It felt like we were fused together, in one body, and I was terrified to think how quickly that would change if she knew I'd been about to kill myself. She'd feel betrayed. She'd be so sad, so angry. She'd look at me like she didn't know me, not at all. She'd be kind for the sake of it. And then she'd walk away from my madness, toward her new, fresh life, as soon as she got the chance. If she got the chance.

As she should, as I hoped she would. But still it made me nauseous.

"Peter Lasky here reporting for *The Apocalyptic Times*," my brother said, holding an invisible microphone to my mouth. "Avery Byrne, so far you've been—shall we say—elusive?" He could have been a reporter with his strong jaw and brick teeth. He could have been a lot of things.

"I told you," I said, "I was writing in the library."

"But with whom!" Peter bellowed.

"Why are you an asshole?" Cass said, and smacked his left calf. "Leave her alone." Before either of them could say anything else, we heard a rustling in the apple trees, and the dog came bounding out, a stick between her teeth.

"Hi, Scouty," Cass said. The dog ran up to snuggle into her. A moment later, Dr. Talley appeared in the clearing.

"Can I join you?" he asked. I said nothing when everyone waved him into the circle.

"So, dude," Peter said as he handed him a cider. "Sorry. *Doctor.* You've been living in our parents' house for about twenty-four hours, and I still don't know what your deal is."

"My name is Dr. Basil Talley, former professor of American Literature. And I don't know what your deal is either."

"Fair," Peter said. "Let's go around the circle and say our deepest, darkest secrets, since nothing matters anymore, and the world is ending."

My mind raced as I tried to think of something true but benign that would still seem convincing. I had plenty of practice; it was exactly what I did every time I went to confession with my parents at Our Lady of Mercy. But, then, I'd had time to prepare.

"How about favorite movie instead?" Aisha suggested.

"I'm stressed," Cass said. "I have way too many favorites."

"Okay," Peter said, waving his arms. "How about the one place you'd visit right now if you could go anywhere in the world?"

"I'll start," Aisha said. "If I could go anywhere in the world, it would be back to Nigeria, but . . ." She pointed at the sky.

"Who's at home in Nigeria?" Georgia asked.

"My parents," she said. "My parents are there. I've been able to video chat with them a bunch, thank goodness."

"No siblings?"

"We lost my sister," she said.

We all murmured, "I'm sorry," and though I'd already known about her sister, I ached for her again. A thick silence settled, and Aisha avoided my eyes. She nervously twisted the cap on her water bottle off and on.

"If I could go anywhere," Peter said, "I'd go to the beach. My parents almost never let us go to the beach when we were kids."

"I'd go see my parents in Brooklyn," Georgia said, "to let them see Teddy in person. But. Yeah." She tipped her bottle back so the rest of it drained down her throat in one gulp.

"I'd go to Fiji," Cass said quietly. "Not because my parents are there, but because it's Fiji. Okay, and maybe also because my parents are there."

Everyone looked to me.

I'd been racking my brain to think of a destination that would make them believe I had desires and an imagination, a bucket list ten miles long. Instead, I ran out of time for a lie and I had to either run away from the circle entirely or go with the truth. When I pictured where I wanted to be, I could only picture the little icebergs in the river. I could only imagine escaping. "I'd go back to Eaton."

"What? Why?" Peter said, flustered. "Booo."

"I feel like I have some unfinished business there."

"That's the most ridiculous thing I've ever heard," he said. "You've been there pretty much every day for the past six months."

"I want to go back to Eaton," I said again. I felt like my glass would shatter if he pushed me any further on it.

"She said what she said." Cass reached back to pat my knee.

"Let the girl go to Eaton." Georgia raised her bottle to cheers. "Avery can go wherever she wants. She's an independent woman."

I wondered, then, if she resented her choice to stay in New Hampshire with our family and see things through to the end.

"We're off track," I said. "Tell us about you, Dr. Talley."
Please.

He looked at the sky, studying it, before he looked back to us.

"My name is Dr. Basil Talley. I'm from Baton Rouge, Louisiana, but I can go anywhere I like by reading a book."

I gripped Cass's shoulders to stop myself from rolling my eyes.

"What were you doing when you found out about the asteroid?" Peter asked, extending his invisible microphone again. Dr. Talley stared down the barrel of his cider before sipping it thoughtfully.

"I was walking through the woods," he said. "My therapist told me to take morning walks to connect with the world, breathe fresh air, smell the roses, etcetera."

Dr. Talley had a therapist? And he just . . . talked about it like that?

"Nature's so healing," Georgia said. "My therapist says it's because it forces you to use all of your senses. To be thoughtful. Present."

"You have a therapist too?" I asked, and looked to Peter, but he didn't seem surprised.

"Actually, I saw you that morning," Dr. Talley said, turning to me. "Running through the trees." I shook my head.

"I was in the library," I said. "Wasn't me." He grinned slowly and wagged his finger at me.

"No, it was you. Red hair. Blue jacket. Those sneakers whipping through the trees like Hermes." Fuck my gold Adidas. I wanted to throw up.

"Must have been on the way to the library."

"Wait, you were *going to* the library?" Peter turned his fake microphone my way. "Or coming back *from* the library?"

"It was nowhere near the library," Dr. Talley said.

"I don't know," I said. "I was in the library."

"She was in the library," Aisha insisted. "Writing a paper for your class."

"I thought you said you were looking for her, Aisha," Cass said.

"She's not in any of my classes this semester," Dr. Talley said.

"I was looking for her," Aisha said. "Then I found her in the library."

"But you said she wasn't near the library?" Peter said to Dr. Talley.

"I was in the library," I said too forcefully, my blood hot in my chest. "Writing a paper for a different class. Then Aisha found me and we came here. I don't know what else to tell you." I leaned away from Cass so she couldn't tell I was shaking.

"Um." She turned around as if to ask me a question but thought better of it. "Let's move on. Please."

"Anyone got any deep, dark secrets they want to share?" Peter asked. *Not again.*

"Ooh, Pete," Cass said, latching on. "That reminds me of the time I stole your Candace Parker jersey because Avery said you didn't wear it and I looked hot in it."

"What?" He reached down for a pinch of snow to throw at me.

"I don't remember saying you didn't wear it, but I definitely said she looked hot in it," I said.

"You're lucky you saved that one until the end of the world."

"Yeah, when I'll be too dead for you to kill me," Cass said.

Georgia choked on a cry, and Peter reached out to take her hand.

"No one's dying here, Cass," he said, his voice tight. The fire crackled in the silence.

"I was kidding," Cass said weakly, but Georgia stood up and started hastily picking up the things strewn about her feet: her jacket, a water bottle, one of Teddy's stuffed animals, a pack of Oreos.

"I'll see you tomorrow," she said. It was only then I realized she'd started to cry. Peter watched her walk toward the house, finished his drink, then stood up himself.

"I should follow her," he said. "You do know we're gonna make it, Cass, right? We're gonna be okay. As long as we stock up enough, we're gonna be okay."

She repeated, "I was kidding, Pete. Swear." He forced a smile, squeezed each of our shoulders, and walked away into the night.

"I should go too," Dr. Talley said, throwing his cider bottle into the fire and reaching for Scout, who was still curled up against Cass's leg. "This was probably a misstep on my behalf. I apologize for ruining your fun."

"No, man, you're good," Cass said.

"Yes, anytime, Dr. Talley," Aisha said. "We truly enjoy your company."

I did not enjoy his company but said nothing, and my cheeks flushed hot remembering the way he'd called my bluff on the library. In front of everyone. He bowed his head and didn't meet my eyes before slipping into the trees again. Once Scout was gone too, Cass climbed into the chair Peter had been sitting in beside me.

"We should sleep," Aisha said. "We need to wake up early. I have to pray at sunrise, and I have more research to do."

"Research for what?" Cass asked. "It's okay to let go right now, Aisha. Just a little."

Aisha folded her mounds of blankets and stacked them on one of the plastic chairs. "Let's not get into this again. You two can do what you want, but I need to know as much as I can. I have plans to save my family."

"You're allowed to breathe for a minute. For a night." We'd spent the day searching for supplies. When we were done, Cass and I had sat in full sweatsuits on the floor of our basement organizing materials while Aisha had stayed fixed to the family laptop.

"Can we help you?" I said, rubbing my hands over the

flames to stay warm. "What are you researching? What are you planning?" What was there to know except precisely when the asteroid was coming, down to the second? Which horrible death we were going to die? What horrors were taking place beyond the edges of the orchard?

Aisha sighed. Cass's and my chairs were set so close together she draped her final blanket over the two of us. "I don't need help. Just wake up early with me, okay? Please?"

"Yeah, of course," I said. "Good night."

"We'll put the fire out," Cass said before reaching down to throw more sticks into the guts of it. Aisha patted each of us on the head, and then she was gone too.

"So . . . what was that about?" Cass said.

"I don't know. What could she possibly be up to?"

"Not that," she said. "Why were you in the woods that morning?"

I looked away from her and tried to decide to what degree I should lie. "I showed you that spot when you visited me. Remember? My favorite place on campus."

"So, you were there?"

"Yeah."

"So, you lied about it because . . . you were with someone?" I bit my bottom lip and tried to quickly rehearse the truth. I wanted to tell her, I did. *I couldn't breathe. I didn't want to live anymore. I was going to kill myself. I was going to drown.* Before I could get the words right, she said,

"You were with that softball player who puts heart eyes on all your Instagram posts, right? UnderhandUndercuts?"

Meredith Wyn.

I looked away from Cass. Decided to lie. Hated myself for it. But it was better, wasn't it? It was better if she didn't know. Why hurt her for no reason?

"We hooked up for a while, but it wasn't anything serious. It's not like I'm talking to her now or anything." At least that much was true. Under our blanket, the outside of Cass's knee was touching mine, and it was all I could think about.

"But you liked her?" she asked.

"I was attracted to her, but it's not like it is with—" *You*, I wanted to say but stopped myself. "—with you and Daisy." Daisy was Cass's hippest, hottest, New York friend. The one who'd ruined my visit. The one who slept in Cass's bed that night while I slept on the cold floor.

Cass smirked a little, but then her face fell. "I wasn't into Daisy, Ave." She looked away from me, into the fire. "I was never into Daisy."

I studied her face for a minute, but she'd set it to stone. My heart felt like a rock, too, dense and jagged, and it pounded against my ribs. *Then why?* I wanted to ask. *Why had it gone down like that?*

She pushed her knee harder into mine. I didn't know if it was on purpose. I pushed back.

"It's okay if you were," I said.

"Don't do that," she whispered, but kept her eyes locked on the flames in front of us.

"Don't do what?"

A wisp of wind pushed the smoke in our direction, and she had no choice but to turn back to look at me. We each shielded our eyes with our hands, and suddenly our faces were hidden from the fire, the orchard, the yard, our house. And they were inches apart.

"Don't pretend," she said, "like you don't know that I love you." Her nervous leg started bouncing again under the blanket, and I slid my hand over to calm it. She steadied, and put her hand on top of mine. Held it there.

Cass loved me. My head spun; my heart hammered. Harder. Harder.

But.

"But I tried to kiss you in New York, and you said—"

"We were drunk, so I wasn't sure you were for real. And you said you hated me, when I tried to apologize—"

"I was scared, Cass! I was scared." Of loving her. Hurting her. Losing her.

"*I* was scared," she said. "Terrified."

And might I, still? Hurt her? Lose her?

But what did that matter?

What did any of it matter?

"Cass," I said. I put my shaking hand on her cheek. "The world is ending. And I am desperately in love with you, and—"

"Avery," she whispered. "Shut up and kiss me."

My lips found hers, and we pushed into each other so hard it hurt. She tasted like smoke and cider. My heart was near her heart. Her hair was in my fist. Kissing her felt like the answer to every question I had ever asked. It felt like the period at the end of a breathless sentence. It felt like we were giants, like I could reach up to swat the asteroid from the sky and we could fold into each other like that forever, so big nothing could destroy us.

A tear fell down my cheek, surprising me. I wiped it away as if it didn't belong to me, and she traced her thumb down my cheek before resting her forehead on mine. There was nothing and everything to say.

We chose nothing.

We chose each other, again.

We spread the blanket on the ground, and tumbled to the frozen grass together. I kissed Cass under the constellations. She held me in the middle of the ice-glass night.

Even if I shouldn't have, even if she deserved more than me—for the first time in my life, I pulled her closer. I let her love me.

one year to impact

After I realized I was fully, deeply in love with Cass, it was already too late. She and Serenity were inseparable during our senior year. Since Serenity attended Manchester West and Cass never got to see her at school, they spent all their free time together. Everything was normal between Cass and me in classes and at practice, or at least I think it seemed that way to her. But I spent most nights locked in my room studying and working out, even after I got into Eaton. I also spent a lot of time on my laptop, typing in incognito Google searches, like, how to know if you're gay or bisexual (or something else?), fail-proof suicide methods, anonymous lesbian chat. I created screen names like redhead04 to fit in with the streaming lines of text that snaked up my screen.

I felt flustered watching X-rated requests pass by at an alarming rate. Surely these were bots or horny men, not confident, cool, queer, lonely women alone in their rooms waiting to talk to me about the afterlife, aliens, or the Sapphic aesthetic of boy bands. And yet, I'd still log on from time to time to see if I could find my reflection in what they were saying. I also used tangled headphones to try to watch lesbian porn in incognito mode and cringed at their long nails tapping at each other with a mild level of repulsion. Their Barbie-waxed pubic hair. The angles of their bodies bent and positioned to be visible to the men off-screen.

Every time, I slammed my laptop shut and felt sick. I didn't want to touch myself until I'd cleansed my brain with thoughts of Cass: the way she laughed, moved, slept. I wondered what it would feel like to undress for her, to let her into me. I wondered what it would feel like for her to let me into her. I didn't know, but I did know it wouldn't feel cheap or nasty. It would feel like a spark in my chest. It would feel like a life I had yet to live. I wanted to be electrified. I thought, *I've missed my chance.*

One night, my parents, Peter, Georgia, and I watched a Red Sox game in what felt like slow motion. It was a school night, so I had my AP English essay notes spread across my lap in the Laskys' living room. I was only half paying attention to the conversation bubbling around me.

". . . and that's two things we've never had in the

family," Mom said, "a priest or a gay." My stomach dropped, and my head snapped up, probably too quickly.

"What's wrong with a priest or a gay person?" I said, immediately defensive. I caught Peter trying to lock eyes with me from where he was sitting on the couch to my left, but I refused to look his way. I might break down.

"I didn't say there's anything *wrong* with them. I said there's no one in our family."

"You can't know that," I said.

"I think I would know," Mom said.

I hadn't planned on coming out to my family, at least not until college. I'd just gotten into Eaton, and everyone was proud and ecstatic, me included. A dream come true. What they didn't know was what I dreamed of, there, exactly: I'd be out from the start, just like Cass had been in high school. People would only befriend me if they were okay with that, and they'd be okay with it, because I'd be a soccer star, top student, beloved by all. The most badass Avery Byrne anyone had ever seen. As for my parents, though, I'd promised myself I would keep it a secret until I was sure, until I had found someone to bring home who could hold my hand and kiss my hair after I'd spoken my truth.

But that day, I was a raw nerve. Tired and agitated.

"You don't know," I said, and then immediately wanted to take it back. But I couldn't stop. I kept going. "People don't always *seem* gay. We're not all just a mash-up of stereotypes."

There was only a beat before Dad picked up on it. "What do you mean 'we'?"

I panicked, and in an instant weighed all my options, opened every door of possibility in my mind. Would they kick me out? Surely, Peter and Georgia would let me live with them. Would they refuse to pay for Eaton? Take my computer? Ban me from hanging out with Cass? I said it anyway.

"I don't know what I am, but I don't think I'm straight." I physically braced myself for the fallout, but a new commercial came on for Puppy Chow.

"Look at that one," Mom said. "I love setters."

"Mom, I think Avery's trying to tell us something," Peter said.

"I'm bi too," Georgia said. "It's not a big deal. It's normal."

"I heard what she said," Mom snapped. "I don't think I have anything to say about it. I think we can all move on." And, yes, I wanted everyone to move on, but not yet. Not when I'd said something big and no one cared.

"Well, I think that's great," Georgia said. "Congratulations." She was wholly unsurprised. My brother had clearly told her about my text concerning Cass and prepped her. I felt annoyed, but also grateful. My parents had to see it wasn't a terrible life, I wasn't alone, people were welcoming now, at least some people. That could be enough.

"Yeah," Peter said. "It's great, Ave. We're proud of you."

My parents continued to stare at the TV. My dad's next comment was about the umpire.

"He's the worst one in MLB history. He looks like a toe."

"I'm going to bed," I said and started to pull my papers together, shoving them into my backpack. The sun hadn't even set.

"Good night!" my parents each said absentmindedly. Peter and Georgia got up to give me a hug before I left. I wasn't sure if they could tell I was shaking.

I lingered in the garage to collect myself among Teddy's strollers, red-and-yellow plastic car, and haphazard rain boots. I'd just come out, technically, and there were no fireworks. But the world hadn't ended either. How many times had I imagined that scene over the past year? In my mind it always ended with tears and prayers and shouting. I think I would have preferred it that way. The silence was so heavy with the words they weren't saying but I knew they were thinking. I pressed my ear back to the door.

"You guys could have been more supportive," I heard Peter saying.

"Why?" Dad said. "She's saying it because all the kids think they're gay now."

"That's not true," Georgia said, but they ignored her.

"I'm sure Cass has something to do with it," Mom said. "I know my daughter. She's not a *lesbian*." She said the word more quietly than the rest. And yes, Cass had something to do with it, but it was feeling more and more like she would never have anything to do with it at all. And my identity still mattered.

I marched myself home and threw my backpack in the doorway. I tried to call Cass, but she didn't pick up. I texted her: **Hey, you free to meet up?** I waited for what felt like an hour for her response, then typed instead: **Just came out to my parents, I think?**

Instead of a text response, my phone lit up with Cass's photo, one of the two of us at soccer camp.

"Hey," I said.

"Avery," she said. "Your text. What are you talking about?"

"What do you mean?"

"You . . . just came out?"

I sat down on my bed. "Yeah."

"Came out as, what, gay?"

"I don't know. I said I'm not straight."

"You're not straight?"

"I don't think I'm straight, no."

"Wow," she said with some bite.

"Wow?"

"Yeah, wow. I'm not mad, I'm hurt. I thought I was your person. And *I'm* gay! You haven't told me anything about this. You like someone?" I wanted to burst out laughing or crying, I didn't know which. Where to begin?

"Can we not do this over a phone call?"

"Do what? I want to know the basics."

"There's nothing to know." *Except I'm in love with you, I can never tell you that, and I know you'll be happier without me.*

"You came out to your conservative Irish Catholic parents, who you hide your *coffee* habits from, and there's nothing to know?"

"I got flustered because my mom said there was no one gay in our family. I said she couldn't know that. I said I might not be straight, that's all. It wasn't a big thing."

"I know I've been busy with Serenity, Ave, but you can still talk to me. About anything, but especially about this stuff. I mean, shit."

Even if there were other girls in the picture, I couldn't imagine telling Cass about them. She almost never talked to me about Serenity. She was coy about what they did, how it felt, what kind of promises they'd made to each other. They'd already picked out their senior year prom suits, I knew that. I'd fully committed to not going, despite a handful of invitations.

"Can we go somewhere?" I said. "I'd really like to get out of the house."

"I'm out with Omar and Serenity, you want to come?"

I bristled. I hadn't been invited in the first place. Why would I take an invitation now?

"That's okay. I'll see you tomorrow."

"Okay. I'm sorry I made this about me, but I do want you to trust me. I'm still your best friend, you know that, right?"

"Yeah, I know."

"Cool." She hung up without saying goodbye, and it left me slack-jawed.

I lay back on my bed and stared at the ceiling while angsty lesbian songs streamed out of my phone. I cried a little, then went into the bathroom to straighten my hair, put on red lipstick, push my boobs up in my lowest-cut shirt. I only knew how to pose myself for boys like Clayton. Is this what girls liked too? I thought again of the time Cass told me I wasn't her type. Was that how all queer girls would feel? I figured I had until the baseball game ended, so I grabbed the keys to the Volvo and started driving toward the first place that came up on Google Maps when I typed in "gay bar."

On the ride, I checked my reflection a hundred times. I tried to imagine what kind of girl would find me attractive. I tried to dream up the girl I would want to wrap my arms around and pull close to me while music played on tinny speakers. I couldn't imagine her face, but she smelled like evergreen trees and tugged me to her by my belt loops. She would run her hands down my hips and whisper something only I could hear. Everyone in the room would pretend to look away as she kissed me—and it would be so easy to kiss her—but they'd all be waiting to see what we'd do next, who we would be together. Before I could finish building my fantasy, I found myself in the parking lot of a dive bar advertising specials on Bud Light. I got out of the car, took a deep breath, and went inside.

Amber lights lit the bar. It smelled like a gym bag. I was relieved there was no one to card me at the door, though it probably helped that it was a Tuesday night. I sat on a tall stool and ordered a Diet Pepsi from the balding man wearing flannel and sucking on a lollipop.

"You here alone, kid?" he asked. "You know this is a gay bar, right?" Did he think I'd stumbled into this hole-in-the-wall by accident?

"I'm trying to meet people."

"You seem like you're probably used to guys chasing you, honey, but they're not gonna do that here."

"I'm trying to meet *women*," I said. As he put my glass down, still warm from the dishwasher, he busted out laughing.

"You won't meet women here." I scanned the room and saw he was right. The only other girl was making out with her boyfriend as her gay friends played pool.

"Where do they hang out?"

He shrugged. "Beats me. There used to be one bar in Boston, the Milky Way. Pretty sure it closed down, though."

"Oh," I said. He walked away and I sat there alone. I sipped my Pepsi and felt my cheeks grow hot. Were people staring at me? Did they think I was strange, for not having friends, for being at a gay bar, for being under-age? Were the boys playing pool laughing at me? I wanted to crawl out of my skin, but instead I ran out of the room and back into the blue evening wind.

Once I was in the driver's seat, hands on the tan leather steering wheel, I didn't know where to go. I didn't want to go home, to my parents who might have questions, or, worse, wouldn't say anything at all. I didn't want to go to Cass and Omar and Serenity, my friends who knew exactly who they were, exactly how they should love and want each other. My friends who didn't want me around.

I saw the moody waves of the Merrimack River rolling between red mill buildings, and I thought, *I could drive right into it.* I could lock my doors and put my foot on the gas and close my eyes, and I wouldn't have to breathe anymore. I wouldn't have to go home or lie to Cass, say I didn't love her. I wouldn't have to go to college or run wind sprints or lie around in my bed sleepless, hopeless, aching every goddamn night.

I wouldn't have to be me.

I wouldn't have to be anyone.

I put my foot on the gas, closed my eyes, and rushed forward. For the briefest second, I felt finally *free*, but then I got so scared—trapped breath choking me—that

I would kill someone else. I slammed on the brakes. My knuckles punched my chest as I lurched forward. I put the car in Park, opened the driver's side door, and ran a circle around it to make sure I hadn't hit anyone. I hadn't. The street was empty. Thank God. *Thank God.* But what if I had? I thought, *I am so selfish. I am so ungrateful, weak, pathetic. I am a loser. A sinner.*

I knew where I needed to go.

When I pulled into the Our Lady of Mercy parking lot, the evening Mass had let out and the stars had started to pop like summer freckles above the building. I scrubbed my lipstick off with a tissue and pulled on a soccer hoodie from my back seat to cover my low-cut shirt. I watched the congregants, some I knew, walk to their cars, huddled into each other. Were they happy? Were they at peace? Were they saved?

When it seemed like my car was one of the only ones in the lot, I went inside. I walked past the stained glass windows I knew by heart, all their stories, all their jewel tones. Though I still went to Mass every Sunday because my parents insisted, and though I still led the Catholic Charities youth group for my college applications, I wasn't as involved as I used to be and I didn't believe in any of it anymore, not really. How could I? I'd be damned. Worse, Cass would be too. During my confirmation, I had stood in front of the congregation in a white dress with Peter as my sponsor. And when they asked me, *Do you believe in the Holy Spirit, the holy Catholic Church, the communion of saints, the forgiveness of sins, the resurrection of the body, and life everlasting?* I stood up tall. I said, *I do.* And then the most Catholic thing possible happened: I felt sick with guilt. Because I knew I had lied.

I was once Our Lady of Mercy's poster child. Now, I was almost surprised when Father Aiden looked up from the altar and waved me to the front of the church. He was in his forties, but he had a baby face and jet-black hair. He might have been the kind of boy I'd had a crush on in middle school—kind, vaguely feminine, nonthreatening.

"Avery," he said, "were you at Mass just now? I didn't see you." His white robe seemed pure in the golden glow of the overhead lights, his smile so simple.

"No," I said, and shoved my hands into my hoodie pouch, suddenly self-conscious about what I was wearing. "I, um . . ." What had I been thinking, going there? What was I supposed to say? I couldn't confess everything I wanted to, of course I couldn't. I never could. "I'm worried about my friend."

His smile dropped, and he motioned for me to sit down with him in the nearest pew. I first glanced around the church to see if anyone was there to hear us, but the only soul was the choir director folding up music stands on the balcony. The clanging echoed through the building.

"So you're worried about your friend," Father Aiden said.

"Right. She, um, recently realized she's gay, or queer or something. And also, she's suicidal. Not because she's gay. Or, I don't know, maybe that's part of it. Not that she thinks being gay is bad! Because it's not bad. It's just . . ." I tried to find the words: *It's just, her parents are disappointed. It's just, she's in love with her best friend who's in love with someone else. It's just, what are people going to think; what are people going to say? It's just, I don't deserve to want, deserve to love, deserve to live.*

"I think I know who you're talking about," he said, and my throat closed with panic.

"You do?"

"That friend of yours, the one who comes to Mass sometimes?" Cass had come with us to Our Lady of Mercy several times over the years after Saturday night sleepovers.

"Oh." I exhaled. "Right. Yeah. Her."

He was quiet for a moment, and brought his folded hands to his chin as if in prayer. I felt sick waiting for him to speak.

"I think you're right to be worried, Avery, and I do want to clarify that while I do not judge, it *is* bad, because it's sinful. It will prevent her from having a full life in the church. You understand, right? She will never be able to enter holy matrimony, and it's unclear if she'll be able to enter the Kingdom of Heaven. It's a risk. Don't you want her in Heaven with you, after all of this?"

"Of course." *But like, in a gay way.*

"As for suicide, well, that's one of the worst sins, in my opinion. Very serious. Gravely serious. God is the master of life. Who are we to play God? Who are we to throw His greatest gifts away? The evilest blasphemy."

I looked at the floor. "What should I do?"

"Well, first, do you know if she has a plan? If she does, Avery, you should know I'm obligated to report it, just like any doctor or therapist would be." My blood went cold. Shit. Was I about to get Cass in trouble?

"No," I said, probably too quickly. "Nothing like that. No plan. She's *very* clear that there's no plan." He nodded solemnly and looked relieved.

"You should encourage her to pray on these things. You should encourage her to seek answers in the Almighty power that is beyond our earthly desires and despair. Bring her to Mass, if you have to. You know what? Bring her next week; I'll write a sermon just for her." *Oh, no.* That was the last thing my parents needed to hear.

"She probably won't come; it's okay. You don't need to do that."

"And, while you're worried about *her,* I'm worried about *you.* You should support her and love her, the way Christ would have, but you must also think about your own salvation. You should distance yourself from this friend. She may try to tempt you with her ways." *Would she ever.*

"Thanks," I said, though I wasn't at all thankful, or faithful. I realized then I had probably come to church to punish myself, to have someone tell me I was all wrong, to confirm it. I wanted someone to say the words my parents were holding back. I wanted the words to burn me.

Outside, the night air was crisp, but my skin felt hot. I wondered, as I buckled myself back into my car, if I should give it all up and become a nun. Want for nothing. Serve something I no longer believed in. Turn my brain off, turn my heart off, die in a million little ways.

When I got home, my parents asked where I'd been and I didn't have to lie, didn't have to sin. They shared a smile, exchanged a hopeful glance that said, *Maybe she can still be saved, then?*

"Church," Dad said, "excellent choice."

"Good girl," my mom said, and kissed my forehead. "You've always been so good. Thank God."

seven days
to impact

I woke up in my bed in my clothes from the night before. I untangled myself from the bonfire smoke of Cass and left her sleeping there, one arm over her head, the other reaching for me. I wanted to crawl back into bed and find every place my skin could touch hers, but the longer we slept, the more likely it was one of my parents would barge in and see us.

I wanted to have the space to love her for a while without feeling their eyes on our every move. What if they reacted poorly, like I knew they would? And how could it ever be worth it, now that there was so little time left, to break their hearts? They'd be disappointed. They'd be scared. They'd think we were damned, and maybe this time they'd even say it. I didn't want any of us to end that way.

I showered to wash the smell of soot from my skin, then went to the basement with my hair wet. As expected, my parents and Aisha were wide awake and already sorting food and making lists. Aisha smiled at me from the corner of the basement where she'd piled all her things, her hair wrapped in a red headscarf, the matching red jeans she was wearing borrowed from my closet. My mom, dressed in green overalls and an Eaton Women's Soccer baseball cap, put down tin cans to hug me.

"Did you get any sleep?" Dad asked as he got down off his ladder. He'd been hanging tarps to divide the concrete space into smaller rooms.

"Think so," I said, but rubbed my eyes.

"Aisha has been awesome," he said. "This girl is a champion, just like on the field."

"We have to do some serious scavenging today," she said, as if to prove his point. "I have ideas."

"I'm in," I said. I counted the little bedrooms of varying sizes. "Why are there only four rooms?"

"Me and Dad will be in that one," Mom said, pointing to one corner, "the Laskys in that one, Aisha in that one, and you and Cass in that one." My stomach flipped. Did they already know?

"Why do Cass and I have to share?"

"This isn't the Four Seasons," Dad said.

"You've been having sleepovers for almost a decade, and now you're going to complain?" Mom said.

"And Dr. Talley?"

"He moved into the Davidson house this morning."

I felt a pang of relief. Mr. and Mrs. Davidson lived in the third house on our cul-de-sac. Though I waved to them when I saw them, I avoided them since I could never shake the shame of the time I almost drowned in their pool.

"The Davidsons are trying to flee the country," Dad said.

"Good luck," Aisha said. "There's no way anyone is getting in and out. Not anymore. Canada and Mexico, *maybe*, but anything beyond that? No."

"So, you're officially staying?" I asked.

"I'm officially staying," she said. "And we're going to make this bunker the best it can be. It has to be perfect."

Footsteps thumped down the stairs, and Cass appeared beside me, hair wet and braided, hands stuffed into the pockets of freshly laundered Kilkenny Knights Lacrosse sweatpants. I missed the smoke and cider. I missed the taste of her skin.

"That's our room," I said, pointing to our corner. She raised her eyebrows. "They're making us share. Because we're best friends, right?" She pulled the sheet back and looked inside.

"Aisha, your room is as big as ours," Cass said.

"I'm blessed, I guess."

My mom came over to hug Cass, too, and held on to her probably a little too tightly.

"We're so glad you're here, sweetheart. We only wish your parents were here too."

"Thanks, Mrs. B," she said. "Wouldn't be anywhere else."

"So happy to see you," Dad said, coming over to hug her too. "Cass and Avery. Let me tell ya. Never did Kilkenny see two better friends." When they let her go, we exchanged a sheepish look.

"Let's crack on," Dad said.

"Yes! Crack on," Aisha echoed, and high-fived my dad. "And go tell your brother too. I have to stay here so I can be on Wi-Fi, so I'll help your parents." I didn't know why she had to be on Wi-Fi, except to talk to her own parents, but I didn't ask questions.

"See? Aisha is a champ," Dad said. "We're going to build new systems for ventilation today. Tomorrow, we'll tackle the bathroom."

"Okay," I said, glancing at Cass. "You ready?"

"After some coffee."

"You're too young for coffee," Dad said. "Your brains are developing!"

"Make sure Peter goes with you," Mom said. "It's not safe."

"What, no quip about women's equality?" I whispered to Cass as we ran up the stairs and grabbed our jackets.

"I have to behave now that I'm dating their daughter."

Was that what we were, then, dating?

"Oh, yeah, *that's* liberating." She shrugged and poured some coffee into a small mug before leaning against the counter and throwing it back. She refilled it, offered it to me, and I did the same. We were about to leave when a ringtone exploded in the kitchen, and our eyes lit up.

We hadn't had cell phone service since it cut out the first night, and our Wi-Fi was spotty at best. The internet rolled in and out, so Aisha and Cass obsessed over their phones—keeping them charged, keeping them nearby, just in case their parents called. The Shagaris had been calling frequently and at all hours, and Aisha would answer her phone from wherever she was praying or doom-scrolling.

Each time a ringtone sang through the house, Cass's eyes lit up, then dimmed as she realized it was Aisha's phone and heard her squeals of delight, her parents' voices. The Joshi-Aguilars had emailed to tell us that they'd called once the day before when we were out scavenging, so we'd missed it. But it was her phone ringing now in the kitchen, her dad's name and face on the screen, and Cass's hands shook as she pounced to answer. I sat beside her in a wooden chair as her trembling hand hit the button to accept.

"Hi, beta," Mrs. Joshi said.

"My Cassandra," Mr. Aguilar added. Their faces were more tanned than usual, and Mrs. Joshi's hair was pinned on the top of her head like a nest.

"Hi," Cass said breathlessly, as we each used a hand to

balance the phone on the table. She bounced her knee beside me, a nervous habit that always made me nervous in turn. I put my hand on her knee to settle her, and she put her hand on mine. She squeezed so hard it hurt. "Why the hell haven't you called me?"

"Wi-Fi is spotty, baby," Mr. Aguilar said. "We miss you so much."

"What have you been up to?" she choked out. "I've been so worried."

"Fiji is beautiful; we've been biking, hiking, swimming. At first it was chaotic with people trying to get in and out, but now it's settled," Mrs. Joshi said.

"It's like a big party now," Mr. Aguilar added. "We wish you were here."

"I wish I was there too," Cass said in her smallest voice. "You have to promise me you'll try to call more. Every day."

"We'll try! We've been trying, diku," Mrs. Joshi said, "but haven't we taught you to be on your own? We're so proud of you."

"I know. I don't know what's wrong with me." Cass ran her fingers through her hair. "No, I *do* know. I'm never going to see you again."

"You see us right now!" Mr. Aguilar said. "We're living in the moment. We want you to do that too hija."

"I'm trying," she said, desperately.

I envied Cass's relationship with her parents, their

often expressed desire for her to fly away to truly become herself, no matter who that person was. My parents knew exactly who they wanted me to be: happy and successful and normal, and I was not that girl. But Cass shouldn't have to live through *this*, with the Joshi-Aguilars on the other side of the world with no way to come home, no way to hold her one last time. My heart broke for her. I gripped her knee tighter.

We talked for about twenty minutes before the Wi-Fi cut out, and after several attempts at getting it back, Cass gave up. Her leg stilled, and her grasp around my fingers tightened.

"I feel like a kid again," she said. "What's wrong with me?"

"There's nothing wrong with you," I said. "You're human." She looked up at me and rolled her eyes a little, but kissed my forehead, anyway.

"Let's go."

Outside, the air was brisk and the snow on the ground shone with an eerie brightness. We darted through the trees toward my brother's house to see if they'd join us on our expedition. After we knocked, Peter answered, but only opened the door halfway.

"We're gonna have to start a little later," he said. His beard looked unruly, and he was still in a T-shirt and slippers. "Georgia's . . . processing." It unnerved me to see Peter so disheveled. He looked like I felt most of the time, like if someone tapped him, he would shatter.

"Would Teddy want to come with us?" Cass asked. "We won't go too far. Promise." I knew Cass had done the right thing by asking, but it also terrified me: the idea of having someone so precious in the back seat of the car. How did anyone have the courage to fully love a child? Maybe everyone did. Except for me.

"That might actually be a good idea," Peter said. He disappeared into the house without inviting us in. When he returned minutes later, Teddy was at his heels, dressed in my hand-me-down pink snowsuit. Teddy's hair was mussed from sleep, and he kept reaching up to smooth it even though his eyes were fluttering shut. "Ready to go for a ride with Auntie Avery and Cass Foi?" Peter asked him. Teddy nodded thoughtfully.

"Foi" was the Gujarati word for "father's sister," and it was Teddy who insisted on everyone using it as soon as Cass taught it to him.

"All right," Peter said, "here's the kid." He handed Teddy's hand to Cass instead of me. "Here's the bag." He slung a boulder-weight backpack on my shoulder. "Snacks, water. The car seat is in the garage."

"We'll take good care of him," I said, though I was swallowing terror as each second passed.

"Bring him home in one piece, or I'll kill you," Peter said.

"Roger that," Cass said and ruffled Teddy's hair even more. "This is gonna be fun, kiddo! You ready?"

"I like fun," he said. "I'm ready."

We circled around to their garage, where a first aid kit was split open on the ground, ointments scattered and Band-Aids curling. I put everything back inside and wondered why the Laskys had left precious items strewn about when we were going to such great lengths to collect them. I used my free hand to grab some tools and a plastic sled from behind their pickup truck, and turned to leave.

A blood-chilling scream filled the inside of the house. I dropped the sled to dash inside, but the door was locked, and Peter's voice soon joined Georgia's in a horrible chorus that made me weak. I understood then that they'd been waiting to break down because they didn't want to do so in front of their son. They'd been waiting, bottling it up, and now they had to explode. Cass covered Teddy's ears and looked at me with panic in her eyes.

I grabbed the sled once again, and the three of us ran through the clearing in the trees to get away from the desperate howling.

"Thanks for hanging out with us, bud," Cass said to Teddy, though his face had gone pale. "After we get some new things for the, uh, blizzard, we'll go sledding!" It dawned on me when we got to my parents' Volvo, we hadn't taken the car seat, but I didn't want to go back to get it. I drove slowly down the barren side streets, while

Cass became a human car seat in the back, her arms wrapped tightly around Teddy's chest and waist. I tried to find a radio station to drown out the echo of the Laskys' screaming, but the airwaves were all static.

I drove into a neighborhood I didn't know and parked in the driveway of a house that seemed abandoned. The street almost felt like a ghostly, parallel version of ours: three houses on a cul-de-sac, each one dark within. We picked the house whose garage door was open. There were no cars inside it, only a John Deere lawn mower and two bikes without tires. Teddy stretched when he got out of the car like he'd come off a two-a-day workout.

"You getting ready to run?" I asked.

"I run a lot," he said, "because at school there are races."

"And you win?" I asked.

He shook his head. "No, but I'm gonna." As if to prove a point, he sprinted around the frozen lawn in a few circles before getting dizzy and sprawling out on the grass. Cass scooped him up in her arms, and he screamed in delight. I wanted to bond with Teddy since I only had days to do so, and because I wanted to show Cass we could have been a family. But what if we survived and then I decided again that I couldn't do it? Then what? I took a deep breath and tried anyway.

"Hey, Ted," I said. "What's your favorite color?"

"Lellow," he said.

"Favorite animal?"

"Scout."

"Favorite character?"

"Buzz Lightyear."

"Can you say, 'I love Cass Joshi-Aguilar'?" Cass chimed in.

"No."

"Please?"

"I love Cass *Foi*."

"Close enough. You're such a good boy, Ted. Can you say, 'Fuck the patriarchy'?" I smacked her arm.

"No."

"Please? Fuck the patriarchy?"

"Fuck the pay-key-airy."

"Close enough! Fuck the pay-key-airy."

"Peter is going to be *thrilled* with us," I said, "but that was the best thing I've ever heard in my life."

We knocked on every door of the house, and found our way in by taking the back door off its hinges with a screwdriver and pliers. As we stepped onto the tile of the kitchen, we called, "Hello?!" to see if anyone answered. Teddy took off running from room to room.

Either the house had been raided before, or its previous owners had taken most things with them. The fridge and cupboards were empty, except for a box of saltine crackers. Wires spilled out of a TV stand, one corner knocked off, raw wood splintering at the edge.

"Ooh, books," I said, running my hand across a full bookshelf.

"When are we going to have time to read?"

"When we're trapped in a basement?"

"Ah. Right."

"Plus, you heard Dr. Talley," I said, deepening my voice. "You can go anywhere in a novel."

"Spare me," Cass said.

"I'm taking a few for good luck."

"Okay, my little valedictorian."

"Salutatorian. Goddammit, Iris Dunn."

"You're the worst."

"Iris Dunn is the worst."

We heard a gleeful shout from upstairs.

"Ladies!" We bounded up the stairs two at a time to catch up with Teddy. He was in a bedroom to the right of the stairs by himself, his arms full of stuffed animals.

"Wow, Ted!" Cass applauded. He tried to pick up more animals, but dropped them.

"Okay, here's the deal," I said. "We don't have room for all of them, but how about you pick three?" He chose a dog, a unicorn, and the largest stuffed rabbit I had ever seen.

"I think we're gonna have to tie this thing to the bike rack using its ears," Cass said, which was exactly what we did after collecting bedding, pillows, towels, first aid supplies, and huge bottles of soap. When we were done securing the rabbit, Teddy clapped.

"Thank you very much," he said.

I wanted to break down into tears. It was so unfair Teddy might only ever be that version of Teddy, but that was how it was, and he was so precious that if I started screaming about it, I would not stop until my lungs collapsed.

We drove to a nearby sledding hill on the edge of the orchard. The snow was patchy, so Cass and I ran down the hill next to Teddy, on a plastic sled, and pushed him forward anytime he got stuck on the grass. He screeched with laughter and ran back up the hill with ease.

It was the first time in a long time Cass and I had watched Teddy alone together. We were, actually, both technically his godparents, a title I'd politely accepted with no real acknowledgment of its reality. A title Cass had accepted as if she'd won a Nobel Peace Prize. I knew it should have been a salve to me, one more person who needed me, one more person I could live for. But I could not look Teddy in the eye without feeling like he knew exactly what I was. I could not stop picturing him diving into a river to come find me. I stood at the bottom of the hill and watched the two of them roll all the way down on their sides.

"Oh God," Cass said, when they reached the bottom. "I'm dizzy. Teddy! Help!" He stood up, ran, and threw himself on her. "This doesn't help!"

"I help!" he insisted, giggling. "I help!"

"Can I try?" I asked him. I chased him to the top of the mound and lay down beside him.

"Ready? Go!" he called. We spun down too slowly, then too quickly. The ground punched me gently on each turn, and the sky popped in flashes. At the bottom, we lay there with our limbs spread out, and shouted at each other, at the sky. While Teddy was busy making a snow angel, Cass kissed me and the world seemed to freeze, if only for a moment, and I was grateful.

When we were grass-stained and snow-soaked, Cass carried Teddy back to the car while I fumbled for the keys. Though we'd had eyes on the car the entire time, someone had smashed the rear window open, half of it now in a pile of glitter on the stuffed animals in the back seat.

"Fuck!" Teddy shouted before Cass and I could react.

"That's right, fuck!" Cass said. I wanted to freak out too, but I realized it could have been worse. They'd only taken some of our cans, and, weirdly, the unicorn stuffed animal. Maybe they only took what they could carry. Maybe they only took what their family needed. Maybe that was more than okay.

We brushed the glass shards out of the car with our bare hands, and Cass put her coat down to make sure Teddy didn't get injured when he crawled into the Volvo that now whistled and chilled as we drove.

• • •

At home, my parents were impressed by our haul but less impressed by the pile of stuffed animals we dumped in the Laskys' room, including the ginormous rabbit Teddy had named Pineapple. We fed him dinosaur Chik'n Nuggets, then brought him through the clearing in the trees and hoped for the best. I knocked on the Laskys' door, and for a minute we met silence, until the door swung open to reveal Peter, red-eyed and messy-haired.

"Thanks for keeping the kid alive," he said, as Teddy wandered down the hall behind him.

"He's alive," I said, "but he may have a, uh, richer vocabulary than he left home with."

"Let me guess. Cass?"

"I am my authentic self," she said.

"I have always loved that about you. Thanks again." Peter shut the door, and left us standing there with our mouths half open.

"Well then," Cass said. But before we could turn to leave, the door swung open again, and my disheveled brother threw his arms around us to pull us into a group hug.

"What's up?" I said, growing concerned as he started to weep.

"Teddy just said he saw you two kissing. And I'm sorry. I'm so fragile right now. But nothing has ever made me happier in my life."

"Aww, Pete," Cass said. "You don't have to cry."

"I do, though," he said. "For so many reasons."

"What's up?" I said again, and he released us and wiped at his eyes.

"It's nothing," he said. "We'll be back at it again tomorrow, scavenging. I promise."

"Okay," I said. "I love you."

"I love you two, too, you crazy kids," he said. "I gotta go, though, okay?" This time he shut the door quickly but gently, and we waved to him as he went.

Back in the basement, Cass and I unpacked the books I'd stolen and put them in our room, along with other random items from around my parents' house: a bamboo plant from the kitchen, blankets from my bedroom, a framed photo of Cass lifting me in the air after I'd scored the winning goal in the soccer state championships. We arranged little bedside tables, lamps, and unlit candles that made the room smell like a fancy mall store. I flipped through my scrapbook of collages and letters from the people I loved most, while Cass ripped T-shirts apart to braid them into a tapestry to cover the concrete wall.

"I kinda like this little room," I said. "You know. For now."

She sat down on the floor where our mattress would eventually be and admired her work. "I like it too," she said. "In New York, this is basically a luxury apartment."

I placed another photo of us on the table and couldn't

help but hold on to it for a beat before letting it go. Pretending we could survive the asteroid was starting to feel a little like a drug. It felt like building a shrine to ourselves. It felt like putting together a puzzle of sad and tiny shards of hope. It felt like it could never be enough to save us. But what did that matter?

six months
to impact

I had always known grief was a type of loneliness, but when I went to college, I learned loneliness was a type of grief.

The day I was due at Eaton, my parents drove me from Kilkenny to Conway in their muddy, silver Volvo. It was late August, but the trees were already tinting orange and the stream water at the side of the highway looked clear enough to drink.

My nerves burned hotter as we got farther from who I was and closer to who I would be: someone new. Someone bold. I'd have new friends who met me every night for dinner and hiked with me up mountain trails on the weekends. My professors would assign books that would change me for the better, and the conversations we had in class would challenge me in exciting ways. I'd find someone to kiss at night under the campus starlight.

And I'd bring her home to Kilkenny during break to show my parents I was loved, after all. Happy. See? They didn't have to worry. I was okay. I'd have *made* it, finally, at Eaton College. I would have nothing left to prove.

"I can't wait to come to your games," Dad said, pumping his fists in the passenger seat as we drove toward my new home, toward the new me. He was already wearing an Eaton Soccer hat he'd ordered online the day I got my acceptance email.

"Studies come first," Mom interjected. She shot him a look and then sent one my way via the rearview mirror.

"We don't have to worry about this one," he said. "She's so good. If she doesn't get straight A's, I'll eat my hat."

Mom shook her head. "Don't let any boys get you pregnant, please."

"*Mom*, God," I said. "I told you, I'm—"

"*Don't* say it, Avery. I can't take it again," she said in a high, tight voice. I didn't know if she meant another freshman-year pregnancy or me saying I was not-straight, but I leaned my head against the cool glass of the window and decided not to push the issue on our last day together. When I didn't say anything, she continued. "Whatever you were about to say, don't say it. Not now, not at school, not yet. Don't tell people that. Especially not your teachers, not your teammates. At least not at first. Give yourself a chance."

A chance at what? I wanted to ask, but again didn't want to spoil the moment. Straightness? Popularity? Salvation? It made me feel sick to know I would eventually disappoint her and that, in my parents' minds, any version of my real happiness would be tied up in my damnation. But they knew better than to say that out loud. It was yet another thing we didn't, couldn't, talk about, but Mom's words from when I jumped into the icy pool still rang in my head all the time: *You go to Hell if you kill yourself.* If you love a woman. If you stray from Christ. *Do you want to go to Hell?* I didn't believe in Hell anymore. But it still mattered to my parents, so it mattered to me too.

"Give yourself a chance," she said again, a bit more softly. "I'm just trying to protect you." We blew past a white wooden sign that proudly declared, *Eaton College.* My heart jumped. We were there, and soon they'd leave, and everything fresh and new and open would begin.

We pulled up in front of my dorm, Kearsarge, a boxy brick building that formed one side of a courtyard. They each took my belongings in their fists and brought them to the unlocked front door. Inside the dorm, the walls were stark white, the lighting fluorescent. My room was on the second floor at the top of the stairs. The space felt clinical and impersonal.

I'd already met my roommate, Aisha, when we visited on accepted student day during my senior spring. She was impressive. Lightning fast on the field. Prospective quantitative social science major. The founder of a non-profit company that distributed motorized bikes charged by solar panels. She quite literally helped people get to work, school, and the hospital, and wanted to work in consulting. International students came early for extra orientation, so she'd already been at Eaton for a week.

When my parents and I entered the room, Aisha was sitting on her bed with two friends who waved half-heartedly. She wore a long, flowing orange dress and turban to match it. I wore jean shorts and a Kilkenny Knights T-shirt. I felt very young and very green.

"This is Avery," my mom said, gesturing toward me. I bristled with embarrassment.

"We've met," Aisha said with a kind but steely smile. "I'm here for soccer too."

"That's great!" Dad said. "We'll see a lot of you then. That's my wife, Laura."

"And he's Seamus," Mom said as she started unpacking my boxes.

"And apparently in this family we introduce everyone except ourselves," I said. All three girls on the bed stared at me blankly.

"You have an accent," Aisha said to my father.

"Irish," my parents said together, beaming. I suspected

they could have ditched their accents if they wanted to, but being noticed in that way allowed them to be fully seen for who they were.

"Nigerian," she said, touching the green-and-white flag hanging on her wall.

"That's like the Irish flag, without the orange," Mom said.

"You know, Avery here was second in her class," Dad said. "Even while playing two varsity sports and holding down a part-time job at the movie theater."

"And, she was the leader of Catholic Charities. She organized food and clothing drives," Mom added. I wanted the floor to open up and swallow me whole, but it didn't.

"No one cares, guys," I said quickly and maybe too loudly.

"I care," Aisha said. "That is very admirable."

"I was head of Catholic Charities in London," one of the other girls said. "Which city did you lead?"

Oh, no. Another Catholic, already? I blushed all over again.

"Oh, um, not a city. It was for, like, my church?"

"That's nice," she said, but she seemed deeply unimpressed.

My parents went back and forth with Aisha while I unzipped my bags and put things in their places. I was torn between wanting them to leave my space and dreading their departure. I spent the whole time they were there wishing they'd leave me alone, but when my dad clapped his hands together and motioned toward the door, my stomach dropped.

"All right, kiddo," he said. "We're off."

"I know you'll make us proud," Mom said, embracing me.

"I'll try," I said, but the words came out breathless. Instead of letting them walk out the door, I followed them down to their car. I thought about getting back in the Volvo and going with them, but they got in without me and waved goodbye. As they pulled out of the parking lot and left me standing there, I somehow felt cold in the wispy August heat.

My dad texted me from the passenger seat: **SO proud of u!! Go Purple Moose! See u at the first game.** I sent him a smiley face back with a purple heart and a shamrock. I sighed and shakily went back upstairs.

I made my bed while Aisha and her friends laughed and gossiped about boys they'd met the night before. I tried to find a lull in their banter to ask for their names, to more properly introduce myself, but the lull never came, and before I knew it, they were shuffling out of the room.

Though Aisha felt very much like a stranger who was polite but wholly uninterested in getting to know me, at least I had someone to walk to the soccer field with early the next morning and for the rest of the week. I'd been

heavily recruited, so tryouts were supposed to be a for-
mality for me, but my nerves choked me every day, and I
started to break down physically during dawn to dusk
weightlifting trials, sprinting competitions, and scrimmages. Aisha made the team with flying colors, and I
made it too, but it was a mistake. I didn't belong on that
roster, and everyone knew it.

Aisha's best friend on the team was Molly Shaw, a
junior who was bound to be captain the next year. She
and Aisha completely jived on the field, ping-ponging
balls back and forth and drilling them into the back of
the net. During scrimmages, Coach Cather paired them
together, calling them a "natural line," and telling us
all to watch their chemistry. Coach was very no-bullshit
and very Canadian, her accent slipping out whenever she
was frustrated. She was almost always scowling, and
she gelled her gray hair back severely.

"I like her, but she's like, *so* gay," Molly told me one
day when she was sitting on Aisha's bed. "Have you seen
her wife? Also so gay." Aisha didn't comment. Anxiety
fluttered in my chest, and I looked down at my textbook
so they couldn't read my expression. I shoved away any
thoughts of coming out to them anytime soon, but total
silence still felt cowardly. *What would Cass say if she were
here?* I thought. And, *God, I miss her.*

"My best friend is gay," I said, my mouth dry. Molly
and Aisha shared a look.

"Oh, obviously gay people are fine," Molly said. "But you know when someone is *so* gay it's like too much?"

I don't remember the rest of what she said, but what I heard was that I couldn't afford to give myself yet another reason to be excluded. I was not on my A game. I wasn't even on my C game. Getting out of bed in the morning zapped about half of my daily energy, so by the time I hit the field or gym every day, I was already drained.

This also meant I was running on empty when I showed up to my classes. I'd registered for chemistry, philosophy, statistics, and the American Short Story class taught by Dr. Basil Talley. My other three teachers barely knew who I was, and I was scraping by based on fumes alone. But Dr. Talley actively *hated* me. During our very first class, I was wearing our team jacket. When we went around the room to introduce ourselves, he stared at me blankly after I said my name, home state, and fun fact (I was born in Ireland).

"You're on the soccer team?"

"Yes."

"Athletes don't get special treatment in my class."

"I, uh, wouldn't expect any."

"Are there any other fall athletes in this group?" A football player and a field hockey player raised their hands. "Ah, well. I have only met one student athlete in my years at Eaton who was academically exceptional. Statistically speaking, I highly doubt all three of you will measure up." The three of us looked at each other slack-jawed, and when he pointed at the girl sitting next to me to introduce herself, I shut my mouth and stared at my hands.

After class, I timidly hung back as the other students filed out of the room.

"Can I help you?" he said gruffly. He didn't even look up at me as he gathered leftover syllabi and papers into an expensive-looking leather folder.

"Thank you for class," I said, hoping to soften what I was going to say next. "I just wanted to let you know I have to leave early from two of our classes this semester for away games. I have this note from my coach." I walked toward him and held it out, my hand shaking. He finally looked at me, took the paper, and put it in the recycling bin behind him without reading it.

"Each student is allowed two absences. That was outlined in the syllabus."

"Oh, right. Just like, if I get sick or—"

"You can miss those two classes. Just like everyone else. If you miss any more, you'll lose one full letter grade per absence."

"Noted," I said, and felt my stomach sink. "Thanks."

"And," he called as I walked through the door, "you lose one letter grade for every day you're late on an assignment."

I had to miss my first of his classes to leave early for our very first game against Holy Cross the next Friday, and my family drove to Worcester to watch me play. The field glowed under spotlights, and I bounced around on my cleats trying to stay warm as the sun went down. My parents clapped and yelled in the stands, so proud to be there and so ready to watch me play, Peter, Georgia, and Teddy beside them.

As soon as the whistle blew to start the game, I already knew I was going to struggle. I passed the ball to Aisha, and she had to jump back to receive it. As she pushed the ball up the field, I couldn't get to it before it skipped out of bounds. For the next forty-five minutes, I was outrun and outmuscled. Bile burned in my throat. I only got two shots and missed them both by a mile, even after one was placed perfectly at my feet in front of the net.

Coach put me on the bench for the second half. I spent the next forty-five minutes watching my bleacher crew get distracted: Georgia braiding tiny plaits into Teddy's hair, my parents chatting to the parents around them, backs to the field. I wanted to cry, but I bit into my tongue and tried to look engaged every time someone looked in my direction.

When the final whistle blew, I smiled as brightly as I could, even though my throat closed. I jogged around the field with the team, high-fiving the girls in white jerseys. At the tailgate in the parking lot, the Laskys stood around me. Teddy was running in circles on a patch of grass with his arms out like an airplane.

"I'm sorry you made the trip down," I said to them once they'd grabbed plates of corn on the cob, burgers, and potato chips. "I sucked."

"It's your first game," Peter said. "You didn't suck."

"Why didn't they play you in the second half? You were getting warmed up," Georgia said a little too loudly.

"It's okay," I said quickly. "I should have scored." Teddy face-planted into the grass, and I held Georgia's plate while she ran over to see if he was all right.

"He's like the Energizer Bunny these days," Peter said. "We all miss you, though, already. Can you come home tonight and we'll drive you back up tomorrow?"

"Nah, it's like team rules we have to go back together."

"Bummer," he said. He had no idea.

After apologizing again to my family and hugging them goodbye, I climbed onto the bus and went to sit in the empty space next to Aisha.

"Sorry," she said, "I promised Molly I'd save her a seat."

"No worries," I said, although I couldn't see any other empty seat and started to have visions of them strapping me to the roof or kicking me off the team all together. I ended up sitting next to Coach Cather, who spent the ride making notes on the roster. I tried not to look at whatever she was writing. I texted Cass to keep from crying.

Your time will come, she wrote. You're Avery freaking Byrne. It's only a matter of time before you're back on top.

She's right, I thought, *I can fix this. I just have to work harder, wake up earlier, train more, lift heavier. I have time. I can fix this.*

Back on campus, I started to head back to my dorm to shower like I always did but realized I'd left my keycard in my gym locker. I was about to push the locker room door open when I heard the girls laughing inside.

"She's not even good!" someone, maybe Molly, said. "I thought Coach said she was gonna be like, the star freshman."

"I set her up perfectly," Aspen said. "She should have scored."

"Definitely a liability."

"I bet Coach is pissed."

I racked my brain, tried to think if they could possibly be talking about anyone other than me, and my throat tightened when the answer was clearly no. Was I surprised? Of course not. They were right. I stood there frozen, knowing I should turn around and hide until they'd all left, but before I could, the door swung open and Aisha stood in front of me. Her eyes widened, and I saw her doing her own mental calculations: Had I heard them? If so, how much?

"Hey, Aisha," I choked out, trying to cut off any questions. "Forgot my keycard." I laughed nervously, ridiculously, and she exhaled.

"Oh, okay," she said. "I'll wait for you so we can walk back together."

"Great," I said, my voice an octave too high. I collected my keycard, and together we crossed the campus in the shadows of the mountains. Our conversation was clipped, forced, as we dissected the game and talked about all the homework we had to get done over the weekend. I wondered if she felt as lonely as I did, but I didn't know how to ask her. Had her voice been one of the ones I heard in the locker room? I wasn't sure, and I couldn't ask about that either.

After she fell asleep, I lay awake in my bed, muscles aching, head spinning. I thought about ways to get better at soccer, and quickly. I thought about how to make the other girls like me, at least enough to stop them from trashing me behind my back. Even if I deserved it. I thought about the papers I had to write and the tests I had to study for, and how much harder chemistry was at Eaton and how it was impossible for Peter to help me over the phone. I thought about how the sun was coming up, reaching through the windows, reminding me I hadn't slept at all, actually. And I hadn't figured anything out. And I was drowning, already. Already. And the year had only just begun.

seven days
to impact

That afternoon, Cass and I spent more time decorating our room in the basement. She ripped old T-shirts apart to make flags for anyone who wanted them: Mexican, Indian, Nigerian, Irish, American. When I hung the Irish flag up, it made me feel like we'd landed on the moon, though it was just our weathered, old basement. It was really coming together: it looked livable, comfortable, even. We'd moved some blankets to the middle of the floor, and the mishmash of our new belongings made it feel not cluttered exactly, but lived in. Every time I shut the sheets to kiss her, I could almost pretend like my entire world was in that little box of concrete, and like nothing at all could end it, no matter how fast or how fiery.

I could almost pretend like nothing could ruin it, not even me or my sadness, my shortcomings, my failures.

The other rooms were shaping up nicely too, though Aisha kept her sheets shut and had barely organized or decorated. Instead, she spent most of her time praying or doing something mysterious on the computer.

After Cass handed me the flag she'd made for Aisha, I went to drop it off at the desk where she was clicking and typing away. She heard me coming and slammed the laptop shut.

"Oh, sorry," I said. "I didn't mean to interrupt."

"It's fine," she snapped, and took the flag from my hands. "Thank you, Cass," she called. She stared at me with bloodshot eyes until I walked away. Then I heard her scrolling and tapping resume.

"I'm worried about her," I whispered to Cass. She furrowed her eyebrows but kept piecing together her Indian flag. "She doesn't leave that desk unless we force her to."

"I don't know, maybe it makes her feel like she has some control. But what is she even reading?"

"No idea. She slammed the laptop shut when I walked over there."

"Hmm," Cass said, a needle between her lips.

Her phone lit up with a text from our old soccer captain, Kayla Powell: K*TOWN END OF THE WORLD PARTY. MY HOUSE: 1849 WINTER HILL WAY. 8 PM. BE THERE. BE FANCY.

"Welp, this is a terrible idea," I said.

"Absolutely not safe at all," Cass said.

"Gonna be a disaster."

"Utter shitshow."

"So, we're going?"

"Obviously."

"We should make Aisha come with us," I said. "I think she needs it."

We told my parents the party was at Milan Leoni's house, because that was only a mile away and because her parents were incredibly vigilant. I did feel a little bad about lying, but I felt like we all needed release, especially Aisha.

She did agree to come, after I quite literally got on my knees to beg her and assured her there would most likely be Wi-Fi at the party. Cass switched from flag-making to outfit-tailoring, and the three of us sat around my bedroom as she turned my old clothes into partywear. With her bare hands, she ripped apart my old, emerald-green prom dress at the seams, and stitched it back together one inch and one thread at a time until it was a jumpsuit.

"I'm tweaking the neckline too," she said, narrowing her eyebrows. "For the cleav." She punctuated the air with her needle. For Aisha, she restructured a gold dress I'd worn one New Year's Eve. For herself, she tailored one of Peter's suits. She pinned it and pressed it until it clung to her body so perfectly I wanted to scream.

Instead, I waited until Aisha left the room to kiss Cass urgently. I draped my arms on her shoulders. She put her hands on my waist. "You're incredible," I said. I really wish I got to see your whole clothing line for Mx. and Match."

"Ugh, I know," she groaned. "You don't understand how good my designs were, Ave. People would have lost their minds. You know how it felt when you got the game winner at state. That's what I imagined it would feel like for me. My clothes. On literal models. On a catwalk. In New York."

"Were you going to invite me or what?"

"I hadn't decided yet," she said sheepishly. "But you should know I designed two looks specifically for you." Cass moved to hold me from behind and put her head on my shoulder. We stared at ourselves together in the mirror. Even I could admit it: we looked *good* together.

"We can still pretend, can't we? That we're on our way to your big show."

She smirked. "Of course," she said. "What will *Autostraddle* say? 'New power couple on the scene: can this soccer star and her fashion designer beau make it last?'"

"What's your fashion line called, anyway?"

"I hadn't titled it yet."

"How about Queer Asteroid?" I said.

"Ooh, yeah. Looks inspired by cosmic chaos, celestial mayhem, and stardust pandemonium."

"The collection that will have you saying, 'Wildfang who?'"

"All of New York's hottest gal pals are *dying* for it. Maybe literally."

As she kissed my shoulder, I thought about how *everything* Cass was: handsome and funny and vibrant and kind. How *nothing* I had been lately. How empty I'd continue to be. Maybe she loved me because she didn't have time to find someone else to fall for, but if we made it out on the other side, it would only be a matter of time before she realized that.

"Would you still want me, if all of this wasn't happening?"

"Absolutely. I've always wanted you, Ave. You get that, right?"

"What about all of New York's hottest gal pals?"

"What about 'em?" she said. "Maybe I could have loved them, too, in another life with much more time. But we got this one. We have this. Loving you is a reflex."

"I love you too, Cass," I said. For the millionth time. For the first time. "What do you think they'll say about us tonight, at Kayla Powell's end-of-the-world party? All our old teammates?"

"You know? I'm a little nervous to see them. But they'll probably think, *Cass and Avery? About. Damn. Time.*"

• • •

Kilkenny was mostly a flat town, but I drove Cass and Aisha in my parents' car—shattered window and all—up winding street after winding street until we reached the top of a small mountain. I had never seen this neighborhood before. I didn't even know it existed. After the last turn, the house appeared all at once. It looked like a mansion Rubik's Cube, as if three or four large houses made of brick, granite, and whitewood had been jammed together and shuffled around. Cars snaked down the street, and the thump of a bass boomed from inside. We climbed out of the car and stood on the grass, side by side, bracing ourselves. Behind the house, the city of Manchester shimmered like fool's gold.

"This *house*," Aisha said, her dress twinkling in the moonlight. She looked brilliant. "It's like *The Great Gatsby* meets *On the Road* meets *The Swiss Family Robinson*."

"Look at you," Cass said. "Dr. Talley would be so proud."

"Speaking of," I said, "has anyone seen him since he moved into the Davidsons'?"

"Nope."

"It's strange he wouldn't say goodbye," Aisha said, though I knew exactly why he wouldn't. It was difficult. It made things real.

Aisha opened the front door to reveal a throng of people with drinks in their hands. Music shook every room.

I grabbed Cass's hand as we stepped through the door. It felt like we were in high school again; all eyes were on us as we slid through the room. I was unsure if they were jealous or disgusted or both, and I didn't care.

Right away, a tall, broad-shouldered man in a tux and pink bowtie shoved red SOLO cups into our free hands. I recognized him instantly. He made my stomach burn.

"Tobias Morrison," I said. Clayton's best friend.

"At your service," he added. "Avery Byrne looking like a snack, how about that?" He bowed when he saw Cass. "Yas queen! I don't remember your name!" He was already so tanked. "And who's this gorgeous, goddess of a woman?" he asked about Aisha. She rolled her eyes and walked away from him. My respect for her quadrupled.

"What's in this cup?" Cass asked.

"Jungle juice," he said, wiggling his eyebrows. "Beer in the fridge, bonfire out back. What do you want, coke? Molly? Weed?"

"We're good," I said, dragging Cass into the crowd. She poured her drink into a potted houseplant and motioned for me and Aisha to do the same.

"We're dying," she said, "not desperate." We squeezed our way through to the kitchen where a dozen claw-foot bathtubs were filled with ice and bottles. She grabbed two Night Shift passion fruit beers and a water for Aisha, and we clinked them together.

"To Queer Asteroid," I said.

"To Queer Asteroid," she echoed.

"Why's the asteroid queer?" Aisha asked, but it was too loud to explain.

We danced in the basement with sweaty crowds of people in ball gowns and three-piece suits. Though she bopped along with us, Aisha seemed distracted and uncomfortable as she tried frantically to get on the Wi-Fi, and then, once she did, checked her phone every few seconds. When it lit up and she answered it, I wondered if she'd asked someone to call her so she could get away from us.

As she climbed up the stairs in a flash of gold, I tried to follow her. I wanted to make sure she was okay, that she didn't get cornered by Tobias or lost in the monstros-ity of a house, but Cass pulled me back to her, into her hips. She made me feel like I could move in the way she did. My whole chest hurt with yearning. I'd wanted this from the moment I'd watched her dance without me at prom.

And my God, the world *was* ending. I didn't care which clowns from our high school saw us and dared to believe we were anything other than beautiful. I didn't care what comments the boys yelled at us or which words girls whispered to one another. I wanted to cry for the old me, the girl who gave a shit, who believed I was so bro-ken I couldn't add queerness to the equation. I had only been hurting myself.

When a slow song came on, Cass pulled her arms away and crossed them against her chest. She looked for an exit.

"What's wrong?" I shouted.

She wrinkled her nose. "Country music featuring Bieber."

I pulled her hands back and put them on my hips. "Please?" I said. She rolled her eyes and pulled me into her. We swayed. It felt childish and campy.

"This song is nauseating," she said. It really was, and it wasn't for us, not at all. It was a couple of men singing about having 10,000 hours to fall in love. We had less than 200, maybe: for me to put my fingertips where her neck met her blazer, to smell her shampoo and cologne from inches away, to kiss her in front of everyone like I had always, always wanted. It was nauseating, but mostly it made me sad. Why had we only figured this out now? It was my fault, but it still hurt more than I could bear.

Tears streamed down my cheeks and onto hers. When I pulled away from her to wipe my nose, I saw she was crying too.

"We deserve our own nauseating love songs," she said, forcing a smile. "I wish I could sing."

"You *know* I can't," I said. "Do you want me to try?"

"Definitely not," she said. "Let's go see the rest of this place." She led me up two flights of stairs into the two-story library where naked people moved in almost every

corner of the room, outfits heaped and wrinkled across
the floor like the afterthoughts they were.

"Oh God," I said, and felt blood flood my face.

"What," Cass replied, smirking, "no orgies at Eaton?"

"If there were, I wasn't invited," I said. "You've been
to an orgy?"

She shrugged a little. "I didn't *participate*, but I do go
to art school. In New York."

"Wish I had pearls to clutch."

"Wait," she said. "Go outside so we can reenter and
play *Beauty and the Beast*."

"Okay."

"I'm the Beast," she boomed. "Close your eyes. I have
a surprise for you, woman I've locked in my home for
some reason the audience will forgive me for in about
ninety minutes."

"How gracious," I said. "Whatever could it be?"

"Surprise!"

"A library! Books! So many damn books!"

"You like it?"

"I love it. Books are my entire personality."

"Then it's yours."

"Do most libraries come with an orgy sideshow?"

"No."

"Can I exchange it for my freedom?"

"Hmm. Also, no."

"Damn." I climbed the ladder that reached all the

way up to the second level and ran my finger along a row of spines. "Want me to read to you?"

"Oh, yeah." She ran a hand through her hair. "Find an olden-timey book and make it dirty."

"And gay."

"Right. Obviously."

The door flew open, and Aisha stood in the doorway looking radiant. *Smiling.*

"Hey," I said. "Why do you look so happy?"

Her eyes went as wide as mine had when she realized who and what else was in the room, but she shook her head to recover and ran over to hug Cass. I slid down the ladder, and she hugged me too. I tried to remember if she had ever embraced me like this. She felt new. She felt lighter.

"I got some very, very, very good news." She was beaming.

"Spill," Cass said, but Aisha glanced at the people having sex around us.

"Not here, disgusting. Come on."

We left the library, climbed down a flight of spiral stairs, and burst into the night. We sprinted off the back porch into the shadows of the massive bonfire fueled by wooden chairs, old bed frames, and small trees. It roared at the sky. We dodged throngs of people until we reached a relatively quiet section of the lawn and huddled together. Still, shouts and sparks cracked behind us. Aisha put one hand on each of our shoulders.

"I found my sister," she said. "She's been in Toronto. Feel my heart, it's racing." She motioned for us to put our hands on the top of her chest.

"Your sister?" Cass asked.

"I thought . . . I thought you said she died." I wanted to be wildly, unconditionally happy for her, but I felt mostly confused.

"I'm careful to say we *lost* her," Aisha said.

"What do you mean?"

"I don't like to talk about this," she said, folding her arms, "because white Americans use it to reinforce their ignorant ideas about being better, smarter, more understanding. Please acknowledge to me you know you're not better or smarter."

"Fully," I said.

"Not white, full agree," Cass said.

"My sister, Rahila—or I guess she goes by Ray now—was like a second mom to me. Twelve years older. I looked up to her so much. She was very funny, very kind. We were so close. She played with me every day, taught me how to tie my shoes, and read me to sleep. Then, when I was six or seven, out of nowhere she was gone. My parents said she went to college. But the years went on and I never saw her. I never heard from her. I Googled her, nothing. I begged them to tell me where she was, why she never called, and they wouldn't."

"She ran away?" Cass asked quietly.

"Ten years later, I was sixteen. I found out from a

classmate that Rahila had been caught kissing another woman. It was the talk of the town when it happened, I guess, but I was young. I never knew. She was forced to leave for her safety." My mouth dried, and Aisha's cheeks glistened in the firelight. Cass put her hand on my back.

"So, she's in Canada," I said. "She's been in Canada this whole time?"

"Apparently so," Aisha said. "We talked for half an hour. I've had her number for *years*, and it's always been a Canadian number. I've texted and called and texted, and she never responded until . . ." She covered her face and started crying. "I told her about the bunker. I told her I want her to be here with me. I want this new life with her."

"She's coming here?"

"If she can find a car, yes. Yes, she's coming here." She rubbed her locket in between her fingers. "I've had this since I was a little girl. She gave it to me."

"Why didn't you tell me about her?" I said.

Aisha wiped her face and put her hand on my cheek. "Queen of secrets wants to know why I had one, eh?"

Cass looked at me sideways. "What do you mean 'queen of secrets'?"

"It's nothing," I said.

"No, I wanna know," Cass pushed.

For the millionth time, I pleaded with Aisha with my eyes. *Don't tell her about the letter. Don't tell her, don't tell her.* It would ruin everything.

"Avery never told me or the rest of the team she's gay."

I exhaled.

"I mean, what was I supposed to say?" I asked, though I felt the shame of a secret lick at my neck. "That I was in love with my best friend?"

"I'm not trying to embarrass you," Aisha said, "but we all knew. About you and——"

"UnderhandUndercuts," Cass cut in. "That softball pitcher. Yeah, I know."

"Well, that. But you in general. We thought it was weird you weren't out, considering Coach Cather."

But the team had to respect Coach Cather. They had no choice but to be okay with who she was, and anyway, she wasn't in the locker room or at parties with us.

"People made comments. About her. About others. And about me, apparently." I hated how my voice cracked when I continued. "I didn't know how you'd feel about sleeping next to me in our dorm room. On our first day, you made it clear you would never change in front of me."

"I'm a very private person," she said, "but you're right. People hate here too. We are what we're taught. But, Avery, it made me sad you felt like you had to hide, like Ray. You should tell people things."

I knew she wasn't just talking about my sexuality.

"You didn't tell us about Ray," I said defensively.

"I didn't want to jinx it! I told you, I have plans."

"I mean, you didn't even tell me she existed on this planet."

"It wasn't my story to tell, not until it had a happier ending."

"It's wild," Cass said. I thought she was going to say that people still went to jail for kissing, for loving, for becoming. That people were killed for it. That maybe some people in some places were safer now that power systems had imploded, that we were all going to die, anyway. Instead, Cass said, "It's wild that after all that, your parents let you play soccer."

"Why?" Aisha asked.

"Soccer's the lesbian gateway drug," I filled in.

"Gayteway," Cass said, spelling the letters in the air with her fingers.

"Really? I have been told it's softball," Aisha said with a smile, "or basketball."

"Or rugby," Cass said. "Or hockey. Or crew."

"Or having sex with women," I offered.

"Nah, that's the lesbian Super Bowl," Cass said.

Aisha cupped her ears. "La, la, la, la, la. Gross. I have heard enough."

"This is why I didn't tell you," I said, only half joking. Aisha rolled her eyes and turned to walk back to the bonfire and the crowd. Cass put an arm around me as we followed her.

Near the flames, we reached a table laden with the remains of s'mores and tipped-over bottles of cider. We opened a new bag of marshmallows, and Cass and I burnt them on long sticks. Aisha spent five full minutes gently twirling hers, getting each one perfectly, consistently golden brown.

"They're spicier when they're basically coal," Cass said.

"This is the first time I have ever done this," Aisha said, "and I already know mine is superior." She winked at us as she popped the marshmallow into her mouth. She made another one to give to me.

"It's perfect," I said. "You're a natural. If my dad were here, he'd make you use cookies instead of graham crackers." Cass pulled her own blackened marshmallow off the end, blew on it, and put it in my mouth, though half of it got on my hands. I dipped them in a large water bucket to try to remove the residual goo, but the water was filled with ashes and dirt, so I wiped them on the grass instead.

"Back me up, baby." Baby. That was new. I hated when people called each other baby, but damn, I loved it coming from Cass.

"Sorry, Aisha," I said. "Cass and I have a long marsh-mallow history." Cass kissed me, and when I heard slow clapping, I expected to look up to see Aisha mocking us for being the most obnoxious couple alive, which would have been extremely fair. Instead, I saw a tall, blond boy walking toward us, barely able to stand up. He sat down on a nearby log and stretched his legs out. The fire flames licked at the soles of his shoes, and he didn't even flinch.

"Clayton," I said. My stomach tightened. I wanted to smack the shit-eating grin off his face, but instead I held Cass's hand tight.

"Avery Byrne. Cass. Other girl. Don't stop because I'm here," he said. "I could use a show."

"You're drunk," I said. "Go home." I could tell by his bloodshot, dilated eyes he wasn't just drunk; he was high too.

"First, I live next door. Second, we're all drunk. Who cares? Are you from Kilkenny?" he asked Aisha. She shook her head and tried to read my expression to see how she should react.

"I went to Eaton with Avery. And now I'm here because we're building a bunker."

"Are you a lesbian too? Is Eaton full of lesbians?"

"I'm ace, if you must know. But I find you repulsive regardless." Aisha was always surprising me. Clayton inched closer to her.

"Hey, let's go," Cass said, but Aisha didn't hear her.

"You want to hear a funny story? I took that one to prom." He pointed at me. He acted like he was whispering, but he was shouting. "I was in love with her for a couple years, right? And I took her to prom, right? I was soooooooo excited. What's your name?"

"You have to earn that," Aisha said. A crowd began to gather around us. I wanted to run away but felt glued to where we sat. I didn't mind if Clayton embarrassed me in front of his cronies; I just didn't want them to hurt us. The feral look in his eyes burned into me.

"So, I took her to my senior prom. Senior! Prom! She didn't even go home with me. In fact, she went to a different party. That's messed up, right?"

"Maybe you're really unpleasant to be around," Aisha said. "That's my first impression."

Clayton stood up and moved closer to Cass and me.

"I was so nice to you, Avery Byrne. Wasn't I?"

"What do you want, a Girl Scout Cookie? We're all in love with Avery. Join the club," Cass said. God, she was hot when she was angry. But Clayton ignored her and inched closer to us, and the look in his eyes chilled any heat in me. He had us pinned against the s'mores table, and the edge dug into my back.

"I kinda feel like you owe me," he said. "Especially now that the world is ending. Come on. I don't mind if it's both of you. In fact, I'd prefer it." He put his hands on our shoulders and rubbed his thumb across my collarbone. I felt the taste of marshmallow rise in my throat, from anger or fear, I didn't know which.

"If you don't let go of us in the next three seconds, I will castrate you," Cass said.

He laughed under his breath, made a big show of releasing his hands, but he was still inches from our faces. He stared down at Cass and said, "You think you're tough because you're wearing a blazer, huh? You think you're like a dude, huh?"

Oh, *hell* no. I thought about pushing him away from us, but the fire was directly behind him, and I didn't want him to fall in.

"I don't owe you anything," I said instead, loudly enough, I hoped, for everyone to hear it. "Leave us alone, Clayton. Back off." He only leaned in closer.

"You broke my heart, Avery Byrne." His breath was hot on my cheeks. "Don't you think I deserve an apology?" I felt everyone watching us. I silently pleaded for one of his friends to grab him by the arm and pull him away. They stood and snickered. They chose him. Though the last thing I ever wanted was for him to see me cry, tears pricked my eyes.

Suddenly, a rush of lukewarm water gushed over Clayton's head, onto the ground, our clothes, and the fire. It sizzled angrily and surprised him enough to make him stumble away from us, try to wipe the water out of his eyes, and yell, "What the hell?" I turned to see Aisha holding the empty handwashing bucket, eyes wide. I grabbed Cass, and she grabbed Aisha, and even though she was wearing heels, she kept up with us as we sprinted away. As we crossed the lawn, the bass thumped. The stars and the city still sparkled, and they both looked so impossibly beautiful.

"Aisha," Cass said breathlessly as we slowed to a walk at the bottom of the driveway. "That was the most badass thing I have ever seen in my entire life."

Aisha burst out laughing, and doubled over to catch

her breath. "I don't know why I did that! I hated that man!" I cackled too as we climbed into the car, Aisha in the driver's seat, Cass as her passenger. When Aisha met my eyes in the rearview mirror, I felt a pang of affection for her.

"I'm excited for Ray to join us," I said. "I want to know her."

"You're going to love her," she said. "I know it."

Cass reached her hand into the back seat to find mine, and Aisha started winding down the back roads of Kilkenny. What was this little family? How did I love it so much? And would it stick if we lived through this? I didn't know, and I almost couldn't bear it, the not knowing. I was everything with them: safe and warm and heading somewhere knowable, somewhere we all called home.

Alone, without them, I was nothing.

five months
to impact

Fall athletes weren't supposed to party during the season, but there was a weekend in September where we only had one home game on a Friday. The captains made it clear we were all expected to attend a Saturday night party with the men's soccer team, and we were all expected to get lit.

Aisha and I got ready with the other four freshmen in our room: Aspen, Grace, Natalie, and Liv. I didn't fit in with them, not really. They talked about which boys they liked, who would be there, who might get together, and the whole time I thought, *Oh my God, I'm such a coward* and *Cass would be so ashamed of me.* But at least if I kept my mouth shut, I could pretend to fit in. I wouldn't have to show up alone. It would look like I had friends.

Aspen made me change my shirt three times, and
Aisha did my makeup, and together we hiked up the
steep, grassy hill that led to the senior apartments. When
we got there, we found them playing beer pong, and the
sophomores cheered and handed us shot glasses filled
with something yellow. They made us count to three
and tip them back at the same time, and cold citrus
burned down my throat.

"Lemon drops!" Keegan said. "They're harmless.
And, Aisha, yours is just lemon juice. Don't worry, this
isn't hazing; it's just fun."

Just fun. Though they kept bringing us drinks for an
hour, and I kept thinking, *If I get drunk, what am I going
to say?*

"Is everyone here?" one of the boys yelled, eventually,
and it felt like a reprieve when they cut the music. It was
tradition, apparently, for all the freshmen to go around
the room and name who they thought was the hottest
person on the other team.

"What if someone's gay?" Natalie shouted. My cheeks
burned, and I looked at the carpet. My mind flashed
back to Ella at church camp. Did Natalie know? How did
people always know?

"Then you don't have to do it. We're inclusive,"
Molly said.

"If you're gay, you have to name someone on your
own team," Ram said.

"Yeah, sure," Molly said with a wave of her hand. Jesus Christ, that was worse; they knew that, right? That was way worse. I scanned the room to find a boy who seemed like a sincere choice, hot enough he'd blow me off, think my crush was cute, but wouldn't pursue it any further. Or, I hoped, they'd call on me last, and then I could copy whoever everyone else named.

"Ladies first," Ram said.

"Whatever," Keegan said. "Alphabetical order." *Well, fuck. Kill me instead. Put me out of my misery.*

"Aisha."

Aisha shrugged as if she couldn't be bothered to care. "Oh, um. Whatever. Femi."

"Aspen?" Aspen acted embarrassed, but I knew she wasn't. She had long, blond hair she'd curled like she was on *The Bachelor*, perfect white teeth, and rosy, pink cheeks without applying blush. She'd gone to boarding school in Newport, Rhode Island.

"Oh my God," she said. "Why me? Okay, umm, this is a sexy team, though! It's hard!" She covered her eyes before yelling, "Okay, fine. Sebastian." The whole room howled in amusement and turned to look at Sebastian, a broad-chested guy who looked like he could be her twin brother. The boys beside him punched his arms, and he, too, pretended to be embarrassed. As the roar dulled down, I felt my heart race and my stomach drop. My turn.

"Aaaaavery," Molly crooned. "Avery Byrne." The longer

I waited, I knew, the more buildup there'd be. The more fear they'd sense on me. I pointed to the floppy-haired brunette in the corner who liked to show off his six-pack by pretending he *had* to wipe his face with his shirt.

"Spencer," I said. More howling, more arm punching. He winked at me, and I looked into the barrel of my red SOLO cup before emptying its contents down my throat. Grace picked Beau. Natalie picked Sebastian, too, and Liv picked Matt. The boys went next, and when no one said my name, I felt both relieved and embarrassed.

After the noise had settled down, I beelined it to the mini fridge and cracked a beer can open. When I turned around, I saw Spencer walking toward me, looking smug. I didn't even think about where I was going. My body walked through the door, into the hall, and into the women's bathroom. I didn't know if he tried to follow me or not.

Inside, under the fluorescent lights, I put my beer can on the sink counter and stared at myself in the mirror. The makeup Aspen had put on me made me look like a different person. I ripped a brown paper towel out of the dispenser, ran the water over it, and started wiping at the thick, black eyeliner.

"It's like permanent marker," I said under my breath as the ink smudged across my face and darkened the towel, but still ringed my eyes.

One of the toilets flushed, and a girl with swoopy blond boy-band hair and an undercut swaggered up to wash her hands next to me. She was wearing a red hoodie and baggy joggers.

"This is why I don't mess with makeup," she said, and I felt my stomach tighten. Oh God, she seemed queer, and good lord, she was hot. My heart pounded.

"I don't usually either," I said. "Or at least not this much. My teammates did this."

"No kidding, what sport?"

"Soccer."

"Sweet. I play softball."

"Cool. I'll have to come to some of your games. See you play." So much for playing hard to get. Or was I even flirting at all? I didn't know what I was doing, but I was so desperate for her to stay in the room, to know who she was, to escape from the soccer party only doors away. My mouth went dry, so I took a sip of my Bud Light.

"You supposed to be drinking during the season?"

I locked eyes with her in the mirror. And then I lied straight to her face: "I do lots of things I'm not supposed to do."

Next, she asked me if I wanted to come to her room. Her roommate had face wipes for makeup, she said. I followed her down the hallway, into her senior suite, which was lit by Christmas lights and the glow of a TV. The Red Sox were up 4–2 against the Yankees, and she handed me a wet little towel. As I wiped again at my eyes in her mirror, I felt her watching me.

"Your hair is like, wow," she said.

"Oh, thanks," I said. "I grew it myself." It was deeply unfunny, and I cringed, but she laughed. Crossed her arms against her chest. Bit her lip.

"I kind of have a thing for redheads," she said. Our eyes locked in the reflection and dared each other to blink.

I said, "Good."

Within minutes we were on her bed, and she was kissing me; oh my fucking God, she was kissing me, and my brain was screaming, *Oh God, I'm gay. I'm gay. I'm SO GAY.* It wasn't just Cass. It was me too, and I was kissing a girl, a hot girl, and her hands were on my skin, and we were tugging at each other's clothes, and my whole body said, *Please, yes, this is what I've been waiting for. This is what I was meant to do.* And, sure, it was a little awkward and I was a bit clumsy and I had to ask her questions, but she wanted me. What was more, I wanted her, and I wasn't afraid.

But after I left, I realized I hadn't even gotten her name, and she had never asked for mine. I wanted to yell about what happened, but I had no one to tell. I couldn't tell Peter because, ew. I couldn't tell any of my teammates. I could never tell Cass, my Cass, and the thought of her made me want to cry.

· · ·

The next evening in the dining hall, I ran into the soft-ball player as I was grabbing a slice of pizza.

"Hey, Red," she said, and smirked at me. My heart fluttered, and I knew I was blushing, though I didn't want to be.

"My name's Avery, by the way."

"Meredith," she said, before leaning across me to grab her own slice and walking away to sit with her friends. I put my tray down at the soccer table, and I heard the other girls snickering around me.

"What's funny?" I said.

"Were you talking to Meredith Wyn?"

"I mean, she said hi to me and I said hi back."

"Avoid her," Molly said. "She'll try to turn you. Trust me."

"She's such a player," Keegan added.

"If it has tits, she's all over it," Josie added.

"Oh," I said. "Good to know."

"I've heard she's slept with half the hockey team."

"Can we stop talking about this?" Aisha snapped. She made eye contact with me briefly, and I had never seen her so angry, so uncomfortable.

"Why'd you leave the party last night, Avery?" Liv asked me. "Spencer was looking for you."

"Wouldn't shut up about it," Grace added.

"I don't know," I said, and realized I couldn't tell them the whole truth. I blurted out part of it, because it was all

I could think of. "Do you ever just feel like you have to get out of a room? Like you want to crawl out of your skin or tear it off? Like you're going to explode if you don't get away from people immediately?"

They all stared at me blankly.

"No," Aisha said quietly. "That's weird."

They moved on to another topic, and I put my pizza down and stared at my hands. I wasn't hungry anymore, and I kind of wanted to leave the room again, but I had to be normal. I had to smile and chat and wait until we were back in our room and Aisha was asleep so I could cry.

Because of the party, my emotional and physical hang-over, and the soccer aftermath (Coach Cather found out we'd all attended and tried to teach us a lesson with wind sprints on Monday afternoon), I had to pull an all-nighter to write a paper for Dr. Talley on an Edgar Allan Poe short story. It wasn't my best work, but I thought it might at least earn me a B. I got the email a week later:

> Avery,
>
> Your thesis is one-sided and while your argument is compelling, one I haven't read before, I'm afraid your subpar grip on grammar and syntax have let you down. I've taken the time to point out where you've erred so you can

fix for next time. Do not let my time be spent
in vain.

Content and ideas: B
Execution: C−
Final grade: C+

I got straight A's at Kilkenny High. An A- was a disappointment. I reread the email repeatedly, looking at the
letters, making sure my name was there at the top.

My next paper also earned me a C+, but I turned it in
a day late after a particularly grueling conditioning ses-
sion and staying up late to obsess over every single word
I wrote. D+. This time, I was unsurprised and tired. I was
so fucking tired, too tired to even cry. But I thought, *I can
fix this, I can fix this, I can fix this. I just have to try harder.*

But my sporadic hours of sleep became even more
scattered as the weeks went on, and I missed a Dr. Talley
class when I fell asleep at my desk accidentally.

The next day, I forced myself to march over to his
office hours in the library, waiting to see if I could talk to
him about extra credit or other ways improve my grade,
to make up for the class I missed.

"Do you have a medical condition? A disability? Was
there a death in your family?" No, no, no. "Then, that
would be giving you an unfair advantage over the other
students. This isn't high school. You don't get to walk

over here and make up rules or rewrite the class. My answer is no."

"Would it be possible to at least get an extension on my Atwood paper?" I was so behind, still in the middle of the reading, and we had to travel to Cornell that weekend, and I had tests in every other class too.

"Again, I ask: do you have a medical condition . . . ?"

I didn't finish the paper on time. I turned it in three days late. I didn't even know why I turned it in at all.

Despite what my teammates said, I hooked up with Meredith again after she found me on Instagram, slid into my DMs, and asked me if I wanted to come over one night at 11 p.m. It was my only escape, from soccer, from school. From myself. I knew she didn't give a damn about me; she didn't care how my day was or how I was doing. And that was better. If she never asked, I never had to lie, or, worse, tell her the truth. Of how lonely I was. How sad. How hopeless.

I lied to Aisha, every time, about where I went. She didn't ask questions, and I kept going anytime Meredith asked me to—until the day the football team was ranking every girl who passed them in the dining hall. When I walked by, someone yelled out, "Six!" When I spun around to glare at them, a senior said, "Never mind, she's one of the girls who goes to Meredith's room."

"Then two," someone said, while another guy shouted, "Eight!"

"You're disgusting, do you know that?" I said, but they yelled, "Oooooh!" and howled with raucous laughter.

That time, I couldn't help myself; I started crying into my fajita soup as soon as I sat down alone in a corner booth. I tried to take a bite, but my hands were shaking and it spilled off the spoon. If they knew, who else knew? Did my whole team know? Were they laughing behind my back, talking about how desperate I must be? Pathetic? I imagined what they said when I wasn't around: *I can't believe Avery, even after we warned her. And the fact she's hiding it? I mean, come on, like we can't tell.* I imagined Aisha snapping, *Stop talking about this.*

That was when I wondered, again, for the hundredth time: Did she hate sharing a room with me? Did they move away from me in the locker room? Did they even want me on the team at all?

The next time Meredith texted me, I didn't respond.

six days to impact

I slept horribly after we got home from the party, nightmares of Clayton's face in the light of the bonfire jarring me awake again and again. Cass and Aisha were on either side of me on the bed in my room, Cass with her head on my chest, Aisha with her head near my head.

When I stirred, Cass woke up too, and she followed me into the kitchen, where we prepared food for my parents: eggs and toast, tea and freshly cut apples. We set the plates out on the table on the back porch, even though it was freezing. And Mom and Dad joined us there, looking out over the apple orchard just as the sun took its sturdy place in the morning sky.

"How was the party?" Mom asked as she blew on her tea to cool it. Cass looked to me to answer.

"It was fun, until people got too drunk," I said. I almost took a bite of something but found I couldn't stomach it. Thoughts of Clayton zipped through my brain.

"What have we always told you?" Dad said. "Nothing good happens after midnight. Or after people find out they only have one week to live." He shook a forkful of apples at us.

"No more parties for us," Cass said. "Probably."

"Well, but you two do take care of each other," Dad said. "That's why I'm never worried."

"I'm always worried," Mom said. "Hey, what time is Peter coming around?"

"I don't know," I said. "I think they'll be back at it today, though." Georgia's shrieking replayed in my brain.

"Oh, wait, you gotta see this," Dad said. He left the table for a few minutes, and when he returned he was holding a half-finished rocking horse fashioned from plywood and disassembled brooms. It was crooked and ugly. It was wonderful. My lungs tightened when I pictured Teddy riding it.

"That's so cute, Dad."

"Wow, nice work, Mr. B," Cass chimed in. "Can you make one for me?"

"Maybe," he said, considering it. "Though I think we'll need all hands on deck today."

"Dad, she's kidding."

"I am absolutely not." He sat back down and continued nibbling on his toast.

"I can't believe Aisha's sleeping in," Mom said. "It's good."

"I think maybe she *can* actually sleep now," I said. "She has some news, but I'll let her tell it herself."

"She found her sister?" Dad asked.

"How do you know about that?"

"She asked us if she could share her room with some-one, and we said yes, of course."

"Then I heard her chatting with her parents and connected the dots," Mom added.

"But they speak in Hausa."

"Not always."

"Wow, you two are good," Cass said, as we exchanged a nervous glance.

Before we could wonder what else they'd noticed, we heard the porch's glass door slide open, and all three Laskys emerged, arms full of bread, cans, rice, wine, and animal crackers. Teddy had already retrieved his gigantic stuffed rabbit, Pineapple, from the basement to carry around the house with him. I knew when the time came, Pineapple would have to get the boot, but Teddy didn't need to know, not yet.

"Hey, family," Peter said.

"We missed you!" Dad said. "Where were you yesterday?"

Peter looked to Georgia to answer. She raised and dropped her arms in her Carhartt jacket.

"I don't know. It sunk in this might not . . . end how we want it to. I thought seriously about going home to Brooklyn. But I'm not. We're not. From everything we've been reading, it's too dangerous for us to travel."

"Way too dangerous," Dad said. "Your parents can't come here? You sure? We have plenty of room."

"My father's old," Georgia said, her voice breaking. "It's too far." Peter put his arm around her, and when I looked at Cass and saw her expression, I wanted to do the same, but didn't know if I should.

Aisha came outside, too, freshly showered, smiling, and wearing jeans and a sweatshirt. It was strange to have all of us there, together, outside the bunker. The morning sky glowed soft and white, and I felt like I could breathe easier than I had in days.

"Good morning," Aisha said. "What's everyone talking about?"

"Nothing," I said quickly. "You want to tell them your news?" Her thousand-watt smile from the night before ripped across her face again as she told Peter and Georgia about Ray, her plan to join us, her hopes for their future together.

"Since this whole thing started, all I have ever wanted is to feel at home again," she said. "With her here, things will be right." No one mentioned the danger, no one echoed, *It's too far.*

"Then let's get moving, eh?" Dad said. He forked one final apple and bit it for good measure.

After Cass, Aisha, and I had yet another successful haul—we found an impressive stash of leftover Halloween candy, medicine, and granola bars—we were sorting what we'd collected when the video call ringtone sounded from Cass's phone. The two of us rushed over to see who was on the other end. The incoming call was from Omar Pérez.

"Holy shit," Cass and I said at the same time. She answered. His face appeared on the screen with a few-days-old beard and a bright grin.

"Omes!" Cass screamed. "I'm gonna cry."

"Don't cry, weirdo," he said. "Wait, that looks like Avery's basement."

"It *is* Avery's basement," I said, and leaned into view. "Hey, Avery."

"Hey, Omar. Are you still in the city?"

"Yeah, I'm at some random guy's house in Queens with some friends. I lost my phone that morning in the chaos, and I've just been kind of winging it ever since. I'm sorry, I shoulda found a way to contact you."

"Yeah, dude, I called you like six times that morning," Cass said. "I thought you might want to come home with me. But I'm glad you're okay. What have you been up to?"

"You know," he said, "partying, clubbing, dancing, living it up. Gonna go upstate, I think, to a new friend's house for the last few days or . . . whatever."

"Like a friend or a *friend*?" Cass said.

He smirked. "His name is Santiago. You're with the Byrne clan?"

"Yeah." She slung her arm around me, kissed my temple. "Where else would I go?"

"Wait, are you two together?"

I looked around the basement to make sure my parents hadn't appeared out of thin air. "Yeah," we both said at the same time, and I waited for him to roll his eyes.

"Wow, damn! Guess I should have seen that coming. Congrats, you two! You finally got the girl." He seemed . . . happy? Sincere? I tilted my head, confused.

"What do you mean?" I said. "You said I should leave Cass alone."

"He did?"

"Prom night."

"Well, yeah, but that's when I thought you were wicked straight. Then you came out last year and I was like, oh, yup. I see it now. My bad!"

"I have *so* many questions," Cass said.

"And I have one for you," he said. "Why aren't you two here in New York? It's where you belong, Cass." She shifted beside me.

"Ugh, why does everyone keep saying this to me?"

"Because it's true. Plus, haven't you heard Mx. and Match is back on? You were so excited for it."

"What? It is?" I felt her whole body light up beside me.

"Yeah, or at least, I heard it from Toby who heard it from Birch. They're going all out. I mean, as all out as you can go right now."

"Oh my God. Holy shit. Do you know when? Why didn't Daisy tell me?"

"I think they said they're throwing it the day before impact. And I don't know! I think they just decided."

Cass looked ready to ask a hundred more questions, but the video dropped.

"*Damn*," Cass said.

"It's out on my phone too," Aisha said, an edge of panic in her voice. Her plate clattered to the floor. We restarted the router a number of times, but the light blinked red. We unplugged and restarted for twenty minutes before staring at each other helplessly.

"It's probably temporary," I said. Aisha walked away from us, wide-eyed, and screamed into a pillow. She started sobbing, and Cass and I exchanged glances. "Cass, you wanna go to Peter's and see if they still have Wi-Fi?"

"Sure," she said and took off up the stairs. I sat on the arm of the couch to be close to Aisha, but also to give her some space.

"You should keep crying," I said, when she emerged

to breathe and wipe furiously at her eyes. "If you want to. If it helps."

"It doesn't," she said, but more tears rolled down her face. She didn't try to stop them.

"It'll be okay," I said, and immediately heard my own insincerity.

"If we don't have Wi-Fi, I can't get in touch with Rahila. She was supposed to be on her way now. How will I check on her? What if she doesn't hear from me and she decides not to come?"

"The Wi-Fi will come back. Or we'll find it somewhere else. It can't be out everywhere." Could it?

"What if she needs me before then?"

"We'll find it, and you can get in touch with her and—"

"Just stop, Avery," she said, her voice high and strained. She clutched her locket necklace and rocked back and forth. "You can say whatever you want, but it won't change the facts."

"You're so close to seeing Ray, though. She'll get here. I know it."

"You don't know anything. Just stop talking."

"You're right, I'm sorry." I was so painfully bad at cheering her up. I was making things worse, even. "Can I hug you at least?"

She sighed, but opened her arms to me. I wrapped mine around her. She felt so cold. There were so many things

I wanted to say, but I knew none of them were what she wanted from me. I couldn't imagine what she was going through: the isolation, the unknowing, the fear.

"It's strange being here," she said, letting me go, "but I am grateful, Avery. I know we weren't really friends at Eaton."

I felt a pang of embarrassment, but more than that, curiosity. What had I done so wrong? Had my mom been right, after all? That I'd never given myself a chance?

"Why do you think that was?"

She bit her lip, considered the question. "It seemed to me you weren't even trying—at school, at soccer. Or at fitting in, honestly. I resented that. I have to try *so* hard. I see now that you were trying, maybe more than I even understand. But also, we're too similar."

"How so?"

"I'm guarded. You're guarded. We are people pleasers and perfectionists, and it is a bad combination. We like to score, but we pass the ball more. We dedicate our lives to other people. I've spent mine looking for my sister." She shook her head and shrugged. "She never looked for me."

"Me scoring is kind of a stretch," I said. She rolled her eyes but grinned. "Ray must love you so much, Aisha. Traveling anywhere is hard right now. She must want this badly."

"What if I don't have time to really know her?" Before I could answer, she put one hand on my bruised knee and rested it there. "What if she hides herself like you do?"

"I only hide the parts that would hurt people," I said.

"I want to know *everything* about my sister's story," she said. "Even the parts that hurt me. Maybe especially those parts." Though I so badly wanted to look away from her, she held my gaze. "Cass will still love you, you know. If you tell her."

Before I could speak, we heard Cass's footsteps on the stairs.

"The bad news is the Laskys' Wi-Fi is down too," she said, leaning on the couch to catch her breath. "The good news is Dr. Talley's is working across the street. You can knock whenever, and he'll let you use it."

"Alhamdu lillahi," Aisha said. "I'm going to go send her a message to say I'll be out of touch."

"Do you want us to come?" I asked.

"No," she said. "I've got this."

Once she left, Cass put her head in my lap and stared up at the Christmas lights. "Should we go to New York?" she said. I ran my fingers through her hair.

"For Mx. and Match?"

"That's part of it, yeah, but not *just* that. New York is full of people like me—queer and Brown and dreaming. I felt most like myself there. It felt like I could be anyone. I want you to feel that way too, even if it's only for a few days. You deserve that. I deserve that."

How was I supposed to do that when I didn't have a clue who I was, who I wanted to be? How was I supposed to do that when the only thing I wanted to be was not alive anymore? I wasn't stable or cool or brave enough for New York. Not at all.

"Shouldn't we stay here? Try to survive?"

"Maybe, Avery." She rubbed her temples. "What if this doesn't work? Honestly, all I want is to forget everything for like an hour. Or, fuck an hour, for a *split second*. I want one tiny, microscopic instant where I feel like we're together for real. I want to pretend like we have a future."

"We might——"

"A future in our old life. Not this one. This one is so sad."

My old life had been sad too, but I didn't say that. I kept stroking her hair, wishing so badly to do something that could cheer her up, at least a little. To do something that would make her feel something other than panic and despair. To do something that would help her forget like she wanted to.

I didn't have much to work with, but I had an idea.

"If we were in our old life and we were going to be together, the next thing I'd do is take you out on a real date."

"Don't play."

"I'm serious. I want to take you on a date. Like, right now. Right here. For real."

"Oh, yeah? Dinner and a movie?"

"Do you really think that's the kind of first date I'd

take you on? Cass Joshi-Aguilar, queen of New York City?" As soon as I'd said it, though, I couldn't think of anything cooler. Maybe a picnic in an abandoned plane? Was there somewhere we could ice-skate? What did people even do in the city? What could we even do around here?

"Excuse me, that's butch queen to you. But, actually, a movie sounds great. Normal, even."

"Oh, well, good," I said. "I happen to know a place. Go get ready."

three months
to impact

In one of our final games of the season, I finally got some playtime. We were up 5–0 against Yale, so we had little to lose. I was still determined to prove myself, and as the minutes dwindled, I felt fatigue and desperation warring in my chest. I could barely breathe, but I didn't care. I got off a few solid shots, I set a few girls up, and time after time we hit the post or went wide or high or got stopped at the sweep line. I could see Coach Cather talking to the seniors sitting on the bench, completely checked out of the game. I wanted to do something that would make her give a damn. The clock was ticking, and someone fed me a long ball I probably wasn't going to be able to reach. I sprinted for it anyway.

What I pieced together was this: I went for the ball at

the same time as their keeper. I planted my foot to strike, and her body pushed me in the other direction.

I'd watched countless girls tear their ACLs and MCLs. Gruesome. They howled while their parents rushed onto the field. In some cases, it ended their soccer careers. In all cases, it required a brace, pain medication, surgery, crutches, and physical therapy. Either the pain or the panic blacked me out, and I had absolutely no memory of falling on the field and screaming.

Later, Aisha would tell me Coach rushed over and the two of them helped me off the field. Aisha held Gatorade to my lips, and I told her I hated the red flavor. I do remember the ice packs and the golf cart ride to the health center where our trainer, Al, took one look at me and said, "Not another one."

My parents drove up to accompany me to my MRI, but it wasn't a torn ACL. It was a bone bruise. It would be sore for a few weeks, and then I'd be fine. It was rest, ice, elevation, and ibuprofen. Mortifying.

I had already missed my allowed two classes in Dr. Talley's class, and the third that time I passed out cold while studying. I didn't want to see him when I was in so much pain either, but the real reason I missed a fourth class was because I couldn't bear to see him face-to-face. I had used up all my anger and embarrassment. I had used up all my shame and sadness. I was just numb, and I chose not to go sit in his class and listen to him chastise me. I used my crutches to limp to the river instead and lay on the dock, daydreaming about sinking to the bottom and never coming up. I couldn't fail his class—my parents would be devastated. I was going to fail his class—what was I going to do?

If I was drowning on land, in oxygen, maybe the floor of the river was the only place I'd be able to breathe. I lay on my stomach on the slippery, splintering wood and put my bare hand in the rolling, freezing autumn water. I thought, again, *I'm so tired. I'm such a disappointment. I don't want to do this anymore. I could kill myself. I should. I might. I want to.*

But, no, I can fix this, still. I just have to try harder.

But I could.

And I might.

I knew I should've been scared, that I was thinking that way. But I wasn't. I did feel like, maybe, Cass could snap me out of it. I felt like I should give her the chance. After my injury, I asked her to visit me at Eaton, and she said, "Ave. Yes. Of course." When she arrived, I was still at physical therapy, so Aisha let her into our room, and by the time I limped back she was snuggled into my single bed, head on her hand, telling a story and making Aisha laugh hysterically.

She trailed off as I entered the room, and Aisha jumped up to help me with my bag.

"Hey, you," Cass said, patting my bed beside her. She sounded the same but looked different. She'd traded in her usual T-shirt and Adidas jacket for a black silk button-up top. Her hair, which was usually half brushed and wavy or thrown up into a thoughtless bun, was slicked back into a tight, straight ponytail. She looked unbearably cool. I felt like I didn't know her.

"What happened, killer?"

I sat down beside her, and she rested her hand on the middle of my back. My pulse quickened.

"I thought you were made of steel. I thought if you ran into a brick wall, it would detonate upon impact."

"Apparently not," I said.

"Mind blown," Cass said.

"You look so . . . New York," I said. I pinched the sleeve of her blouse.

"You look so . . . New Hampshire."

"I mean you look good, just . . . different."

"I look good, she says. Aisha, did you hear that?"

"I like your look," Aisha said. "Very put together." Aisha, too, looked very put together, as usual. It was a Friday morning when she had no classes, and yet she was dressed in a starched, pressed blue button-down with matching accessories. I felt their eyes travel to my own sweatpants and fleece jacket and knew they couldn't throw that compliment my way.

"I should put real clothes on to get on your levels."

"Oh, stop," Aisha said, "you're injured." *Broken* felt like the more appropriate word, but I didn't correct her. And anyway, this was what I wore when I *wasn't* injured.

"I'm here to wait on you hand and battered knee," Cass said. "And"—she got out of bed and rooted around in her duffel bag—"I brought you something."

She pulled out a gray, plastic block and a smaller drawstring bag.

"This was my dad's old cassette player. Look, you can still use the headphone jack and everything. And this"—she opened the bag and dumped its contents onto my bed—"is thirty-two books on tape. The NYPL was cleaning house."

"This is . . . I mean, thank you," I said, picking up the tape closest to me. "*Atlas Shrugged*, Cass?"

"Ew," she said, taking it from my hand and chucking it into the garbage bin across the room. "Sorry, I grabbed them all. I know there are some good ones in there, though, see? Virginia Woolf. James Baldwin. All those olden-timey books you like."

"The classics."

"Sure."

"This is really thoughtful."

"You're welcome. You're going to be laid up a lot, and you used to read to me all the time, and I won't be here, so."

It was a sweet gift, it was so, so, sweet, but all my brain heard was, *I won't be here.* I choked on my words. "Thanks. It's weird not being able to run."

"You should take up shadowboxing," Aisha said. "It's one of the best cardio workouts when you can only use your arms. Gets your heart rate up quickly."

"Good idea," I said. "Would you wanna practice with me?"

"Once soccer is over," she said. "Sure."

Soccer was never over. There was spring practice and travel scrimmages and weight-lifting sessions and summer training. Okay, so I was going to have a tape read to me and punch at thin air and sit in my bed while Cass went back to New York and Aisha went back to the team—and was I feeling sorry for myself? Yes, I was, but not in a way where I felt like I deserved anything more. In a way where I was resigned to it. I was ready to let them go so I could let go too. An uncomfortable silence hung stale in the room.

"What were you talking about before I came in?"

"She was telling me about her parents visiting New York," Aisha said.

"My mom unwittingly took us to a burlesque show, but then once it started, she didn't want to seem like a prude, so she made us stay, and anyway, it was one of the most uncomfortable hours of my life. I am dead now. RIP me. Spread my ashes in the Atlantic."

"Is accidental burlesque a New York thing?" I asked.

"Apparently! It happened to be going down at this tapas restaurant."

"Oh, no."

"Oh, yes. At one point my dad leaned over to me and said, 'This is an art, you know.' Yeah, Dad, thanks, I got that."

"Ohhh, no."

"Ohhh, yes."

After Aisha left to hang out with Molly, Cass traced her fingers along the photographs I'd hung on my wall and stopped to rest on one of the two of us: a clichéd orchard portrait, both of us hanging out of a tree, white paper bags filled to the brim with shining fruit.

"I love college," she said, "and New York. I *love* New York. But I do miss home. New Hampshire in general."

"Yeah, it's pretty here."

"Do you walk around campus and be like, 'Oh my God, I live *here*? And it looks like *this*?'"

Did I? I couldn't remember the last time anything felt beautiful to me.

"The first few weeks, maybe," I said, "but I guess you get used to it and then it's just . . . you know." I knew most people wouldn't get used to it. Most people would fall in love with the world again and again and again every time the leaves shifted a shade.

"What's up with you?"

"Nothing. What do you mean?"

She sat on the end of my bed and studied my face. I looked down at my hands and was afraid to look back up at her, afraid she'd read me.

"You're different."

"So are you."

"You're like . . . I don't want to be like, 'Smile, woman!' but seriously, I don't think I've seen you smile once today. Your voice is flat."

"It's not a great time for me." I gestured at my knee.

"No, it's more than that. See, like, when I FaceTime Serenity, we can talk for over an hour and she won't ask me one single question about my life. She goes on and on about life at UCLA, and it's like she doesn't care at all what I'm up to, and that sucks. But when I call you, we talk for over an hour and you won't tell me one goddamn thing about you. That sucks too. You ask me questions, and then the call's over and my parents will be like, 'How's Avery?' And I'm like, 'Honestly? I have no clue.'"

"Wait—what's going on with Serenity?"

"See? That's exactly what I mean."

"There's not much to tell."

"Tell me one thing. One single thing about your life right now."

I bit my bottom lip, and though it was wildly embarrassing, I let tears pool in my eyes and slip down my cheeks.

"I'm failing a class."

"*What?* That's absolutely ridiculous. Why?"

I was going to tell the story but surprised myself with what came spilling out instead. "Everyone's straight or rich or both. I haven't made a single friend outside of soccer, and the team doesn't even like me, but it's all I have. I tried to sign up for a volunteer group, and they told me they'd put me on an email list, and I never heard from them again, and I'm too tired to follow up. I'm somehow cold all the time. I hate most of my classes except philosophy. I'm behind in *everything*, and I'm not smart enough. My lit professor hates me. I'm a total loser, Cass."

"Oh, Avery, no," she said, but it wasn't pitying. It was its own type of pleading. She knelt on the floor next to me and took my hands in hers, though I could hardly feel them. "I wish you could see you how I see you. You're at Eaton, Ave. Of course, everyone is amazing. But you are too. So what if you need some time to readjust?"

"I'm not good enough, Cass."

"You are." She touched my chin. "You're the best person I know. If you're not good enough, then I'm definitely not good enough. And, Avery?"

"Yeah?"

She leaned in to whisper, "Fuck that."

I smiled despite myself, for what did feel like the first time in forever. But it was Cass making me laugh, making me feel grounded in my body again. That was the beauty of her, not the beauty of me. And when she was gone, that beauty would be too.

"Listen," Cass said. "You're Avery freaking Byrne. I've been living in your shadow our entire friendship. You have been the best at quite literally everything, and I've been there to be your sidekick every step of the way. Finally, I have my own world where I'm the star."

"Cass, you've always been—"

"Let me finish. This feeling of being not good enough? That's new for you, but most mortals feel it all the time. As a long-time mortal, I can let you in on a little secret: the only person who can decide if you're good enough is you."

I had never felt good enough, not even when I was topping lists or scoring goals. Not then, not ever. Certainly not now.

"I'm not good enough," I said again. I knew that it was true.

"Avery, come on. This conversation is painful. You're so determined to be defeated." I heard the irritation in her voice and wanted to cry. She didn't understand. She wasn't like me. She was fully alive. She knew how to dream and wish and want. I was empty.

"Yeah, Cass, I get it. I'm pathetic. You've made your point."

"Christ. I'm not saying you're pathetic. I'm saying you need to find something here just for you, even if it's a new you that you don't know yet." I wanted to stop talking about it. I didn't like that she was seeing me in this state. I didn't want to be in the room with her anymore.

"There is one place that's all mine," I said. "One place I really love here."

"Will you show me?"

"Okay," I said. "It's nothing special. It's this dock on the river I like to sit on to read or whatever. It looks like basically all the rest of New Hampshire."

"If you love it, I'll love it too," she said. "Take me there."

I did, though it took me longer than normal to get there on my crutches, and of course it felt anticlimactic and unimpressive. As soon as we got to the edge of the water, I wanted to turn around and leave. It didn't feel like ours or like something I wanted to share with her or anyone. I didn't tell her it was where I went when I wanted to kill myself, which was almost all the time.

"That's basically it," I said, and moved to guide us back through the trees.

"Whoa, whoa," Cass said. "I love it here. This isn't a weird New York flex, but I haven't tasted air like this in forever. Can we sit?"

We dangled our legs over the edge and watched a row of ducks ride the current like a roller coaster.

"I think Serenity and I are breaking up," she said. It was my turn to put a hand on her back.

"Oh, Cass. I'm so sorry. What happened?"

"Nothing exactly. I mean, there's that whole thing where she doesn't ask about my life at all. But now that we're apart, I don't feel this pull to her the way I used to. When I have a free minute, I don't think, 'Hey, I want to talk to Serenity.' When I picture my future, I never see her in it. I know that sounds harsh, but I asked her the same thing, I asked her what she imagined for us, and she said she has never thought about it, not even once."

"Woof," I said. "That feels like bare minimum."

"Right? And what's worse? I wasn't even hurt or disappointed. It's what I expected, actually. I've tried to think about our future, and I come up blank, which is why I asked her in the first place."

"Maybe it's like you said; maybe you both need to readjust."

"I think when it's over, it's over, you know?"

I tried to picture my own future, and all I could see was beach after beach of winter sand, colorless and chilled to the touch. Rushing waters. Like Aunt Devin.

"I'm sorry then," I said. "I know you loved her. You went through a lot with her. It's still going to be hard and sad."

"Yeah, it will. Expect drunken two a.m. phone calls. Maybe some crying, I don't know. Brace yourself."

"When you think of your future, what *do* you picture?" I knew I wouldn't make the cut, but that was fine.
I wanted her to be okay without me. I needed to know
she would be.

Cass smirked. "Graduating. Getting a job as an underpaid, overworked intern alongside a bunch of white trust
fund kids. Waitressing nights and weekends to pay rent
in a shithole apartment infested with mice. Maybe getting
a job at some boutique where, again, I'll be underpaid.
And then I'll squirrel away money until I can branch out
on my own, make my own clothing line so young queer
kids can feel like themselves." Her vision was perfect for
her. I found myself smiling, despite myself.

"They'll be lucky to have you," I said.

"Who?"

"Queer kids. The world."

"You know what's funny, though?"

"What?"

"In every version of my future, I see myself back here
in New Hampshire in the end. With you." My heart sank
a little. I was starting to realize more and more that was
an ending I couldn't give her. As if on cue, a loon sang
sadly nearby.

"You don't want to come back here. You deserve the
world, Cass," I said.

She slung an arm around me. "You too, Ave. But you
should know: in the movie of my life, you're in every

frame." Another group of ducks tumbled by. "Come visit me in New York when you're healed up. You'll see."

But before I went to visit Cass, I showed up to every single practice and every single game for the next two weeks until we were eliminated by Dartmouth in the semifinals. Only then did Coach Cather call me into her office.

"Listen, lady," she said, suddenly soft and therefore suspicious. "You've been a good soldier for me this year. You've never complained, you put your head down and worked, and you supported your teammates. Those qualities are going to take you far in life."

"It's been a great experience," I lied. "I hope I can contribute more next season, though."

"That's the thing, Avery," she said, leaning back in her chair. "You were our most promising recruit, but you've struggled. With us, and with your classes. I have this note from Dr. Basil Talley here."

"You don't have to read it," I said, my throat closing. She ran her hand through the gel of her hair and sighed.

"You failed his class, Avery."

So it was official, then. I felt nothing. I hadn't been back to his class all semester. I hadn't opened a single email from him. It wasn't a surprise.

"You're going to be on academic probation next semester. If you're going to be on the team, you need to show major improvement this spring. At practice, once you heal up, and in your academics. We can set you up with a tutor. Would that help?"

I didn't need a tutor. It wasn't that I didn't know how to do my work. I just couldn't.

"No," I said. "I'll get it together. I'll fix it."

I'm already trying my best, I didn't say. *I'm depressed*, I didn't say. She leaned forward and put her chin in her hands.

"So next time you're in my office, we'll be talking about how much progress you've made, right?"

Not a chance in hell.

"Of course."

I showered under hot water until I couldn't feel my skin. I opened my mouth and let the water in, swallowed it, and let it burn like tea. *I'll fix it*, I started to think again, but there was nothing left to fix. It was over.

I was over. Things would never get better. *I* would never get better. This was it. This was my very best, and it wasn't nearly enough. The other familiar thoughts washed over me, through me: *I'm so tired. I'm such a disappointment. I don't want to do this anymore. I could kill myself. I want to. I shouldn't. I shouldn't. I shouldn't.*

But I could.

I might.

And for the first time, I added, *I will.* I started to plan.

six days to impact

After showering, drying my hair, and putting on a soft gray sweater I knew she loved to touch, I drove around the neighborhood a few times so I could pick up Cass. It was ridiculous to spend full, precious minutes of the rest of my life driving around in circles, but Cass wanted this. And I wanted to give it to her, this proper date in this pretend future where we could be together for real, for longer. I drove into my own driveway, walked up my own walkway, and knocked gently on the front door, where she told me she'd be waiting. After a few beats, she opened it, and though there shouldn't have been any shock to the moment—I'd seen her only minutes earlier—I felt like I could melt right through the ice and into the ground.

"You look—" I shook my head, couldn't finish. She was the same person, but she was radiant, all new glow and old gravity. She was wearing a faux leather jacket, ripped black jeans, and black boots. She ran her hand through her hair, tilted her head, and smirked.

"I look what?"

"You look sexy as hell." I stepped up to pull her into me, hip to hip. I kissed her and felt her shaking under my hands. I glanced nervously toward the windows of my house to make sure my parents weren't watching us, but nothing flickered in the windows, so I kissed her again, longer. "Let's go."

We held hands as we drove, and I took my eyes off our abandoned back roads more than I should have.

"What would your parents have done in our old life if we'd decided to date?" she asked.

"I thought we're pretending we're in our old life," I said.

"Oh, yeah."

"I think they'll eventually come around to it. They've always loved you, you know that."

"My parents are probably already planning our wedding and shit."

"Do you think we'll get married?"

"Avery, this is our first real date. Clingy much?" She winked at me, and I rolled my eyes. "I mean, yeah, I'd like to think so. But you're gonna have to move to New York with me."

"I don't even know what I'd do there. It's so big and I'm so small."

"Well, what do you want to do?"

What a question. I shrugged and felt a familiar pop of panic in my chest.

"I really don't know," I said. "That's the problem."

"It's not a problem to be nineteen and unsure of what you want to do with the rest of your life."

"But you know *exactly* what you want. I feel like you're always so sure, and it scares me because I'm never sure of anything. You knew you were gay before you even fell for someone. You knew you wanted to go to Pratt. You knew you wanted to go into fashion. For me, it's different. I never want anything, so it's like . . ." I threw my hands in the air and had to whip them back down to steer around a corner.

"So what? I'm a Scorpio. I've got a good gut. Or maybe I trust mine more. Or maybe I forgive mine more. But, who's to say I wouldn't fall for some guy some day? Get into fashion and be like, 'Screw this'? What if I'm not even a woman? Maybe I'm nonbinary, I don't know! I don't know everything, Ave. I make decisions, but they're nothing more than predictions. I don't know my future either."

"You're right, but I hope you know I love you no matter who you are. Always will. You do know that, right?"

"Yes, but it's nice to hear. And the point remains, Avery, you *choose* to be excellent at so many things. I know how hard you work. I know how good you are. The question isn't if you're too small for New York; the question is how you'll fit the entirety of you into that city."

"All right," I said, and hit the steering wheel enthusiastically. "Okay. We'll live in New York. At least for a few years." She pumped her fist.

"Good. And when we get wildly rich, we'll build our own log cabin somewhere in New Hampshire so we don't forget our roots."

"Good."

"Great."

"Perfect."

I knew that wouldn't happen, but damn, it was nice to pretend.

I parked haphazardly in the familiar, abandoned cinema parking lot and for a second felt like I was back in high school, going to work. As we got closer, though, I saw the glass door was shattered. Movie posters flapped in the wind. I almost wanted to cry seeing it that way, but it was more important I didn't ruin the moment, so I held Cass's hand to guide her over the shards of glass. A pinball machine was still playing an electric version of *The Addams Family* theme song, and though the rest of the place was desolate, it was enough of a spark of life for me to imagine the bustling weekend crowds, the sticky-handed children, my high school classmates bouncing into their first dates.

Like we were.

I flipped the lights on, and Cass sprinted toward the concession stand.

"Bad news," she called. "Popcorn machine's empty."

"Good news!" I ripped open the cabinets where we kept the un-popped kernels. "I knew no one would know to steal these." I filled the machine to the brim, and we watched the popcorn come to life in all its staccato glory. Butter perfumed around us, and my mouth watered for the salt. Cass hopped on the counter to reach over the top and pulled out a fresh handful.

"Hotttt," she cried but grinned wider than I'd seen all day. She threw pieces at me to catch in my mouth. I caught one after the next and took a step back in between each until she pelted me in the face and chest. I jumped up beside her, and we fed each other popcorn until we felt sick, and then we filled up buckets to take in with us anyway. We opened the door to the first theater and stumbled into the dark. Our laughter echoed and softened the terrible silence. We put our buckets and soda cups in the back row, and I led her up to where we kept the movie hard drives.

"We probably only have what was playing before— sorry—what's been playing these past few weeks."

"Blah, it's been like puffy superhero sequels and white men running around in suits and *Frozen 4* and—"

"Oh my God, wait!" I opened the door to the next room, where they stored old reels for special events. I scanned the titles until I found the one I was looking for and pulled it off the shelf, cracked it open, and smiled. I handed the reel to Cass.

"You're kidding," she said, and shook *Saving Face* like a tambourine. "I could cry."

Together we hauled a projector out of the adjoining closet and dragged it to the screening room. We put on the movie and sprinted down the stairs to take our seats in the back row. She folded into me.

It was easier than I thought it would be to lose ourselves in one of her favorite movies, in the familiar scenes, in the dialogue and darkness. She slid her arm around my shoulder and squeezed mine. I buried myself in her chest. I'd invited Cass here to help her forget, but I hadn't realized how badly I needed to forget, also—not just the doom of our days, but also the sadness of before. I hadn't known how badly I needed to feel it: That we could have been together, in our old life. That we were together, now, and I felt beautiful and loved and free. And what if I even deserved it?

My stomach sank a little as the credits rolled. It was over, and the rest of our days were waiting for us on the outside, but there was nothing and no one forcing us to leave.

"Hey, Cass?" I said, and sat up to face her.

"Hey, Avery?"

"Do you want to be my girlfriend?" She covered her

face, threw her head back. "Don't leave me hanging," I said after what felt like minutes.

"I know, it's silly considering, I mean . . . What I mean to say is yes, Avery. Finally."

It was kind of, absolutely silly. And yet I was floating, and it still felt like it meant something and everything. She ran her thumb across my cheek and said, "We were never just friends, were we?"

I tried to remember. Had there ever been a time when my heart didn't race around her? When my hands weren't drawn to her hands? When fighting with her didn't feel like the end of the world? When she wasn't untangling my life? When we weren't tangled together?

"No," I said. "I guess we never were *just*."

On our way out, we passed the vending machines filled with tiny plastic toys, cheap metal rings, Ninja Turtle tattoos, and mini Slinkys.

"Brace yourself," she said and kicked one of the machines over. The glass fractured on the floor, and she reached down to carefully extract two clear plastic capsules. She got down on one knee on the musty rug in the middle of glass and soda stains, and I got down on one knee across from her.

"Avery Devin Byrne," she said through a smartass grin. "From the moment you asked me to be your girlfriend four and a half minutes ago, I knew someday I'd be asking you to be my wife."

"That's a big commitment, Cass," I said, matching her expression. "I'm only nineteen."

"All the more time to be married, then, yeah?"

"I thought you don't believe in marriage as an institution because it's the hooks of the patriarchy latching on to—"

"Oh my God, Avery, say yes."

I kissed her. "Yes, Cass, I'll marry you."

"Dope."

"I hate you."

"You love me."

"I do." She put the rings on our fingers, hers black, mine blue.

Outside it was as dark as the inside of the theater, and though everything was the same, something had shifted between us. I was supposed to stop forgetting as we drove away from the theater. I was supposed to resume remembering that we were at the end. But I couldn't, and what was more, I didn't want to. I wanted to ride into more days than we had left. I wanted to grow big enough for New York City, or some city like it. I wanted to figure out what would keep me going day after day in my life, my new life braided with Cass's new one. Tangled, again.

"I don't want to go home yet," I said.

"Me neither. Let's go somewhere we can be alone."

"I know just the place."

We parked the car on the far end of the orchard, about half a mile away from our house. Cass chased me through the aisles. She caught me every so often and pulled me to the frozen ground. She pinned my hands above my head and kissed me too hard on the mouth. I wouldn't have cared if she'd drilled herself through me.

Beyond the apple trees, the frozen duck pond, the shuttered summer ice cream shop, there was a big red barn with a lock Peter had taught me how to pick with the help of any small twig. I pushed the door open and flipped on a row of white lamps suspended by electrical cords. The orchard owners, the Connor family, insulated the barn back when they were trying to turn it into a wedding space, but they never got the funding. The air was as hot as our breath. There was nothing inside except bales of hay, tractors, and the ghostly smell of blossoms and goats. We took off our jackets, laid them on the straw floor, and got on our knees. We kissed again, longer, harder.

Together, we pulled her shirt off, and her bare chest opened for me. I could have screamed, but instead I ran my hands up her until I held her. She leaned forward to kiss the center of my neck and lifted my sweater up over my head. We lay on our sides and pressed our skin together everywhere. I ran my fingertips over all of her, and she inhaled quickly. I moved down to kiss her nipples before sliding down even farther to hold her hips and unbutton her black jeans. She helped me slide them off and then took off her underwear. I kissed her thighs before sitting up for a minute to take off the rest of my clothes. To take her in. She raised her eyebrow as if to ask a question.

"You're perfect," I said to answer it. "So. Painfully. Perfect." I could hardly get the words out. She turned her head to the side and ran a hand through her hair before turning back to me.

"Avery," she said, reaching up for my hand, pulling me back down to kiss her again. "You have no idea." I shivered, and she rubbed my arm to warm me. Then she flipped me over, kissed her way down my body, pulled her hair back, licked her fingers, and started. My brain numbed and my blood warmed.

"Tell me what you like," she said.

And I did, and I did, and I did, until my whole body tensed, and my thighs shook. She held on to me while I came. I ran my hands through her hair.

"God, Cass," I said, as she kissed my legs and moved up to kiss my chest.

"God, Avery," she said. Before my breathing evened, I pushed her gently onto her back and spread her legs apart. She laughed a little and leaned back into the floor with her eyes on the ceiling. "Sometimes it takes a little while for me to cum," she said.

"Lucky for us," I said. "We have all the time in the

world." She laughed, but only once, ready for me to get started. I mimicked what she'd done on me for a bit, but I followed her lead as she guided me to where she wanted me to lick and suck and kiss. I cupped her hips with my hands. I mapped the ways I made her chest rise and fall.

"That's right," she said when my tongue found the right pacing. "Don't stop," she said, when I found the right place to pull. "God, Avery," she said again, when I put my fingers inside her and pressed. "Right there," she kept saying, "yes," until she shook in my hands and I felt her closing and opening on me until she melted into the floor.

We breathed heavily when I climbed back up to lie beside her, the hay under our jackets digging grooves into our skin. We were coated in sweat, smelling like each other, pressing our skin together, running our hands through each other's hair.

The electric lamp swung above us. It was the best thing I had ever done in this body. Cass was me, and I was Cass, and we were maybe dying. *And here*, I thought, *here I am. Finally alive.*

two months to impact

A lot of people were surprised when Cass announced she was going to Pratt Institute for fashion design, but I wasn't. I'd seen her sketchbooks, magazine collections, and collages, which she stockpiled under her bed and brought out whenever we were lying around.

When I told Peter, he scrunched his nose and said, "Cass? Like, Cass Cass?"

I understood what he meant, but still used the moment to be self-righteous on her behalf. "Why not Cass?"

He shrugged. "I've never seen her wear anything other than jeans or soccer shorts."

"She wore a suit to prom and her quinceañera."

"Okay, but fashion design?"

"She wants to design a fashion-forward, sustainable, affordable line for queer people."

"All righty then," he said. "I'm still going to give her a hard time about it."

"She'll expect nothing less."

In the beginning of December, right after she had broken up with Serenity, I went to visit her at Pratt—and technically Omar, too, since he was studying at Juilliard. It was my first time in New York City, and she took me to a party in a bright white gallery loft where everyone was so hip and so beautiful it stung. She wore brand-new faux leather pants I really wanted to touch. I felt like a middle schooler wearing jeans and an Eaton Soccer jacket. Every eye in the room flickered over me, as if to make sure I knew being an athlete didn't make me special. Was I even an athlete anymore? I crossed my arms, trying to be cool, or to at least disappear, but I audibly gasped when someone opened the curtains and, through the window, the Empire State Building sparkled in the night before us.

"What, you've never seen it before?" someone said.

"Just in pictures," I said, and there it was, capped with neon, so close I could almost touch it.

"It's literally just a tall building," said someone else. "So touristy."

Cass introduced me as her "friend from high school." I felt sick every time she said it. I met Birch, the girl in a kilt. Orion, whose hair was every shade of the rainbow. Daisy, the girl with three nose rings, impeccable eye makeup, and a shaved head. They orbited around Cass, hung on her every word. I felt both jealous and justified. I'd wanted nothing less for her, but I wanted that for me, too, and I hadn't found it at Eaton.

"Are you a lesbian too?" Daisy asked me.

"Oh," I said, thinking about Meredith, my ears getting hot. "I think so."

"You think so, huh?" She smirked a little. "That's so cute."

"She's definitely queer," Cass said loudly, almost as if to reassure Daisy. She handed me a clear plastic cup that reeked of liquor. "She came out to me senior year."

"Aw, she's a baby gay!" she squealed. It almost felt like I wasn't in the room anymore. I took a swig of whatever it was in the SOLO cup so I didn't have to say anything else.

Cass's friends drank things I'd never heard of: 99 Bananas. Triple sec. Hennessy. I'd psyched myself up to tell her that night how bad things really were, so much worse, even, than when she visited a few weeks earlier. I thought about telling her how I had failed, so completely. I thought about telling her how much I thought about suicide, which was most days and every night. I wanted to do it. I was going to do it. But wasn't it only fair, to give her a chance to talk me out of it? I planned on telling her after a drink or two, after my nerves were dulled and my inhibitions shot. But instead, I had three or four drinks of something green apple flavored, and I forgot what I wanted to say, exactly.

I didn't think Cass was purposely ignoring me, but she kept getting swept up in different conversations with random people, and I'd have to either worm my way in or stand there silently, smiling, pretending I knew what they were talking about. I went to the bathroom about a dozen times just to be able to breathe, just to have something to do. I prayed Omar would show up to the party like he said he was going to so I would have someone I at least trusted and knew. He didn't.

Although every single person in the room seemed like they were head over heels for Cass (myself included), Daisy seemed particularly obsessed with her.

"Don't you love Cass's new hair?" she said as she grabbed Cass's slick, straight ponytail with her fist and ran her hand down it. It looked like it hurt, but Cass's expression didn't change.

"Looks great," I lied. It did in theory, but it made her look like a stranger, and it kind of broke my heart. "I thought you always wanted to cut your hair short, though, Cass, when you went to college."

She opened her mouth to answer, but Daisy answered for her. "I told her she doesn't have the cheekbones for that."

I stared at Daisy and her own shaved head, and the liquor started to hit me.

"Cass has the cheekbones for anything," I slurred. "How dare you?"

"No, she's right," Cass said, and put her hand on the

small of my back to steer me away, like I was embarrassing her. "I look much better this way. Let's head out."

In the night air, just the two of us, it felt right again.
We felt like ourselves again. By that time, Cass and I
were drunk enough to pretend like we were drunk
enough to hold hands on our long walk back through the
sparkling, screaming city streets. We swung our arms.
Talked too loudly. Took up space. Puffed our breath into
the air. She stopped to show me places where she'd met
someone interesting or visited a designer's studio. We
stood still in Koreatown to scream-sing whatever song
was playing in a nearby karaoke bar. We stumbled into a
deli where a small old man greeted Cass by name and
sold us bagels from that morning for fifty cents.

"This is Ricardo," she said. "He's my pal." Cass's life
was suddenly everywhere, and there were so many people
in it. And yet, she was holding *my* hand. And *damn*, that
bagel was ridiculously good.

"Most of my friends are fashion goddesses," she said,
as we spilled into her dorm room. It was half the size of
mine, but somehow more charming. More homey. "But
as you saw, Daisy was wearing a straight-up bikini top in
December. I know she's intense, but she's really well connected and she likes me. I have to stay on her good side."
We kicked off our boots and climbed into her raised twin
bed with all our clothes on. We stared at the ceiling with
the lights still off.

"I mean, hey, her outfit was cool. Maybe she's ahead of our time," I said. "She can pull it off." I felt our legs cross under the blankets, and my heart quickened.

"Not much to pull off," Cass said. Her hand reached around for mine. I adjusted my position so she could find it. "Maybe she's actually Aquaman. That would be a good disguise. Or, what's the word? Alibi?"

"Alter ego?"

Cass finally found my hand, and squeezed. We turned to face each other, and I could feel her breath. My blood played a full-out concert on my eardrums. I thought I was going to kiss her. Was I going to kiss her?

Cass let go of my hand. She rolled away from me and turned toward the wall.

It felt like I'd been punched in the ribs.

"Hold me," she said.

I did. I wrapped my arms around her body. God, I had been so close, *so close* to kissing her. But holding her was just as good: I felt the heat of her back on my chest. Her shampoo smelled like lilacs. It blossomed in my lungs. Even when we'd shared beds in the past, we'd curled to the edges so there'd be enough space between us. We'd pretended like we needed that space. We'd pretended we wanted it.

Now, drunk as hell, we shut up and breathed and stopped pretending. I kissed her hair; I figured I could play it off as an accident if she jerked away. But she held on to my hands. She pushed back into me harder. I kissed her hair again, this time more obviously. My knees fit into the back of her knees. God, I'd waited years for this. But the moment was also tinged with something darker: a sense we were ruining something precious, because we could. Because we were careless and young and single and boozy. Because we were lonely. For a second, I forgot she deserved someone better than me, someone vibrant and alive and wanting. For a second, I allowed myself to want her. For a second, I hoped she might want me.

"Turn around," I said, my mouth going dry. She did, and we breathed into the inches between us. She was right there. All I needed to do was lean forward and meet her. She was right there, and all I had to do was believe someone like Cass could love someone like me, even when she had all those beautiful people to choose from. "Do you want this?" I asked. Her eyes searched mine, and I thought she might start to cry.

"I don't know, Avery. I—"

There was a knock at her door. We untangled ourselves quickly.

"Cass, it's Daisy," a voice said. "Are you there?"

"It's after midnight," Cass called back. "Are you okay?"

"I got locked out of my dorm. Again. Can I stay with you, angel? I'm cold as balls." Cass sighed and didn't look at me. She got up to open the door and flick on the light. Daisy came in, clutching her leather jacket closed over her bikini top. She stripped it off and hung it on the back of a chair.

"Avery," she said. "I forgot you were here." Sure she did.

"I am," I said. She looked harder at me on the bed.

"Oh God, did I . . . ?"

"No," Cass said. "Not at all." Ouch.

"We weren't, I mean, I have a sleeping bag," I said, unsure why I was defending myself.

"Good," Daisy said. "I cannot fall asleep on floors. And I love to cuddle. Especially with you." She started running her hands through Cass's ponytail, and I wanted to scream.

Cass looked at me apologetically but didn't say anything—and she didn't kick Daisy out. Instead, she helped me unfold my sleeping bag and positioned it in the tiny space between the twin beds, in case her roommate came back from whatever party she was at. I crawled inside and watched Cass climb into her own bed, where Daisy wrapped her arms around her, and Cass held on to her just as tightly. They fell asleep with their bodies pressed close together, a mirror image of me and Cass only minutes before. Hot tears pooled on my cheeks. It took all my energy to gulp down the sobs bubbling up like vomit.

Cass didn't need me anymore. And maybe I'd just ruined us forever.

Maybe that was okay. Maybe I should, once and for all, let her go. Let her be happy.

I gathered my things and slipped out the door as quietly as possible. I stood in the city streets, so different from my mountain town and evergreen school. I expected, I guess, for Cass to come after me. But she didn't. *How could she?* She didn't know I was running on my bruised knee down the blocks with open lungs and one last crumpled sob in my chest threatening to expand.

When I called Omar, he picked up. "Can I stay at your place tonight?"

"Sure," he said. "Why? Trouble in CaveryLand?"

"It's a long story," I said, but when I got there, he was half asleep. And I was grateful, because I didn't have to tell it.

six days to impact

Cass and I held hands driving home from the barn. My muscles felt so spent, and I fantasized about falling asleep in the basement on our mattress under the Christmas lights while my whole family and Aisha—and maybe Ray—slept around us. If Toronto was around ten hours from Kilkenny, and presuming Ray drove almost straight through, she should get to our house sometime the next day. I shivered with excitement for them.

As we pulled onto McIntosh Court and toward the cul-de-sac, I let my body relax in a way I couldn't ever remember feeling, not ever. I felt wanted. I was already home, and I was going home.

I slowed the car when I saw my house lit up in every room, the glare bright against the darkening sky. The front door was wide open. It was never wide open, and it looked wrong. My whole body iced, and a scream caught in my chest. I pulled over.

"Who the hell is that?" Cass said, pointing to the side of my house where someone had parked a black Escalade haphazardly on the lawn.

"I don't know." EDM music cut the night, and we ran toward the house and the sound, my raging blood distorting it into a haunted fun house soundtrack.

"Get back, get back!" I whispered as a man in a black jacket ran out the front door, a black trash bag clutched to his chest. We ducked behind some trees before he saw us, though we must have made a sound, because he looked up and dropped a corner of the bag. Cans rolled out and clinked on the brick walkway.

He bent over to pick them back up. Cass grabbed for me in the darkness and caught my wrist.

"What's our move, Ave?" she whispered.

"Where's everyone else?" I considered going to the Laskys', but they were the last people I wanted to put in danger, and what would they do? Who could they call and how? It was better to leave them alone. And Dr. Talley . . . By the time I got to his house and back, everything might be over.

Cass was shaking. I didn't know what was happening inside my house, but I knew I had to go in and help them. I didn't have a choice. It was my family; it was Aisha. I was disposable. It was okay if I didn't make it out.

"I'm going in," I said. Cass clawed for my arm, dug her fingers into it.

"You're not," she said. When I jerked to get away from her, she grabbed my face in her hands and pulled me until I was inches away from her. She rubbed one thumb across my cheek. "You're not."

"They could die," I said. "They could be hurt. We don't know what's happening."

"What are you gonna do? Go in and take out however many assholes are in there?"

I didn't have time to explain to her why I should be the sacrifice if we had to make one. I wrenched myself away from her and sprinted closer to the house. I heard her say my name behind me, a broken, gargled sound. I almost turned around, I almost stopped, but I didn't.

I could die, I knew that. It could have been the last time her breath was on my cheeks, the last time her eyes were my suns, but what choice did I have? I was the only one who could, who should, put myself in the middle of these people and my family.

The man had gone back into the house, and the blaring music masked any noise inside. I stepped into the unnatural light and onto the hardwood floor of our front foyer. I ducked into the dining room to the left just in time to miss someone climbing the stairs from the basement. From the weight and pacing of the shoes, I guessed it was another man, or perhaps the same man, carrying bags of all the things we'd carried home.

I heard muffled yelling in my parents' room, the farthest down the hall. I could pick out the accents: Irish. I slipped up the flight of stairs, cringing when one stair moaned beneath me. I slunk toward the door, and though I knew the steps well, white bursts of panic blurred my vision. What *was* my plan? To kick the door in and threaten someone who had been able to subdue multiple people? To climb onto the roof, manifest a grappling hook, swing feetfirst through the window? Without even the rough outline of a plan, I turned the copper knob and pushed it in.

Immediately two guns pointed at my face. I threw my hands up but stepped farther into the room. My parents were tied up with ropes on their bedroom chairs, and their heads snapped to look at me. Where was Aisha? Once my vision focused, I seized in fear.

"Clayton?" His face was as close to me as it had been when I danced with him on prom night, as close as it was to me at the end-of-the-world bonfire: his crooked teeth, shock of white-blond spiked hair, cold blue eyes.

"Avery Byrne," he said, lowering his gun for a second as my parents screamed my name. "Funny meeting you here." At least he wasn't drunk or high this time. The other guy, a stranger to me, though he looked like Clayton, pinned me to the floor and pushed his knee into my chest. I coughed until he eased up a little, enough for me to breathe.

"I'll do what you want," I said. "Let them go. Let them live."

"We're not going to kill anyone," Clayton said. "We're not monsters."

"So, what's your game?" I heard Mom asking from a mile away. "You're going around threatening to shoot people, raiding houses?"

"Pretty much," the strange guy said with a laugh. For fun, he shot three times at the ceiling. The kickback crushed me in three quick pulses. Plaster and dust rained down onto my parents, and I tried to scream, but the sound died in my chest where his knee dug in. My parents shook their heads to clear their eyes. I tried, again, to scream. In rage. In fear. But I could barely catch the air to breathe. *Is this what it will feel like, when it ends?* I thought. *Is this what it will look like—everything white with dust and ash?*

"Dammit, Nolan. Don't waste bullets," Clayton said. Nolan. His brother.

"Have a little fun," Nolan said, finally releasing me as he stood up. Clayton shot once, right above me, and plaster showered onto me too. We heard whooping from downstairs.

"That's it." Clayton lowered his gun. "Let's move."

"You're sick people," Dad cried as they started to leave the room, my parents still tied up with ropes. Clayton hustled after Nolan but paused in the doorway. He reached down into his pocket and threw me a pocketknife.

"Sorry, Avery Byrne," he said. "It's just . . . you owed me, right?" I crawled for the knife, flicked it open, and rushed to cut the ropes around my parents' wrists and feet. I could hardly do it. My hands shook with rage. "Hurry up," Clayton said. "I need that back." I clung to the pin-holes of my vision as I tossed the knife back to him.

"Clayton," I barked after him. He doubled back one more time. "If you see Cass, don't let them hurt her. Please."

"I'm not a monster, Avery Byrne," he said again.

I hoped she was still hiding or had gone to Peter's, that she loved herself enough not to follow me in.

The EDM music outside faded away into silence. My parents rubbed their reddened wrists. We stood together, the three of us, shaking. I tried to cry to get a piece of the ceiling out of my eye. I heard the gunshots ring in my head over and over.

"Are you okay, Avery?" Dad said.

"I'm fine," I said. "Are *you* okay? What happened? Where's Aisha?"

"We thought she was with you," Mom said. "Where were you?"

"Tell me what happened."

"Where were you?" she said, more frantically.

"I was at the movies with Cass," I said, and, without even mentioning the barn, knew it was a terribly wrong answer. She let out a strangled sob, and the grenade of guilt I was harboring detonated as I realized: I hadn't locked the door after I'd picked Cass up on our own front stairs.

It was my fault. I hadn't locked the door.

"Just tell me what happened," I pleaded.

"I woke up with a gun in my face," my mom said. "It was a man who smelled like cigarettes. He tied us to these chairs. And then they all went back downstairs."

Oh God.

I ran downstairs, and my parents followed me. In the bunker—could I even call it a bunker anymore?—we stood surrounded by shredded cardboard boxes, tipped-over milk crates, and upended apple cartons. The food we'd hoarded, saved—gone. The toys and art and games—gone. The sanitation supplies, the communication devices, the medications—gone. Our photographs, Cass's handmade flags, my collage scrapbook with all our tattered memories—gone, gone, gone. The blank pages would always stay blank, now. Pineapple the bunny remained, but he looked sad in his corner all alone. I couldn't breathe. It was all my fault, and now no one would survive. A wave of deep, heavy sadness surged in my chest and brought me to my knees. This was true, total heartbreak. This was horror.

"They took everything," Mom said. She was eerily calm, which told me she'd gone into military mode, a type of disassociation that was at the very least productive but at the very worst inhuman. She knelt to grab me by the shoulders.

"Go check on your brother and find the girls."

I felt like I did days ago, on the Eaton campus. I was eager to have something to do, someone to help. I hated myself so much, so deeply. All I wanted to do was sprint away from what I had done—the unlocked door, the empty basement. I ran toward the Laskys' and almost tripped on a tree root in the pathway between our houses. When I caught myself with my bone-bruised knee, I winced.

Their lights were on too. I knocked on the front door and called out so they'd know it was me. The door opened quickly, and Cass stood there like a statue. Her face crumpled as she turned and walked away from me. I followed her into the foyer and did a double take. The walls of the front hallway were splashed with colors—paint in bold jewel tones fumed and dripped as if the world were melting around me. The smell of it made me even weaker than I already felt.

In the kitchen, Peter and Georgia sat at the counter on barstools. Their complexions were paper white. It looked like Cass had walked in on something wild— Georgia was in her powder-blue prom dress, and it was splattered with paint. Cass hyperventilated, then fell into Georgia's arms, not mine. Peter crushed me against his chest, and held me for too long before letting me go.

"They took everything," I said.

"Fuck," Peter said, and I couldn't quite read his tone.

"More like 'fuck you,'" Cass said, lifting her head. I bristled.

"Excuse me?"

"Why did you go in, Avery? Why?"

"I was the one who left the door unlocked, Cass. And my parents were in there. I had to."

"You didn't *have* to do anything." Her voice dropped to a whisper. "You know what *I* had to do? I had to listen to four gunshots. Four. And I had to do the math on that."

She pushed past me into the bathroom and slammed the door. I looked at Peter's and Georgia's faces: pale, empty, and I knew. I'd made a mistake coming home from Eaton. I'd ruined everything for everyone. Of course I had.

"Is Aisha here?"

"No," Georgia said.

"So," Peter said, "everything?"

"All of it." I didn't mean to whisper. "Everything."

Georgia stared at Peter and seemed to communicate something with her eyes he understood and I didn't. We could start again, but there was no way we could recover what we'd had. We could already taste our exhaustion, and resources were scarcer every time we left the house. Peter reached out, pulled me into them. I could smell the paint striped on their clothing.

"I'm sorry, Avery," he said. He wept into my hair. "I'm sorry," he said again.

I couldn't breathe, otherwise I would have asked questions. I couldn't speak, otherwise I would have said I was sorry too. I couldn't do anything at all except lean into them, feel his tears on my cheek, and fall carefully, perfectly, completely apart.

one month
to impact

By winter break—before the asteroid, before the river— I'd decided I would never be happy again. I would never even be okay. I hadn't told my parents about my failing grade. I hadn't told them I would probably never play soccer again. I had completely forgotten how to hope for anything, and the thought of living through another semester brought me to my knees. The depression was more physical than anything. I was so fatigued that any spark of life genuinely surprised me. So sad, any lick of happiness stung.

I remember the night I last felt that sting. Winter break was almost over. We were celebrating my birthday early, though it wasn't for another few weeks. We were doing it because I had to go back to campus, but also because we always celebrated it early or late. Since my actual February birthday was the anniversary of Aunt Devin's death, Mom could never hold it together. She always spent that day in her bedroom crying, and I didn't blame her. Most years I wanted to lock myself in my own room and cry too. It felt like the date meant something, like it was my fault somehow.

It felt like I would be, should be, next.

But on my fake birthday, I stood in our wood-paneled kitchen, watching Cass and Peter hold blowtorches. It was the first time I'd seen Cass since I visited her in NYC. It was the first time I'd *talked* to Cass since I visited her, since she had made it abundantly clear I was no longer a star in her life. Though things were cold between us, we were pretending they were normal because it was my birthday and the unspoken rule is when it's someone's birthday, you suck it up and behave. Still, I was surprised she'd bothered to come at all.

She wore her New York uniform: tight black pants, loose black button-down shirt, and a long silver necklace that danced down the center of her chest. Long, slick ponytail. She and Peter bumped shoulders, laughed together, and I stayed a few feet away because I didn't want to get burned. Dad looked on as they shot out flames, a small smirk on his face, not chastising them but not encouraging them either. Peter turned into his high school self when he was around Cass, which I both loved and hated. She held a blowtorch out to me.

"Fancy a light, Avery?" Her eyes didn't leave the flame. I shook my head.

"I'm good," I said, but no one heard me under Peter howling, "Burn like the fires of hell!"

Mom ran down the stairs to yell about Peter's language, and her irritation snapped to horror when she saw the scene on the counter. The white icing she and Dad had carefully covered in strawberry slices had been staked and flambéed.

"You'll burn the house down!" she yelled.

"We won't," Peter said, shooting me an amused glare. "It's fine."

"We are internet-ly-trained professionals," Cass added.

My father shrugged. He didn't like confrontation, but he was entertained by Cass and Peter's shenanigans. Sometimes he'd join in even when I didn't.

"It's not fine," Mom said, but she folded her arms in defeat and came to stand by my side. "This is Avery's birthday, not yours."

"Unbirthday!" Peter said, and Mom glared at him. She didn't like to be reminded why we always picked a random date.

Once the wicks were lit and the candles melted into hooks and puddles between strawberry slices, Dad put his arm around my shoulder and Mom hit the light switch. The oak and granite of the kitchen flickered and faded, but the five of us stood solid. In the darkness, our faces caught the cake shine like little plastic planets hanging from a mobile.

"The big nineteen," Peter said, folding his arms across his old UNH Manchester sweatshirt. Georgia was at home with a sick Teddy, who'd been vomiting all day with no end in sight. Peter looked as exhausted as I felt, his brown, curly hair haphazardly pushed out of his face and his eyes framed by shadows, but his smile didn't waver even when he yawned. Cass swung her arms to orchestrate a harmonized version of "Happy Birthday," but my family wailed miserably, and she covered her ears in mock disgust.

It was the first time we'd all been together in a while, just us, just like that. I almost never got to go home because of soccer, and the two times I did, we were almost never in the same room, or even in the same house. Peter's family was, rightfully, his priority. My parents had filled their empty nest by becoming even more involved at Our Lady of Mercy. They had started to move on, which I understood. Which I wanted.

I blew on the sheet of fire and put out every candle on the first try. Peter stuck a blue one bottom-first in his mouth.

"Wacha wish for?" he asked.

My heart chilled. It hadn't occurred to me to wish for anything, but I couldn't tell him or any of them I didn't want anything. Not anymore.

"If I say it," I said, "it won't come true."

"You know, you can't *ask* the universe for what you want; you have to *demand* it."

"Behold," Cass said with arms outstretched, "the straight, white, cisgender male." Peter grabbed a fistful of unused candles to chuck at her. "Such a majestic creature! So entitled! So commanding! So brave! Ow!"

"Get out of here," Peter said, but his smile, impossibly, grew wider.

A strawberry burned the roof of my mouth. I savored it.

After cake, my brother dragged me outside to set off Roman candles. I stood on the graying wood of our porch in my sweatpants as Cass and Peter ran down the stairs to the grass. They knelt beside the neat stack of firewood, the landscape of my life stretched out behind them: our little yard, our sledding hill, and the Purple Finch Apple Orchard sleeping under the stars. Cass tilted the red paper candle toward the trees with her steady hands. Peter struck a match against a log and carried the flame across his chest, where it whistled and wiggled in anticipation. I looked at the black canvas sky as they chanted quietly:

"Three . . . two . . . one . . ." Then the bullets roared, glittered, shivered, and hung themselves near the moon.

I could have told Peter and Cass right then, on my last birthday, in the orchard, how completely lost I felt, how suicidal. Peter was great with secrets, but not when he was worried about me, and of course he would be. And Cass? I'd tried to tell her in New York, I did. But the distance between us had been expanding each and every day since then. There, under the pink-and-white lights of the fireworks, she felt planets away.

When the smoke cleared, Cass wordlessly handed me a flashlight, her fingers brushing mine, her smug smile one I almost recognized. Peter gestured for us to follow him. It was frigid outside, and frost kissed the ground, but we chased each other through jagged rows of apple trees, trying to tag each other. My eyes danced between the fading grass and the open night before me, and I ran quickly but carefully to avoid loose roots or rogue iced cores. My left knee ached with each step. When I looked up, my light caught on a figure between the aisles of apple trees. Cass. She let her own light splash across my face. "You got me, but I got you too!"

For a split second, there it was: My brain soaked with serotonin. My eyes welled up with some sort of vague, beautiful hope. There it was for the first time in such a long time—not happiness, exactly, but something that lodged in my chest like an amethyst. It was there, painfully, and then it was gone, and it carved a cavern bigger than the one there before.

Suddenly, I couldn't see Cass, or my brother, and I didn't know where they'd gone.

"Come back," I whimpered, but I knew the feeling wouldn't.

They wouldn't.

They'd darted off into the night, smiling and shouting, heading for the orchard's lookout tower, where Peter had hidden his weed in high school.

"Come on, Avery!" Cass called. That should have hooked me, but it didn't. I stayed where I was, and they kept running, and it was okay. It was right. It was how it had to be.

Instead of following them, I walked back to the street. All three houses on the cul-de-sac were asleep but still glowing. The light in Peter's house looked gold, warm, and insular. I imagined him going home to be with Georgia, their baby monitor crackling beside them as they drifted off into each other. I knew I'd never have that. I wasn't going to make it to that. I felt that if there were tomorrows for me, I would surely be able to taste them.

I stood there for however long I could without moving, letting the pain register in my brain and the cold in my ribs. I heard Peter and Cass calling my name, but all I could do was stand there and cry, because everything was so beautiful, and I didn't know how to feel it.

I walked in moonlight back to my house.

Cass and Peter were slouched against the railings of the back porch.

"Where've you been?" Cass said, but she couldn't stop giggling.

"What's so funny?"

"Ugh, don't worry about it," Cass said.

"Cass was just telling me all about her scandalous life in New York," Peter added. He gave her a knowing look.

"I'm sure she was," I said bitterly. I walked into my kitchen and toward the stairs. She caught me in the living room.

"Avery," she said. "What's your problem?"

"What's *my* problem?" I bit my lip and simmered. "My problem is you talking to my brother about other girls on my porch on my birthday. Especially after what happened in New York."

"First of all, I was not talking about other girls. Second of all, it's not actually your birthday." When I turned to leave, she grabbed my arm gently to make me stay. "Wait. What happened in New York is my friend locked herself out of her room, Ave. It was cold out. That's it. That's all." I could almost feel the tile of her floor on my back again. Could almost hear her friend's laugh as she crawled into bed with Cass, where they both slept on the embers of my body heat.

"You could have kicked her out. You could have made her sleep on the floor."

"What, in *your* sleeping bag?"

"Oh my God," I said. "Forget it. You're missing the point."

"Ave," she said. "What *is* the point?"

I wanted to say, *We almost kissed and then we didn't.* But I was scared my parents would hear it. I wanted to say, *You're selfish.* But she wasn't, not really. She had no obligation to love me in the way I loved her. I wanted to say, *You broke my heart that night.* But that was unfair, too, since I hadn't even told her how I felt about her.

I wanted to say, *I love you* and *I'm going to kill myself soon,* and *I am so sorry for how that will hurt you.*

Instead, I said, "The point is, I don't even like you anymore. No, I hate you right now, Cass. I hate who you're becoming in New York."

Instead, I watched her face fall. She took a few steps away from me.

"Wow," she said. "Wow."

A silence bloomed between us and pushed us apart. She left the room and didn't look back. And I thought, *Well, good.* She could stand on my porch with Peter, and they could laugh together, the two of them so happy, the two of them taking in everything they deserved. The two of them the way they'd be when I was gone, except for maybe when they'd cry in their bedrooms like my mother did once a year.

My parents were already in bed, heads down and dreaming. I didn't get in trouble for coming in too late.

I didn't wake anyone up as I slipped under my covers, drenched in every type of salt. I stayed up thinking about Cass, about how she looked as she ran away from me. How I would never see her again.

I stayed up thinking about the thing my family never talked about. What Devin Did on my real birthday. The thing *I'd* decided to do on my real birthday when I got back to school, because it felt fitting. Because it was the one gift I could give myself. *I'm so tired. I'm such a disappointment. I don't want to do this anymore. I could kill myself. I want to. I can. I might.*

I will.

I didn't sleep. It didn't matter. Morning came anyway.

six days to impact

In the harsh light of the Laskys' kitchen, I kept replaying the night on a loop: Picking Cass up for the movie. Driving away, the unlocked door behind us. Loving her in the barn while my parents were tied to chairs. The gunshots, the plaster that still clung to my hair. All of it, everything, was my fault, and I knew it. I should have locked the door. I should have. *I never should have come home in the first place*, I thought. *I shouldn't be here. Maybe then this wouldn't have happened. Everyone would have stood a chance.* Peter and Georgia held on to me too tightly, and Cass hid from me in the bathroom. I couldn't breathe.

"I have to find Aisha," I said, untangling myself from their limbs. She was probably at Dr. Talley's, but I had to know for sure.

I rang the doorbell at the Davidsons' old house, and Scout barked until Dr. Talley peeked out of the upstairs window, then shut the shades. A minute later, I was sitting in the kitchen chair where I'd sat years earlier after almost drowning in the Davidsons' pool, dripping wet, wrapped in a towel, while Mrs. Davidson called my parents.

Dr. Talley put two glasses in front of me. One with water that tasted too much like grass, another of whiskey. I was about to remind him I wasn't twenty-one yet, but then I remembered myself, this new world where the rules had shifted. Scout curled up at my feet and thumped her tail against the wood floor.

"Where's Aisha?"

Dr. Talley put a finger to his lips. It had only been a few days since I last saw him, but it seemed like he'd lost weight. His hair was stringy, greasy, uncombed. His sweater vest was on inside out. I ran my hands through my own hair self-consciously. Did I look just as ragged and sour?

"She's in the office upstairs. She fell asleep on the laptop keyboard waiting for the internet to come back. I put a blanket on her. She has since moved to the couch." We both sipped our whiskey and water and averted our eyes.

"Your Wi-Fi's not working?"

"It *was* working," he said. He tapped on his phone a bit. "Now it's not."

"Do you know if she got in touch with her sister?"

"I believe she got an email out, yes."

"Thank God," I said. "I don't know what we're going to do if Wi-Fi's out permanently."

He chuckled. "I spent much of my life without Wi-Fi," he said. "You'll manage."

He may have meant it to be encouraging, but it felt condescending. My familiar rage toward him returned, but I swallowed it with a side of whiskey.

"What have you been doing here?"

"Reading, mostly. Writing here and there. Walks with Scout."

"What's the point of writing right now?"

He stared at me blankly. "What's the point of writing ever?"

"There may not be anyone to read it."

"You assume to know the entire future of human existence. Also, curious you assume I write for other people. Writing is an act of worship, of study, of care."

"Is this another thing your therapist had you do?" My question sounded terribly earnest, and I felt a little spark of shame. "Along with morning river walks?" *And what else do they say?* I wanted to ask, but stopped myself.

"Actually, yes. I try to reach outside myself, even when I'm alone. Inside myself, well. That's a darker tale." He poured more whiskey into my glass, and though I knew I should protest, I didn't. I should go help my parents, help the Laskys, reconcile with Cass. I should go upstairs and wake Aisha and tell her—oh God, oh God, I would have to tell her—that everything was gone. Just in time for her sister's arrival. I took another swig and let it burn.

"Why were you depressed?" I asked.

"Why is anyone depressed?"

Hell if I knew. It was in the soil of who I was as a person. It wasn't something that had roots and therefore a way to weed it out.

"Most people have reasons, though, right?" Most people were justified in feeling the way they did. Most people weren't like me.

"My wife died ten years ago. My days are tedious. I live a life of isolation."

"I'm sorry about your wife," I said, and felt, strangely, like I wanted to hug him. I didn't.

"She was a tremendous woman. An excellent poet. She, too, taught at Eaton. Died of cancer. Can't imagine what she would think of all this." It made sense, then, why he might be miserable, depressed. He'd suffered a huge loss. He did have a reason, after all. Unlike me. I took another sip of whiskey.

"Did you ever try to kill yourself? After she died?"

"No."

"Why not?"

"That would be like typing 'The End,' at the beginning of my third act. Structural travesty."

I nervously swirled my whiskey glass, and the single ice cube in its center clinked in our silence. "I was at the river that morning," I said. "You were right about that."

He studied me. "Are you trying to get me to ask you why?"

"No," I said quickly, though I guess I was. The whiskey had started to burn through the puppet strings holding me up.

He sighed. "Why were you at the river?"

"I was going to drown myself," I said. Who was he going to tell?

"You're a much better writer than that." His cruel comments on my papers blazed in my brain. I felt the water rising to my eyes, but I tried to push it down.

"Do you even remember me from class?"

"Of course."

"I was struggling so much. You were kind of mean to me." The words sounded silly leaving my mouth. I felt like a petulant child.

"I did not see your depression," he said, "because you did not show me your depression."

"I couldn't get my papers done. I stopped coming to class. You told me I was lazy and uninspired and entitled."

"Correct. You seemed lazy and uninspired and entitled."

"You failed me without even asking questions."

"You deserved a failing grade." When I said nothing, he continued: "My job was to teach you about American literature, not to counsel you through depression or proactively monitor your well-being. When I called you lazy and uninspired, did you come to me and say, 'I'm depressed'?"

"Obviously not."

"I was a despondent, weary professor. Not a mind reader, licensed therapist, or doctor. Did you see my depression?"

He was as smug as ever, but I felt myself soften toward him. I hadn't seen his depression, of course. I hadn't bothered to consider it.

"No," I said, "but you were the adult in the situation."

"I hate to break it to you, Avery," he said, "but you are also an adult now. A brilliant one. Your technical skills needed improvement, but you knew how to write about the endless spectrum of human emotions, suffering not least among them. It is not preposterous I assumed you would communicate with me if you needed to."

I bit my bottom lip to keep from crying, and bit harder because I hated myself for breaking down in front of him.

"You're right," I said, once I'd steeled my throat. "I guess I just . . . needed you to see me."

"You have to allow yourself to be seen. How many people have you told about the severity of your depression?"

"Only Aisha," I admitted. "And then, not fully." He raised his water glass to me.

"Before you were lazy and uninspired in my class, you were passionate and inspired. Did you have to go to Eaton? Who made that choice?"

"I got into an Ivy League school. How do you not go?"

"Easily, if it's not the right place for you. If you can't afford to be happy there."

"I couldn't have known." My voice trembled remembering how hopeful I was, how beautiful the grass and brick and open sky looked on my first day. How convinced I was that everything could change for the better. It only got so much worse.

"I understand there's pressure—parents, society, money, our desire to be successful above all else—but I'd imagine your parents would rather have a college dropout daughter than a dead one." I stared into my glass, and I couldn't help myself. My tears finally fell. He reached over to rub my shoulder quickly and awkwardly, and his voice softened. "There are things in life we can't control. There are circumstances we cannot escape. Eaton College is not one of them. You could have transferred. You could have found another path. College is far from the only path to a successful, happy life."

"I couldn't transfer, not with the F you gave me. And it wasn't really about Eaton. I would have drowned anywhere."

"It seems to me like you've been functioning quite nicely in Kilkenny. All things considered."

"I have purpose here."

"Purpose?"

"Helping everyone with the bunker. Loving Cass."

"In other words, living for others." Why did people keep saying that?

"No. They've done things for me too."

"I didn't say they haven't done anything for you. I'm saying *you* haven't done anything for you."

I opened my mouth to protest but couldn't find words.

"And couldn't you have made that your life? Helping people? Maybe you wouldn't have been rich, but you could have made a living working for a nonprofit, diving into journalism, working as a community organizer."

"I tried to get involved at school. Everyone was better than I was. At everything. I couldn't even get a volunteer shift."

"Do you understand how big the world is? How small you are? How little a handful of no means? You have to get up and look for yes. The world is yours for the taking."

I heard Cass's words from my unbirthday ringing in my head, and I smiled despite myself: *Behold, the straight, white, cisgender male.*

"There's nothing I want," I said slowly. "Nothing I wish for."

"At the bonfire, you said you wanted to go back to Eaton. That you had unfinished business."

"I meant killing myself."

"You could kill yourself anywhere. I don't think that's what you meant."

"It is what I meant."

"Fine," he said, wearily, "but you're still alive. You keep making that choice." He yawned, tilted his head back, and poured the rest of his whiskey down his throat. I mirrored him, poured my own glass down my open throat.

"Dr. Talley, why did you come here anyway? Why didn't you leave us in Boston?"

"Though it's not my *job* to ensure the safety of my students, I actually do care. Despite what you think of me, I wanted to make sure you and Aisha got out alive." Or was it that he was lonely too? Or was it that he was terrified?

"Thanks, I guess," I said. "I should go." I stood up and startled the dog. "If Aisha wakes up, will you tell her I'll come back for her? Maybe tell her to sleep here for a little bit?"

He raised his eyebrows. "Is there something I should know about?"

"Some men broke into our house. Took everything. I want to tell her myself." He offered me more whiskey, but I declined it. I had to go. I had to talk to Cass.

I was breathless and dizzy by the time I got back to my brother's house. Georgia let me in after I knocked on their door again.

"Peter's up with Teddy," she said. As I walked through the hallways of their home, I was able to process what I hadn't before: The walls were painted into murals with outrageous reds, punching blues, and simple golds. On one wall, a beautiful, devastating willow tree. On another, flowers grew from the ears of a little boy who had planted himself in an orange clay pot. In the kitchen, colors bled into other colors like waves and a sun set deep into the water.

"Damn," I whispered, touching a wall to see if the paint was dry. My fingertips came away clean.

"Do you like it?" Georgia asked, her voice tinged with a tired joy.

"I love it," I said. I meant it. They had painted every wall and ceiling and door perfectly, brilliantly. Splotches of color stained the rugs and soaked into patches on furniture.

"When did you do this?"

"Yesterday," she said. "Last night. Today."

"Why?"

"Don't you ever just want to leave a mark?"

I touched another wall with my fingertips, and when I pulled them back to me, they were wet with blue paint. I streaked it across my jeans. "Who's it for?"

"What do you mean? It's for us."

It was like everyone knew they were worthy of art except for me. She caught my arm in the hallway and looked me in the eyes.

"You're going to be okay, Avery," she said. "No matter what. You hear me?" I nodded, but it caught me off guard. Exhaustion washed over me. I looked at my watch and saw it was after 2 a.m. As if time mattered.

I found Cass in their living room curled up on the couch, a bottle of white wine in her fist. Her eyes were red, and she barely looked at me when I sat next to her. Sufjan Stevens played on their speakers, and I wanted to crawl out of my skin.

"Aisha's asleep at Dr. Talley's," I said.

"Okay," she said, still not looking at me.

"We should sleep too."

"Why?"

"It's late."

"So?"

"I need to report back to my parents. Are you coming or not?"

"I'll sleep here," she said simply.

"Fine," I said. I tried to kiss her good night, but she pulled away and balled up into the corner of the couch. I wanted to unfold her, but I didn't know how. How could she not understand my parents needed me too? Especially now?

I found my parents still awake and assured them everyone was fine, as if any of us were fine. Mom scrubbed muddy boot prints out of the white carpet upstairs. Dad swept the basement where broken glass, dust, and dirt gathered in small piles. The Christmas lights still twinkled around us.

"We'll start again tomorrow," Dad said, but I knew he couldn't mean it.

"Dad, what can I do to help?" He stopped sweeping and wiped sweat from his forehead. I could still see the rope burn on his wrists.

"Get some sleep, sweetheart. The work will be here in the morning."

I wanted to argue, but my body had started to shut down, maybe in part because of the whiskey. I could barely keep my eyes open. As I trudged up the two flights of stairs to my bedroom, I had to use the railings to pull myself up each step.

I wondered, obsessively, if Cass hated me for leaving her at Peter's, but when I woke up in a cold sweat hours later, her head was on my chest, her hand was on my hip, and she was drooling on my T-shirt.

I lay there pulsing. I tried to practice the words for a morning apology: *I'm sorry for luring you home when you could be with more beautiful people in a more beautiful city living the rest of your life with sparkle and burning and novelty.*

Instead, she was here with me in a house that was no longer a bunker, no longer a home. Instead, she was here with just me. Just me. How could that ever be enough?

five days to impact

I woke up to Cass's hand under my shirt, my legs wrapped around hers, and the sound of someone sobbing from a floor away. It took me a minute to shake sleep, but once I did, I bolted upright.

"What is it?" Cass whispered.

"Aisha," I said. "Oh, no." Apparently, she hadn't heeded my warning to stay at Dr. Talley's until I went to get her, and why would she? That had been my wishful thinking at best—cowardice at worst—and now she was here. Her sister could be here any hour now, and she would arrive to *this*. I pulled myself out of the covers.

"Where are you going?" Cass said.

"To comfort her." Wasn't that obvious?

"What about me?" I'd assumed her body on my body meant she had forgiven me for running into the house the night before. For leaving her behind. For risking myself. I assumed wrong. I lay back on the bed and tried in vain to ignore my friend's crying. I put my hand on Cass's cheek, and she pushed it away. How could I apologize sincerely? I didn't regret what I did. I would do it again.

"I'm sorry I scared you," I said. "I didn't know what else to do." She grabbed my hand and put it back on her cheek. Her skin was so soft.

"You could have died," she said. "I'd have no one, Ave. I'd be alone. I'd die alone."

"I mean, you'd still have the Laskys and Aisha and—"

"Jesus Christ," she said. "You really don't get it, do you?"

"Get what?"

"Who you are to me. *What* you are to me. I thought we were each other's first priorities. I thought we were a team of two. You ran off into a fucking heist without even thinking about what might happen to me."

"That's not what happened, Cass. I was worried about everyone in the house. I didn't think it was either-or. How could I have known they had guns? How could I have known it was Clayton?"

"Holy shit, it was Clayton?"

"I didn't mention that?"

"Why don't you tell me anything?"

"This is the first time we're even talking about it."

"Why don't you tell me *everything*?"

"What are you talking about?"

"Why does Aisha call you the queen of secrets?"

I looked away from her. Wasn't this the moment? The moment I should tell Cass about the river? She was practically begging me. But she was already so mad at me.

"Remember? She said it because I didn't tell anyone I'm queer at school."

She put her head in her hands and massaged her forehead. Aisha's sobs continued to slip under our door.

"Fine, go be with her," she said. She didn't have to tell me twice. I ran from that room, from the chance to tell her anything real.

In the kitchen, Aisha sat at the table with her head bowed. My parents looked relieved when they saw me. They'd already told her what happened, obviously, so the only thing left for me to do was sit beside her and feel guilty.

"We'll fix it," I said, and even before she leveled me with a withering glare, I knew it was the worst thing I could say.

"Stop fixing," she whispered, but she grinned a little too. "You are unbelievable."

"Shit, sorry," I said.

"Stop swearing," Mom said at the exact same time

Aisha said, "Stop apologizing." There was nothing I could do to make things better. There was nothing left to fix. Everything I did made things worse, for everyone. I was so tired and frustrated I wanted to cry too, but this was Aisha's grief, not mine. And it was all my fault. I wanted to disappear. *I could. I should . . .*

"Did you email your sister last night? At Dr. Talley's?"

"Yes," she said. "I said she should still come here. She has a map and a car. When she's going to get here is anyone's guess, though."

"Maybe today?" I asked.

"Maybe, but I can't think like that." Aisha inhaled sharply.

The doorbell rang, and our eyes went wide with surprise or hope or fear. All four of us jumped up to answer it, but Cass ran down the stairs and beat us.

The Laskys stood on the steps, even though all three of them had keys to this house.

"Can we come in?" Peter asked, and Cass stepped aside to let them.

"What can I get you?" Mom said. "We still have some apple pie, would you like that?"

"It's okay," Peter said. "Can we get everyone in the living room?" My heart sank. He'd gathered everyone in the living room when he announced they were pregnant with Teddy, when they rented the house next door, when their cat, Butterfly, was put to sleep.

After we all sat down on chairs or couches, Georgia and Peter looked at each other, speaking without saying a word. Teddy sat on Peter's lap, his eyes glued to a picture book. My parents both looked like they hadn't slept for even an hour. Mom's hair, usually brushed and flowing, was balled up in a scrunchie on her head.

"Come out with it," she said. "What do you have to say?" Peter breathed for a few seconds. He was shaking.

"We wanted to stay here," he said, "for a chance to survive. But now that survival is off the table, we're going to New York."

"I want to see my parents again," Georgia said. "We've been living here. We haven't seen them since Chanukah. It's only fair."

"We could drive to Brooklyn and get them," Mom said. "We can all be here."

"It's not just that, though," Peter said quickly, but he'd started to cry. "I can count on one hand the times I've left New England. Same for Teddy."

"It was nice pretending with the bunker and all," Georgia said, "but that's gone. It's as dangerous here as it is anywhere else."

My brother was leaving. They were all leaving. I might never, ever see them again.

"We weren't pretending," Dad said, but there was no bite in his voice. "There was a chance. There still is."

"We may have nothing except for a few days."

Georgia's eyes were big and wild. She twisted her ruby wedding ring. Her tattoos were smudged more than usual. "We want to make the most of them." If Teddy knew what they were talking about, he didn't let on. He turned the page of his book and smiled at me conspiratorially.

"If cell phones and Wi-Fi don't come back," Dad said, "we'll never be able to talk to you again."

It was my fault. For leaving the door unlocked. Karmic retribution for the pool and the river and everything else I'd ever done. But wasn't it also right? They *should* go see Georgia's parents. They'd been living with my parents all this time. She was right, it was only fair.

"We might never see you again," Mom said. *And it was my fault.*

"We might never see Teddy again," Dad said. *And that was my fault too.* A full minute went by before Peter finally looked them in the eyes.

"I know," he said, "and we want to be with you all in the end, but we can't. I'm so sorry."

"Can't we come with you?" Cass asked. "Avery and me and your parents and Aisha and Ray and—"

"We're not leaving the house," Mom said.

"I have to wait for my sister," Aisha said.

"I don't agree with this," Dad said. "It's not right."

"What's right, Dad? Nothing is the same anymore," Peter said. "I have to do what's right for my family."

As if we were no longer a part of it.

"We're thinking of leaving tomorrow night," Georgia said. My vision tunneled.

"We were thinking tomorrow we could have one more perfect day with you all," Peter said. "Will you come to the beach with us?"

I couldn't bring myself to speak. I didn't cry, because I knew if I started, I wouldn't stop until the earth made me. I pumped my lungs with sheer willpower.

"Sandcastles!" Teddy said then. His eyes were alight, sparkling, wanting. I never, ever, ever wanted their light to go out. I wanted them to see everything this world had to offer. In fact, I wanted that more desperately than anything I'd ever wanted: for him to love this world in the ways I couldn't.

"We'll come to the beach," Mom said, but she promptly ran out of the room, probably to cry in her bathroom. Dad followed her, and Cass, Aisha, and I were left alone with the Laskys in a sickening silence.

"At least you all have each other," Peter said. "Ray is coming, and Avery, you have Cass and . . ." He trailed off, probably knowing what he was saying was nonsense. No one could ever replace him. Cass held my hand, but I couldn't feel my body.

"We should go," Georgia said. "We have a lot to do."

My mom reappeared in the doorway in a completely different outfit: a floor-length cotton dress with faded blue flowers. She ran a brush through her hair.

"If you're leaving us," she said, "you're going to do one more thing for me."

"What's that?" Peter said.

"We're all going to church."

I wanted to groan out loud but thought better of it. Georgia did groan audibly, but it was quiet enough so Mom wouldn't hear.

Our Lady of Mercy, we'd learned previously, had also been raided and set aflame. It was on fire for over twenty-four hours before collapsing in on itself. A man had died trying to save the Jesus nailed to the cross above the altar. The congregation had started holding midday vigils in Manchester with other demolished churches along the Merrimack River.

"I'll stay here," Aisha said, "in case Ray arrives."

"You can't be here alone," Mom said.

"I'll be fine," she said, and she said it with such authority we believed her.

"We'll pray for you," Mom said.

"Thank you," she said and smiled softly, "and I'll pray for you too."

After lunch—bread and peanut butter that had been stored at Peter's—everyone except for Aisha got ready. It took me three tries to find an outfit my parents deemed appropriate (we settled on blue pants and a button-down), and then we all piled into trucks and cars. Mom was tight-lipped as she drove the freezing, whistling Volvo down the battered highway. I sat in the back with Cass, feeling both nothing and so much it made me weak.

We pulled up to the edge of the Merrimack River and parked along the concrete walkway as the Laskys parked their truck beside us. The redbrick buildings that had once been textile mills, a home to so much pain, seemed sleepy now. Resigned.

We had to walk half a mile to get to the site where members of Our Lady of Mercy's parish and others had congregated next to Amoskeag Falls. A few dozen people were standing in clusters by the dam, watching the water tumble over into the slushy body of the river.

When we got to the crowd, parishioners handed candles to everyone except for Teddy even though the sun was still white in the sky. Every so often the wind would extinguish one and we'd relight it with the others. We watched the flames live and die, catch and pop. As clouds covered the winter sun, the little lights got brighter, stronger, steadier. Their smoke seemed angry. Their wax dripped onto fingers. When a man had a panic attack a few feet away from us, everyone with candles formed a circle around him as he crouched on the ground, head in his hands.

"The Lord is with you," they all said. "The light of the Lord is with you." I bit my lip, unable to believe them, but the man's breathing settled slowly, and he was soon able to stand. Dad blew his candle out so he could hold Teddy. Mom wrapped her arms around Peter and Georgia. Father Aiden climbed on the concrete ledge of a fence and began to speak. He looked like a young soccer dad in jeans and a fleece jacket, the only indication of his priesthood evident in the clergy shirt poking out from underneath.

"Good afternoon," he said, and then again, louder, "good afternoon!" The voices around us echoed his call, then hushed. "I feel blessed you are able to join us today for this celebration of life, for this time to honor the people we have lost, and to anticipate our journey home to our Heavenly Father and Lord Savior Jesus." The crowd murmured amens and hallelujahs. "There will be no communion today, because we lost everything in the fire, but we should not despair. For Jesus has given us his body time and time again, and soon it will be our turn to return our flesh to him."

Cass and I raised our eyebrows. She placed her hand on the small of my back. I looked to see if my parents noticed anything, but they weren't looking at us. I leaned into her.

"Now, you're used to me preaching, and you all know me—if you wanted me to, I could stand up here and talk until the end of time. But we are people of God and we've read his words. You've listened to mine. I want to hear yours too. We've been here to spread the word of Jesus

Christ of Nazareth, and we are here to bear witness to each other. If there's anything you'd like to confess to me privately, I'll be here all night, but if there's anything you'd like to share with the congregation—a favorite memory, a hope for the future, a Bible passage—I'll open up the floor."

The first to speak was a woman who talked about cheating on her husband. She talked about what she'd learned from it, how regretful she was, how she found the grace to forgive herself, and how she hoped she'd still be let into Heaven. I could only hear every other word she said, because the river raged behind her. More people got up with Father Aiden to speak about their children, their hopes for the afterlife, and the people they'd missed along the way. My stomach clenched when my mother moved away from us to stand in the speaker's line. I made a face at Peter, but he shrugged before moving closer to us and putting an arm around me.

When it was Mom's turn, parishioners helped her stand up on the concrete wall's edge. She looked beautiful in her resoluteness. She made me so proud, but I was still terrified of what she was going to say. I buried my head into Cass's shoulder and waited for her words.

"For those who don't know me, my name is Laura Byrne," she shouted over the waterfall. "I ask for your prayers because our son and his family—who we love— are about to travel, and because our house was robbed last night. Men broke in and stole everything we have been collecting over the last few days." The crowd whispered, and some people shouted sentiments of sympathy.

"The real reason I wanted to come up here, though, was to ask for forgiveness with the congregation as my witness. From God, for all the ways I have failed Him. From my sister, Devin, for all the ways I failed her." My lungs and heart stopped pumping. Mom was talking about Aunt Devin in front of *everyone*. And she felt like she'd failed her.

I had never heard her describe it that way. *What Devin Did* was always something Devin did to her, the way that Devin failed, the hurt that Devin had caused.

"I also want to ask for forgiveness from my children, for not ever talking about your aunt. And I especially want to ask for forgiveness from my daughter, Avery." I blushed warmly as heads turned toward me and Cass. "When she told me she was gay, I didn't hug her. I didn't tell her I love her. I want everyone to know I'm proud of her, and I don't give a damn what any of you think about that. Except for you, Lord."

"Did Mom just swear?" Peter whispered.

"And also," Dad shouted from where he was standing, still rocking Teddy back and forth, "we're proud of her girlfriend, Cass." I almost choked on air. Cass whipped her hand away from my back as if that was what had tipped them off.

"You told them?" she whispered.

"No!" I said. She blew her own useless candle out to put her arms around me, fully. I got redder, I was sure, and felt heat sink through me. But as someone helped Mom down from the wall and Dad smiled at us from where he stood, I surged with love for my parents. Their words were an act of kindness, of recognition. In that moment, I felt like I was enough. We were enough.

The look I gave my father must have read like a question mark, because he rolled his eyes. "We weren't born yesterday," he said in a gentle voice. I felt so exposed. I felt so relieved.

"You're lucky, Avery," Cass said.

It was true. It had always been true. So where did my darkness come from? Why was I the way that I was? How dare I?

When Mom joined us again, I hugged her, and Cass did too, and I looked at her quizzically. Before I could even ask the question, she answered.

"I saw you kissing on the steps yesterday."

"Oh, no."

"Oh, yes. The front door is glass, you know, Avery. My heart cheered! And then I was afraid. But, well, here we are. Nothing left to lose. And so, nothing left to fear. I can't protect you any longer, girls, but I can love you."

Though people kept on getting up to speak, Father Aiden sat on a rock near a particularly volatile part of the river to hear confessions. I moved to get in line, but Cass raised an eyebrow at me.

"Really?" she whispered, both bemused and curious.

"I'm not going to get absolved," I said. "I just have something to say to him." Mom, Dad, and the Laskys got in line behind me, and I realized how lucky we'd been to get near the front. The line snaked all the way down the river toward the mills.

"What do you have to say?" Cass asked.

"It's a long story," I said, looking over my shoulder at my family.

"You're going to tell things to that man," she clarified, "instead of me."

"It's not like that," I said and turned away. "I'll tell you later."

"You've gotta be kidding me, Avery."

"Whatever, Cass, fine," I said. "Let's go." But it was my turn.

"What? No, not after all that," Cass said, and then bitterly, "you obviously have something to say."

Mom pushed me forward too. "Ask for forgiveness," she said. I tumbled forward to stand in front of Father Aiden, his raven hair flickering in the wind.

"Hello, Father," I said and made the sign of the cross. I sat down on a rock across from him.

"Hello, Avery," he said.

"It was me," I said. He cocked his head in confusion.

"Remember when I came to you in the church that night? And I told you I had a friend, who was gay. Who was suicidal."

"Yes, I recall."

"It was me. You heard my mom; I'm gay. And on the morning we all found out about the asteroid, I was going to kill myself." I had never in my life been honest with him before. I had never stood in front of him, in front of God or Jesus or the Holy Spirit, and said anything true out loud. I visibly trembled; I felt scared and horrible and exhilarated and free.

"Oh, dear," he said, his composure rattled. He looked for the first time like he was at a loss for words. He offered his hand to me, palm up, and I took it. He leaned forward so I could hear him. "That's a mortal sin, Avery. You know that. So you're here to atone? To ask for forgiveness?"

I resented him for caring more about the sin than the why, more about my failing than my pain.

"No," I said. "If there's a God or Gods, they'll forgive me or they won't. I came here to tell you that you shouldn't ever, ever tell a child or anyone they're wrong or sinful or blasphemous for being who they are. You shouldn't ever tell anyone they're damned for being sad, for struggling."

"But, Avery, God—"

"You're not God. You're a man. You're human too. And you've been so very wrong."

When he said nothing, I started to walk away, but he stopped me.

"Do you still want to kill yourself?"

I should have been prepared for that question. I should have answered, "Yes!" emphatically, quickly, definitively. But the answer was no, I realized. Even though I hated myself, the answer was no. I didn't want to die.

"I'm still here, aren't I?"

After everyone else had their turn speaking to him, all seven of us stumbled back to the cars arm in arm.

"He said my penance is to shave my head," Cass said. "That's how bad it was."

"No!" Dad yelled, and I grinned at his sincere outrage.

"That's what he said!" Cass shrugged. "I don't make the rules."

"You're not shaving your head," Mom said. "Not in my house."

"Mom," I said, shaking my head.

"Not in my house!"

"Okay, okay, okay," Cass said. "But blame the man in the sky, not me."

Back at the house, Cass pulled me into the bathroom. She took scissors out of the drawer, let her hair down, and shook it.

"We're not going to shave it," she said, "per your

mom's request." She put the scissors on the counter. I picked it up, opened the blades.

"How short?"

"I don't know. Just chop it. Just start." I pulled some of her hair to the side, the silk of it making my heart race.

"Just chop it?"

"Just chop it." My fingers shook as I pressed down, a lock of her hair falling to the floor. "Shorter," she said. "As short as it can be where I can still run my hands through it."

"What if I fuck it up?"

"Fuck it all the way up, baby."

It was a strange release. It was a loss. It was a becoming, the thing that Cass wanted most of all, and so it was beautiful. Her hair slipped through my fingers, hit the floor, and spiraled into art. When I was done, she beamed at me in the mirror.

"You look like a different person," I said.

Her smile fell a little bit. "Is it the cheekbones?"

"No, what? Fuck Daisy. You look *handsome*. Hot. Perfect. You look like *you*." She ran her hands across her head and tilted her face to different angles in the mirror. I kissed the top of her head, tasted her shampoo—not her normal lilac but the Market Basket kind my parents had hoarded. My hands were on her shoulders. Her hands were on my hands. She made eye contact with me in the mirror.

"I want to know what you said to the priest today. Every single word." My brain started spitting out lie after lie. I tried to decide what the best one would be. "If you love me, Avery, you'll tell me the truth. I'm tired of secrets between us." I took a deep breath and chose my words carefully.

"I told him he shouldn't tell kids it's a sin to be who they are," I said, "like he once told me."

"That's it?"

"Well, no." Of course it wasn't.

"So . . ." *I should lie*, I thought. It was the smart thing to do. The selfish thing. It was the only way I wouldn't lose her, us. But she wanted the truth, and I loved her, and if I lied, it would be a betrayal. My heart sunk, so deep. I would lose her either way.

"Cass, I don't want to hurt you."

"It hurts more not knowing," she said. "I'll tell you what I said too."

"I don't know if I can say it out loud."

She left the room, returned with two pens and a piece of paper, which she ripped in half.

"Then we'll write it down." She gripped her pen in her left hand and started scribbling. Blood roared in my ears as I did the same. I couldn't help but feel like I was about to end my whole world. But did I have a choice?

I was going to kill myself that morning. You called me just in time. I stared at my own words, wishing I could crumple the paper up and swallow it.

"On the count of three," Cass said. "Three . . ." I closed my eyes and thought about running. "Two . . ." I took another deep breath and held it in my lungs. "One . . ." I held my paper out and forced myself to keep breathing. She took the paper away from me, and when I opened my eyes, I was holding hers.

I unfolded it to read her handwriting. I exhaled as I processed it, but when I tried to inhale again, there was no oxygen in the room. My eyes read her words over and over and over to be sure, and each time I felt weaker and weaker.

I want to go back to New York. I'm going with the Laskys.

five days
to impact

I stared at Cass's words and backed away to sit on the
edge of the bathtub. She caught herself on the sink.
When we finally dared to look at each other, there was
too much and nothing to say. I felt so cold.

"Why?" she asked, finally. What a question.

"I'll ask you the same."

"Why were you going to kill yourself, Avery?"

"I didn't want to live anymore," I said slowly. "No,
that's not true. I didn't know how to."

She studied me. "What were you going to do?"

"Drown myself in the river." She put a hand over her
mouth. I looked at the tile of the floor. I couldn't bear it,
how I was hurting her, how I was changing us. Why
hadn't I lied? Why hadn't I buried it?

"Why are you leaving?" I said, if only to interrupt her own line of questioning, but it was like she didn't hear me. She stood frozen, silent. She looked at me like she didn't know me, and I could practically feel the wheels turning in her head as she decided what a terrible person I was, as she tried to calculate how I could do that to my family, to her. And what could I say? I wanted to close the distance between us, to hold her, to apologize again and again until she forgot what I had told her, but I knew she wouldn't want me to touch her. I had ruined everything, and as usual I only had myself to blame.

The doorbell rang, and Cass dropped her hand to her heart as we heard Aisha and my parents charging to open it. We waited until we heard it: a gasp, a squeal, and sobbing.

We said it at the same time: "Ray."

We still had so much to say to each other, so much to answer to, but we shoved the papers in our pockets before bolting out of the bathroom and down the stairs to where Aisha was hugging a woman with gold rings on every finger. When they separated, I could see she was so clearly her sister. Though Ray had long braids and an eyebrow ring, their faces were the same shape, their eyes burned in the same brilliant way.

"Look at you, Aisha," she said. "My baby sister not so baby anymore."

"Look at you, Ray," she said. "You made it. I can't

believe it." They started speaking Hausa, and after a moment, Aisha waved us down the stairs so we could meet her. "This is my Eaton roommate, Avery, and this is her girlfriend, Cass." That stung, suddenly.

"Nice to meet you," Ray said. She reached down to open some of the plastic bags around her feet. "I brought food from home," she said. "Only things that would last for the drive. Kilishi, dabino, and alkaki."

"Oh, wow," Aisha said, clutching one of the containers to her chest. "This is the best gift in the universe. Should we eat? Let's eat."

In the kitchen, Aisha and Ray unwrapped the food while Cass and I set the table with the only remaining dishes we had left, cheap plastic plates and bowls in varying colors. I was intoxicated by the idea of eating something other than stove-cooked apples. Sweetness and spice stirred the air. I still felt sick from my conversation with Cass, but my stomach pulsed with hunger.

"Cass, your hair!" Mom gasped as she put down a pitcher of water. We all broke into laughter despite ourselves.

"You just noticed, Mrs. B?"

"I've been a little distracted!"

"I told you it was part of my penance."

Mom clutched her heart as if she believed Cass.

"I like it," Dad said, helping himself to another serving of alkaki. "It's very dapper."

"A true ally." Cass smiled at me before we remembered ourselves. What she knew, what I knew. What I had planned to do. What she still planned to do. My eyes filled with tears, but I shook them away. I couldn't ruin this moment too, not for Aisha and certainly not for Ray. Except I'd already ruined it—irreparably—by leaving the door unlocked, letting the Fielders in.

"I have some bad news," Aisha said to Ray. "Like I told you, we were preparing the basement to try to survive this. We collected so much food, Ray. So many things. You should have seen it."

"Yes, you told me."

"Some men broke in last night," Dad said. "They had guns. Tied us up. They took everything." For a horrible moment, everyone was quiet, and guilt burned in my chest. I thought if someone didn't say something soon, I might have to run from the room.

"Is everyone okay?" Ray asked, breaking the silence.

"Yes," Aisha said. "Everyone's okay."

"We have a little food?"

"Yes, we still have some saved at our son's house next door," Mom said.

"And we can still stay here?"

"Yes, of course," Dad said. Ray took another bite of her food.

"Then it's not bad news," she said. "We're all here. As it should be."

I exhaled, but still felt nauseous and guilty.

"And did you know," Dad said, "this town is home to the first Irish potato on American soil?"

Cass avoided eye contact as we continued eating. I thought she might be trying to bite back her own tears. Ray told us about her drive here, the people she met, the things she had seen. She told us about her life in Toronto. She owned her own Nigerian restaurant, lived in a high-rise building where she could see the city skyline, played in a women's ice hockey league for fun on the weekends. She said she lived with teammates. She said they were her family. She said she had been happy.

"It must have been hard to leave your parents, though," Mom said, "and your sister."

Ray put her glass of water down. "Of course it was," she said, her voice catching. "My heart has always been broken."

"You didn't have to leave," Aisha said gently.

"I did."

"Mom and Dad loved you. Still do. There are others, you know. So many others. I had friends who—"

"I didn't know how to make it work back then, being there, being me. I'm sorry. You were better off without me, Aisha."

"That was never, ever true." Aisha grabbed Ray's hand across the table, and we all sat in silence and tried to swallow food. "Never."

"We'll discuss it later, but I cannot get over what a beautiful person my baby sister has grown into," she said. Aisha's smile could have lit the room. "It's nice to be here with all of you, and you two." She gestured to me and Cass. "I didn't know what to expect coming here. I didn't know if Aisha would really love me for *all* of who I am, but hearing her talk about you made me realize she would. She did. Thank you for being you."

"Thank you for being *you*," I said. "You too, Aisha." If I had to name the emotion swelling inside me, quieting every other terrible feeling: pride. For the first time I understood why people used that word. It wasn't just a slogan. I *felt* it.

After we placed all the dishes in the sink, Cass and I stared each other down near the bathroom.

"Let's go somewhere we can actually talk," I said. We got our coats and went out into the fading day. We trudged wordlessly through the fallen apples. We opened the barn's big red door, flipped the lights on, and sat together on a bale of hay. I wanted to get on my knees and beg her to forget what I'd written on that piece of paper, to plead with her to let us start over. I could confess something different, unburden her. I could bury it all again, if she'd let me, and we could be in love again, for however long. We could be a team.

But before I could say anything, she hugged me under the string lights, in the barn that smelled like apple blossoms. Then she gently pushed me away to look at me and said, "So. You were suicidal."

I couldn't say it, so I nodded.

"And you were going to jump in the river that morning."

"Right." I braced myself for her anger, her hatred, her hurt.

"Come here," she said softly, and pulled me by the hand. She leaned up against a bale of hay, and I lay with my back to her chest. She held me to her, and I felt her tears, finally falling, in my hair. "I don't even know what to say, Avery. I'm probably not going to say the right things."

"There's no right thing," I said. We sat there for a minute breathing while she collected her thoughts.

"I'm sorry you felt so alone. I'm really, really happy you're still here. I'm thanking every single God I got to love you like this. I'm angry it seems like I'm the last to know."

"You're not," I said. "Aisha knows because she found one of my goodbye letters that morning."

"What did the letters say?"

I tried to think back to the night before the asteroid. It was so hard to remember who I was, what I thought. I'd stayed up through the previous two nights cleaning my side of the room as Aisha slept, deleting photos, and writing erratic letters purposely designed to look like homework if she were to wake up and get suspicious.

"I don't fully remember, but I probably said you shouldn't feel guilty in any way, that my decision had nothing to do with you and that my time with you—every single minute—was the best of my life. It probably said you're my hero and always would be. It said I hoped I was wrong, that there was a heaven and I'd meet you there and read to you until time ended or something else began."

"And then something else began," she said. I waited for her to tell me she was scared of me. Disturbed. Wounded. Instead, she said, "I've thought about it too. Many times."

"Suicide?"

"Yeah. I never had a plan or anything, but sometimes I'm so damn tired. I have the best parents and friends and all these ideas for my future, but it felt like the world told me over and over again it was not built for me. It did not want me to be happy. It did not want me to survive, not really."

"And what did you do? When you felt like that?"

"Usually I'd call you or Omar. You'd make me laugh, and you'd remind me why I loved the world and myself and fuck everything else. I love you so much, Avery."

"Why do you want to leave me, then?"

"I don't want to leave you. But if we're not going to survive here, I want you to come with me. Come with us. We're still so young, Ave. There's so much more we can do and see. You can see my show, all my designs. We can go upstate with Omar, and we can run around the city at night under the lights, and this time, this time I will kiss you on every street corner. This could be the best adventure. I want to do this. I have to." She didn't say *we*.

I thought about getting in the car, leaving my parents behind forever, driving to Brooklyn. I imagined the fire and the grit of that city. It felt claustrophobic. It felt wrong, and even with Cass beside me, it felt lonely. I imagined myself shrinking down to the size of a pin, until I was no one and nothing at all. I couldn't go, but I didn't want to tell her, didn't want to say goodbye to her. Maybe she didn't have to go either. Maybe there was still a chance for the bunker to work. I turned around to face her, my knees between her knees, my hands on her cheeks.

"What if we can get the food back?"

"What do you mean?"

"What if they're out raiding houses? We can break in while they're away. We'll take the truck, smash some windows. Take back whatever we can. Rebuild. We can still do this. We can still live through this."

Cass bit her lip, considering. "And you want to? Live through this?"

"Yes," I said, and I was telling the truth. "I do. I really do."

"They have guns," she said. "It's dangerous."

"We'll be careful. This time, I won't go in alone. This time, we'll do it together."

"Ride or die," she said. "Hopefully not literally."

"Definitely not literally."

"And if we fail?"

"Then we fail, and you go to New York, and at least we'll know we tried. At least we gave it a shot."

She gripped the front of my jacket and pulled me in to kiss her, feel the heat of her breath on my skin. We kissed like we were desperate. Loved like if we did it hard enough, we could save the world.

"You'll tell me, right, Ave?" she said. "If you ever feel suicidal again?"

"I'm not anymore. You don't have to worry about—"

"I'm not worried. I'm open. I'm grateful you finally trusted me. Please keep trusting me? Please? In all the time we have left?"

"Yes," I said. "Okay. You'll tell me too, right? If you feel that way?"

She played with my jacket zipper. "Yeah, I'll tell you. I'll tell you everything, always."

"Team of two," I said.

"Team of two," she echoed.

For the next hour we stayed there, rested, and pre-pared. And I was home, there, beside her.

I was honest and unhidden. Nowhere on Earth I'd rather be. No one else I'd rather be. My cells were still. My breath came steady. We napped, if only briefly, the closest we'd ever been.

five days
to impact

Cass and I sat side by side in the car and drove into the screaming, neon, sunset sky. I held her hand as I pushed the gas pedal harder and familiar country houses blurred. The town of Kilkenny was mapped on my bones, and I barely had to look at the street signs to navigate. Clayton knew where I lived, but after the party at Kayla's, I knew where he lived too. And that was where we were headed, up winding hills and shaded gravel roads. Blood pounded in my ears, in my chest, and in my hands. I wondered if Cass could feel it.

When we got to his house, I backed into the driveway across the street from his. I gripped the steering wheel and Cass tighter to stop my hands from shaking.

"That's it, huh?" she whispered, as if anyone could hear us.

"Think so," I said. His house wasn't as big as Kayla's, but it was close, all-white brick and blue shutters. The Fielders had so much and it wasn't enough. He had so much and wanted more, and as much as it disgusted me, I kind of understood it: Did he think maybe the next stolen, flashy thing would save him? Or was I giving him too much credit? Did he want to hoard and destroy because he felt like it was his right?

At first, we couldn't tell if anyone was home, because their garage was closed, so we sat in silence, Cass's head on my shoulder, and watched for shadows in the windows. But as the final wisps of daylight faded from the sky and darkness settled, a light flickered on in one of the first-floor rooms. Panic rattled in my ribs.

"Damn," I said.

"At least we know," she said. "But now what?"

"We either wait or we gamble."

"Gamble on what?"

"That we can take 'em. That we can sneak in. That they won't kill us."

"Cool your jets." Cass put her hand on my thigh to hold me in place. "We can wait." We could, but we both knew our time was limited. In the morning, the Laskys expected us at the beach. In the evening, they would leave. Forever. And there was an empty seat in their packed truck with Cass's name on it.

The more I pictured them leaving, the more I started to spiral. My breath quickened. My skin crawled. I wanted to drive the car straight into the house, tear the walls down, take the Fielders by surprise, and peel off into the night again. But the more practical thing, the only real thing I could do after an hour of waiting in the tightening darkness, was unbuckle my seat belt.

"Ave," she said, and looked at me with questions in her eyes.

"I won't go in," I said, then checked myself. "*We* won't go in. Let's get close enough to hear what's going on inside. Maybe they'll say something about leaving, about where they're keeping everything." She sighed but unbuckled her seat belt too.

"I don't love this," she said, "but I trust you. Let's roll."

We opened our doors as quietly as possible and got our weapons out of the back seat: two hammers, a lacrosse stick, a baseball bat, and Cass's sewing needles. We had plastic trash bags stuffed in all our pockets. We were ready to grab anything and everything we could. Under the cover of fresh darkness, we creeped along the tree line around to the back of their house. A splintered wooden porch stretched across it and ended next to a rust-red bulkhead, a metal hatch leading down to their basement. We crouched on icy leaves and watched lights flicker on and off in different sections of the house. We watched the windows and counted figures as they moved in the shadows.

"There's someone on the second floor," Cass whispered.

"Two on the first," I said. That meant we could

pinpoint all three of them: Clayton, Nolan, and their dad. Maybe they didn't have another parent? It had never come up in our countless hours of intimate, enlightening conversation. I put the baseball bat on the ground to rub Cass's back. She wasn't shaking. She felt solid. I felt ready. I scanned the house to make sure there weren't any security cameras.

"We're gonna have to get closer," I whispered. We had to hear their voices to know who was where, and to listen for the creaks of their weight on the floors.

"Okay," she said, grabbing the bat. "All right. Let's go." We ran, still crouched, and fell into a crawl. We were close to the porch when a shadow grew larger in the kitchen, and I heard a shuffle at the door. Someone turned the porch light on, and I dropped a hammer to grab Cass's jacket and pull her with me under the deck as the door slid open above us. Pain zapped through my knee as we crouched, and I swallowed a yelp. I stared at my hammer a few feet out from the porch with a sinking feeling in my stomach. I looped my pinky finger with Cass's. Now, we were both shaking. Footsteps moved above us.

"You're going out to party again, man? That's not cool," one voice said.

"What does it matter, Clay?"

"Just does." I heard clicking, a whoosh, and then the smell of fire and charcoal drifted through the cracks in the wood above us. They'd lit a grill.

"It's not like I'm hurting anyone."

"You're kinda hurting me. You're supposed to be helping me steal more shit."

"We'll go again tomorrow. We're totally stacked. We could live forever."

"Not forever."

"Long enough. Might as well have fun before we're stuck eating cold beans."

Yes, please, I thought, *please go party.* Could we possibly get that lucky?

"Maybe," Clayton said. "Who's gonna be there?"

Their conversation circled back to the details of the party: whose house it was at, who'd be in attendance, what kind of drugs they'd scored. Then, the sizzle, smoke, and scent of steak expanding above and around us. Cass mimed gagging beside me, and it was making me feel physically ill too. But then Clayton said, "Fine, sure, whatever. I'll come."

I nearly cried out with relief. This was really happening. God, it could *work*. We'd still have to get around their father, sure, but we could get in and get enough if he was upstairs. We could make this happen. Cass would stay. My brother would too.

After a few minutes of banter, we heard Nolan and Clayton plate the steak, take the food inside, and shut the door behind them. We both audibly exhaled.

"That was close," I whispered.

"But they're leaving," she whispered too.

"Let's go watch the garage, see when they leave."

We army-crawled out from under the porch and sprinted back to the trees. We crouched near the side of the house so we could see the garage doors. I didn't know how long we'd have to wait. We watched our breath cloud in front of our faces, in and out together. And then, as my knee began to throb, we heard the most magical, thrilling sounds possible: the gears of the three-car garage door opening, the black Escalade revving its engine, tires screeching on the driveway.

Then we saw something else, something that almost, *almost* made me believe in God again: they'd left the garage door wide open, and the only light on in the house was on the top floor. We took one look at each other, stood up, and sprinted.

The door inside was locked, but Cass pulled one of her sewing needles out of her pocket and was able to slip it into the tiny hole of the lock and easily push it until it clicked. We held our breath as she slowly pushed the door forward.

In an instant, we were in their mudroom. Alone. Lacrosse sticks lined the walls, random sneakers covered the floor, and the smell of laundry detergent permeated the space. For a few seconds, I completely forgot to exhale. Country music howled upstairs.

We moved into their kitchen, where Cass and I each

opened a plastic bag and started collecting things from the counters: potato chips, cans, jars of peanut butter. When I opened the fridge, it was stuffed so full a bowl of cherries fell out. The ceramic shattered when it landed, and the fruit shot out like marbles all over the floor.

I started to pick them up, their juice staining my hands, but Cass hissed at me.

"Avery!" I looked up at her and saw her eyes wide with fear, and then I heard it: another set of feet clomping down the central stairs. Mr. Fielder. I looked around for an escape, and pointed to a door open a few feet away from us. Cass took off and I followed her, almost tripping down the first few stairs. I caught myself on the railings. They led to the basement.

We tumbled down the remaining plywood stairs, Cass tugged a string that flipped on a dim light, and suddenly we stood surrounded by our old life, my old things. I fell to my knees, wrecked by longing. I reached out to touch a blue sweater I knew Mom had brought over from Ireland. I held it to my chest and took it in.

Cass was already in action, grabbing boxes and cans and throwing them into her bag. The boxes from our basement were strewn about, not carefully stacked and organized the way I remembered them. Still, I ripped open lids and tore open the sides to rescue medical supplies and granola bars. I reached into one of the plastic tubs and felt pain rip across my fingers. I'd grabbed broken glass. When I pulled my hands to my mouth to suck the blood away, I saw the glass was shattered in a frame, and the photo behind it was me and Cass after the state championships. Clayton had taken my future because he needed it, but he'd taken my past because he could.

I was supposed to focus on the food, but I shook the glass off the photo and put it in my back pocket. My heart broke when I touched the unfinished rocking horse Dad made for Teddy, because I knew I couldn't carry it. Then my hand hit a soft fabric and I grasped at it desperately. I saw a flash of forest green, then wrenched the scrapbook out from everything weighing it down and flipped through the pages. It was still there, all of it, unharmed, every page I knew by heart. Every world I'd built, every world Cass and I had built together.

"Look," I said, holding it up, and she grinned across the room.

"Ah," she said, "the museum of all my thinly veiled love letters."

I opened my mouth to say, *I saved each and every last one of them*, but instead we heard the door at the top of the stairs squeak open. We dropped our bags and dove behind boxes to hide. One of my bags of cans spilled everywhere, and my heart turned to ice in my chest. Because of the way we were hidden, neither of us could see Mr. Fielder come down the stairs, but I was positive he'd heard either us talking or my cans clanking around on the cement. Cass and I held our breath and our eye contact from across the room. She had both hands over her mouth, trying not to breathe, trying not to scream. I felt the same way: shaken up, boiling over. Ready to pass out. Ready to explode.

The next sounds, boots on concrete, Mr. Fielder pushing boxes, humming, "Hmm," the blood knocking against my skin.

With our eyes locked, our lungs full, fear ripping through our every cell, the invisible rope between Cass and I tightened, braided, burned.

And then something horrible happened. The man said, "Where the fuck—" And in that instant I knew, and I could see that Cass knew, we had made a grave miscalculation. It wasn't Mr. Fielder in the basement with us. It was Clayton. I'd know his voice anywhere. It was only feet away.

"—is my box of hair gel?"

Maybe things would have been different if the Escalade didn't have tinted windows, if we'd seen he wasn't in the car with Nolan. Maybe we could have stayed quiet if we'd been side by side, looking ahead instead of at each other. Maybe we could have kept it together if our nerves weren't already electric.

But the car did have tinted windows, and we weren't side by side, and our nerves were already electric. We had the right eye contact at the worst possible time. Cass and I started laughing.

I tried to stop. I did. I really tried. My whole body ached with the trying, with self-loathing, with knowing I ruined everything. We ruined everything. At least we ruined everything together.

But it still hurt, all of it: When Clayton yelled, when he found me first. When he tilted his head, squinted his eyes, opened them wide with recognition.

"Avery Byrne?" He looked me up and down. "What do you think you're doing?"

"I'm taking our stuff back," I said through painful, awful laughter.

"Pretty sure it's my stuff now," he said, and shouted up the stairs for his father to come help him.

In the corner of my eye, Cass was a flash. She grabbed the bat and ran across the basement and up the stairs that led to outside. Metal clanged as she tried to unbolt the doors above her to free us, and Clayton turned to chase her.

"Clayton!" I called to stall him, and he hesitated. "What happened to you, huh? You used to be, I don't know, kind of nice." It was my final lie.

"Yeah, and what did that get me?" he snarled. We both heard the boom of Cass getting the big doors open, pushing them to their sides, escaping. I got to my feet, and Clayton and I both raced after her, me still clutching the scrapbook, him tugging on the back of my jacket, trying to rip me down to the ground. We wrestled each other up into the night.

Outside in the cold starlight, Cass stood a few yards away from us.

"Run!" I yelled, but of course she didn't. Their back porch door slid open again, and Mr. Fielder was above all three of us holding a hunting rifle. He wore a backward hat and a camo jacket. I heard the click of the safety of his gun.

"Who's this?" he said. "Your ex?"

"No," I said as Clayton said, "Yeah." His cheeks reddened, and he reached toward me to take the scrapbook out of my hands. I tried to yank it away, but he got a grip on it and held firm.

"What's she doing here?" Mr. Fielder called, then noticed Cass and the open bulkhead. "And what's *she* doing here?" He motioned to her with the barrel of his rifle, focused it on her, and my whole body tensed. What had I been thinking? Raiding this house was my idea, getting our stuff back was my idea, and I had put the person I loved in danger. I watched her drop the bat, and put her hands up in the moonlight. I wished I could reach them. I wished I could hold them.

Instead, I slowly got to my feet and marched forward until I was between Cass and the gun. I looked Mr. Fielder in the eyes.

"We're not taking anything," I said. "Not a single thing. Let us go. Please."

"I don't know if I want to," he said, a sick grin spreading across his face.

In the quiet seconds that followed, I stared down the barrel. My muscles withered. I heard a voice shrieking inside, an echo of what I'd thought when talking to Father Aiden: *I don't want to die, I don't want to die, I don't want to die.* It bubbled through me, caught in my throat.

And, then, for the first time, it also said, *I want to live.*

For an instant, the world spun around me, because I realized it was true. I did want to live. And I was going to make that happen, even if only for a few days.

"I love you," Cass said in a small voice behind me.

"I love you too," I said, just loud enough so she could hear me.

"On the count of three we run?"

"Ready?" I said. "Three, two . . ."

But she took off first, and Clayton went for her, and I realized he'd left the scrapbook behind on the ground. I arced my run just barely so I could swoop down and grab it, and even though pain ripped through my knee, I was euphoric when my skin felt the fabric.

Clayton and his father hurled slurs at us as we crossed their dead lawn under the night sky, but Clayton slipped on black ice before he could even touch my beautiful friend, my favorite person, the love of my life.

I hope he thanked every single God, because I would have wrecked him. While Clayton lay on the ground, and his father shot once into the sky to scare us, Cass and I sprinted across the front lawn, made it into the car, and locked the doors behind us. I turned the keys in the ignition and pushed the gas pedal as hard as I could.

We sped down the back roads, main roads, and all the way back to our house on McIntosh Court without saying anything at all. I parked, and we ran to the barn, throwing ourselves down together onto the hay. We caught our breath. We cried. We had tried. It wasn't enough.

"I'm sorry, Cass," I whispered. "Don't leave me. Don't go to New York."

"Oh, Avery," she said, and kissed my tears away. "I can't stay here. Not like this. I can't. Come with me. Please."

I tried to think of what to say, because as badly as she wanted me to come with her, as badly as I wanted to see her designs and watch her face light up brighter than city lights as she saw them come to life, I knew I couldn't.

I clutched her shirt in my fist. "On the first night, in the orchard," I said, "you said you've been chasing me your whole life. But I've been chasing you too, Cass. The second I had to map my own course, I couldn't do it. I don't want that to be my story."

"Of course not."

"You've been saying you want to really know me. I haven't let you, not because I don't want to, but because

I don't think *I* know me." She put her hand in my hair and pulled me closer.

"So, what are you saying?" she sobbed.

"I guess I'm saying I don't want to go to New York." Though my voice shook, it felt right. "I want to trust my gut. I want to want something that's mine. I want to be my own person, even if it's only for a few days. If I never have that, what do I have? If I never have that, how can I fully love you?"

She studied my face, put her hands on my shoulders, and rubbed her thumbs across my collarbones.

"You know for sure, Ave?"

Wasn't it strange I could say so? Wasn't it terrible? Wasn't it right?

"I know for sure," I said. "I'm so sorry."

"Don't be sorry. It's nice to hear you want things, Avery. But, goddamn, I'll miss you like crazy."

"You definitely want to go to New York?"

"Not even want," she said. "I think I need to. It's the place I've felt most like myself. I want to feel that way again before . . . whatever happens."

"I know," I said. I tried to memorize the heat of her and the way it felt to love her. I stroked her hair and liked how it felt short, my fingers sliding right to the tips.

"You'll stay here?" she said. I couldn't answer her. I couldn't leave my parents. Could I?

"I don't think I know yet," I said, surprising myself.

"Avery," she said, and held my face, kissed my forehead. "You deserve your own world."

"It doesn't mean we love each other any less," I whispered.

"I have never loved you more." She sat up, reached across my body, and grabbed the scrapbook. "Let's read through this together tonight," she said, "and then . . ." She skipped to the blank pages, counted them, and ripped half of them out. "I'll take these. You take the rest. When we're apart, we'll both write our stories, what happens to us. What it looks like. What we feel. That way if one of us makes it and the other one doesn't . . ."

"We'll have left something behind," I said.

"Answers," she said, "and a whole museum of thinly veiled love letters."

We held each other and cried. We spent the night in the barn, and everything was holy. And when we finally fell asleep, tangled together for the last time, I realized I was crying not because of our goodbye or our sorrow or our fear. I was crying because everything was so beautiful, and for once, I knew how to feel it.

one perfect day

We packed two cars for the beach in the morning: my parents' car with snacks, games, and blankets, and the Laskys' truck with all the things they and Cass wanted to bring to New York.

We met Peter in his driveway. He wore jeans, a button-down, and a tie. He sat on the hood of his truck and leaned back to look at the afternoon sky, and his curls fell out of his eyes. It was still cold enough to see our breath if we blew hard enough. The trees cut the sun into a crooked geometry on the driveway, and he tried to catch it on his palms. He was here in front of me in color, in flesh. For the last time.

Their front door opened, and Georgia walked down the stairs with Teddy two steps behind her. She was

364 ★ JEN ST. JUDE

wearing her wedding dress, a white lace floor-length gown, but she clutched a black sweater to her chest. The sight of her knocked the breath right out of me. Peter stood up to meet her.

"Since we had a shotgun wedding, we thought we'd do something more official today. Make it a happy memory."

Was it a memory if it only lasted for a few days?

Teddy was wearing his Buzz Lightyear Halloween costume without the helmet. Peter had accidentally dropped it on the pavement last October when he was trying to balance it and a plastic pumpkin full of candy. The plastic screen cracked right down the middle, but instead of crying, Teddy said, "Buzz didn't actually need it either, remember?"

Georgia's hair was curled and pinned up with fake white lilies of the valley.

"Hi, Cass Foi," Teddy said. "Hi, Auntie Avery." He posed like a muscleman, then spun around and stumbled. Then he did a double take on Cass. "Your *hair.*"

"Hey, Buzz," Cass said for both of us. "Don't I look great?" He nodded but didn't seem so sure. My parents came through the trees and opened their arms for him to run and jump into. I didn't want any of us to move, to get in the car, to drive away. I wanted the world to end right there, right then. As it was.

It didn't.

Mom and Dad got in their car, and Cass and I sat in

the back seat of the Laskys' truck holding hands. We pulled out of the driveway, down the street, through disconnected stoplights, and onto the empty highway where the trees bent sadly over us. The truck hummed, and for a second, I thought the next forty minutes were going to be the quietest and loudest of my life.

"Teddy, I want you to ask us every question you've ever had about the world. Any and all of the questions you can think of. Do you understand?" Peter said.

Teddy nodded, looking at Georgia. "Why do only girls wear flowers in their hair?"

"Anyone can wear flowers in their hair," Peter replied.

Georgia pulled a lily bead from above her ear. "Would you like some of my flowers?"

"No. Why can't I be Buzz Lightyear all the time?"

"You can be Buzz all the time."

"Forever?"

"Yes, forever."

"Why do I get to be Buzz Lightyear forever?"

"You were born to be Buzz Lightyear forever," Peter said, like he believed it.

"Do you have snacks?"

Georgia asked me to get the snacks out from a bag that sat between Cass and me. I did, and grinned when I saw that instead of chocolate and cake and ice cream, she'd still packed apples and peanut butter and yogurt.

"Why are you sad, Mom?"

"I'm not sad."

"But you were crying."

"I wish we could stay a little longer, that's all." She smoothed his hair. He reached out to touch her and got peanut butter on her dress. She rubbed it in.

"You look pretty today," Teddy said.

"Your mother is the most beautiful woman on Earth," Peter said, taking his eyes off the road to look at his family.

"Is Santa going to be able to find me?"

"Yes, of course."

"Will I go to school?"

"Only if you want to."

"I don't want to." We all laughed, and the sound bubbled around us.

"What questions do you have for Cass Foi and Auntie Avery?"

"Why do you kiss?"

"We love each other," I said.

"Do you have a baby?"

"No, bud," Cass said.

"You coming to York?"

"New York," Peter said.

"Yes," Cass said, as I said, "No."

I didn't want to cry. I didn't want to scare him. But I thought I was about to shatter. It was like Cass knew I was about to detonate, so she leaned over and exhaled on the window until there was a patch of fog. She drew a heart with a shooting star like an arrow through the middle. She put her initials at the top: CJA. She put mine on the bottom: ADB. We watched it fade away.

"Daddy, what makes you happy?" Teddy asked. Peter tilted his head to the side.

"Playing with you. My students. Walking around Boston with Georgia in the sweat of July." He was speaking slowly. "My old cat, Butterfly. Sitting on the roof with Cass and Avery. Our beautiful house. Apple picking in October. Getting stranded on a boat in a rainstorm. And today, right now. I think I'll dream of this forever."

"Going to the beach?"

"Right. The beach. And your mom with these flowers in her hair. And you, my superhero. And Avery and Cass being together and in love like I wanted them to for so long." He caught my eyes in the rearview mirror, and I gave him the small gift of a smile.

"Why aren't you coming?" Teddy said to me.

"I have things I have to do," I said and touched his cheek. "But I'll be okay. Don't worry."

I saw his eyes searching me for answers I couldn't give him. I thought for a second I'd revealed something terrible, because a darkness flickered in him and he looked worried and knowing, but then his face melted back into its usual, even glow.

We pulled through the pebble parking lot to the edge of the beach, and my parents parked beside us. The whole world was yellow and gray and washed with blue. Seagulls screamed above us, and even through the closed windows we could hear the ocean chanting as the sun slipped into the corner of the dashboard and fractured into beams.

"Let's go," Teddy said. "Let's go!"

He tried to wiggle out of the door to chase after my parents, who had started walking away from their car and toward the beach.

"Be careful, Teddy!" Georgia called.

Please don't go, I thought. *Please don't leave me.* But the doors opened, and Georgia, Peter, and Teddy ran away from all of us. I sat in the back seat with Cass while Peter put his arms around both of my parents and walked toward the shore.

I couldn't breathe. Cass moved closer to me, and I put my head on her shoulder until I stopped gasping for air.

When I lifted my head, all I could see through the window were shoes lined up on the concrete wall and the ocean stacked above them. We listened to the screaming of the seagulls and the cycle of waves until we opened the car doors ourselves and cold air washed over us.

I took off my sneakers and set them in the line, and Cass did the same with her boots. We hit the sand at a run and headed toward the speckled sky, the water's edge, where my family sat on blankets. Teddy and Peter drew in the sand with sticks. As Cass and I approached, their etchings came into focus. There was a spaceship and the words *To infinity and beyond!* There were other things: hearts and a house and a dog. They'd built a small fire to hover around, and we sat down beside it.

We spent the hours building sandcastles, dipping our feet in the freezing ocean, talking about our favorite memories, singing our favorite songs. I drew my own things in the sand. Cass drew her shooting star heart again, this time bigger and bolder and for everyone to see. I watched my parents and brother smile at their children, despite everything, because of everything, and their bravery melted me completely. I could be that brave.

"Teddy," I said, "do you want to go on a walk with me?" He looked at his parents to ask if he could, and they both nodded. I took his hand, and we walked toward the big boulders that marked the end of the beach. We picked up seashells and stones. He put them in his jacket pockets, and I helped him climb up on the rocks.

"Buddy, I'm sorry I didn't spend more time with you over the past year," I said.

"It's okay," he said. "You have school."

"I did," I said, "but I still could have tried to see you more. I wish I did. I miss you."

"You play soccer too."

"I do."

"And you're sad." I helped him jump from one rock to another.

"I'm not sad; I'm happy to be here with you right now."

"No, you're *always* sad."

"What do you mean?"

"Nana said you're sad like Aunt Devin." My blood chilled as I looked back at my family, who were too far away to hear us.

"Nana said that?"

"Yeah. She said don't go near the water."

"I won't," I said. "You shouldn't either." A bitter, freezing wind picked up and raged around us. Teddy ran into my arms to hide from it, and I exhaled. Even with my sadness, he trusted me to keep him safe, to keep him warm. He still ran to me, and I opened my arms and closed them around him.

"Why you sad?" he asked when it was quiet again. We looked to the water together.

"It's okay to be sad," I said. And as I said it, I believed it. It meant I was feeling something. It meant I was alive. I might never be fully, completely, totally happy, not exactly, but I kept finding things to pull me to the next day and the next, and sometimes life even felt beautiful. Sometimes I even felt something in my chest that felt like real, fluttering hope. Couldn't I keep doing that for the next few days, and, if it came to it, beyond that? "Will you still be my buddy, even if I'm sad sometimes?"

He nodded. "I'll be your buddy when you're sad too." He pulled out a rock from his pocket, a small gray one that glittered when it caught the sunlight.

"For you," he said, showing me his little teeth.

"Thank you so much," I said. "I'll keep it forever." I gave him my favorite stone too, a smooth one softened by the ocean, and he put it in his pocket.

"I keep it forever," he said. That felt like enough.

After we got back to our little spot on the sand, Teddy dove into his mother's arms, and I sat next to Cass again. As the daylight hours and our food dwindled, my hand gripped Cass's tighter and tighter. We pressed against each other as the sun slipped away.

"I wish you would stay," I said just once.

"I wish you would come," she said.

"Oh, no!" Georgia said suddenly. "We forgot to do it."

"Do what?"

"Get married again."

"Oh, right," Peter said. "Who's gonna officiate?"

"Me!" Teddy said.

"Okay," they said, and pulled blankets tighter around their shoulders while he sat in the middle of them. My dad handed ciders to everyone except for Teddy.

"Teddy, say, 'We are gathered here today to celebrate the union of these two people,'" Peter said.

"We gather today to these two people," he said.

"Great. Who will be together in sickness and health, for rich or for poor, for asteroid or for eternity."

Teddy stuck his tongue out but continued. "Be together for sickness and rich, asteroid and eterrity."

"Close enough. We love each other. We're married again. The end," Georgia said.

"We marry. The end," Teddy said. They kissed, and we all toasted them. "Now you!" Teddy pointed at me and Cass.

"No, we're not married," I said.

"You're not married *yet*," Peter said.

"Peter, don't." I didn't want to cry, but tears bubbled over. I wiped them away, embarrassed, but when I looked at Cass, I saw she had tears in her eyes too.

"Let's do it," she said. "Fuck it." I rubbed Teddy's stone in my pocket and waved him over.

"Okay," I said. "Work your magic." He sat between us and looked to Peter for cues. We held hands and let him lead.

"Say you're here to form a union," he shouted.

"Here for ma union," he echoed.

"Between two people who love each other."

"Why do you love each other?" Teddy asked. We each took another sip of cider. Cass opened her mouth to speak.

"I love you," she screamed over the rushing air, "because you're my home."

All my life I'd been telling people I loved them. I'd been so careful with those three words, careful to say them too much and careful, too, to mean them. But maybe it wasn't those three words that even mattered at all; maybe it was the "because" that was the important part, the real part. I'd been leaving that part unspoken, assuming people knew why or how I loved them, but how could they ever know? It was Teddy who brought it out of me. Of course it was.

"I love you because you have been my greatest adventure," I yelled. Cass smiled and held my hands harder.

"Now you say, 'You may now kiss the bride,'" Georgia yelled at Teddy.

"No," Cass said, and bent down to whisper in his ear.

"Fuck the pay-key-airy!" Teddy shouted with glee.

"Oh, for Heaven's sake!" Mom shouted. As my family laughed around me, I kissed the person I had loved for so much of my life, and the world spun, and the day was almost gone.

While the sun continued setting, my parents and the Laskys packed up their cars with our blankets and wrappers and shells. I hugged Georgia and Teddy and Peter. Peter: my Peter, my brother, my best friend. He kissed my hair.

"I'm sorry," he whispered, his voice breaking. "I love you, Avery."

"Don't be," I said. "I love you too."

Cass dragged me a few feet away where she kissed me, and I kissed her, and I didn't want to let go.

I memorized the feel of her. The smell of her. The taste. Beautiful, Brown, golden, loud, brilliant Cass Joshi-Aguilar: my detangler, my hero, my sidekick, my teammate, my heart.

"I have to go," she said. "I'm so sorry."

"I have to stay," I said, "but I'll write to you." I didn't know if she would ever get to read my words on those scrapbook pages, but I had to pretend. I had to. We folded into each other. We breathed. We let go. We got into separate cars: she with the Laskys, me with my parents. And as the tires hit the highway, our worlds split into two. I put my face against the chill of the backseat window and wept.

I missed them all so much.

There was no other way.

We drove under the same moon.

We drove toward the same star.

That was the only thing we could follow.

four days
to impact

When we pulled into our driveway, the world was so dark. My parents turned around to smile at me in the back seat, and I smiled at them too, however forced, however tired. I put my hands forward, and they held them for a moment, and then together we all went inside our house without Cass, without Peter, without Georgia, without Teddy.

On the couch, Aisha and Ray were in pajamas eating leftovers. A fire burned in the fireplace. They both glowed, but when they saw my face, their faces fell too.

"Come here," Aisha said.

"No," I said, "it's okay. I should sleep. It's been a long day."

"Come here," Ray said, and the two of them slid apart so I could sit between them.

"They're gone," I said, falling into the couch. "All of them."

Aisha pulled me into her. She rubbed my back. "I'm so sorry, roomie," she said. My parents sat together on the brick ledge of the fireplace. They both cried, and we watched the fire pop. The stars taunted us outside the skylights.

"You will see them again," Ray offered, and though none of us knew if that was true, we didn't dare say anything. Cass's final words to me rang in my head, and the colors of the Laskys' hallways flashed in my mind. Now that their house was empty, who did those murals belong to? Georgia said they'd painted the walls for themselves, like that could be enough. The collages in my scrapbook were the only things I had ever made for myself.

"Have any of you seen their paintings? The murals they did in their house?" I asked. No one had, so we bundled back up to go next door.

We entered, turned on the lights, and though the silence was nearly unbearable, the colors bloomed. I held on to my parents as we moved around the first floor, remembering. We all climbed the stairs to the second floor, and Aisha hit the lights there too.

I gasped in the hallway at the landscape of Amoskeag Falls. In Teddy's room, his handprints in rainbow all over the walls. I pressed my own palm against them, across blob-like shapes of paint mixed to brown that were surely meant to be trees or people or dogs. I felt devastated I'd never truly told them how much their art meant to me, how it stamped the world.

I found Aisha and Ray in the main bedroom on their knees in front of a royal-blue sky. In it, a single star. Three houses. An apple orchard. Ten silhouettes. Eleven, if you counted the dog. And in Peter's handwriting, in silver paint:

Good luck, brave and beautiful strangers.
Aren't we the lucky ones
walking into the night, all eyes on the same star?
Aren't we the lucky ones?
We were here for a time to dream.
We still are.

Again, I touched the paint, and this time it came off on my fingertips. My parents joined us, and we stared at the words until they burned into our brains.

"You two should take this room, this house," Mom said to Aisha and Ray. "It's more cheerful than ours."

"Are you sure?" Aisha said. "It's their house. Their paintings."

"They're not here," Dad said. "You are."

Together, we moved their things from our house to the sisters' house. As we arranged everything in the different rooms, it felt like building the bunker again. It felt good to practice survival. It felt good to build something for the future, no matter how short it might be.

Back at our house, I sat with Mom and Dad around the fireplace and warmed my hands. It was so quiet, the three of us: no raging waters, no screaming newscasts, no video call ringtones blasting in the basement. So still. I pictured Aisha and Ray sitting on that couch earlier, so open to each other and so happy because of it. I wanted to open up to my parents like I had to Cass, like Ray had to Aisha. But Aisha *wanted* to hear her stories, even or especially if they were painful and ugly. I wasn't sure my parents could handle knowing how broken I was, what I almost did, now that the world was ending. I couldn't do that to them. I realized, though, there was a story I wanted too. Needed.

I took a deep breath and dared to say it: "I want to know about Aunt Devin." When my parents exchanged a weary look, I wondered if I'd crossed a line, even after what Mom had said at the river. But she just sighed, left the room, and came back with the shoebox. She spread photos across the floor, and we all got on our hands and knees to touch them, to share them.

"This is all I have left of her," she said. "Imagine?"

"I've seen these photos before," I admitted. "A long time ago. Peter and I found it once when we were kids."

"I know." She smiled gently. "Why do you think I found a new hiding place for it?"

I held a photo of Aunt Devin carefully between my fingertips. She wore a plaid skirt and a white polo shirt and leaned on a golf club. She looked so much like me, not just in her coloring but in a certain expression she wore. I'd seen it in the mirror so many times, not sadness, exactly, but an exhaustion that had nothing to do with the body. It was like there should be a light there and there wasn't. It was like she should be dreaming, but she couldn't.

"What was she like?" I asked.

"She was bright and funny and kind. We fought as kids, especially over clothes and this one very sparkly bicycle, but never in my high school years. I guess I always knew she was prone to sadness. She was so serious all the time. But I didn't know how bad it was."

"Do you know why?"

"I don't think there has to be a 'why,' sweetheart. When I joined the Defence Forces, I got wrapped up in my own life. I was busy, sure, but I met your father, and I didn't call home as much as I should have. I didn't write to her as much as I should have. I think she felt very alone once she moved from Kilkenny to Dublin. She had a string of bad relationships, got let go from her job at a restaurant, I don't know what else. It was like she lost sight of God and family and country. It was like she lost sight of herself. When I got that call . . . Oh, Avery. I was holding you in my arms. You were less than a day old. I was supposed to be so happy, and I was, to have my baby girl. But I held you and I cried."

"That must have been really hard, Mom," I said. "I can't imagine."

"It was."

"But it wasn't your fault. It wasn't anyone's fault."

"That's why we moved you from that Kilkenny to this one," Dad said. "It was too sad, always too sad. We thought we could escape it."

"She wrote you a letter," Mom said. I went cold. "She left it on her dresser with the others before she died."

"Do you still have it?"

She rooted around in the shoebox and pulled out an envelope. "I've never read it," she said. It was sealed. "I didn't give it to you, because it didn't feel right to have her haunt you."

I took the envelope from my mother's hand and carefully ripped it open. My hands shook as I pulled out a simple piece of loose-leaf paper, creased in three places, with blue ink.

> Dear Avery (and other future kids Laura may have),
>
> You will be born any day now, and if you're reading this, I am not there. I am sorry because I wanted to meet you and I hope I get to someday, somewhere else. I want you to know I did have happy moments and I love

your mother and father a lot. My hope is you
live a life worth writing about. Don't worry
about being beautiful or good. Didn't help me!
You're better off without me, but I believe in
you, little Byrne.

With love and apologies,
Devin Walsh

I closed the paper and rubbed it between my fingers.
My life had never been better without her, not ever. Had
I lived a life worth writing about? What I wouldn't give
for a book of Aunt Devin's life: her fears and hatreds, her
small happiness, her gaping sadness. Who hurt her and
who did she hurt? What did she love and taste and learn?
Why had she taken all of that with her?

I knew why, but I missed her still.

"What did it say?" Mom asked.

"Can it just be mine?" I asked. She looked worried but
smoothed my hair.

"Of course," she said. "You've always scared me,
Avery, because of how much you remind me of her. But
she was wonderful too. I'm sorry I made it seem like a
bad thing."

Maddeningly, another voice rang in my head, Dr. Talley's: *Your parents would rather have a college dropout
daughter than a dead one.* I knew I couldn't or didn't want

to tell them the whole truth of what happened, not after losing Peter. Not after holding Devin's photos in our hands. But I could still let them know me.

"I think I've been depressed for a long time," I said. "I've felt very broken and wrong, and I don't know why. And I'm sorry, because you deserve so much better. You've given me the best of everything."

"We deserve the best," Dad said, in a small voice that grew stronger, "and that's still you."

"You're ours," Mom said. "We love you. Although that makes me very sad to hear." I felt like their child, but I also felt like the adult Dr. Talley told me I was too. I could let them be broken. I could be broken too. It wasn't anyone's fault, and I didn't have to fix it. The world was ending, but hadn't it always been?

"Did you want to go to New York with Cass and the Laskys?" Dad asked. What a word: *want*. And I could picture it then for real, for the first time, wanting something. I pictured not the wreckage of New York City but the mountains of Eaton's campus, a return to a life I'd hoped for but never got to love.

"No," I said, and though they seemed relieved, I continued, "but I think I need to leave for a few days to be alone. I can't even articulate why, but I think that's the point. For once I want to trust myself, even if I don't have the words for everything."

"Where will you go?" Dad asked.

"Back to Eaton," I said. "I feel like I have unfinished business there. I feel like I need to begin again."

"Can I ask for one more morning?" Mom said.

"Of course."

"I'm sorry about the bunker," she said, and I knew what she meant was she was sorry she couldn't save me, had never been able to save me.

"You did everything you could," I said. "I love you because you have never given up on me, because you've always been my biggest fans, because you are smart and kind and bighearted. I am lucky to be your daughter."

"We were lucky to be your parents," Mom said.

"Were? We still are," Dad said, and Peter's words echoed in my head until sleep came: *Aren't we the lucky ones? Aren't we the lucky ones? Aren't we the lucky ones?*

three . . . two . . .

In the morning, my parents and I ate cookies and apple crisp, drank coffee together for the first time ever, then walked to the edge of the orchard where the ground had only begun to thaw. The sun kissed the trees, the maze I knew by heart, the place I went to be lost, and the place I went to be found. Mom and I dug little holes with boots and shovels, and Dad handed out grafted branches to each of us. We tied them to stakes with burlap and ribbon.

We planted trees for the eleven of us: my parents, me, Peter, Georgia, Teddy, Cass, Aisha, Ray, Dr. Talley, Scout. And we planted one more for Devin. She belonged. Mom prayed the rosary, and we knelt with her. For a second, I was back on the dock of the river with the ice on my skin.

And then came a rush of my tears, tears that didn't hurt this time. I imagined myself thawing, cracking into my own chest with a shovel, planting something. And that was what I planned to do.

"We're proud of you," Mom said.

"We love you," Dad said. I hugged them one last time.

I said goodbye to Aisha and Ray, who were moving furniture around Peter's old house, making it their own bright, beautiful, colorful world. Aisha hugged me tightly, then told me to wait. She took her gold locket off and put it on me instead.

"I can't take this," I said.

"You can," she said. "Just try to bring it back to me."

"But I don't have anything for you."

She gestured toward the house, toward Ray. "I have everything I need now."

I started to walk away from her, but she called for me once again.

"Hey, Avery?"

"Yeah?"

"You're a good friend."

"You're the best friend," I said, and somehow, somehow I made myself walk away from her.

I said goodbye to Dr. Talley, who seemed indifferent but offered me Scout's leash.

"Take the dog," he said. "It's her home. She'll be happier there."

I hesitated, but I took her leash. "Scouty," I said, as I walked with her across the lawn, "looks like it's you and me, girl." Her head perked up and her tongue flopped out. It looked like she was smiling uncontrollably. Oh, no. Did I have a dog voice? She was disoriented, but she loved me. It was so ridiculous, and it was so admirable. I put my face in her neck, and I squeezed her, felt like we belonged to each other. I let myself be loved irrationally. I let myself love her in the same way.

Though my heart became my whole chest as I got into the Volvo with the broken window, I put my foot on the gas and steered into my separate life. Scout was in my back seat, tail thumping, breath jumping. My parents stood in the driveway holding each other, waving to me, and just like that, our world ended. Mine began.

The drive up north was quieter than I expected. Eaton's campus was muddy, gray, and whispering. Glass from shattered dorm windows glittered on the ground. My room had been raided, most of my things taken, but I was expecting that. They'd left the bedding, and I was grateful. Eaton had never felt special to me, but that was because I had never felt any kind of special at Eaton. Now it was a different world because I was a different person. It was a different space because it was finite. It was right simply because I had chosen it, because it was mine, because I could rewrite the ending I'd chosen before. I could become someone different.

In my two days alone, I woke up for both sunrises. Neither was spectacular, but I savored every wisp of pastel cascading across the sky. I laced up my sneakers to run around the purple and brick grounds with Scout at my side, to suck in sharp air, to feel every single muscle move, to have a body, to listen to my own mind. I blasted soccer balls at the back of the net for no reason other than to hear the whoosh of it. I read beautiful books I'd been meaning to get to while leaned up against the bark of an ancient tree. I felt alone. I felt like everyone was there. I talked to them out loud when I missed them the most. There were so many people to miss, but my cells were still. My breath came steady.

I talked to Scout for a while until neither of us needed words. Dr. Talley was right: this was her home, and though there were moments when I probably projected longing into her eyes, she seemed comfortable and eager to roll on her back with her legs up in the air and to sleep on some pillows on the carpet. I let her lick my face. I let her love me even though she had no reason to, and I loved her too, so much, even though I could lose her.

On the second night, I was sleeping fitfully, but she woke me up from a patch of calm with her whining.

She spun in circles with her tail between her legs. She scratched at the window and then clawed at the door. I pulled wool socks on and found my old slippers under my bed. I followed her into the hallway and was going to crack the front door to let her slip out when I noticed an eerie glow burning beyond the glass panels. My ribs shook. *It's here early*, I thought. *It's hit somewhere and this is ... what? Radiation? Neurons? Electricity? Some type of heaven?*

I stepped onto the concrete walkway and saw the lights for what they were: green-and-purple northern lights sleeping above the tree line. They pulled me across campus, my arms outstretched, reaching for something I knew I could never touch.

"Do you see this?!" I yelled to Scout in a scratchy, unpracticed voice. She cocked her head at me before running ahead to sniff at some bushes. "Do you see this?!" There was no one around. I had to lie down on my back to still myself. I wished desperately for my parents, Peter, Georgia, Teddy. Ray. Aisha. Cass.

It was just as well I was alone. I didn't have the words for the majesty in the sky, but it was mine, it was mine, it was mine alone, and I deserved to have something that wonderful. Everyone did.

On a frigid night—the night before the asteroid was supposed to make impact—Scout snored beside me as I sat cross-legged on my bed, writing my memories of the past nineteen years and the last nine days down on loose-leaf paper. I glued every finished page in my scrapbook. I wrote about summers in the ocean, on lakes, at church camp. I wrote about autumns in our apple orchard, at Halloween. I wrote about winter at the end of the world—I wrote about my parents, Peter, Georgia, Teddy, Cass—and then, finally, I tried to imagine spring:

> *I am someone too. I'm Avery Devin Byrne: vulnerable, smart, fun, hardworking, sensitive, observant, and kind. I finally believe it, and if anyone is ever reading this, you should believe it too. I am someone worth mourning, celebrating. My aunt Devin was too. So are you.*
>
> *At least for now, I know what I want to do with the rest of my life, if tomorrow comes or even if it doesn't: I want to help people, though I'll have to see what people need in New Hampshire or New York or anywhere beyond. It pains me to admit Dr. Talley had a point: one version of my life was unlivable, but not every version will be, and I am allowed to go searching. I want to help people not because I'm a savior and not because I need saving, but*

because we need each other. I know I need
everyone. I always will.

If I get more days, there are still things
I want beyond that too: To find a therapist,
maybe go on medication, try things and
try things and try things until everything
gets a little easier. To forgive myself when
it doesn't. To play soccer and lacrosse again,
even just for fun. To find my way to the
people who make me feel like home. To
let new people know me: all my sadness,
memories, and hope. To know them too. To
love them. To love me too.

Did I believe what I wrote in those scrapbook pages? Did I believe I could love all of who I was, including my screaming flaws, my biggest failures, and my cruel, relentless brain?

I wasn't sure, but I could choose to try. I did believe this for certain, finally: There is no one so broken they are completely unsalvageable. There is no life so hopeless tomorrow can't be at least a little better. I did believe that.

I flipped through the book's pages. I reread my life. I tried to see it through someone else's eyes, and my heart pounded. There was still a blank page I wouldn't have time to fill.

I was doing well on my own—and it had been so necessary to be alone, to be at Eaton—but I couldn't help it: I wished Cass were there to paint the blank page with her kaleidoscope colors, to read my words, to watch me close the book and walk away into my new life. She'd be proud of me, I knew, for choosing myself. For *becoming*.

I didn't need Cass, but I missed her in a wild way: her strong hands and her new hair and her smug smile. How she looked in the sunshine. How she looked under the moon. So I dragged Scout into a freezing night to sleep, cuddled together, on frozen grass under New Hampshire stars and feel *everything*: sadness and terror and euphoria and chest-breaking longing. For the life I had. For the life I missed. For a future that might not be a future at all. I let my tears run. I let Scout kiss them away. Somehow, I found sleep.

...one...

I'd mused for years on where to hide my body, and I'd once settled on the Saco River—a hungry stretch of icebergs and fog that slipped by the edge of campus. On my final morning, the day the asteroid was scheduled to hit at 11 p.m., I shut the scrapbook. I went to the river with Scout. We sat at its edge, where loons wailed, and crew boats beat steady against the docks. I was not alone, and the shore no longer felt like an opening. It felt like something was closing, and it was right. The river had seen the worst and the best of me, and all the while, I was enough.

There was a rustling in the trees behind us. Scout started barking, and before I even turned around, I *knew*. I felt her there, in the stutter of my heart, in the ache in my chest. I felt her in every cell of me, and then I heard her too:

"Avery freaking Byrne."

I turned around, and there she was, Cass, standing only a few feet away in the brush. She was still wearing her New York uniform—tight black pants, a black jacket, and a long, silver necklace. She ran a hand through her short, wavy hair and sat down beside me.

"Cass." I wrapped my arms around her, held her tighter than I ever had, and Scout wiggled next to us, happily.

"If you haven't had enough time, I'll go," she said. "I swear I will. But if there's room for me in this new world of yours, I'd really love to see it." I didn't want to start crying, but I did.

"Stay," I said, "we have all the time in the world." She kissed me, and it felt like the first time. She ran her thumb across my cheek, and we sat side by side on the dock to watch the water.

"So? What happened in New York?"

"New York was everything, of course. The Laskys are safe. Teddy freaked out when we hit the city. His eyes were as big as saucers. We ate pizza, Avery. Pizza."

"And Mx. and Match?"

"Oh my God, it was epic. I'm not even gonna be humble about it; my pieces stole the whole damn show. People *loved* them, Avery. They were cheering and yelling and . . . I was made for it. Even Daisy said so."

"Well, if Daisy says so," I teased, and she pushed me with her shoulder. "You didn't want to stay there?"

"No. I mean, I felt so *cool* and proud and excited—until a model I didn't even know started walking down the runway in one of the looks I designed with you in mind and my heart, just . . ." She mimed an explosion. "As soon as she changed into someone else's collection, I grabbed all my favorite outfits and started running."

"Please tell me I get to wear them."

"Oh, yeah. That's the whole point. It wasn't the same, being there. Or I wasn't the same. I loved it, but I didn't *need* it to feel like myself. At least not right now. I need to be . . . here."

"How did you even find me? And what are you even doing here?"

She put her head on my shoulder, and I put my head on hers. She smelled like lilac and forest and home. We laced our fingers together.

"I went to your house first, and your parents told me where you were." She threw a pebble in the water with her free hand. "Last time we sat right here, I told you I saw myself back in New Hampshire in the end. Now it's the end. If we live through this, though, you gotta promise you'll *consider* living together in the city."

For the first time when I pictured it, it felt open. Welcoming, even. For the first time I felt big enough to fill it. "I promise."

"I wasn't gonna bring it up, but you *did* say you'd go anywhere for me. No pressure."

"Yeah, yeah. You're right. I did. New York, it is."

"Good. Did you write on your scrapbook pages?"

"You know it," I said. "I'll let you read them. Whenever you want." I'd let her know me, fully, finally, even if it was the last thing I ever did.

"My little overachiever." She pulled her scrapbook pages out from her jacket pocket and unfolded them.

"Did you write about New York?" I asked.

"God, no. I'm a shit writer; I don't know why I suggested that."

I rolled my eyes and slung my arm around her, as she showed me page after page of *Dear Avery* scribbled out and tossed them one by one into the river. But on the final page, she'd made me one last collage: a perfect universe of ripped magazine edges, bright colors, stars, birch trees, cityscape oceans.

"For you," she said and squeezed me a little too tightly. "Now whaddya say we go sailing?"

My heart rose again.

In my dorm room, I pasted her collage on the final page of my scrapbook. She changed into a navy suit with yellow plaid piping, and I changed into the outfit she'd made for me: a sky-blue-and-yellow plaid jumpsuit that made my eyes pop. It fit like a glove, better than any clothes I'd ever worn.

"You're amazing. I can't even tell you how much I love it."

"You look *perfect*."

"I look like . . . *me*."

"Exactly." She ran her hands through my hair to untangle it, then wrapped her arms around me from behind. I took us in, one last time, the two of us together. *Finally. Again.*

Next, we threw our stuff in the car and crossed thirty miles to Lake Winnipesaukee. We drove around with the windows down, Scout in the back seat, until we found a boat to steal.

"There she is," Cass said as we pulled over for a sailboat called *The August*, blue and white and docked to someone's abandoned cabin, waiting to be untied.

We took our shoes and socks off and ran into the icy water. Cass raised the sails and showed me which ropes to tie and pull, and Scout ran around the deck barking. The wind caught us, took us out. My hair haloed around me. It was winter, but Cass was still golden. She smiled so easily. Can you imagine? In my life, I got to love her.

"I'm happy," I said, as she swung around to sit next to me.

"It's not the ocean," she said, "but in a way, I like it better. Oceans, rivers, they're like hope for what's beyond us. But lakes remind me there's beauty where we are."

I thought about how close I'd been to dying in that river, to not being there in this moment on the wild water, in the middle of trees and mountains and an unforgiving sky.

My God, the things I would have missed.

We sailed until the sun set, in the middle of that lake, too full of love for any type of fear. The light dimmed. The color faded. I swear I read a version of Peter's words in the constellations as they bloomed above us:

Here we go, the brave and the beautiful.
Here we go, all eyes on the same star.
We were here for a time to dream.
We still are.

I didn't have paint, and I'd already filled every inch of my scrapbook, but I thought to myself, *I still am.* We still were: Cass and I in the middle of the water, hands clasped together, the dog barking at the sky like she might be able to protect us. When the time came—when the asteroid burned in the sky like lightning, like a firework, like a fluttering, melting birthday candle—I would close my eyes. I would wish for more.

resources

THE TREVOR PROJECT

The Trevor Project provides free, confidential counseling to LGBTQIA+ young people via text message, phone, and online chat. Visit their website for helpful resources on LGBTQIA+ topics and issues.

• TheTrevorProject.org
• Text START to 678-678 or call 1-866-488-7386

988 SUICIDE AND CRISIS LIFELINE

If you are afraid that you might hurt yourself or are feeling suicidal, the 988 Suicide and Crisis Lifeline (previously known as the National Suicide Prevention Lifeline) provides 24/7 free, confidential support over the phone and online.

• 988lifeline.org
• Call 988

SAMHSA'S NATIONAL HELPLINE

SAMHSA's National Helpline is a confidential, free 24/7 information service, in English and Spanish, for individuals and family members facing mental and/or substance use disorders. This group provides referrals to local treatment facilities, support groups, and community-based organizations.

- Samhsa.gov
- Call 1-800-662-HELP (4357)

CRISIS TEXT LINE

Crisis Text Line provides free, confidential crisis intervention via text message. Text HOME to 741741 from anywhere in the United States, anytime, about any type of crisis, and a live, trained crisis counselor will help you handle the situation.

- CrisisTextLine.org
- Text HOME to 741741

NAMI

The National Alliance on Mental Illness is the nation's largest grassroots mental health organization dedicated to building better lives for the millions of Americans affected by mental illness.

- https://www.nami.org/Your-Journey/Kids-Teens-and -Young-Adults
- Call 1-800-950-NAMI (6264)

acknowledgments

This book is my whole heart. During the decade I spent writing this novel, I went through countless drafts of both the story and myself. If you encouraged or supported me, I love you. You're on every page.

Thank you, especially to:

My agent, Erin Harris, for your dedication, thoughtful edits, and incredibly hard work—all during one of the most challenging times in human history. I am forever grateful you took a chance on this book (and me) and fought so hard for it when it counted most. You are excellent at what you do, and your continued support means a lot to me.

My editor, Camille Kellogg. I think the world of you. I never dreamed I'd find someone who understood this book quite like you did, and it has meant more to me than I could ever say. Your editorial insight, instincts, and empathy changed this book so much, all for the better. You are as brilliant as you are kind, and working on this story with you has been (and will always be) one of the most meaningful creative experiences of my life.

Everyone at Bloomsbury Children's for your beautiful work and love for this book. Especially: Diane Aronson, Erica Barmash,

Faye Bi, John Candell, Mary Kate Castellani, Erica Chan, Jennifer Choi, Nicholas Church, Phoebe Dyer, Beth Eller, Alona Fryman, Lex Higbee, Donna Mark, Kathleen Morandini, Andrew Nguyen, Daniel O'Connor, Laura Phillips, Valentina Rice, and Sarah Shumway.

I am in awe of—and impossibly grateful for—all you do. The fantastic team at Penguin Random House UK (especially Anthea Townsend and Charlotte Winstone) for your support and enthusiasm. The wildly talented Mary Metzger for the cover of my dreams.

My wife, Krupa. Can you imagine? In my life, I get to love you. I'm savoring it—our life—with its bonfires, postcards, long walks, and late nights in electric cities or our living room. Our years together have felt like a universe only ever expanding, collecting beautiful, good things all the while. Your passion for living has made me a happier person. Our story has made me a better writer. You are at once my home and my greatest adventure. I love you, I love you, I love you. (Thank you to our beloved dog, Juni, too. You will never read this unless technology gets really cool really quickly but you deserve to be included.)

Our baby, Zariah. At the time of writing, you are exactly one month old, and I already adore you so completely. It is the gift of my life to love you for all of who you are and will be: your sorrows and dreams, worries and joys, heartache and wonder. I hope you discover worlds beyond my wildest imaginings, and like Cass and Avery at the lake, find beauty right where you are. When I'm with you, Z, I always do.

My family. Mom and Dad, for instilling in me a love of reading and writing at an early age and for always believing in me. I'm proud to be yours, and so deeply appreciative of everything you've done for me. Andrew Barret, the coolest, most creative person I know. I won the sibling lottery and feel so lucky, all the time, to go through life with you. Tony Clements for over a decade of ridiculous and perfect memories (and the rest of the Clements family for making our family bigger and more fun). The Murphy and Cox families for shaping so much of my childhood. My second family for the late-night card games, idli sambar, and for welcoming me so completely into your lives: Jagat Shah, Rita Shah, Ashish Shah, Rose Paca-Shah, my amazing nieces and nephews (JJ, MJ, CJ, KJ, EJ, and DJ), Sandy Ruszczak, Nick Ruszczak, and Nicholas Ruszczak.

The professors and mentors who helped me turn the pages: Jenny Boylan (your end-of-semester note was one of the biggest reasons I kept writing this book), Bill Holinger, and Lindsay Mitchell. Emily Danforth for your incredible generosity and for taking so many of us under your wing. The big-hearted Kelly Quindlen and absolutely magical Adrienne Tooley: this book would literally not be here without you. Thank you for your mentorship, but more important for your friendship. You changed this story and my life.

Jas Hammonds: forever grateful for the number of times you've read this novel, the ways you've supported me, and the moments you've lifted me up when I needed it the most. Jas, I have thought of you as my twin star these past few years, but it's been the most incredible thing to watch you burn brighter and brighter. You mean so much to me, and I'm unbelievably grateful our Averys brought us together.

To my other Lambda family members: I simply do not know what I would do without you. Each and every one of you is kind, thoughtful, hilarious, and talented. Octavia Saenz, you add neon to my world. Thank you for being this book's godmother, your other-worldly art, and breathtaking words. Lin Thompson, we are cut from the same cloth, and I love losing myself in your incredible worlds. Kirt Ethridge, I am blown away by your gentle thoughtfulness and care for the people around you. JD Scott, you are one of the most fabulously funny people and a poet in all mediums. Your care packages have saved me more than once. Avery Mead, your guidance and friendship have changed me, and I am constantly in awe of your blooming. Sacha Lamb, you are a voice of reason and one of the most trustworthy, measured people around. Barrak Alzaid, Kay Ulanday Barret, Kate Bove, Tia Clark, Amal Haddad, Caitlin Hernandez, and Amos Mac: I am so grateful to have met you, so proud of all you're doing, and hope our paths cross again and again.

Kate Cochrane and Isla Lassiter; you're my writing hotline, my trusted readers, and some of my very favorite authors. Kate, thank you for being my ~~Dartmouth~~ Eaton consultant. I love your Roy Kent energy, humor, loyalty, and kindness. Isla, your stories break my heart and heal me every time. It's wonderful to watch you build worlds and travel through ours with your deep emotions and love of everything strange, gorgeous, and haunting

The rest of The Thirstiest; thank you for letting me be a total [thirsty] disaster all the time and matching my energy. Keena Roberts, for your sincerity, advice, and solid friendship. Anita Kelly and Meryl Wilsner, for your gender-panic-and-other-things comfort. The Pride Five: Kate Fussner, Caroline Huntoon, Ronnie Riley, and Justine Pucella Winans. Thank you for opening your hearts up so quickly, and trusting me so fully. I'm lucky I found you. This world is so much less lonely with you and your stories in it. My Bloomsbury buddies, Gabi Burton and Trang Thanh Tran, and '23 friends (so far): Isa Arsén, Jenna Miller, Vicki Johnson, and

Miranda Sun—it's an honor to be here beside you and your magnificent, heartfelt, life-changing books.

Early readers who were often the reason I kept going (beloved friends and writer/artists whose words have and will change the world): Lara Ameen, Terri Bello, Carey Blankenship, Léa Colombo, Nico Colton, Jordan Francoeur, Connor Garstka, Jessie Hansen, C.J. Heid, Amanda Helander, Caitlin Keller, Lakshya (you solved my ending!), Whitney LaMora, Vitória Lima, Chloe Maron, Kyrie McCauley, Briana Miano, LC Milburn, Dana Murphy, Cole Nagamatsu, Layla Noor, Shelly Page, Gianye Palmer, Nekee Pandya, Neha Shah, Daniel Sanchez Torres, Addie Tsai, Jas Saunders, Birdie Schae, Jordan Silversmith, and Jenn Vandehey. Dahlia Adler, Brandy Colbert, Robbie Couch, Leah Johnson, Rachael Lippincott, and Tucker Shaw for taking the time to blurb this book; I'll treasure your words always. My first-ever book club: Deanna Saunders, Ray Saunders, Claudette Jean-Louis, Maxine Jean-Louis, Chris Saunders-Fields, and Aurora Fields.

More dear friends for the treasure of your support, love, and kindness: Thais Afonso, Caroline Barnaby, Bethany Baptiste, Payal Beri, Sophia Brohmier, Mandana Chaffa, Elayna Mae Darcy, Sami Ellis, Stanny Ethridge, Glen Frieden, Doug Gracie, Elle Grenier, Emily Hobbs, Imogen Hobbs, Colleen Keenan, Priya Parikh, Amanda Pyron, Tess Malone, Emily Marcum, Molly Marcum, Amanda Maynard, Caitie McKean, Jess Mehta (you're so much more than my dentist), Haley Neer, Isabel Plourde, Anna Read, Amy Reed, Ashlee Reed, Joelle Russo, Lisa Ryan, Andrew Sanders, Amy Shah, Chitra Shah, Brett Solimine, Chaloe Tyler, Sonia Uppal, Cora Van Hazinga, Katherine West, Katie Wyle.

My various, necessary literary communities: A League of One's Own, My YA Tin House Cohort, My Harvard writing crew (especially Rob Medley, Jimmy Matejek-Morris, Ben Sunday, and Sarah Zeiser, who were there from draft one), *Chicago Review of Books*, and *just femme & dandy*. The people who donated to my Lambda retreat: thank you times a million. Pride@BCG and BCG Chicago, who convinced me that work can feel like family. My Chicago Sky friends. The musicians who carried me these past few years: The Aces—your music has brought me real, unexpected *joy*. It feels like home. Hayley Kiyoko—this book would literally not be gay without you. MUNA—the sad and sentimental queers of my heart. Taylor Swift—*folklore* was the most beautiful salve during the most terrible time.

The children (and young adults) in my life: I want the whole world for you; all the birthday candles, all the fireworks, all the shooting stars. But if you need a buddy when you're sad, you know where to find me. I'm here. Please write about your wonderful, unforgettable, magnificent lives; or just have the courage to tell someone about them (collages work too).

And, finally, thank you from the very bottom of my heart to you, reader, for taking the time to read Avery's story. My life—and this world—will always be better with you in it. Tomorrow will come. It will, I swear it. I'll meet you in the morning.